NATIVE
TONGUE

NATIVE TONGUE

Suzette Haden Elgin

Afterword by Susan M. Squier and Julie Vedder

The Feminist Press
at The City University of New York

Published by The Feminist Press at The City University of New York
365 Fifth Avenue, New York, NY 10016
www.feministpress.org

First Feminist Press edition, 2000

Library of Congress Cataloging-in-Publication Data

Elgin, Suzette Haden.
    Native tongue / Suzette Haden Elgin ; afterword by Susan Squier and
    Julie Vedder.— 1st Feminist Press ed.
        p. cm.
    Originally published: New York: DAW, 1984.
    ISBN 1-55861-255-6 (h.c. : acid-free paper) — ISBN 1-55861-246-7
    (pbk. : acid-free paper)
    1. Language and languages—Fiction. 2. Languages, Secret—Fiction.
    3. Women—Fiction. I. Title.

PS3555.L42 N38 2000
813'.54—dc21   00-042958

The Feminist Press would like to thank Joanne Markell and Genevieve
Vaughan for their generosity in supporting this book.

Printed on acid-free paper by Transcontinental Printing
Printed in Canada

08 07 06 05 04 03 02 01 00   5 4 3 2 1

PREFACE

There is a sense in which no book can be said to be "ordinary" today; we are well aware of that. When the publication of as many as ten books in a single year is unusual, even the most undistinguished volume would not be ordinary. But when we say that this is no ordinary book, we mean a good deal more than just that its format is rare.

First, we believe this book to be the only work of fiction ever written by a member of the Lines. The men of the linguist families have given the world a vast body of scholarly work and other nonfiction. Their women have made substantial contributions to that work, duly acknowledged by the authors in their introductory notes and prefaces. But *Native Tongue* is not a work of scholarship, or a teaching grammar, or a book of science for the general public; it is a NOVEL. And it gives us a sense of participation in the linguists' lives during the first quarter of the 23rd century that we cannot gain from any history of the time, no matter how detailed, no matter how abundantly documented. Very little fiction on that subject exists, even from the pens of nonlinguists; this book is the unique example *from* a linguist, and as such it is beyond price. We owe a major debt to the scholar who found the manuscript and who saw to it that it reached our hands; we deeply regret that our ignorance of that scholar's identity prevents us from expressing our appreciation more effectively. It is a miracle that this document was not lost; we are grateful for the miracle.

Second, although we would have had no difficulty making the material available in the traditional publishing media of computer-disc or microfiche, that was not what we wanted. From the very first reading, we felt strongly that this should be a *printed* book, printed and bound in the ancient manner. It is very special; it seemed to us that it deserved an equally special form. It took almost ten years, and the efforts of hundreds of persons, to secure the necessary monies and to find craftsmen with the necessary skills who were willing to provide them for what we could afford to pay—even for this limited edition.

We cannot tell you who actually wrote *Native Tongue*. It was signed simply "the women of Chornyak Barren House." It must have been written in scraps of time, at odd stolen moments, at the cost of sacrificing much-needed sleep, for the women of the Lines had no leisure. If anyone has evidence that might shed light on the mystery of its authorship, no matter how fragmentary, we ask that you share it with us; we promise you that it will be treated with the utmost discretion and respect.

It is with great pride, then, and with a sense of profound accomplishment, that we urge you to read on, and to keep this volume among your treasures and in a place of honor.

—Patricia Ann Wilkins, Executive Editor
(*Native Tongue* is a joint publication
of the following organizations:
The Historical Society of Earth;
WOMANTALK, Earth Section;
The Metaguild of Lay Linguists, Earth Section;
The Láadan Group.)

Chapter One

Section 1.   The nineteenth article of amendment to the Constitution of the United States is hereby repealed.

Section 2.   This article shall be inoperative unless it shall have been ratified as an amendment to the Constitution by the legislatures of three-fourths of the several states within seven years from the date of its submission.

(Declared in force March 11, 1991.)

ARTICLE XXV

Section 1.   No female citizen of the United States shall be allowed to serve in any elected or appointed office, to participate in any capacity (official or unofficial) in the scholarly or scientific professions, to hold employment outside the home without the written permission of her husband or (should she be unmarried) a responsible male related by blood or appointed her guardian by law, or to exercise control over money or other property or assets without such written permission.

Section 2.   The natural limitations of women being a clear and present danger to the national welfare when not constrained by the careful and constant supervision of a responsible male citizen, all citizens of the United States of the female gender shall be deemed legally minors, regardless of their chronological age; except that they shall be tried as adults in courts of law if they are eighteen years of age or older.

Section 3.   Inasmuch as the aforementioned natural limitations of women are inherent, such that no blame accrues to them thereby, nothing in this article shall be construed to allow the mistreatment or abuse of women.

Section 4. The Congress shall have power to enforce this article by appropriate legislation.

Section 5. This article shall be inoperative unless it shall have been ratified as an amendment to the Constitution by the legislatures of three-fourths of the several states within seven years from the date of its submission.

(Declared in force March 11, 1991.)

SUMMER 2205. . . .

There were only eight of them at the meeting; not the best of numbers. Not only was eight a very small number to accomplish business efficiently, it was an *even* number—which meant that in case of a tie they'd have to give Thomas Blair Chornyak an extra vote, and he always hated that. It smacked of an elitism that was completely contrary to the philosophy of the Lines.

Paul John Chornyak was there, still putting in his oar at 94, when Thomas ought to have been able to proceed without the old man's interference. Aaron was there—he had to be, given the final item on their agenda, which concerned him directly. They'd managed to scare up two of the senior men by comset, so that the faces of James Nathan Chornyak and of Thomas' brother-in-law Giles were with them in blurry irritation, after a fashion. Adam was there, only two years younger than Thomas and quite properly part of the group; Thomas relied on his brother for many things, not the least of them being his skill at deflecting their father's digressions and convincing Paul John that his words had been attended to. Kenneth was there because, not being a linguist, he could always get away from whatever he was doing to come to meetings; Jason was there because the negotiation he was involved in was hopelessly stalled on a technicality about which he could do nothing, leaving him marking time until the State Department could straighten it out.

Either of the last two could have solved the problem of the even number by courteously excusing himself—but neither one would do it. It was Jason's opinion that since Kenneth was only a son-in-law, and not even a member of the Lines by birth, it was *his* place to take himself off to whatever it was he ought to be doing instead of butting in here. And it was Kenneth's opinion that he had as much right in the meeting as Jason had—he hadn't given up his birth name and taken Mary Sarah Chornyak's name for his own for nothing. He was Chornyak now, as much as any of them, and he knew very well that one of the things he had to do was underline that fact firmly at every opportunity, or the other junior men would bury him at the bottom of the pecking order. He wasn't about to leave.

It was awkward, and Thomas briefly considered asking James Nathan to drop out; but they'd waked him up for this, and he hadn't been happy about it. He'd been up all the previous night and well past breakfast time interpreting in one of the Third Colony crises of which there seemed to be an inexhaustible supply, and he'd been obviously exhausted. Now they had him awake, it would be less than tactful to suggest that he go back to bed, sorry to bother you but we thought we needed you at the time. . . . No. It wouldn't do, and he let it pass. If he had to vote double, so be it; they'd all survive. And their meetings were always small at Chornyak Household lately, except for the Semi-Annuals that were on permanent schedule and for which everyone kept a free day on his calendar. The way the government was pushing into space these days, and every inch of the push to be negotiated with the whole apparatus of treaties and purchase agreements and establishment of formal relations, it was hard to find *any* linguist under the age of 60 with an hour to spare for household affairs.

He would settle for what he had, Thomas decided, and be grateful it wasn't just himself and old Paul John and Aaron. They would have made a pitiful quorum, just the three of them at the table all by themselves. The table's shape, the standard blunt-tipped A without a crossbar, was ideal for the Semi-Annuals; you could really pack the men in around it, and still have ample space for threedies and holograms in the solid area at the top of the A. But when you had only half a dozen, you either rattled around with each of you established at some arbitrary point to fill out the geometry or you huddled in a little knot at one end and felt dwarfed. Today they had opted for the rattling around. His father at his right hand, the comsets clear across the room out of the way of people's heads, and the other four men laid out like the points of a compass. Silly ass procedure.

He got them through the first seven agenda items with dispatch, and no need for any tie-breaking. The one thing he'd been a little uncertain about, the contract for REM80-4-801, ran into no opposition at all. Sometimes there were advantages to a meeting with a substantial percentage of inexperienced junior participants. He'd had his arguments ready, just in case; but either none of the others saw the dangerous opening in subparagraph eleven or none of them cared enough about it to spend time arguing over it. The other items were routine . . . they went through the whole list in just over twelve minutes flat.

And now there was this last matter to be taken up. Cautiously. Thomas read it out for them, keeping his voice casual and adding no elaborations, and then he waited. As he'd expected, Aaron made a point of looking bored past all bearing; he had the Adiness Line's skill with facial expression, plus the ease of long practice, and he managed to look excruciatingly uninterested.

"This matter is open for discussion," Thomas said. "Comments?"

"Frankly, I don't see any need for discussion," observed Aaron at once. "We could have settled this whole thing by memo, to my way of thinking, and god knows I've better things to do with my time. As do we all, Thomas—I'm sure I'm not the only one strangling in federal deadlines."

Thomas wasn't ready to say anything yet; he raised his eyebrows just the precise fraction indicated, rubbed his chin gently with one hand, and waited some more—and Aaron spoke again.

"I'm willing to accept the fact that you had to add this to a formal agenda; you've convinced me of that," he said. "And we've done it. It's on there, a matter of record. For all the curious world to see and applaud. And that's quite enough time wasted. I move we vote, and be done with it."

"With no discussion at all?" Thomas asked mildly.

Aaron shrugged.

"What's to discuss?"

That brought Paul John into it; he was old enough to find the arrogance of this particular son-in-law less than amusing, and too old to be impressed by either his brilliance with language or his astonishing good looks.

"You might find out, if you'd let somebody else talk," said the old man. "Why don't you try it and see?"

Thomas moved quickly, not interested in seeing Aaron and Paul John started on one of the sparring sessions they both took such delight in. That *would* be a waste of time. "Aaron," he said, "this meeting is not entirely window-dressing."

"No. We had to discuss those contracts. And vote on them."

"Nor is this last item window-dressing," Thomas insisted. "There is a reason, a very good reason that has nothing to do with just putting it on record, for us to give it our consideration. Because we do feel—and, I might add, we are obligated to feel—more than just a ceremonial regard for the woman in question."

"And I would remind you that in purely economic terms the woman is fully entitled to that regard," Kenneth put in from the far end of the table, right leg of the A. He was nervous, and he hadn't the skill to hide it in either voice or body-parl, but he was determined. "Nazareth Chornyak has borne nine healthy infants to this Line," he said. "That's nine Alien languages added to the assets of this Household. It's not as if she were an untried girl."

Thomas saw Aaron allow the barest sign of contempt, the most carefully measured flicker of disdain, to move over his face; then it was replaced with a false and cloying kindness that would also be attached to whatever he was about to say. It wasn't a fair contest in any way; poor Kenneth, straight from the public and brought into Chornyak Household with the public's bottomless ignorance of all linguistic skills . . . and Aaron William Adiness, son of Adiness Household, second only to the Chornyak Line in the linguist dynasties. Kenneth was a duck in a barrel, and Aaron enjoyed duck-shooting too much to let it pass.

"At times, Kenneth," he said sympathetically, "it is overpoweringly obvious that you were not born a linguist. . . .You don't learn, do you?"

Kenneth flushed, and Thomas felt sorry for him, but he didn't interfere. In some ways Aaron was right—Kenneth didn't learn. For example, he hadn't yet learned that time spent playing Aaron's little games was time spent feeding Aaron's giant ego, and therefore time wasted. Kenneth fell for it, every time.

"It isn't the woman," Aaron said pleasantly, "who adds the Alien languages to the Household assets. It is the MAN. The *man* goes to the trouble of impregnating the woman—who is then coddled and waited upon and indulged sickeningly, to ensure the welfare of his child. To attribute any credit to the woman who plays the role of a receptacle is primitive romanticism, Kenneth, and entirely unscientific. Re-read your biology texts."

RE-read. Presupposed, Kenneth had read them already and learned nothing from the experience. Neat. And typical of Aaron Adiness.

Kenneth sputtered, and flushed darker.

"Damn it, Aaron—"

Aaron went sailing on in the conversational stream; Kenneth was scarcely there at all, except as the recipient of his compassionate instruction. "And you would do well to remember that if it weren't for the intervention of men only females could ever be born. The human race would degenerate into a species composed entirely of genetically inferior organisms. You might want to think that over, Kenneth. It might be well to keep those very basic facts in mind, as an antidote to . . . sentimental tendencies."

And then he leaned back and blew a superb row of smoke

rings toward the ceiling, and he smiled and said, "Let us not confuse the pot with the potter, dear brother."

At the other leg of the table, Jason chuckled in appreciation of the tired joke. Thomas was disappointed. Later he might have a few words to say to his son about cheering on the one who held the gun when the target was a duck sitting in a barrel. He was a good deal more satisfied with what happened next, when the reproof came from the comset screen where James Nathan's face was wavering and flickering against the fluctuations of the household power mains.

"Damn all, Adiness," said this other, more capable son, "the only reason we aren't through with this and able to get to those deadlines you were so worried about five minutes ago—and the only reason *I* am not back in my bed, where I certainly ought to be—is because of your love affair with your mouth. None of us, and that includes Kenneth, who has my apology for your bad manners, needs an idiot recitation of information known to every normal human being by the age of three. Now I'm going to take it for granted that you're through, Aaron . . . and I suggest you *be* through."

Aaron nodded, all courtesy and aplomb, smiling easily, and Thomas knew he considered the rebuke well worth the pleasure he'd had toying with Kenneth, né Williams. Aaron had never considered Kenneth's input of fresh genes sufficient justification for his presence. He'd opposed taking the fellow into the house as husband for Mary Sarah in the first place, and he'd made no secret of the fact that his opinion was unchanged, even after seven years. Kenneth, he was fond of remarking, was "positively girlish." Not in Kenneth's hearing, of course, but always where the insult would be sure to get back to his brother-in-law rather promptly.

"Nazareth is barren now," said Jason, aware that he'd been the only one to laugh at Aaron's quip and anxious to demonstrate that there was more to him than that. "She's nearly forty years old, and she was no beauty even when she was young. What earthly need has she got for *breasts*? It's absurd. It's a non-issue. It wasn't worth five minutes, much less a meeting. I agree with Aaron—I move we end this discussion, vote, and adjourn."

"And do what? Let her die?"

Paul John cleared his throat, and the senior men looked politely at the ceiling. They were going to have to spend more time with Kenneth, that was obvious. Perhaps a few words to Mary Sarah . . .

"Christ, Kenneth, that's a stupid thing to say!" That was

Jason, feeling his oats. "There's plenty of money in the women's Individual Medical Accounts to cover all the treatment Nazareth needs. Who said anything about letting her die? We don't let women die, you moron—do you believe everything you read in the news about linguists? *Still?*"

Thomas sighed then, loud enough to be heard, and caught a sharp glance from Aaron. Aaron would be thinking that he was tired this morning. Tired, and—to the well trained eye—on a thin edge of strain. Aaron would be thinking it was high time Thomas stepped down and passed the running of this Household on to someone younger and more able, preferably Thomas Blair 2nd because Aaron knew he'd be able to push him around. Thomas smiled at Aaron, acknowledging the thought, and let his eyes speak for him—it'll be many a long year yet before I turn Chornyak Household over to anybody, you conceited bastard—and then he raised one hand to end the argument between Kenneth and Jason.

"See here—" Kenneth began, before Thomas cut him off.

"Linguists do not say 'see here,' Kenneth. Nor do they say 'Look here' or 'Listen here' or 'Get this.' Please try for a less biased manner of expression." Thomas was a patient man, and he intended to keep trying with this stubborn and impetuous youngster. He'd seen far rougher diamonds in his time—and the four children Kenneth had sired for them so far were superb specimens.

Kenneth obviously didn't understand what difference his choice of sensory predicates made here in the bowels of the great house, miles from any member of the public who might risk contamination from his flaws of phrasing, but he had learned manners enough to keep his opinions to himself. (He couldn't keep it off his face, of course, but he didn't know that, and they had no reason to tell him.) He nodded his apology, and started over.

"Perceive this," he said carefully. "There is also plenty of money in the women's IMAs to pay for the breast regeneration. I keep the accounts, remember? I'm in a position to know what there is and what there isn't money for. It's a piddling sum of money . . . only a cell or two to be implanted, and some rudimentary stimulation to initiate the regeneration of the glands. *That* is elementary biology—and elementary accounting! It's about the price of a wrist computer, as a matter of fact, and we've bought forty of those this year. How do we explain that we're unwilling to authorize that small a sum for the benefit of someone who's been so efficient and so sturdy and so productive a 'receptacle'? I'm well aware I wasn't born a linguist—even without Aaron's constant reminders—but I am a member of this Household now, I am entitled to be heard, I am *not* ignorant, and I tell you that I am uncomfortable with this decision.''

"Kenneth," said Thomas, and the kindness in his voice was genuine, "we value the compassion and the quality of empathy that you bring to us. I want you to know that. We sorely need such input. We spend so much of our time sharing the worldviews of beings who are not human that we are far too likely to become a little other than human ourselves. We need someone like you to remind us of that, from time to time."

"Then, why—"

"Because whatever we can afford in the way of actual monies, actual total numbers of credits expended, we cannot afford to spend them on sentimental gestures. And I'm sorry if it distresses you, Kenneth, but that's all it would be. We all regret that, but it remains true. The rule which says NO LINGUIST SPENDS ONE CENT THAT THE PUBLIC MIGHT VIEW AS CONSPICUOUS CONSUMPTION holds here, as it holds for every Household of the Lines, with absolute rigor.''

"But—"

"You know very well, Kenneth, because you come from the public—and unlike Aaron, I don't consider that a deficit—you know that no member of the public would indulge a middle-aged and barren woman in the manner that you are proposing. Do you want us to be the Household responsible for another round of anti-linguist riots, son? For the sake of one foolish woman, already overindulged her whole life long and now making the usual feminine mountain out of a pair of thoroughly worn out mole hills? Surely you don't want that, Kenneth, however sympathetic you may be toward Nazareth's demands.''

"One moment," said Aaron flatly. "I'll clarify that. Nazareth has not demanded anything; she has merely asked.''

"Quite right," Thomas replied. "I overstated the case.''

"But the point remains, Thomas; the point remains. I'm sure Kenneth has now come to see this matter in a less . . . maudlin light.''

Kenneth stared down at the table and said nothing more, and they all relaxed. They could have just overruled him, of course, without the chitchat. That option was always open to them. But it was preferable to avoid that sort of thing whenever it *could* be avoided. Linguists lived too much and too deeply in one another's pockets for family feuds not to be a substantial hindrance to the normal conduct of affairs—and with 91 under this roof Chornyak Household was one of the most crowded of them all. You tried for peace, in those circumstances . . . and Aaron's readiness to sacrifice that peace just to score a point or two was a major reason why Thomas would see to it that he never had an opportunity to achieve any real power in this house. It was Aaron who *truly* did not learn, and apparently could not. And without Kenneth's excuses.

"Well, then," said Paul John, rubbing his hands together, "we're agreed, are we? We'll authorize the transfer of funds for the treatments to destroy the diseased uterus and breasts of the lady and order that done at once, and that is *all* we will do. Correct, gentlemen?"

Thomas glanced around the table, and at the comset screens, and waited a few polite seconds to be sure nobody wanted his attention. And nodded, when it became clear that they didn't.

"Anything else?" he asked. "Anyone not clear on the new contract in from the Department of Analysis & Translation on those mirror-image dialects? Anyone want to protest the terms they're offering? Remembering, please, that it's a computer job from start to finish . . . not much effort there. Any personal business? Any objection to recording the vote on Nazareth's medical care as unanimous? No?"

"Good," he said, and brought the side of his hand down on the table in the chop gesture of adjournment. "Then we're through. Aaron, you'll see to it that your wife is advised promptly of our decision and that she goes immediately to the hospital. I want no media accusations later that we delayed and endangered her life, no matter how trivial that may seem. It's no more to our advantage to be accused of callous mistreatment of a woman than of lavish spending of our misgotten billions. You'll see to it?"

"Certainly," said Aaron stiffly. "I'm familiar with my obligations. And quite as sensitive to the problem of public opinion as anyone else in this room. I'll have Mother take care of it right away."

"Your mother-in-law's not available at the moment, Aaron," said Thomas. "She's sitting in on some kind of folderol with the Encoding Project this morning. Get one of the other women to do it in her place, or do it yourself."

Aaron opened his mouth to make a remark. And closed it again. He knew what his father-in-law would say if he objected again to the time the women wasted in their silly "Encoding Project." It keeps them busy and contented, Aaron, he'd say. The barren ones and those too old for other work need something harmless to do with their time, Aaron, he'd say. If they weren't involved in their interminable "project" they'd be complaining and getting in the way, Aaron—be glad they are so easily amused. Don't look a gift horse in the mouth, Aaron. No point in going through all that yet another time.

Furthermore, Thomas was right. Those rare retired women who weren't interested in the Project's addlepated activities *were* forever under foot, interfering just because they were bored. He said nothing, and headed quickly out through the side door, up the stairs, and into the gardens, where one of his sons was waiting for him to come discuss a problem in translation. He'd been waiting too long, thought Aaron in irritation. At seven even a male child can't be expected to have unlimited patience.

He was halfway down the path to the garden, already at the banks of orange day-lilies, that the women grew in profusion because not even the most fanatical anti-linguist could consider them an expensive waste, before he realized that he'd forgotten to send his wife the message after all. God, but women were a nuisance with their unending complaints and their fool illnesses. Cancer, for godsakes, in 2205! No male human had had cancer in . . . oh, fifty years at least, he'd be willing to bet on it. Puny creatures, women, and hardly worth their keep—certainly not worth their irritation.

His annoyance at having to go back to the house and carry out his promise very nearly caused him to rip up by the roots an inexcusable yellow rosebush, half-hidden among the day-lilies. Only one, but it was asking for trouble. He could hear the citizens now. "Work and slave and bleed for every *cent* and don't even have money to keep the *slide*walks decent because half our taxes go to the effing Lingoes, god curse them all, and they throw it all away on their underground palaces and their effing *rose* gardens . . ." He could imagine the slogans, the jingles, the media solemnly discussing the actual figures for rosebushes purchased by linguists in the period from 2195 to 2205—the media were fond of decades because it was so easy to run up the statistics for ten-year chunks. And he'd bet that the luscious yellow rosebush was one more of those little acts of sabotage Great-Aunt Sarah so enjoyed slipping past the accountants.

He reminded himself for the fifteenth time—somehow he must find space in his schedule this year to confer with their Congressional lobbyists about the legislation that would forbid females to buy anything whatsoever without a man's written approval. This business of letting them have pocket money, and making exceptions for flowers and candy and romance media and bits of frippery was forever leading to unforeseen complications . . .

astonishing how clever women were at distorting the letter of the law! Like the chimps, futzing around with their instructions in the military, and getting into pranks you'd never forbidden because never in your wildest fantasies had you *foreseen* them. Who'd have thought you had to formally teach a chimp not to shit on its weapons, for example?

He would have preferred to see "No Females Allowed" signs in *all* places of business, himself. But once again he had to bow to the argument that the creatures were a lot less trouble if they were allowed to spend their idle hours wandering around looking at things in the stores instead of doing all their buying by comset as men did. There was no end to it, always another concession to be made—and it was a certain amount of consolation to be able to say that the women of the Lines, linguist women, *had* no idle hours.

If anything could have tempted Aaron William Adiness-Chornyak to such black blasphemy as the concept of a Creatress, it was the seemingly irrational creation of females. Surely the Almighty could have had the simple gentlemanly courtesy to make women mute? Or to see to it that they had some biological equivalent of an Off/On switch for the use of the men obliged to deal with them? If He hadn't had the ingenuity to do without them altogether?

"Count your blessings," his own father would have said. "You could have been born before the Whissler Amendments, you know. You could have lived in a time when females were allowed to vote, when females sat in the Congress of the United States and a female was allowed to call herself a Supreme Court Justice. You think about that, boy, and you be grateful."

Aaron chuckled, remembering the first time he'd heard about that. He'd been seven years old, the same age as the boy he hurried now to meet. And he'd been punished, made to memorize a dozen full pages of useless noun declensions from an equally useless artificial language, for standing there seven years old and shocked silly enough to call Ross Adiness a liar. He had forgotten those sets of noun endings long ago, but the shock had never left him.

"Nazareth?" Clara said, and stopped short to stare.

Nazareth Joanna Chornyak Adiness, twin sister of James Nathan Chornyak, eldest daughter in this Household, mother of nine, looked like nothing so much as a battered servomechanism at that moment. Ready to be traded in. Ready for scrap. The unsavory image struck the woman Aaron had sent to deliver his message, struck with a force that she hastily suppressed. It would be inexcusable for her to pass the men's decision along with a look of repulsion on her own face as its accompaniment.

But there *was* something repulsive about her. Something about the gaunt body, the graying hair drawn viciously back and skewered to the head with cruel pins, something about the rigid posture that was the reaction of a dogged pride to intolerable exhaustion and strain. She did not look anything like a *noble* wreck of a woman, or even a tortured animal . . . could you, Clara wondered, torment any machine into a state like Nazareth's?

And then Clara caught herself, and shuddered. God forgive me, she thought, that I could see her that way. I will *not* see her that way! This is a living woman before me, she told herself sternly, not one of those skinny cylinders with a round knob atop that scuttles silently through the houses and workplaces of nonlinguists doing the dirty work. This is a living woman, to whom harm can be done, and I will speak to her without distorted perceptions.

"Nazareth?" she said gently. "My dear. Have you fallen asleep there?"

Nazareth jumped a little, startled, and she turned away from the transparent walls to the Interface where her youngest child was serenely stacking up plastiblocks under the friendly gaze of the current Alien-in-Residence.

"I'm sorry, Aunt Clara," she said. "I didn't hear you . . . I'm afraid my mind was a million miles away. Do you need me for something?"

Putting it off, Clara gestured with the point of her chin at the child, now laughing at some comment from the A.I.R. "He's doing well, isn't he?"

"I think so. He seems to be putting sentences together already . . . little ones, but certainly sentences. Not bad for just barely two years old, with three languages to sort out at once. And his English doesn't seem slowed down at all."

"Three languages," mused Clara. "That's not so bad, dear. . . . I've known them to lay on half a dozen, when there weren't so many infants available."

"Ah, but you remember Paul Hadley? Remember how worried we all were? Three years in the Interface with that northern Alphan, and nothing in *any* language but a half dozen baby words."

"It turned out all right," Clara reminded her. "That's all that matters. That sort of thing happens now and then."

"I know that. That's why I worry that it might happen again. Especially this time."

Clara cleared her throat, and her hands made a small useless gesture. "It's not likely," she said.

Nazareth raised her eyes, then, and looked at her aunt. Her face was the faded yellow of cheap paper.

"You've come from the men, Aunt Clara," she said, "and you're trying to avoid telling me what they decided. It's no good . . . we could find a dozen frivolous topics to postpone it with, but you will eventually have to tell me, you know."

"Yes."

"It's not good, is it?"

"It could be worse."

Nazareth swayed then, and put one hand against the Interface wall to steady herself, but Clara made no move to go help her. Nazareth allowed no one to help her, and she had good reason.

"Well?" she asked. "What have they decided, Clara?"

"You're to have the surgery."

"The laser surgery."

"Yes. But not the breast regeneration."

"Are the women's accounts so low as all that?"

"No, Natha—it wasn't a financial decision."

"Ah. . . . I perceive." Nazareth's hands moved, one to each of her breasts, and she covered them tenderly, as a lover might have covered them against a chill wind.

The two women looked at each other, silently. And in the same way that Clara ached for the woman who must accept a wholly avoidable mutilation, Nazareth ached for the woman who had been ordered to carry that message. It was the way of the world, however. And as Clara had pointed out, it could have been worse. They could have refused to authorize the surgery—except that the media would have seized on the story as yet another example of the difference between the linguist and the normal human being.

"You're to go right away," said Clara when she could no longer bear the sight of that blind anguish. "There's a robobus due by in about fifteen minutes, that stops at the hospital. They want you on it, child. You needn't take anything with you—just get yourself ready for the street. I'll help you if you like."

"No. Thank you, Aunt Clara, I can manage." Nazareth's hands dropped, to be clasped behind her back, out of sight.

"I'll have someone authorize the transfer of credits to the hospital account, then," said the older woman. "No need for you to have to sit there waiting for it to be verified. I can have it done before you get there, if I can find a man not occupied with anything urgent.''

"Like the tobacco accounts.''

"For example.''

"If it can be done,'' said Nazareth stolidly, "that would be a pleasant development. If not, don't worry about it. I am one of the most accomplished wait-ers in the Line. Another few hours won't do me any serious damage.''

Clara nodded. Nazareth was always accurate.

"Any instructions about the children? Anything I should see to?''

"I don't think so. Judith and Cecily know my schedule, and if there's anything not on the usual list they'll know about that—they'll alert you. You might tell them to check my journal in the mornings to be certain.''

Clara waited, but Nazareth had nothing more to say, and at last she made the useless gesture again and murmured, "Go in lovingkindness, Nazareth Joanna.''

Nazareth nodded, lips tight and gray in the stark face. The nodding small jerky motions like a windup toy, such as you could see in the museum collections, went on and on, until Clara turned helplessly and left her there. Nazareth did not look again at little Matthew or at the AIRY, except to arrange her body in the obligatory parting-posture of PanSig that politeness required. It was not the Alien's fault, after all.

Think about that, Nazareth instructed herself. Think about the Alien-in-Residence. Use your unruly mind for something constructive. This is no time for wild thoughts.

The Alien was interesting, by no means always a characteristic of AIRY's. She looked forward to knowing more about its culture and its language as Matthew grew older and became capable of describing them. Three legs rather than two, and a face was more "face?'' . . . tentacles, in a mane from the top of the head down the entire spine, tentacles that either reacted to something in the environment and moved in reflex or were under voluntary control . . . There had been lengthy discussion before it had been accepted, some question as to whether it was truly humanoid. It had taken the unanimous vote of the Heads of the thirteen Lines to put it through and get the contract approved, and the old man at Shawnessey Household in Switzerland had taken considerable persuading.

My child, she thought, her back turned to him. My little son. My last son, my last child. And if they made an error, if that being is not truly humanoid, *my* child who will be a vegetable, or worse.

There you go again, Nazareth, with your mind that does not behave! She clicked her tongue, "tsk!", and clasped her hands more tightly. Better to occupy that mind with the interesting characteristics of this latest AIRY, or a review of the current inventory of her children's linguistic skills. Better to occupy that mind with anything at all but the bitter gall of the simple truth, vile in her throat.

Make herself ready for the street, they had said . . . what did they want of her? She looked down at herself and saw nothing to criticize. No ornament. A plain tunic with modest sleeves to the elbow, in a color that was no color. Clingsoles on her feet, nothing more. Her hair she knew to be orderly. No one could have looked at her and thought "There goes a bitch linguist!" unless they spotted her for a degree of impoverished appearance that could only be the result of having a choice about such things.

She would leave her wrist-computer; there was nobody who did not have one, and hers was plain and worn. She would need it in the public wards, to be able to contact the Household from time to time.

I am all right as I am, she thought. Ready for any street. And any data that the hospital might want from her was easily available from the tattoos in her armpits.

Nazareth went out to the front of the house to wait for the robobus. She did not bother to get anything at all from the room she shared with Aaron. She did not touch her breasts again.

Chapter Two

The linguistic term *lexical encoding* refers to the way that human beings choose a particular chunk of their world, external or internal, and assign that chunk a surface shape that will be its name; it refers to the process of word-making. When we women say "Encoding," with a capital "E," we mean something a little bit different. We mean the making of a name for a chunk of the world that so far as we know has never been chosen for naming before in any human language, and that has not just suddenly been made or found or dumped upon your culture. We mean naming a chunk that has been around a long time but has never before impressed anyone as sufficiently important to *deserve* its own name.

You can do ordinary lexical encoding systematiclly—for example, you could look at the words of an existing language and decide that you wanted counterparts for them in one of your native languages. Then it's just a matter of arranging sounds that are permitted and meaningful in that language to make the counterparts. But there is no way at all to search systematically for capital-E Encodings. They come to you out of nowhere and you realize that you have always needed them; but you can't go looking for them, and they don't turn up as concrete entities neatly marked off for you and flashing NAME ME. They are therefore very precious.

(Chornyak Barren House,
Manual for Beginners, page 71)

WINTER 2179 . . . .

Aquina Chornyak was bored. It was a boring negotiation, on a boring contract, for a boring treaty amendment, with a set of almost stupefyingly boring Aliens-in-Transit. You never expected an A.I.T. to be exactly stimulating company—that wasn't what they were on Earth for, in the first place, and there was no reason to anticipate that what a Terran found stimulating would be anything they found stimulating, or vice versa, in the second place—but sometimes there were a few glimmers of interest in the waste of bureaucratic drivel.

Not this time. The Jeelods were so nearly Terran in physical appearance that it was hard to remember they *were* A.I.T.s . . . no amusing tentacles or tails, no pointy ears, no twin noses. Not even an exotic mode of dress to provide diversion. They were short and they were stocky, a bit more square than was typical with Earth humanoids, and they had long beards. And that was it. In their baggy coveralls they looked like a trio of . . . oh, maybe plumbers. Something of the kind. It was boring. And who cared (except the Jeelods, of course, since if they hadn't cared they wouldn't have demanded the negotiation), who cared if the containers Terra shipped them weapons in were blue or not?

They cared. They'd made that clear. Blue, they had said, was a color shocking to every Jeelod, an insult to the honor of every Jeelod; it was a *twx'twxqtldx* matter. Aquina could not begin to pronounce that, but she hadn't had to; she was here only as backup and social translator for Nazareth, who was the native speaker of REM34-5-720 for Earth. Nazareth could say it, as easily as she might have said "twaddle." And Nazareth had tried patiently to explain what the word meant.

If Aquina understood it correctly herself, making those shipping containers blue was about equivalent to the Jeelods having shipped freight to Earth in containers smeared with human feces . . . curious how the same idiot taboos turned up in so many humanoids from all over the universe. But the Jeelods weren't going to participate in handling the matter the way two Earth cultures would have done it, in a similar situation.

"You mean making the containers blue is like smearing shit all over them?"

"Damn right!"

"Jeez, we didn't know. Our apologies, okay? What's a color that's okay with you guys?"

"Make 'em red."

"You've got it."

And the meeting would be over. No . . . there was clearly something else going on here, and it couldn't be done that way. (And to be honest, there were Earth cultures that couldn't have done it that way either.)

Every time Nazareth tried to explain it, speaking first in flawless REM34-5-720 to the Jeelods, and then in flawless English to the representatives of the U.S. Government, the same thing happened. The Jeelods went pale, turned their backs, sat down on the floor, and covered their heads with their hands—a position, Nazareth said, indicating that they were not present in any legal sense of the word. These periods of legal absence lasted, per Jeelod cultural imperatives, exactly eighteen minutes and eleven seconds. After which they would seat themselves at the conference table again and Nazareth would give it another try. Poor kidling.

If *she* was bored, Aquina thought, at her age, Nazareth must be at the end of her tether completely. Eleven is not a patient age, even for a child of the Lines. And unlike the men from the State Department, who had started going out for coffee for exactly eighteen minutes and three seconds every time it happened, Nazareth had to stay there in the room. No telling *what* the A.I.T.'s would have offered up as reaction if their interpreter had left the room during their ritual of insult.

They were fifteen minutes and a bit into the latest episode, and Aquina sighed and considered going for coffee herself; as mere backup, she could presumably be spared. But it would be complicated, since she'd have to find an agreeable male to escort her. And it wouldn't be kind . . . She was fond of Nazareth, who was something pretty special in eleven-year-old girls. Aquina glanced at her fondly, wishing she could tell her a joke or something to ease the tedium, and saw that the child had her head bent in total concentration over a small pad of paper. Scribbling something on it, with the tip of her tongue sticking out between firmly clamped lips. Aquina touched her gently to get her attention, and then she signed a question at her; with their backs turned, the Jeelods would never know that the Terrans were using sign language.

"You drawing, sweetlove? Can I see?" she signed.

The child looked uneasy, and her shoulders curled protectively toward whatever it was.

"It doesn't matter," Aquina signed. "Never mind—I didn't mean to pry."

But Nazareth smiled at her and shrugged, signing. "That's okay," and passed her the little tablet to look at.

Now that she had it, Aquina didn't know what she had; it wasn't drawings, certainly. It appeared to be words, but no words she'd ever seen before. Nazareth would be far ahead of her in REM34-5-720, because it was her responsibility to be far ahead—it was her native language, as much as English and Ameslan were. But these words couldn't be REM34-5-720. Aquina knew the rules for word-formation in the language . . . these were something else. ·

"They're Encodings," signed Nazareth, seeing her puzzlement.

"What?"

"Encodings," Nazareth fingerspelled it, to be sure of it, and Aquina stared at her open-mouthed.

Encodings! What on earth—

Before she could ask, she heard the swift hiss of clingsoles behind her; the State Department men were coming back. Nazareth sat up straight in the interpreter's booth, where she and Aquina were sufficiently hidden from view to spare the delicate egos of the males the humiliation of really seeing the women . . . on whose services they were completely dependent in this interplanetary transaction. Nazareth's whole attention was on the Jeelods and their Terran counterparts, and she left the little tablet in Aquina's hands. Nazareth knew her obligations, and she fulfilled them. Aquina heard her speaking, easily producing the impossible consonant clusters with their impossible modifications of clicks and glottalizations and squeaks, trying to find a way of expressing their objections that would not force them to be "absent" from the negotiations again.

Which left Aquina free to study the tablet, casually at first, and then with a steadily increasing excitement. Encodings, the child had said! New language shapes, for concepts not yet lexicalized in any known language . . . Encodings, Capital-E, was that?

She stared at the neat symbols; children of the Lines, trained to do phonetic transcription by the age of six, did not produce anything but tidy symbols. The words themselves she recognized now—they were Nazareth's attempts at Langlish, and they were pathetic. Given the resources that Langlish offered to a coiner of words, they were bound to be pathetic; and given the very very little that Nazareth could know about Langlish, they weren't even top quality pathetic. But she was excited nevertheless.

It was the concepts themselves, the semantics of the forms that

Nazareth was trying to make speakable; they made her heart
race. They might well exist in some language she did not know
about, sure, and that would have to be checked; but then again
they might not. And if they didn't, well—if they didn't, they
were like finding a carteblanche disc on the slidewalk, with
nobody around to see you pick it up. It would be easy enough,
now that Nazareth had written down the semantics, to put the
proper shapes to them, to make them words . . .

There was a fine dampness on her forehead and on her palms;
she looked at the child beside her as she would have looked at a
truly interesting Alien. And saw that Nazareth was exasperated,
and not with the Jeelods—Aquina must have been missing cues,
and being about as much use as a no backup at all. The tablet
would have to wait, and Aquina signed a hasty "Sorry, Natha!"
and turned her attention to her work. Nazareth had more than
enough to do just trying to solve this tangle of language and
custom, without having to take the notes on it and look up forms
in the lexicons and make nice at the government flunkies when
they got agitated. Aquina put the tablet firmly out of her mind,
and bent to her work.

It was nearly midnight before she got back to Chornyak
Barren House and could finally talk the whole thing over with
someone. First there had been the interminable series of
"absences." By her count, twenty-nine of them, before Nazareth had at last found a pair of equivalent utterances in the two
languages that would serve the purpose and offend neither group
of negotiators. Then there'd been the long wrangle over what
color the containers should be in the future . . . there was no
point, Nazareth had advised them, in choosing another color and
then finding out that it was also taboo, with all of this to be gone
through again.

Aquina had been just barely able to follow what the child was
doing, and she hadn't known half the words. (That was the
problem of having only an informal backup, instead of another
native speaker, of course—but when the only other native speaker
wasn't walking yet, you did the best you could.) Nazareth had
told the Jeelods a story, the way you'd tell any story; and all
through it she had salted in, one by one, the Jeelod color
terms—all eleven basic ones, and a few additional common ones
for good measure. She knew what she was doing, that was
obvious; presumably this was the Jeelod equivalent of beating
around the bush until a safe point was reached. As each color
term was introduced into the story, there'd be a certain twitch of

Nazareth's shoulders, a certain flicker of her tongue, a certain sniffing noise . . . surely a body-language unit of Jeelod, by the patterning, although Aquina didn't know its significance. And the child had watched with an impressive intensity as she spoke, looking for something from *them,* some scrap of body-part that would give her the clue she needed. While the government men fidgeted. They had no patience at all, as usual; Aquina had wondered what rock the government found them under. Also as usual.

Finally, *fin*ally, there'd been the proper color, and no unpleasant reaction to contend with from the Aliens. Then there was the matter of drawing up the new treaty clause to specify that color . . . and that had not been easy, for reasons that were no doubt clear to Nazareth Chornyak but that she had been too exhausted by then to bother trying to make clear to the rest of them.

And when it was all over, negotiation successfully concluded, Jeelods homeworld bound and happy, contract all signed and sealed and delivered, Aquina and Nazareth had been kept waiting while the government morons complained at length to the Chornyak man who'd come to retrieve them and take them home. Nazareth was incompetent, etc., etc. Aquina was no help, etc., etc. Disgraceful waste of time and money, etc., etc. If this was the best that the linguists could do, the government could only say et cetera et cetera.

Their driver had listened gravely, nodding once in a while to keep the stream of plaintive piddle flowing and get it over with; and eventually the flunkies had run out of anything to complain about. At which point he'd suggested that if they were truly dissatisfied with Nazareth and Aquina they should feel absolutely free to hire a different interpreter/translator team for their next contact with the Jeelods.

There *was* no other team, of course, since Nazareth Joanna Chornyak was the only living Terran who could speak the Jeelod's language with even minimal fluency. There were two Chornyak infants learning it from her, of course, so there'd be someone to step into her shoes at a later date and to serve as formal backup. One of them was nine months old, and the other was going on two . . . there wasn't much you could expect of them in the way of negotiating skills for quite some time to come. The flunkies knew that, and the linguists knew they knew that, and it was all just as silly as the Jeelods and their absence rituals. And seemed to take just as long.

"Eighteen minutes eleven seconds," Aquina had muttered to the weary girl beside her, while they waited for it to be over; and

Nazareth had giggled, and then said something genuinely gross in gutter French. All taken, they weren't in the van until nearly eleven, and even at that hour the Washington traffic was so heavy that it was another twenty minutes before they boarded the flyer . . . and Nazareth would have to be up at five-thirty for the next day's routine, as always, and in another interpreting booth by eight o'clock sharp. Such fun, being a child of the Lines!

And fun being a woman of the Lines, too, of course. There were plenty of women still awake at Barren House at midnight, and they were busy enough—and tired enough—to welcome an excuse for a break and listen to what Aquina had to tell them. She started with a small and dubious audience; just herself and Nile and Susannah and a new resident named Thyrsis that she didn't really know well—who'd decided for some as yet unexplained reason that she preferred being here to living at Shawnessey Barren House. No doubt she'd tell them about it, in her own good time. Aquina began with those four, and then as she talked her audience grew steadily.

"I don't think I understand," put in Thyrsis Shawnessey the first time Aquina paused. "In fact, I'm sure I don't."

"That's because Aquina's so excited. She never can talk straight when she's excited . . . fortunately, she's always bored at negotiations, or lord knows what kind of things she'd have brought upon us by now."

"How can you be excited, Aquina, at this hour of the night?"

"Because it *is* exciting," Aquina insisted.

"Tell us again."

Aquina told them, trying not to get ahead of herself, and they listened, nodding, and Susannah got up and made three pots of tea and poured it all round.

When she was satisfied that everyone was settled with the steaming cups, she called Aquina to a halt, saying, "Now let me just find out if I have this straight, without all the exotic touches. What you're telling us is that that child, all on her own, has been writing down Encodings and making up words to fit them in Langlish. Without any help or instruction from anyone. And nothing in the way of information about Langlish, really, except the scraps the little girls pick up running back and forth between here and the main house . . . the bits and pieces they see us fooling with at the computers, and such. Have I got it right, Aquina?"

"Well, it was pissy Langlish, Susannah—you'd expect that."

"I surely would."

"But you have it right. Considering what she has to work with, she'd done very well. You could tell the forms were supposed to *be* Langlish, at least. And that's not what matters anyway; it's the semantics that matters, damn it. And I had a chance to ask her a thing or two while we were waiting for the men to wind up their dominance displays and let us come home—she's been doing it a long time, she says.''

"That would mean a month or two, at her age."

"Maybe so; maybe not. She says she has lots more pages at home. She's keeping a notebook, like I kept a diary. What wouldn't I give to get a look at that notebook!"

"You really think this is important, don't you, Aquina? Not just a little girl playing, but really important."

"Well, don't you?"

"Aquina, we weren't there—we didn't see what she had written. And you can't remember very well. How can we judge, with so little data?"

"I copied one of them."

"Without asking her."

"Yes. Without asking her." Aquina was used to being in trouble with her housemates, and used to being on the wrong side of their ethical lines; she didn't bother being defiant. "I thought it mattered, and I still think so. Here . . . please, look at this." And she showed them a sample of what had been on Nazareth's tablet.

> To refrain from asking, with evil intentions; especially when it's clear that someone badly wants you to ask—for example, when someone wants to be asked about their state of mind or health and clearly wants to talk about it.

"Well?" she demanded after they'd looked at it long enough to understand it. "Say something!"

"And she gave this a lexicalization as a Langlish word?"

"Well, hellfire and heavengates, woman, Nazareth doesn't know that there's any other woman-language *but* Langlish! Naturally that's what she tried to do. But can't you see? If she can formulate semantic concepts like these, *we* know what to do with them!"

"Oh, but Aquina," Susannah objected, "then the child would expect to see them turn up on the computers in the Langlish program. And that would mean the men would have access to them. We can't have that, and you know it."

There was a chorus of agreement, and Aquina shook her head

fiercely and shouted, "I NEVER SAID—" and then abruptly lowered her voice and started over. She was too tired to yell, even if it had been appropriate.

"I never said that we would *tell* Nazareth we were using them; lord, I'm not completely stupid!"

"But then how would we get them?"

"I'll get them," said Aquina. "I'm Nazareth's informal backup for all the Jeelod negotiations, and they're back with some fool complaint about every two weeks. I'll have plenty of boredom time with her to find out where she keeps that notebook. Not in the girldorm, that's for sure . . . I never would have. But she never has any opportunity to take it far from either this house or the big house—it's in a tree, or down a hole, or something. And she'll tell me."

"And then?"

"And then I will—very carefully, so she'll never know—go every week or so and copy off whatever she's added."

There. Now they were shocked. They knew all about breaking eggs to make omelettes, but it didn't help them any; they had about as much political sense as Nazareth, even when you put the whole bunch of them together.

"You can't do that," said Nile flatly, pulling her shawl tighter around her as a sudden lash of sleet rattled the window beside them.

"Why can't I?"

"How would you have felt if somebody had done that with your diary, when you were little?"

"There's a difference."

"Such as?"

"My diary was only important to *me*. Nazareth's secret notebook is important to every woman on this planet, and every woman beyond, and all women to come. The two things are not the same at all."

Susannah reached over then and laid her hand, gnarled with arthritis and swollen with blue veins, but sure and strong and kind, over Aquina's hand.

"My dear," she said gently, "we understand you. But please do think! Living as we do, all of us in communal households from the day we're brought home from the hospital—and on the public wards before that, lord knows!—and no instant away from the Household except the time we spend shut up with one another in interpreting booths . . . Aquina, we have so little privacy! It's so precious. You can't violate Nazareth's privacy by sneaking her notebook from where she's hidden it away, just because she's a child and won't suspect you—that's despicable. I don't believe you mean it.''

"Oh, she means it!" said Caroline, joining them with a mug of black coffee. Caroline didn't care for tea, and wouldn't drink it to be polite. "You can be sure she means it!"

"Indeed I do," said Aquina.

Susannah clucked her tongue, and took her hand away; and Aquina wished for her own shawl, but against the chill inside this house, not the chill of the weather. She could not understand why it never stopped hurting, having all the other women set against her. She'd be fifty-five years old tomorrow, more than half a century, and she'd lived here in Barren House so many years . . . and still it hurt. She was ashamed, to be so soft. And sorry she'd told them, but it was too late for that.

"I will find out where she keeps the notebook," she said between her teeth, "and I will check it every week or two to copy what's been added there, and I will bring that data back here for us to work on."

"You'll work on it all by yourself if you do."

"I'm used to that," said Aquina bitterly.

"I suppose you must be."

"And because Nazareth will never know about it, she won't be looking for those words in the Langlish computer displays—and they'll be safe. But we will have the good of them."

"Shame on you."

"I'm not ashamed," she said.

"Takes eggs to make an omelette?"

Aquina firmed her mouth and said nothing; she hadn't learned not to be hurt, but she'd learned not to let them bait her.

And then, because she was so tired and she felt so alone, she started to tell them what she thought of their damnfool ethics, but Susannah cut her off instantly. And Belle-Anne, drawn from her bed by the subdued racket of their arguing, rosy as an angel, and her yellow hair loose down her back, came in to help. She rubbed Aquina's taut shoulders, and poured her a fresh cup of tea, and there-thered her generally until she was soothed and Susannah had the subject well changed and onto neutral ground.

What was a real shame, they were saying, was that it would be so long before they could have Nazareth *with* them. With them and working on the woman-language in all her spare moments, with full knowledge of what she was doing.

"Do you know," asked Nile, "that Nazareth's mother told me the child's language-facility scores are the highest ever seen since we've been keeping records? Clear off the scale! They're expecting tremendous things of her . . . and such luck that it was her they gave that awful Jeelod language to; she has no trouble with it, apparently.''

"She won't be any use to us for . . . oh, what, forty years?" Aquina hazarded, her voice thick with resentment even under Belle-Anne's stroking and soothing. "She's eleven now . . . she'll marry, perhaps marry into another Household, and she'll have the obligatory dozen children to give birth to—"

"Aquina! Don't make it worse than it is! Thomas Blair Chornyak will never let her get out of his sight—you can count on that. And it's not a dozen children she'll have to produce, that's absurd!"

"All right, half a dozen, then. Six children, seven children, whatever you like—lots of children. And every instant given over to working on the government contracts, hardly time to get up out of childbed before she's back in the interpreting booths again . . . until she's worn out at last, and the menopause comes to bless her.''

"Even then," Caroline put in, "she may not come to us. Not if her husband wants her to stay with him—not if she wears well. Or if she's lucky and the man's fond of her beyond just her body.''

"Or if she's useful to him somehow," said Thyrsis, with a sharp note to her voice that caught their attention. So that was it . . . she'd come to Chornyak Barren House against her husband's wishes, because she was useful to him in some way, clever at something he liked having her do. And if she'd tried to go to Shawnessey Barren House he'd have been close by to be forever pressuring her to come back to the main house. They would be interested in knowing how she'd managed to get around his authority, come the time she felt free to tell them more.

"Damn and damn and damn," mourned Aquina. "That's forty years or more *wasted*. Don't you understand that? Don't any of you understand that?''

"Aquina, it's not as though the whole Encoding Project was dependent on Nazareth—we are all working on it. And women at the other Barren Houses are working on it, Be reasonable.''

They soothed her, all of them. Soothed and coaxed, anxious to restore her perspective on this in spite of her distress. She was overtired, she would feel better about it in the morning, she would see that it was just that she'd been under such a strain. On and on. . . .

Aquina let them talk, and she kept her own counsel. Tomorrow, first thing, what she would do was go looking for Nazareth and begin trying to find out where that notebook was hidden. Her own priorities, thank god, were properly ordered.

Chapter Three

The only way there is to *acquire* a language, which means that you know it so well that you never have to be conscious of your knowledge, is to be exposed to that language while you are still very young—the younger the better. The infant human being has the most perfect language-learning mechanism on Earth, and no one has ever been able to duplicate that mechanism or even to analyze it very well. We know that it involves scanning for patterns and storing those that are found, and that's something we can build a computer to do. But we've never been able to build a computer that can acquire a language. In fact, we've never even been able to build a computer than can learn a language in the imperfect way that a human *adult* can learn one.

We can take a language that's already known, and program a computer to use it by putting the language into the computer piece by piece. And we can build a computer that's programmed to scan for patterns and store them very efficiently. But we can't put those two computers side by side and expect the one that doesn't know the language to acquire it from the other one. Until we find out how to do that (as well as a number of other things), we are dependent on human infants for the acquisition of all languages, whether Terran or extraterrestrial; it's not the most efficient system we can imagine, but it's the most efficient system that we have.

(from Training Lecture #3,
for junior staff—U.S. Department of Analysis & Translation)

SPRING 2180. . . .

Ned Landry had been pleased with his wife Michaela, as well he might have been, since she had fit his bill of specifications almost to the last and most trivial detail. (There was that slight tendency to poor muscle tone in the hips—but he wasn't a fanatic. He knew that he couldn't expect total perfection.) It had cost his parents a tidy sum to pay the agency fee for her, but it had been well worth it, and he had long since paid them back with interest. Just picking a wife from among whatever gaggle of females happened to be available in his circle of acquaintances had never appealed to Ned; he had wanted something with quality guaranteed, and he had never regretted waiting. It had been a little annoying, having his own marriage nothing but a list of specs in a file when his friends were well on their way to being heads of families already—but they envied him now. They all envied him, and that pleased him.

Michaela did all the things he wanted a wife to do. She saw to his house and his meals and his comfort and his sexual needs. She kept so smoothly running a setup that he never had time to think, *I wonder why Michaela hasn't* . . . done something or other, because she always *had* done it; often it wasn't until after she had seen to some detail, some change, that he realized it had been a thing that he wanted. The flowers in the vases were always fresh; clean garments appeared as if by magic in his gardrobes; a tunic that had seemed to him about to show signs of wear either appeared so expertly renovated that it looked new, or was replaced between one day and the next . . . never once did he have to miss something or do without anything.

Ned had only to mention in passing that a particular food sounded interesting, and in the next day or two it would appear on his table—and if he didn't care for it after all, it would never appear again. Household repairs, maintenance, cleaning, the small garden of which he was justifiably proud, any sort of household business matter, upkeep on his assets and his collections—all these things were attended to in his absence. His only contribution to the perfect serenity of his home was to look over the printouts his accountant provided for him at the end of every month and sign or refuse the authorization for spending whatever sums Michaela had requested.

It was a blissful existence; he treasured it. Except at his work, where no woman's influence could intrude and there was therefore no way Michaela *could* smooth the waters, Ned Landry was spared even the memory of irritation. And she was always there, her butter-blond hair in the elegant chignon he liked so much for the contrast if offered when, in his bed, she let it down to fan over the pillows like a net of pale silk.

He valued Michaela for all the things that she did, he knew her worth, and he saw to it that she was rewarded not only by the customary birthday and holiday gifts expected of any courteous husband but with small extra ones that he had no obligation to make. He was careful not to establish any pattern that might lead her to take that kind of indulgence for granted—when you had something as fine as Michaela in your pocket, you didn't act like an ass and take chances with her. He had no intention of spoiling her. But once in a while, seemingly for no reason, he would bring her some pretty trinket, the sort of foolishness that women always liked. Ned prided himself on understanding what women liked and on his ability to provide it, and Michaela was worth every credit and penny she cost him. Michaela was a thoroughbred, and superbly trained, just as the agency had guaranteed that she would be.

But the thing that mattered most to him about his wife, the thing that was the heart and core of the marriage for him, was none of those usual things. He could have hired almost anyone to do what she did around the house, including the sexual services—although he would have had to be exceedingly careful about that last. He would have been obliged to give orders rather than having his order anticipated, but he could have managed that. He could have bought servomechanisms to carry out many of those orders. And anything he had no permanent arrangement for, he could have dialed up by comset in a matter of minutes.

What really mattered to him, the one service that he could not have simply purchased, was Michaela's role as listener. Listener! That was beyond price, and had come as a surprise to him.

When he got home from work in the afternoon, Ned liked to unwind for a while. He liked to stand there, maybe pace a bit, with a cigarette in one hand and a glass of straight whiskey in the other, and tell her about his day. What he'd said, and what so-and-so had said back, the sonofabitch, and what he'd said *then*, and how it had showed the sonofabitch, by god. The good ideas he'd had and how they'd worked out when he tried them. The ideas that should have worked, and would have if it hadn't been for so-and-so, the stupid jackass. And what he just happened to know about the stupid jackass that might come in handy one of these days.

He liked to pace a while, and then stand there a while, and then pace some more, until he'd gotten rid of the energy from the morning, talking all of it out of his system. And then when he'd finally loosened up he liked sitting down in his chair and relaxing with the second glass of Scotch and the fifth cigarette—and talking some more.

That listening function of Michaela's meant a tremendous amount to Ned Landry, because he loved to talk and he loved to tell stories. He loved to take stories and draw them out to a great length and polish them until he found them flawless. Adding a new detail here, inventing a bit of embroidery there, cutting a line that didn't quite meet his standards. To Ned, that kind of talking was one of the major pleasures of a man's life.

Unfortunately, he was not *good* at it, for all his excruciating effort, and nobody would listen to him long if they could help it. Talking to people other than Michaela meant that second of attention that tantalized his need; and then the sudden withdrawal, the blank eyes, the glassed-over face, the restless body, the furtive looks at the timespot on the wrist computer. He knew what they were thinking . . . how long, oh lord, how long? That was what they were thinking, no matter how much some of them tried not to show it, for the sake of politeness.

He didn't understand it. Because he was a man of taste and intelligence and sophistication, and he really worked *hard* at being a raconteur, at shaping and polishing his narratives until they were works of oral art. It seemed to him that if people were too stupid to realize that and appreciate the skill with which he used language, it was their fault, not his . . . he more than did *his* part, and it was his considered opinion that he did it very very well indeed. Nevertheless, it frustrated him that people didn't want to listen to him talk; it was their fault, but he was the one who paid.

Except for Michaela. If Michaela thought he was boring and pompous and interminable and a windballoon, no tiniest flicker of that judgment had ever showed on her face or in her body or in her words. Even when he was talking about the injustice of a man such as he was being afflicted with seemingly innumerable allergies—and Ned was willing to admit that his allergies were probably not the most gripping conversational topic of the season, he just needed to talk about them sometimes—even then, Michaela always looked interested. She didn't have to answer him, because he didn't have any desire for conversation, he just wanted to be listened to, *attended* to; but when she did answer, her voice never carried any of that taint of impatience and boredom that so irritated him in others.

Michaela listened. And she laughed at the lines that he considered funny. And her eyes brightened at just the places where he meant the tension to build. And she never, not once, in three years of marriage, said, "Could you get to the point, please?" Not once. Sometimes, before he really got a new story worked out, or when he was just bullshitting along about the morning and hadn't had time to make stories out of it, he would realize that he had maybe wandered off his subject a little, or said something more than once . . . but Michaela never showed any awareness of that. She hung on his words. As he *wanted* them hung on—not slavishly, but tastefully. That was the difference. He could have paid some female to listen slavishly, at so many credits the hour, sure. But you'd know. You'd know she was only listening because of the money, like some kind of a meter running. It wouldn't be the same. Penny for your words, Mr. Landry? Sure . . .

Michaela was different, she was a woman with genuine class, and there was nothing slavish about the attention she gave him. It was careful attention, it was intense, it was total; it was not slavish. And it fed him. When he got through talking to Michaela, somewhere into the down slope of the afternoon, and was at last ready to do something else, he was in a state of satisfaction that wiped away the rebuffs he got from others as if they'd never happened. At that point Ned believed that he really *was* one of those irresistible talkers, one of those men that anyone would feel privileged to sit down and listen to for hours, as it seemed to him that he ought to be. He knew his stories were as good as anybody else's . . . hell, he knew they were better. One hell of a lot better! People were just stupid, that's all; and Michaela made that trivial.

It was that particular thing that the baby ruined for him, when it came. He could have put up with all the other stuff. Having Michaela look tired in the morning instead of showing her usual fresh perfection was annoying; having her attention distracted during lovemaking because the baby was crying was irritating; twice he'd had to point out to her that the vases of flowers needed to be seen to, and once she had even let him run out of Scotch. (That did get to him, considering that all she had to do was push one button on the comset to get it delivered . . . but still, he could have put up with it.)

He understood all these things. It was her first baby, and she wasn't getting as much sleep as she wanted; he was a reasonable man, and he understood. She had a lot of things to do that she wasn't used to doing, it was hard on her, sure. Everybody knew you had to coddle new mothers, like you had to coddle pregnant women. He was willing. He was confident that she would be able to get herself straightened out and back to normal in a month or two, and he didn't mind giving her all the time she needed. He had no respect at all for a man that didn't treat his woman fairly, and he wasn't that kind of man.

But it had never entered his head that the baby wold interfere with the time of *talking* to Michaela! Jeezus, if it had, he would've had her sterilized before he even married her. There were brothers to carry on his family line, and nephews all over the place for him to adopt at a suitable age if he wanted somebody to carry on the "son" role under his roof.

He'd no more than get started telling her how that goddam wimpoe of a technician had come up with yet one more stupid change in procedures, no more than get through a couple of sentences, when that effing baby would begin to squawl. He'd be right at a point in a story that he was starting to get perfect, one he'd only been telling a while but was beginning to see shaping up just right, just at a point where it was crucial for a person not to miss even one of the words he was saying, and the effing *baby* would start up!

It happened over and over again. And it made no difference whether he ordered her to go shut the brat up or ordered her to let it squawk—in either case, although of course she did exactly as he told her, he did not have her attention any longer. She wasn't listening to him, not *really* listening; her mind was on that little goddam tyrant of a puking kid. This was a possibility that he had never considered, something nobody had ever mentioned to him, something he hadn't been prepared for. And it was something Ned would *not* tolerate. Oh, no! Michaela's full attention was a major factor in his wellbeing, and he was bygod going to have it. He was making no compromises on that one.

The fact that he could pick up a ten thousand credit fee for the kid when he volunteered it, plus a guaranteed percentage if it worked out—with the money coming in quarterly for the rest of his life, mind—that was a pleasant little extra. There were things he wanted to buy, and the tenthou was going to be handy. He didn't mind it. He could afford to put a chunk of it into something pretty for Michaela, since in a way it was her kid too. But he would have volunteered the little effer for Government Work even if he'd had to pay *them* instead of getting a nice bonus to his account, because he wasn't about to have his life spoiled by a creature that weighed less than fifteen pounds and didn't even have teeth yet. No sir. This was his household, and he paid for it and for everything in it and for its upkeep, and he was bygod going to have his life as he had arranged for it to be. Anybody who doubted that just hadn't taken a look at his track record.

There was also the appeal of what it would be like to have his kid be the very first one ever to crack a nonhumanoid language . . . that, now, would be *very* nice. He didn't see any reason why it shouldn't happen; it was going to happen sometime, why not with *his* kid? It made sense. And he could imagine it, how he'd feel, being the one responsible for having finally broken the choke hold the effing Lingoes had on the taxpayers of this country! God *damn*, but that would feel good! People would suddenly find his conversation pure gold, if it turned out like that. Yeah. Ned could have really gotten to like it, if it happened.

You didn't tell a woman you were going to do something she might be silly about, of course. You did it, that's all; and afterward, you told her. Right away, so you could get the crap over with, her bawling and all that shit. Or you waited as long as you could put it off, so you didn't *have* to put up with the crap. Depending. This was one of the do-it-now times, since there wasn't anything Ned could use as a plausible explanation for the baby not being there when Michaela got back from the party at her sister's that he'd given her permission to go to.

She'd been surprised when he said she could go. It wasn't like him. He didn't approve of her being away from the house at night without him, especially now when it was important for her to get all her strength back so she could go back to her morning job at the hospital. The money she made as a nurse was useful to him, it went into a special account that he had big plans for, and every week that there wasn't any credit on his account for her services caused him a pretty good twinge. It bruised him, losing that money.

But the party had been a lucky break this time, and he'd done a really great job of telling her how she'd earned some fun and she could stay until midnight if she wanted to. It had gotten her away long enough for the fellow from G.W. to bring over the papers to be signed—and that very handsome transfer of credits— and for Ned to turn over the baby along with all its clothes and toys and stuff. He'd been scrupulously careful that there was nothing left to remind her of the kid, even though that meant he'd had to go up and check out its room personally, and he was allergic as hell to the No-Toxin spray they used in there, it made him cough and choke and swell up like a toad. He wanted to be absolutely certain all the kid's stuff was gone.

He suspected that Michaela had a holo of the baby somewhere on her person, maybe in that locket she wore all the time, and he'd have to get that later when she was asleep. No point in going through a scene about it and having her get herself all upset about it, that wasn't the way to handle a woman. And except for the hologram, there was nothing at all. The records he'd need if Government Work ever tried to renege on something were all in his computers, backed up with his accountant's computers, and a hard copy in a lockbox at his lawyer's. There was nothing for her to see, nothing to smell, he'd fixed it like there'd never *been* any baby. As there never should have been. He'd been guilty of poor planning, not seeing that; he was willing to admit that. He could have avoided all this hassle, if he'd just given it some thought.

And he was proud of her, because she took it like the true lady he knew her to be. He'd been prepared for a scene, and was ready to put up with quite a lot of female hysterics and nonsense, considering. She didn't say a word. Her eyes, dark blue eyes just like cornflowers, he loved her eyes—her eyes had gotten big; and he'd seen her give a kind of jerk, like she'd been punched and the wind knocked out of her. But she didn't say anything. When he told her she had to go down to the clinic in the morning and have a sterilization done before it happened again, god forbid, she only paled a little bit, and got that cute look she had sometimes when she was scared.

She'd asked him a few questions, and he gave her easy answers that didn't tell her any more than she needed to know. He'd signed the baby over, and that was the end of it. He reminded her that it was something any right-thinking American would be proud to do, because it was a heroic sacrifice for the sake of the United States of America and all of Earth and all of Earth's colonies, for chrissakes. He explained to her carefully that as long as the Lingoes wouldn't do their godgiven duty and put *their* babies to work on the nonhumanoid languages, as long as they kept on with their effing treason, it was up to normal people to step in and show them that bygod we could do it ourselves without their help, and to hell with them. Everybody knew that the Lingoes knew how to get the nonhumanoid languages, if they didn't get such a jolly out of keeping it a secret . . . he spent quite a bit of time making it clear to Michaela that all of this was the fault of the linguists. And he told her how the President would probably send them a personal note of thanks—no specifics, of course, since the official line was that the government had *no* connection with G.W.—but they could get away with telling a couple of close friends.

It was going to make a hell of a story, especially if the President *called*, and they'd told Ned that sometimes he did; he already knew how he was going to start it. When Michaela told him she didn't understand why the agency was called Government Work if the government wasn't supposed to have anything to do with it, he realized that that would be a nice touch to the story, too, and he patted her fondly on her little butt and explained about the old saying. "Good enough for government work," they used to say. Whatever that had meant.

He didn't tell her about the money, because he didn't want her getting any ideas, and women always *did* get ideas. He could just imagine her, talking about the fountain that his shit of a brother-in-law had let Michaela's sister wheedle him into putting in their front hall, maybe saying that with ten thousand credits he ought to be able to get her one like it. Nah. He was going to get her something nice, but he'd get her something she ought to have, not some piece of junk she just thought she wanted because some other woman had one. And he'd let it slip, toward the end of their discussion, that he might be planning something a little special for her. You had to hand it to her, after all; for a woman, she was pretty goddam sensible.

"You know, Mikey," he said, feeling expansive about it all, and so damn proud of her for not carrying on, "for a woman, you're pretty damn sensible. I mean that."

She smiled at him, and he admired the lovely curl of the corners of her lips—he had specified a smile like that, when he was still looking. "Thank you, darling," she said, pure sugar, pure sweet sugar, not even a pout because he'd called her "Mikey" and she hated that. Hell, it was *cute*, "Mikey" was! He didn't mind saying "MiKAYluh" in front of company, he'd humor her about that most of the time, but he liked calling her "Mikey," it suited her. Thinking about it, he said it again, and reached over to pull the hairpins out of her hair so she'd have to put it up again. She looked distressed, and he chuckled. God she was cute when she was upset . . . he was a very lucky man, and he'd see to it that she got something really special this time.

"Let me tell you what happened today at the goddam meeting," he began, watching the swift movements of her fingers repairing the havoc he'd wreaked in the silken hair. "Wait till you hear, sweetheart, it was just about the dumbest goddam piece of puke MetaComp has tried to pull yet, if you know what I mean . . . and you always do know what I mean, don't you, sweet lady? Let me tell you—this is a good one. We were all sitting there—"

He stopped, and he took a long leisurely drag on his cigarette, letting her wait for him to go on, enjoying it. He let the blue streams of smoke curl from his nostrils, grinning at her, holding it, holding it . . . and then, when he was ready, he went on and told her how it had been. And she listened, with her full attention, just like the way it had been before the baby, not a word about it being three o'clock in the morning or any of that stuff. God, it was good to have his home back again, *his* home, the way it was meant to *be*! He felt so good he made it through four glasses of Scotch, and he knew he wasn't going to be awake for the special Saturday breakfast he always had her order for them. Ham and eggs and waffles and strawberries, by god, and if the strawberries gave him hives, well they gave him hives. He was entitled. But he wasn't going to be awake for all that, not this morning.

It didn't matter. Whenever he decided to wake up, she'd have that breakfast ready for him, no matter what time it was. He could count on her. Life was just purely great.

Michaela was solicitous the next day, bringing him the Null-Alk capsules before he lifted his head from the pillow, and admitting at once that it was her fault he hadn't taken them before he went to sleep the night before. Sitting there beside him murmuring her sympathy until the pills took hold and he felt like himself again. There were lots of advantages to having a wife that was a trained nurse, besides the money it brought in. When you didn't feel good, it was gratifying to know there was somebody there that knew what to do, or knew when it was time to call somebody else because it was more than a woman could deal with. It was a comfort.

"I love you, honey," he said from the pile of pillows she'd fluffed for him. Women liked to hear that. And he felt like indulging her this morning, just knowing that he had the whole day—hell, the whole rest of his life—to look forward to now, without the effing baby.

He was just lying there, beaming at her and getting ready to have her bring him the special breakfast—with double strawberries—when he heard the noise.

"What the hell is that?" he demanded. It sounded like it was coming from his dressingroom.

"What, darling? Do you hear something?"

"Yeah . . .yeah, there it goes again. Don't you hear it?"

"Ned, darling," she said, "you know my ears aren't sharp like yours are . . . I don't hear a thing. It's a good thing you're around to take care of me."

Damn right it was. Ned stubbed out the cigarette and took a swig of the coffee she'd brought him right after the pills, laced with Scotch the way he liked it. "I'll go check it out," he said.

"You could just tell me where to look, Ned," she suggested, but he shook his head and threw back the covers.

"Naah. I'd better go see for myself. Probably a monitor that's gone bad. I'll be right back."

It wasn't until he was inside his dressingroom and had closed the door behind him that he saw the wasps. Four of them, *goddam* it, angry ones, *furious* bastards, buzzing and buzzing in there! He reached behind him for the door, he had to get out of there fast . . . shit, they were as big as effing hummingbirds! He'd seen them before outside, meant to mention them to Michaela and have her see to them, but how the fuck did they get in *here*? And it was not until he knew they were going to get to him no matter how carefully he moved that he realized something was wrong with the door, oh jeezus there was something wrong with the door, the plate that you pushed to open it from the inside wasn't there, there was oh jeezus just an empty fucking space there where it was supposed to be!

He started yelling for Michaela then, thanking god reverently and sincerely that she had never, not once, kept him waiting for *any*thing!

Michaela surprised him. She kept him waiting a very long time. Long enough to be certain. Long enough to put the insects down the vaporizer. Long enough to fix the door assembly so that it opened the way it always had, from either side, and wipe everything clean of her fingerprints. Long enough to see that there were fingerprints of *his* on everything they should have been on. It was often useful, being a nurse; you had to know lots of things that women weren't usually taught anything about. Lots of things that were going to come in handy from now on; oh, yes.

Only when she could step back and see nothing out of the ordinary in any way except the body on the floor did she scream for help and faint appropriately across the threshold in the clear view of the security monitor. *Care*fully, being very sure she did herself no harm. She had to take excellent care of herself now, did Michaela, because *she* was now the one who had all the big plans.

Chapter Four

I suppose every single one of us that comes here, knowing that his work will mean contact with extraterrestrials, thinks that *he* will be an exception, that he'll find a way to make friends with at least some of them. You figure you'll get the Lingoe to teach you a few words . . . "Hello! How *are* you? Nice whatsit you've got there!" That kind of thing. You think, we can't just go on forevermore being strangers, right? But when the time comes, and you get *close* to an Alien, you understand what the scientists are talking about when they say it isn't possible. There's a feeling that comes over you. It's not just fear, and it's not just prejudice. It's something you never felt before, and something you'll never forget when you've felt it once.

You know how you can find things under rocks that will just about go crazy digging in and curling up, trying to get away from the light? That's how you feel, when you're close to an Alien, or even when you're in contact with one by comset for more than a minute or two. You wish you had something to burrow into. Everything goes on red alert, and everything you've got to feel with is screaming ALIEN! ALIEN! You're glad then, let me tell you, you're very glad then, that you're not expected to be friendly. Just polite, that's all, even after all the training they give you here. Just polite.

(U.S. Department liaison staffer,
in an interview with Elderwild Barnes
of *Spacetime*)

The fervent emphasis that the government placed on traditional Christian values and on getting-back-to-one's-Vacation-Bible-School-roots (never mind that it put a steady drag on American culture, like hanging lead weights on one side of a wheel, pulling all of life at a crazy angle back toward the twentieth century) was a big help to Brooks Showard in his cursing. He didn't have to be inventive about it and use the resources of his Ph.D. to dredge up exotic oaths. The sturdy fundamental godams and hells that had served his forefathers, glazed now with time like candied fruits studding an otherwise plain loaf of bread, served him perfectly well.

"God damn it to hell and back," he said, therefore. "Oh god *damn* it all the way to hell and back, with side trips for the eager! Oh, *shit*!"

The other technicians had pulled back from the Interface, the oh so perfect and according to specs Interface, where Brooks stood holding the infant. They had formed themselves into a little gro.p, that could behave as if it had nothing to do with whatever this regrettable latest development turned out to be. Who, them? They were just passing by. Just happened to be in the neighborhood, don't you know . . .

"You get on over here!" he bellowed at them, shoving the baby under one armpit and shaking his free fist at them like the maniac, raving ranting maniac gone clear outaspace, that he considered himself to be at this moment. "You get on over here and look at this mess, you shits, you're as guilty as I am in this! Get your asses on over here and *see* this!"

They moved an inch, maybe. And Showard began a steady dull cursing, bringing Job's beard into it along with the private parts of the Twelve Disciples and a variety of forbidden practices and principles. They weren't going to come over there to him. They weren't going to participate in this, share the guilt, spread the horror around, not willingly. He was going to have to take it *to* them, the cowards! And it might be that next time he wouldn't have the guts to go inside the Interface after what was squirming there either, and then they could all be cowards together in Christian fellowship, couldn't they?

Behind him, safe in its special environment, the Alien-In-Residence *existed*, so far as anyone could tell. If it had died, presumably the various indicators on the walls would have told him that—that was the theory, anyhow. You couldn't say that the AIRY sat, precisely, or that it stood, or that it did anything, or was in any particular state. It *was*, and that was all it was. If what had happened to the human infant was of any concern to it, there was no way to know that, and might never be any way to know that. Sometimes Showard wasn't sure he saw the AIRY, really; the way it flickered (??), and never any pattern to the flickering (??), it drove the Terran eye to a constant search for order until there were great flat spots of color floating in the air between you and the source of the sensory stimulation. And then there were the other times, when you profoundly wished that you *couldn't* see it.

The linguists called theirs Aliens-in-Residence, too, called them AIRY's for short like the technicians did; but theirs were different. It was possible to look at one of theirs and at least assign labels roughly to its parts. That thing was a limb, say. That little lump there might well be a nose. There was its rosy butt, you see. Like that. It was possible to imagine that the creature *had* obligingly taken up "residence" in the simulated and sealed-off environment you had built for it within your house, and that it was delighted to visit for a while and share its language with your offspring. God knew the Lines had offspring to spare; the Lingoes bred like rats. But Brooks couldn't imagine the thing inside *this* Interface being allowed to take up "residence" in a human dwelling. Did it even *have* "parts"? Who could tell?

And now, there was this baby.

"Gentlemen," said Government Work Technician Brooks Everest Showard, holder of a secret rank of Colonel in the United States Air Force Space Command, Division of Extraterrestrial Intelligence: "I am sick unto death of killing innocent babies."

They all were. This would be, they thought queasily, the forty-third human infant to be "volunteered" by its parents for Government Work. The ones that had lived had been far worse off than those that had died; it had not been possible to allow them to go *on* living. The thing that the Colonel carried under his arm like a package of meat must already be dead . . . it was something to be grateful for.

There were plenty of bleeding-hearts who called them, the G.W. staff, "mercenaries." And so they were. You might do what they did for money; you surely would not do it for love. They liked to think they did it for honor and glory, sometimes, but that was wearing a little thin. And the parents? You couldn't help wondering sometimes whether the parents, if they'd been allowed to see what went on here, would have considered the generous fee they had been paid to be an adequate compensation. You wondered if those who had volunteered baby boys would be interested in *keeping* the posthumous Infant Hero Medal in its black velvet box with the solid silver lock . . . if they'd had a little more information. The obligatory top secret classification on the procedure, the signed-for-in-advance permission to cremate—can't chance Alien bacteria or viruses getting into the environment, you understand that, of course, Mr. and Mrs. X—they helped. But you wondered.

"Well, Brooks," one of them said finally. "Happened again, I guess."

"Oh! You can talk, can you?"

"Now, Brooks—"

"Well this kid can't talk! It can't talk English, it can't talk Beta-2, it can't talk anything and it never is going to talk anything!" An obscene jingle ran crazily through his head, turning him sick . . . ALPHA-ONE, BETA-TWO, SEE ME MAKE A BABY STEW . . . sweet god in heaven, make it stop . . . "You know what it has *done*, thanks to our expert intervention in its exceedingly brief life?"

"Brooks, we don't want to know."

"Yeah! I expect you don't!"

He advanced on them, inexorably, shaking the dead baby the way he had shaken his fist, shaking it in front of him like a limp folded stuff, and they saw the impossible condition that it had somehow come to be in. He made certain they saw it. He turned it all around for them so that they could get a clear view from all sides.

None of them threw up this time, although an infant that had literally turned itself inside out by the violence of its convulsions, so that its skin was mostly inside and its organs and its. . . . what? . . . mostly outside, was something new. They didn't throw up, because they had seen things just as bad before, if you were interested in trying to rank abominations on a scale of awfulness, and they weren't.

"Get rid of it, Showard," said one of the men. Lanky Pugh was his unfortunate name. Doubly unfortunate because he was shaped like a beer keg and not much taller. Doubly unfortunate because when he told you his name you might be inclined to grin a little, and to forget the respect that was due a man who could play a computer the way Liszt might have played a metasynthesizer. "Vaporizer time, Showard," said Lanky Pugh. "*Right* now!"

"Yeah, Brooks," said Beau St. Clair. He hadn't been there as long as the rest of them, and he was looking green. "For the love of Christ," said Beau.

"Christ," Brooks ranted at them through gritted teeth, "would have had nothing to do with this! Even Christ would have been too merciful to raise *this* thing from the dead!''

The man allegedly in charge of the group, who had not had the guts to go into the Interface after the baby when it had seemed to them all to suddenly explode in there, felt as if he had to make some kind of leadership gesture. He cleared his throat a couple of times, to make sure that what came out wouldn't be just a noise, and said, "Brooks, we do the best we can. For the greater good of all mankind, Brooks. I think Christ would understand."

Christ would understand? Brooks stared at Arnold Dolbe, who watched him warily and backed off a step or two more. Arnold was not going to take a chance on being handed that baby, that was very clear.

"God allowed *His* beloved Son to be sacrificed, for a greater good," explained Arnold solemnly. "You see the parallel, I'm sure."

"Yeah," spat Showard. "But God only allowed crucifixion and a whipping or two, you pitiful pious shit. He would not have allowed *this*."

"We do what we have to do," said Dolbe. "Somebody has to do it, and we do the best we can, like I said already."

"Well, I won't do it again."

"Oh, you'll do it again, Showard! You'll do it again, because if you don't we'll see to it that you take the whole rap for this all to yourself. Won't we, men?"

"Oh, shut *up*, Dolbe," Showard said wearily. "You know what bemdung that is . . . one word about this, one word, and we will all—every one of us, right down to the lowliest servomechanism that cleans the toilets in this establishment—be *dumped*. Just like the babies, Dolbe. Mercilessly. Permanently. We'll disappear like none of us had ever existed. And you know it, and I know it, and everybody knows it. So shut up already. Be your effing age, Dolbe."

"Yeah," agreed Lanky Pugh. "There'd be an 'unfortunate incident' that just conveniently happened to vaporize everything out to about two feet past the G.W. property lines. *With* no danger whatsoever to the population, of course, no cause for alarm, folks, it's just one of our little routine explosions. Shitshingles, Dolbe . . . we're all in this together."

Brooks Showard laid the horrible pile of distorted tissues that had only recently been a healthy human infant down on the floor at his feet, and he sat down beside it very gently. He laid his head on his knees, wrapped his arms around them, and began to cry. It was only by the quick intervention of Arnold Dolbe that the servomechanism speeding across the floor to pick up what it interpreted as garbage was intercepted. Dolbe snatched the baby from under the edge of the cylinder and almost ran to the vaporizer slot . . . and when he had shoved the body through it he rubbed his hands violently against the sides of his lab coat, scrubbing them. There goes your *boy*, Mr. and Mrs. Ned Landry, he thought crazily, and have *we* got a medal for *you!*

"Thank you, Dolbe," sighed Lanky. "I didn't want to look at that thing any longer, either. It wasn't really . . . decent."

Lanky was thinking of Mr. and Mrs. Ned Landry too. Because he was the one who had to dump all the data out of the computers after each failure, and he remembered stuff like the names of the parents. He wasn't supposed to. He was supposed to dump it out of his head at the same time. But he was the one who had to write the names down on a piece of paper before he dumped them, and he was the one that had to transfer the names to the data card in his lockbox, so there wouldn't be any chance of *losing* what had been dumped. Lanky knew all forty-three sets of names by heart, in numerical order.

In the small conference room, with Showard in reasonable control of himself once again, if you ignored the shaking hands, the four G.W. techs sat and listened while the representative from the Pentagon laid it out for them. Neat and sweet, wasting nothing. He wasn't overpoweringly pleased with them.

"We have *got* to crack that language," he told them bluntly. "And I mean that one hundred percent. Whatever that thing in the Interface has for a language, we've got to get at it—it sure as hell can't use *Pan*Sig to communicate. We absolutely must find a way to do that—communicate with it, I mean. With it, and all its flickering friends. This is a matter of the utmost urgency."

"Oh, sure," said Brooks Showard. "Sure it is."

"Colonel," snapped the Pentagon man, "it's not a question of just wanting to chat with the things, you know. We need what they've got, and we can't do without it. And there's no way of getting it without negotiating with them."

"We need what they've got . . . we always 'need' what something's got, General. You mean we *want* what they've got, don't you?"

"Not this time. Not this time! This time we really do have to have it."

"At any cost."

"At any cost. That's correct."

"What is it, the secret of eternal life?"

"You know I can't tell you that," the general said patiently, as he would have spoken to a fretful woman he was indulgent with.

"We're supposed to take it on faith, as usual."

"You can take it on anything you like, Showard! It makes no difference to me what you take it on. But I sit here, empowered by the federal government of this great nation to support you and a rather sizable staff in the carrying out of acts that are so far past illegal and criminal, and so far into unspeakable and unthinkable, that we can't even keep records on them. And I'm here to give you my sacred oath that I'm not going to participate in that kind of thing for trinkets and gewgaws and a new variety of *beads*; and neither are the officials who—with tremendous reluctance, I assure you—authorize me to serve in this capacity."

Arnold Dolbe flashed his teeth at the general, trying not to think that the uniform was quaint. There were good and excellent reasons for keeping the ancient uniforms, and he was familiar with them. Tradition. Respect for historical values. Antidote to Future Shock Syndrome. Etc. And he wanted to be certain that the general remembered him as a cooperative fellow, a real Team Player in the finest reaganic tradition. He meant to see to it that the general was fully aware of that. He felt that a brief speech was in order, something tasteful but still memorable, and he thought he was not overstating the case when he considered himself to be topnotch at the impromptu brief speech.

"We understand that, General," he began, all sugar and snakeoil, "and we appreciate it. We are grateful for it. *Bee*lieve you me, there's not one member of this team, not one man on this team, that doesn't support this effort all the way—those without a need to know always excepted, of course. Not that they don't support the effort, that is—they just don't know . . . in detail . . . what it is that they're supporting. We *do*—those of us in the room—we do know. And we feel a certain humility at being chosen for this noble task. Colonel Showard is a little overstressed at the moment, understandably so, but he's behind you all the way. It's just been an unpleasant morning here at Government Work, don't you see. And yet—"

"I'm sure it has," said the Pentagon man, cutting him off in a way that hurt Dolbe deeply. "I'm sure it has been bloody hell. We know what you men go through here, and we honor you for it. But it's something that's got to be done, for the sake of preserving civilization on this planet. I mean that, gentlemen! Literally for the sake of preventing the end of humankind on this green and golden Earth of ours—the *permanent* end, I might add. I'm not talking a few decades in the colonies while things cool off and then we can move back planetside. I'm talking the *end*. Period. Final. Total.''

He said it as if he believed it. It was in fact possible that he *did* believe it, if only because he was a good soldier and you cannot be a good soldier if you think that those up the chain of command from you are telling you lies. And of course they were good soldiers too, and they wouldn't think that those who had fed them the same line were lying to *them*. Nobody knew precisely where the buck stopped in this business. The general had a feeling that the buck went around and around on a möbius strip. Sometimes he wondered who was in charge. Not the President, certainly. It was one of his primary duties to make certain that the President never knew much about this little twig on the executive branch. The general had no illusions about the Pentagon not being part of the executive branch.

He steepled his fingers, and he looked at them long and hard, noting automatically that only Dolbe began to squirm under his gaze.

"Well, gentlemen?" he asked. "What are you going to do now? I've got to take some kind of reasonable answer back to my superiors—no details, mind, just a rough idea—and they aren't feeling all that patient these days. We've run out of fooling around time, gentlemen. We're right up against the wire on this one.''

There was a thick silence, with the general's fingers drumming lightly on the table, and the air exchange whirring high and thin, and the American flag jerking limply every now and then in the mechanical breeze.

"Gentlemen?" the general prodded. "I'm a very busy man."

"Oh, hellfire," said Brooks Showard. He knew. Either he did the talking, or they'd all sit there until the end of time. Which, to hear the general tell it, wouldn't be all that long. "You know what we've got to do next. You know perfectly well. Since you government/military shits are too chicken to slap every last goddam linguist into prison for treason or murder or inciting to riot or pandering or sodomy or whatever the hell it takes to make the fucking Lingoes cooperate—"

"You know we can't do that, Colonel!" The general's lips were as stiff as two slabs of frozen bacon. "If the linguists had any excuse, *any* excuse, they'd withdraw from every sensitive negotiation we have underway with Aliens, and that *would* be the end of us! And there wouldn't be one damn thing we could do about it, Colonel—not one damn thing!''

''—since, like I said, you're too chicken to do that and do it right and make it stick, there's only one thing left. You fellows want to keep your pretty hands clean, I'm sure. But *we* fellows have got to steal us a linguist infant, a baby Lingoe. On your behalf, or course. For the good of all mankind. How's that for Plan B?''

They all squirmed, then. Volunteered babies, that was nasty. But stolen babies? It wasn't that the effing linguists didn't deserve it, and it wasn't that they didn't have babies in hordes and swarms enough to console themselves with if they came up one short. But the *baby* didn't exactly deserve it, somehow. They were willing to go along with the religious party line, after a fashion, but none of them was really able to swallow that stuff about the sins of the fathers being visited, etc. Stealing a baby. That was not very nice.

''Their women whelp on the public wards,'' Showard observed. ''It won't be difficult.''

''Oh dear.''

The general could hardly believe he'd said that. He tried again.

''Well, by heaven!''

''Yeah?''

''Is that the *only* alternative remaining to us, Colonel Showard? Are you absolutely certain?''

''You have some other suggestion?'' Showard snarled.

''General,'' Dolbe put in, ''we've done everything else. We know that our Interface is an exact duplicate of those the linguists use. We know our procedure is exactly the same as theirs—not that it's much of a procedure. You put the Alien—or better still, two Aliens, if you can get a pair—in one side. You put the baby in the other. And you get out of their way. That's all there is to it. That's what we do, just like that's what they do—we've tried it again and again. And you know what happened when we tried the test-tube babies . . . it was the same, only it was worse somehow. Don't ask me to explain that. And we've brought in every computer expert, every scientist, every technician, every—''

''But see here, man—''

''No, General! There's nothing to see. We have checked and rechecked and re-rechecked. We have gone over every last variable not just once but many many times. And it has to be, General, it has to be that for some reason known only to the linguists—and I *do* feel, by the way, that it constitutes treason for them to keep that knowledge to themselves—for some reason known only to them, only linguist infants are capable of learning Alien languages.''

"Some genetic reason, you mean."

"Well? Look how inbred they are, it's on the fine line of incest, if you ask me! What are we talking about? Thirteen families! That's not much of a gene pool. They bring in the odd bit of outside stock now and then, sure, but basically it's those thirteen sets of genes over and over. Sure, I'd say it's a genetic reason.''

"General," Beau added, "all we're doing here is sacrificing the innocent children of nonlinguists, in something that is never going to work. It's got to be an infant born of one of the Lines, and that is all there is to it.''

"They deny it," said the general.

"Well, wouldn't you deny it, in their place? It suits the traitorous bastards, controlling the whole goddam government, doling out their nuggets of wisdom to us on whatever schedule happens to strike their fancy, living off the backs and the blood of decent people. And if we have to murder innocent babies trying to do what they ought to be doing *for* us, well, shit, *they* don't care. That just puts every American citizen, and every citizen of every country on this globe and in its colonies, all the more at their mercy. *Sure* they deny it!''

"They're lying," Showard summed up, feeling that Beau St. Clair had said about all he was going to say. "Plain flat out lying.''

"You're sure?"

"Damn right."

The general made the noise a restless horse makes, and then he sat there and chewed his upper lip. He didn't like it. If the Lingoes suspected . . . if there was a leak . . . and there always were leaks . . .

"Shit," said Lanky Pugh, "they've got so many babies, they'll never miss one, long as we can get by with a female. *Can* we get by with a female?''

"Why not, Mr. Pugh?"

"Well. I mean. Can a female *do* it?"

The general frowned at Pugh, and then looked at the others for explanation. This was beyond him.

"We keep telling Lanky," Showard said. "We keep explaining it to him. There is *no* correlation between intelligence and the acquisition of languages by infants, except at the level of gross retardation where you've got a *permanent* infant. We keep telling him that, but it offends him or something. He can't seem to handle it.''

"I should think," said the general, "that Mr. Pugh would want to stay abreast of at least the basic literature on language acquisition. Considering."

The general was wrong. Lanky Pugh, who had tried to learn three different foreign human languages, because he felt that a computer specialist ought to know at least *one* other language that wasn't a computer language—and had had no success—was not about to keep up with the literature on native language acquisition. If Lingoe females could learn foreign languages . . . Alien languages, for chrissakes! . . . when they were only babies, then how come he couldn't even master passable *French*? Every linguist kid had to have native fluency in one Alien language, three Terran languages from different language families, American Sign Language, and PanSig—plus reasonable control of as many other Terran languages as they could pick up on the side. And he'd heard that a lot of them were native in *two* Alien tongues. While he, Lanky Pugh, could speak English. Just English. No, he didn't like it, and he didn't want to take any close look at the question. It was something he carefully did not think about any longer.

". . . throw his ass right out of here," Showard was saying. "But it just so happens that he *is* the top computer tech in the whole world, the top hands-on man, and it just so happens that we can't do without him, and if he chooses to know absolutely nothing *but* computers, that's his privilege. That's all he's required to know, General, and he knows that better than anybody, anywhere, anytime. And nevertheless, we are not going to crack Beta-2 with a computer. Sorry."

"I see," said the general. He said it with utter finality. And he stood up and picked up his funny hat with all the spangled stuff on it. "None of my business, of course. I'm sure Dolbe here runs a tight ship."

"General?"

"Yes, Dolbe?"

"Don't you want to discuss—"

"*No*, he doesn't want to discuss how we do this cute little kidnapping caper, Dolbe!" shouted Brooks Showard. "For gods *sakes*, Dolbe!"

The general nodded smartly.

"Right on target," he agreed. "*Right* on target. I wish I didn't know what I already do know."

"You asked us, General," Showard pointed out.

"Yes. I know I did."

He left, with a smile all around, and he was gone before they could say anything else. The general got in, he did his business, he got out. That was why *he* was a general, and *they* were in the baby-stealing business. And the baby-killing business.

The only question now was, which one of them was going to do it? Because it would have to be one of them. There wasn't anybody you could trust to go snatch a linguist baby out of a hospital nursery. And it had better not be Lanky Pugh, because he was the only Lanky Pugh they could get, and he couldn't be spared. They didn't dare risk Lanky Pugh.

Arnold Dolbe and Brooks Showard and Beau St. Clair stared at each other, hating each other. And Lanky Pugh, he went after the straws.

Showard had thought he might feel nervous, but he didn't. His white lab coat was the same one he wore at work. It wasn't as if he had on a disguise. The corridors of the hospital were like the corridors of hospitals and laboratories everywhere; if it hadn't been for the constant bustle and racket that went with changing shifts and visitors coming and going he could easily have been at G.W. The only concession he'd made to the fact that he was actually in this place to kidnap a living human child was the stethoscope that hung round his neck, and he had stopped being aware of it almost at once. People passing him mumbled, "Good evening, Doctor" automatically, without needing anything more than the antique symbol of his calling to identify him, even after he reached the maternity ward. Any other profession, they'd have switched a hundred years ago to something less grotesque then an entirely nonfunctional and obsolete instrument like the stethoscope—but not the doctors. No little insignia on a corner of the collar for them. No tasteful little button. They knew the power of tradition, did the doctors, and they never missed a beat.

"Good evening, Doctor."

"Mmph," said Showard.

Nobody was paying any attention to him. Women had babies at every hour of the day or night, and a doctor on the maternity floor at ten minutes to midnight was nothing to pay any attention to.

The call had come in twenty minutes ago—"A bitch Lingoe just whelped over at Memorial, about half an hour ago! Get your tail over there." And here he was. It was no consolation at all to him that the baby was a female, but he assumed Lanky would be pleased.

This was an old hospital, one of the oldest in the country. He supposed it must have fancy wards somewhere, with medpods that took care of every whim a patient had, with no need for the bumbling hands of human beings; but those wards were high in the towers that looked down over the river. With private elevators to make sure that the wealthy patients going up to them, and their wealthy visitors, didn't have to be offended by the crudity of the rest of the buildings. Here in the public wards there was very little change from what a hospital had looked like when he'd had his appendix out at the age of six. For all he could tell, except for the nurses' uniforms and the computers at every bedside, it looked just like hospitals had looked for the last century or so. And the maternity ward, since it served only women, would be the last place anybody would spend money on renovation.

A light over a booth at the end of the hall showed him where to go. The night nurse there was bent over her own computer, making sure the entries from the bedside units matched the entries on the charts. Very inefficient, but he supposed she had to have something to do to make the night go by.

He pulled the forged charge slip from his coat pocket and handed it to her.

"Here," he said. "Where's the Lingoe kid?"

She looked at him, ducked her head deferentially, and then looked at the charge slip.

BABY ST. SYRUS, it read. EVOKED POTENTIALS, STAT.

And the indecipherable scrawl that was the graphic badge of the real doctor of real medicine.

"I'll call a nurse to bring you the baby, Doctor," she said at once, but he shook his head.

"I haven't got time to wait around for your nurses," he told her. As rudely as possible, keeping up the doctor act. "Just tell me where the kid is, and I'll get it."

"But, Doctor—"

"I have sense enough, and training enough, to pick up one infant and carry it down to Neuro," he snapped at her, doing his best to sound as if she were far less than the dirt beneath his valuable feet. "Now are you going to cooperate, or do I have to call a man to get some service around here?"

She backed down, of course. Well trained, in spite of being out in the big wide world of the ancient hospital. Her anxious face went white, and she stared at him with her mouth half open, frozen. Showard snapped his fingers under her nose.

"Come on, nurse!" he said fiercely. "I've got patients waiting!"

Three minutes later he had the St. Syrus baby tucked securely into the crook of his arm and was safely in the elevator to the back exit that led out into a quiet garden of orange trees and miscellaneous ugly plants and a few battered extruded benches. One light glowed over the garden, and at midnight you couldn't see your own hand in front of your face out there—they'd checked that.

It was so easy to do that it was ridiculous. Out the door of the elevator, baby firmly tucked against him. "Pardon me, Doctor." "Not at all, pardon *me*." "Pardon me, Doctor." "Good morning, Doctor." They were very scientific in this place. Sixteen minutes past midnight and they were saying good morning.

Down the corridor, turn right. Another corridor. A small lobby, where another night nurse looked at him briefly and went back to her mindless fiddling with records. Another corridor. "Good morning, Doctor." An elderly man, carrying flowers. "God bless you, Doctor." Almost bowing. Must be nice, being a medicoe and getting all that adoration. "Thank you," Showard said curtly, and the man looked absurdly thrilled.

And then he was at the door. He felt a faint tingle at the back of his neck, walking toward it . . . if he were going to be stopped, if some alarm had already gone off and they were after him, this was where it would happen.

But nothing happened.

He opened the door, pulled the blanket up over the infant's head, making sure it could still get enough air to breathe, and he was outside and headed for the flyer parked at the edge of the lot for him. With the Pink Cross/Pink Shield stickers on its doors.

It was, as they used to say, a piece of cake.

Chapter Five

Oh, chiddies and chuddies, do you DO you want to come in out of the dark and cog ALL that's happening? You do you DO! I know you do, you want to dip and cog the WHOLE waxball in its nicewrap, don't you, my sweet chiddy-chuddy fans? OH YES! Well, here I have a little bit of something for your neurons to chomp, yes, I do . . . how about a Lingoe Story to start our mutual day, this mutual day? It's not easy, getting into a Lingoeden, you know—but for you I'd go through fire and toxins, and I DID I DID and oh these eyes were data-saturated door to DOOR!

Did you know that every Lingoeden has as many servomechanisms as it has rooms, my luvvies? At 300 M-credits the unit? Well, that's rational, that's reasonable, that's so no Lingoe ever has to bend over to pick up any least thingthang, you cog . . . might sprain the giant brain, and we can't have THAT, oh woe no!

And did you know about the baths in the dens—oh, chiddies and chuddies, I SAW this, with my own taxpaying eyes, I saw it—every least knob and toggle and button and switch has the family crest outlined on it in seed pearls and solid gold . . . isn't that QUARKY, luvaduvs? Have you checked your facility lately, luvaduvs? Just to see if maybe you've got a little gold horsey standing on its hind legs inside a circle of seed pearls? Maybe there's one of those on YOUR waterswitch, hoy boy . . . why don't you go look? And if you can't find yours, why, you could just run next door to your friendly nabehood Lingoes', could you NOT, and borrow yourself a cup of pearls and just a smigwidgen of gold? And why NOT? Isn't it your taxes, chiddies and chuddies, that fill up the Lingoe treasure vaults, way down WAY DOWN in their underground castles? You go right over there and ask . . . but WATCH IT! You have to get past the laser guns on the doors, like I did! Oh hoy hoy hoy, our aching backs, luvaduvs . . . our aching backs. . . .

> (by Frazzle Gleam, comset popnews caster,
> COMING AT YOU program,
> August 28, 2179)

The message on the private line, all certified debugged and then scrambled and rescrambled because there was no such thing as a truly debugged line, and the codes changed daily because even if you did all that you couldn't be sure—the message said, "Emergency meeting in DAT40, 1900 hours." Room 40, Department of Analysis & Translation . . . that would be one of the soundproof rooms in the lowest of the sub-basements. He remembered it from other times. No air, either too much heat or too much cold, and no bathroom facilities closer than a good brisk five minute walk. Damn.

Thomas was tired, and he had work to do, and he'd had other plans for this evening if he'd managed to get that work done. It had by god better be an emergency, but there was no way to find out except by going over there. That was the whole point of the private line and the debugging and the scrambling and the code changes.

By the time he got there he was thoroughly irritated. He'd wasted thirty precious minutes circling over the flyerpad on the building's roof, waiting for permission to land, and ten minutes more waiting for some fool visiting potentate complete with cameras to clear off so that it was safe for him to leave the flyer. He was tired, and he was cold, and he was hungry, and he had nine thousand things on his mind, and he charged into Room 40 in a way that made the two men in there already exchange swift looks and sit up straighter in their chairs.

"All right!" he said as he sat down. "What is it?"

"It's an emergency," said one of them.

"So you said," said Thomas. And "I don't suppose there's coffee?"

"Scotch if you like," said the other, before the first—who knew better—could stop him.

Thomas Blair Chornyak stared at the fellow as he stared at everything he couldn't see any good excuse for.

"No man who needs the use of his mind drinks anything stronger than a very good wine," said Thomas. "Now do you have coffee or not?"

"We have coffee," said the first fellow, and he went and got it and set it down in front of Thomas. He knew better than to put it in anything but a real cup, and he knew better than to bring it any way but black. He also knew enough to hurry. Dealing with a man who was the absolute top dog linguist in the world and all its outposts, you hurried.

"There you are, sir," he said. "Black. And now to business."

"Please."

"Sir, we have some difficult news."

"And?"

"Sir, we want you to know that this action was taken very reluctantly—VERY reluctantly."

"For the love of the gospels, man," said Thomas wearily, "will you spit it out or let me go back to my work?"

It came out in a rush, because the government man was worried. They'd promised him there'd be no trouble about this, but he found that hard to believe. If it had been him there would have been trouble. A lot of trouble. And he wasn't even somebody important.

"Sir, a baby of the Lines has been kidnapped from the maternity ward at Santa Cruz Memorial Hospital."

Chornyak did not so much as blink. He might as well have said that the sun had come up that morning in the east.

"Federal kidnapping, I assume," he said. And they nodded.

"Female or male?"

"Female, sir."

"Mmhmm."

The junior man looked at his companion out of the corner of his eye, signaling confusion and now-what and a bunch of other stuff; the senior official, who'd been at this a long time, paid no attention to him. They'd wait; and when the Lingoe godfather chose to speak, he'd choose to speak. And if he was going to raise hell, well, he'd raise hell. And there was not one thing anybody could do about it, except if he used the needle he had in his pocket, and he wasn't sure he could do that.

"Explain," said Thomas at last. "Please."

He was being excruciatingly polite. If he were pulling out your toenails one at a time, he would be excruciatingly polite.

"My name is John Smith, Mr. Chornyak," said the senior official.

"Yes. I've worked with you before."

"I was instructed to explain to you that in the interests of our efforts to acquire the Beta-2 language of the primary Jovian lifeforms it became necessary for us to take temporary custody of one of the infants of St. Syrus Household . . . somewhat abruptly."

"Became necessary."

"Yes, Mr. Chornyak."

"I don't follow you, Smith."

He told him. He told him about the dead infants, about the meeting with the technicians, about the final decision that it had to be a linguist baby the next time.

"You were supposed to be advised of this in advance," Smith lied. "But when news came in of the baby's birth in California there wasn't time to talk to you first—we didn't know when we'd get another chance like that, you see."

"And where is the baby now?"

"In one of our safe houses, sir."

"Your friend here—does he have a name?"

The junior man cleared his throat uneasily and said, "Yes, sir. I'm Bill Jones, sir."

Thomas carefully entered that information on his wrist computer, and smiled at them. John Smith and Bill Jones. Sure. And they all lived happily ever after.

"And when does the baby go into the Interface?"

"In three weeks, Mr. Chornyak. We can't wait any longer than that, in view of the current crisis."

"Ah, yes. The current crisis. Which is?"

"We don't know, sir. We aren't told. You know how that is, Mr. Chornyak. Need to know."

"All right, I'll assume the existence of the current crisis for the moment—it's that or stay here all night, obviously. Given that assumption, Smith, do you suppose you could just explain to me, without a lot of fluff and quaver, why this extraordinary crime has been authorized—no, that's not strong enough—has been committed by the government of the United States? Against a Household of the Lines, to which this government owes much and from which it has suffered no injury? Kidnapping—" A corner of Thomas' upper lip twitched, once. "—is a crime. It is not a trivial crime. It carries the death penalty. I suggest that you explain to me why an official of my government has felt justified in kidnapping one of my relatives."

Smith hesitated, and then said, "Sir, we explained to you."

"You explained to me that you have failed in your experiments using human infants in the Interface with the lifeforms. Yes. I understand that. That does not surprise me—you were told that you would fail. What I do not understand, however, is why that set of entirely predictable events lead in some inexorable manner to this crime."

Feeling that if he was ever to seem more than a cardboard character in this exchange this was his moment, Jones spoke up.

"Perhaps you'd let me handle that, John," he said carefully.

"By all means, Bill. Have at it." Smith shrugged. It wasn't going well, and it probably wasn't going to get any better, but he didn't intend to let that bother him. He'd met with Chornyak before, on different but almost equally uncomfortable occasions. He'd met with linguists hundreds of times. And he knew that there was absolutely nothing an ordinary citizen could do if a linguist decided to structure an encounter in such a way that that citizen would look like a perfect ass. That was one of the skills the Lingoes learned, it was one of the things they trained their brats in from birth, and it was one of the reasons they were hated.

Jones appreciated it greatly when the Lingoe putting him down was a male, at least . . . when it was one of the bitches, he got physically sick. Oh, they observed all the forms, those women; they said all the right words. But they had a way of somehow leading the conversation around so that words came out of your mouth that you'd never heard yourself say before and would have taken an oath you couldn't be made to say . . . He knew all about linguists. You couldn't win, not face to face with one, and he knew better than to try. Let Jones beat himself to death on that rock if it appealed to him; he'd learn.

"Sir," Jones began, "it's like this."

"Is it," said Thomas.

"We of the federal government have of course heard and read the official statements of the Lines to the effect that there is no genetic difference between linguist infants and the infants of the general population. And we are capable of appreciating the reasons for that position, in view of the regrettable friction between the Lines and the public." He stopped, and Thomas tilted his head a fraction, and Jones felt deeply inferior for no reason that he could understand; but he was into it now and had no choice but to go on. They'd been told to be very careful with this man.

"You know what he can do, don't you?" the chief had said to them, holding on to his desk with both big fists and leaning at them like a tree. "That man, all by himself, can just give an order. And every single linguist in government contract service would just stop what they were doing. That means every last interplanetary negotiation we have in progress—business, diplomatic, military, scientific, you name it—every last one would simply STOP. We can't do a damn thing without the Lingoes, god curse their effing souls and may they fry one and all in hell. But that man, may he fry especially slowly, holds this government hostage. Do you understand that, Smith? You, Jones, do you remember that?"

And why, thought Jones, bewildered, had the government then sent *him*? Smith, maybe . . . he understood that Smith had experience in dealing with linguists. But why him? Why not some real superstar?

Smith, who was watching him in mild amusement, knew the answer to that question. The government, which was composed of bureaucrats, felt that sending anyone obviously important to deal with Thomas would give Thomas an indication of the way he owned us all, and that that would be a tactical eror. As though Thomas himself were unaware of the facts of the matter . . . So they sent a team. One experienced ordinary-looking agent, with no spaghetti and no flash, just your average government token. And one very junior bumbler to set him off. Poor Jones.

"So, Mr. Chornyak," Jones labored, "we of course understand the motivation for that stance on the part of the Lines—but we also know that it isn't really in accordance with the facts. That is, we know that in actuality the genetic difference does exist."

"All that inbreeding," Thomas murmured courteously; and Smith chuckled inside as Jones swallowed the bait.

"Exactly," said Jones happily.

"Unnatural practices."

Jones looked startled and declared that he hadn't said that.

"There is some other sort of inbreeding, Mr. Jones?"

"Well, there must be."

"Oh? Why must there be? We could establish the sort of systematic genetic difference you suggest—claiming, by the way, that the linguist Households deliberately lie—we could only establish that sort of systematic genetic difference by systematically fucking our first cousins, generation after generation. Switching to sisters would do it even faster, though it might give us some other kinds of genetic differences. Two-headed babies. Armless babies. Headless babies. That sort of thing."

"Mr. Chornyak, I assure you—"

"Mr. Jones, I assure *you* that I did not leave my home, where I have important duties to see to on behalf of the government you claim to represent, and fly here through vile weather and a traffic pattern managed by lunatics, to listen to you attack the sexual habits of my family."

It was too much for Jones, entirely too much. He had no idea how he'd gotten to the point where he now found himself, and he sat there opening and shutting his mouth like a toad.

"Mr. Chornyak," said Smith, moved by pity, "do come off it."

"I beg your pardon?"

Stop torturing my associate, Chornyak. It's not nice. You are behaving like the Ugly Linguist. And the fact that he makes it so easy doesn't make it any more sporting."

Thomas chuckled, and Jones looked infinitely confused.

"We don't believe you," Smith went on. "This is no news to you at all. We've been telling you we didn't believe you ever since we found out what linguists were for. And it's got diddly to do with your sexual practices, in which the government hasn't the slightest interest."

"It is scientifically . . . drivel," said Thomas.

"So you tell us. And we don't believe that either."

"And?"

"And we have put up with it, because you have us by the short hairs as always. Forty-three human infants have now died in our valiant attempts to go along with the arrangement it pleases you linguists to impose upon us. And how many computer scientists are now barely capable of cutting out paper dolls from trying to deal with all this I can't imagine."

"Eleven, as of yesterday," said Thomas.

"How do you *know* that?" demanded poor pitiful Jones.

"They know everything," Smith told him. "It gets boring after a while."

"So," said Thomas, "you decided that you had to have a linguist infant, because only a linguist infant could acquire the language you call Beta-2. Despite the fact that there is no evidence whatsoever that there *is* any such language. And even if you had to steal the infant. Rather a primitive act, stealing a human being, don't you think?"

Smith was not going to be led down a path at the end of which he would hear himself admitting that he didn't consider linguists to be human beings. Not a chance. He said nothing at all, and Thomas went on.

"Mr. Smith," he said, "Mr. Jones, I swear to you—" and to

Jones' astonishment he suddenly looked just like the pictures of Abraham Lincoln at his most tender and trustworthy . . . "—that we of the Lines are now and always have been telling you the simple truth. Never mind the dubious genetic theory involved; we'll ignore that. But the reason that you cannot put a human infant into an Interface with a non-humanoid Alien without destroying that infant utterly has nothing whatsoever to do with whether you use an infant of the Lines or not. It has to do with the fact that no human mind can view the universe as it is perceived by a non-humanoid extraterrestrial and not self-destruct. It is as simple as that.''

"So you say," said Smith stubbornly.

"So we say, yes. And so we have always said. We tried, very early in the days of the Interfaces, because it did not happen that in early exploration of this galaxy we encountered only humanoid Aliens. Sometimes we did, yes; but just as often, we ran into sentient beings who were crystalline, or gaseous. You will recall the infamous encounter with the population of Saturn, which was a liquid—the Lines lost three infants to that one. And when we saw we had reached a limit that could not be breached by technology, we halted there. The United States government would be well advised to do the same.''

"It cannot be true of every non-humanoid Alien species," declared Smith. "That's ridiculous."

And Thomas thought that no, it wasn't ridiculous at all. It was distressing, but it was not ridiculous. No human being could hold his breath for thirty minutes; that was a natural barrier, and one learned not to fling oneself at it. No human being, so far as he knew, could share the worldview of a non-humanoid. It was not ridiculous.

"If you people are willing to keep trying," said Thomas reasonably, "and if you don't mind risking the sanity and the lives of your infants in this quixotic series of gambles, that's your business. But we linguists are genuinely tired of having you blame the results of your stupidity on us.''

"Mr. Chornyak—"

"No. You listen to me. What you sit here saying to me is very easily summed up, Smith. It goes like this. One: we linguists do know how to Interface with non-humanoid Aliens, but we won't— for some mysterious reason. Our inherent wickedness. Our monstrous greed. Just for the hell of it. Who knows? We just won't. Two: you non-linguists have made a real try at using your own babies, and they've all died horribly, or worse than died. Three: since that comes directly from our refusal to help, we are to blame for those tragedies—we, the linguists, not you who actually put the babies in the Interface time after time after bloody time and watch them suffer unspeakably. Four: since we are to blame for all that, and since humanity really and truly needs to grab off these non-humanoid tongues, you the government are thereby by god ENTITLED to one of our babies. It's not kidnapping, it's our just desserts after your patient forbearance long past the point of sweet reason. We *owe* you one of our babies!''

Jones had always prided himself on being a sophisticated and reasonable man, and on being free of the primitive emotion of prejudice. Watching the threedies of the anti-linguist riots, he had marveled that man could so turn against his own kind and could excuse such brutality for a reason that was no reason. Once, for the color of a man's skin. Now, for whether a man came out of the households of thirteen families of this world— out of the Lines. He had watched and felt contempt, thankful that he could not be like that, pleased that no such baseness tainted *him*.

His stomach twisted, now; sick, he realized that the hate he felt for the elegant man who sat there mocking them—hate that rolled through him as he had once seen pus roll from a wound— *was* prejudice! He hated this man with an entirely irrational blood lust. He would have taken pleasure in thumbing out his eyes. For a few words, and no doubt a few gestures. He'd been warned that a linguist could control you with gestures and you'd never suspect, when he was in training. "With the tip of their little finger, men!" the instructors used to snap at them. "With nothing more than the way they *breathe*, they can control you!" He'd learned that for the exams, he'd learned all kinds of crap for exams, but he hadn't believed it. He believed it now. Because it couldn't have been the words that Chornyak was using. Shit, he'd read those words in a hundred right-wing magazines, heard them in a hundred bars when tempers were running high, it was what anybody at all would have said in an off-guard moment, it could not be the words . . . No, the man had done something to his mind, he'd gotten at him somehow . . . with the tip of his little finger. With the way he breathed.

It did not occur to Jones that one way to avoid some of this, although it wouldn't save you from what linguists could do with the modulations of their voices, was not to *look* at the linguist while he talked. He stared at him, as fascinated as a snake in a basket. Smith, on the other hand, looked at the ceiling when he wasn't speaking directly to Chornyak and looked a little past him when he was, and he knew that Jones had been told to do the same. Jones hadn't learned it, because he hadn't believed it mattered.

"Mr. Chornyak," said Smith, "we know how you feel, and you know how we feel, and it's all very cosy. The question is not how we feel about this—nobody likes it, whatever you may think—but what the linguists will do."

Thomas sighed and shook his head slowly.

"What *can* we do?" he asked. "I can imagine the reaction I'd get if I called the FBI and reported that a government agent had kidnapped one of our babies. We are as helpless in the face of government barbarism as any other citizen, Mr. Smith, and we will do what any other citizen does. We will go through the motions. Call the police, report the baby missing, pretend for the sake of its parents that a search is being made . . . And then we will comfort the mother in her grief as best we can."

"You don't know—"

"I do know. The baby will die, as all the other babies die. Or it will be mutilated so horribly that it will have to be put to death in the name of decency, as has also happened. And we will comfort the mother in her grief, as best we can."

Thomas knew precisely what Smith was thinking. Why, Chornyak, he was thinking, don't you threaten us with what you really can do, and with what every one of us knows you really can do? Why don't you threaten to pull out the linguists, every last one of them, and plunge the world into chaos? Why do you pretend that you are just a citizen like any other citizen?

Well . . . let him wonder. Thomas had no intention of telling. Nobody knew, or would ever know, except when time came to pass on the leadership of the Lines. Then he would have to explain to the next Head that that trump card was being held for one situation—for the time when the government, after murdering who knew how many hundreds or thousands of innocents in their Interfaces, finally stumbled upon that unique non-humanoid species whose perceptions could be tolerated by humans. On that day, which might be ten thousand years away, or ten days, the government would suddenly decide that it was in the Interfacing business and could do the job of acquiring Alien languages on its own. And it was then that the government would hear the linguists' terms: either the Lines kept *that* part of the Interface industry as they had all the rest, or every linguist involved in negotiation, no matter how crucial, would walk out and participate no more. It was not the intention of the linguists to see their own offspring wasted in this random search for the chance

species that would break the perceptual barrier between humanoid and non-humanoid; on the other hand, it was not the intention of the linguists to see their power lost to the government or
the public.

Governments, and people in general, were likely to take power
and do damn fool things with it, like carrying on nuclear wars
and cutting each other up with chain saws and laser scalpels. The
linguists had a way to curb some of that, an awesome power for
all its limitations, and they would keep it in the Lines where it
would never be subject to the follies of bureaucrats or simple
ignorance.

Thomas had a responsibility, and sometimes it was unpleasant.
Sometimes, when he listened to the very little boys in the
Household complaining that they didn't understand why they had
to do without everything just because stupid people thought
linguists made too much money, and how they thought it was
sucking up to go on like that . . . sometimes he was tempted.

He remembered when he'd been a little boy like that himself.
It was during one of the times when energy was wasted,
inexcusably—a time of government "market adjustment." There
had been a kind of portable force field that whirled around the
outside of the body and could be set to keep the temperature
within a certain range. It let you do away with winter clothing,
and it made it possible to wear ordinary clothing in summer with
total comfort. It hadn't lasted, because even the rich who loved
such toys quickly found such squandering of resources intolerable.
But while it was available, the children had had a good time.
They had discovered that if you got a few of these fields whirling
at top heat setting and a few others at maximum cold, you could
get a baby tornado going in the middle of the circle of children,
and you could watch it suck up leaves and grass, and if you were
daring you could stick your finger into its center where everything was totally still.

Thomas had stood there, six years old and bundled in a plain
cloth coat, stamping his feet against the cold and rubbing his
frozen fingers together. The other children were in a little park
that he had to pass on his way to and from school, and they were
blissfully comfortable in that cold in light shorts and shifts—
except for the ones who were providing the maximum cold
settings, of course. They were cold like Thomas, colder even.
But they were having fun. He would never forget how he had
watched and longed to play that game, wanted to have a baby
tornado to play with, wanted to be part of that circle . . . he'd
gotten chilblains, standing there. And no sympathy.

"You're a little fool, Thomas," they'd said to him at home. "Linguists can't have such stuff, and you know it, and you know why. You've been told a thousand times. People hate us, and we do not choose to feed that hate for trivia. People believe that we are greedy, that we are paid millions of credits to do things that anybody could do if we'd only tell them how—we do not choose to feed that perception, either. Now go study your verbs, Thomas, and stop whining."

Thomas caught himself sharply—he'd been woolgathering, and the two men were watching him silently.

"Well?" he said. "You've won. Are you satisfied?"

"You're free to go, Mr. Chornyak," said Smith wearily, "if there's nothing else you want to talk about."

"You called me here, man, not I you."

"As a courtesy."

"Ah. Courtesy. I value courtesy."

"We didn't want you to hear about the . . . incident . . . on the news, Mr. Chornyak. And your orders are that no contacts between you and the government are to be held in any other way than this, unless they are the ordinary routine of linguistics. We did as you requested—and that also is courtesy."

"I will be sure to inform Mrs. St. Syrus of your courtesy," said Thomas, bowing.

"You won't, either," blurted Jones. "That's not what you'll do, you . . . you filthy Lingoe! You'll—"

Smith sighed. That was really a bit much, he thought. He'd been prepared for clumsiness, that's why they picked Jones; but this was a little more than he thought justified by the role. Now Thomas Chornyak's face would register faint distaste . . . ME ARISTOCRAT, YOU CAVEMAN . . . there it went. And he wouldn't say a word. And then he would start entering data in his wrist computer . . . there he went.

Smith often thought that if he could just spend a few months, round the clock, with some linguists, he could learn to do the things they did. So much of it was so obvious. Except that there must be something else that wasn't obvious, because when he tried the things he thought he'd picked up in his observations they never did work. Never.

Dear sweet Jesus, how he hated Lingoes.

Hurrying down the hall with the two men, Smith disgusted and Jones humiliated, Thomas almost ran into an equally hurried group coming round a corner. Four men in dress uniforms and a woman all in black . . . a lovely woman. In such a place, at such an hour?

"Funny thing, that," he noted. "What's going on?"

"Her name is Michaela Landry, Mr. Chornyak," said Smith. "She was the mother of the last volunteer baby Interfaced—we told you about that. Her husband died almost immediately after having the baby picked up . . . a freak accident . . . and she's been brought in to accept the Infant Hero medal in the man's place. It's all top secret, sir, of course."

"I see. And now she will go back to her parents' home, I suppose. Poor woman."

"No, sir. She's completely alone, no family of her own at all. But her husband's brother took her in, and he's given her permission to work."

"What kind of nursing does she do?"

"She was in the public hospitals before this, sir, but after what's happened, understandably enough, she doesn't feel she can face any more of that. She's looking for a post as a private duty nurse . . . and we'll see that something just happens to come her way very quickly. Poor thing's had about enough, without having to sit around alone thinking about it."

"It's a very sad story," Thomas said, stepping into the private elevator that would take him to the roof, "and a damn shame all around."

"Oh, she won't stay mopey long," Smith said. "Somebody will marry her within the year . . . she's a lovely piece."

"So she is," Thomas agreed.

And he went home to wait for the contact from St. Syrus Household, which should come early tomorrow morning, if not sooner.

Chapter Six

The curious 20th century aberration in cultural science that led briefly to such bizarre phenomena as women practicing medicine, sitting as judges—even as a Supreme Court Justice, incomprehensible as that seems to us today—and filling male roles throughout society, can be rather easily explained. Men are by nature kind and considerate, and a charming woman's eagerness to play at being a physician or a Congressman or a scientist can be both amusing and endearing; we can understand, looking back upon the period, how it must have seemed to 20th century men that there could be no harm in humoring the ladies. We know from the historical records, in particular the memoirs of great men of the time, how often the women's antics provided them with occasions for laughter—very welcome in the otherwise serious business of their days. (There was, for example, the famous Equal Rights Amendment hoax so cleverly set up and maintained for so many years by members of Congress . . . we've all laughed heartily over that one, I'm sure.)

It may seem radical—I know I will be hearing from some of my more conservative colleagues—but I am inclined to feel that I might welcome a little of that same comic relief today. Life is such a grim business; a laugh now and then, especially if the source is a female sufficiently beautiful and shapely, would be almost worth the trouble of having her blundering about in Congress!

But unfortunately we cannot allow ourselves that sort of luxury. Our forefathers did not know—despite the clear statements of Darwin, Ellis, Feldeer, and many others on the subject—they did not have scientific *proof* of the inherent mental inferiority of women. Only with the publication of the superb research of Nobelists Edmund O. Haskyl and Jan Bryant-Netherland of M.I.T. in 1987 did we finally obtain the proof. And it is to our credit that we then moved so swiftly to set right the wrongs that we had, in our lamentable ignorance, inflicted. We saw then that the concept of female "equality" was not simply a kind of romantic notion—like the "Nobel Savage" fad of an earlier era—rather, it was a cruel and dangerous burden upon the females of our species, a burden under which they labored all innocent and unawares . . . the victims, it can only be said, of male ignorance.

There are some who criticize, saying that it should not have taken us four long years to provide our females with the Constitutional protection they so richly deserved and so desperately needed. But I feel that those who criticize are excessive in their judgments. It takes time to right wrongs—it always takes time. The more widespread the problem, the more time required to solve it. I think that a span of four years was a remarkable speedy resolution, and a matter for considerable pride—let us, gentlemen, lay those criticisms to rest for once and for all.

(Senator Ludis R. G. Andolet of New Hampshire,
speaking at the Annual Christmas Banquet
of the New York Men's Club,
December 23rd, 2024)

SUMMER 2181. . . .

Michaela was more than satisfied with the post she'd found. Verdi Household was surrounded by old oaks and evergreens, tucked into the arm of a bend in the Mississippi just outside Hannibal, Missouri. It was nothing at all like Washington D.C., although she'd been warned to expect that its summer heat would make Washington's seem almost pleasant in retrospect. The house would have been called a mansion if it held an ordinary American family; for the throng of linguists it was adequate, but no more than that, and could not have been considered luxurious. As for the grounds, Michaela suspected that they might have been criticized if the public had known much about them, because the Verdis had a fondness for gardens and didn't appear to have spared much expense in those behind the house. But out in the country like this, with a stretch of woods between them and the highway, no one was likely to know. Linguists didn't have visitors because they didn't have time; and they adamantly refused to allow members of the press on their grounds.

In spite of the crowding in the house, the Verdis had found a room with its own bath for Michaela, and a window overlooking the river. She was in the corner of the house on an upper floor, and to get down to the common rooms she had to go all the way around an outside corridor and across a walkway that went over the roof of the Interface. When she'd first arrived, that had worried her, and she'd gone immediately to the senior woman of the Household to express her concern.

"I'm concerned about my room, Mrs. Verdi," she had said.

"But it's such a nice room!"

"Oh, yes," she said hastily, "the room itself is beautiful, and I am most grateful for it. But I can't get to my patient in less than four minutes, Mrs. Verdi, and that's alarming. I've clocked it by three different routes, and four minutes is absolutely the best I can do—it's that bridge over the Interface that slows me down."

"Oh, *I* see!" Sharon Verdi had said, the relief on her face telling Michaela a good deal about the shifting and crowding they must have done to give her the room she had. "Oh, that's all right . . . really."

"But four minutes! A great deal can happen in four minutes."

For example, you can die in four minutes," thought Michaela. It had not taken Ned Landry four minutes.

"My dear child," the woman began, and Michaela guarded her face against any betrayal of how she despised the idea of being a linguist's dear child, "I assure you it's no problem. Great-grandfather Verdi has nothing serious wrong with him, you know; he's just very old and weak. Until the last few months we've always been able to assign one of the girls to sit with him, taking turns . . . he just wants company."

"But now you think he needs a nurse?"

"No," Sharon Verdi laughed, "he still just needs company. But he has taken it into his head that he wants the same person all the time, you see, and there's nobody we can spare on that basis. And so we need you, my dear—but you won't have crises to deal with. Nothing that requires you to get to his room in ten seconds flat, or anything like that. One of these nights he will go to his just reward peacefully, in his sleep; he's sound as a racehorse. And until then, I'm afraid that your major problem is not going to be rushing to emergencies, it's going to be boredom. That man can barely sit up without a strong arm to help him, but there is *nothing* wrong with his voice, and he can talk any one of us into a coma. You'll earn your salary, I promise—and want a raise."

"Ah," said Michaela. "I understand. Thank you, Mrs. Verdi."

"You're quite welcome . . . and don't worry. Nothing he needs won't wait five minutes, or fifteen for that matter. And if he ever should have a touch of something or other that makes you feel you really need to be closer, there's a very comfortable couch in his room where we could put you up for a night or two."

Michaela had nodded, satisfied. True, she would be taking the old man out of this world a bit more quickly than the Verdis anticipated; but while she was serving as his nurse, he would have the best care she could provide him, and no corners cut. She was an excellent nurse; she had no intention of lowering her standards. And she was awfully glad to be able to stay in the spacious corner room, where she could lean out like Rapunzel and watch the river.

Stephan Rue Verdi, 103 and not more than 99 pounds dripping wet, lived up to his billing. He was as formidable a talker as she'd ever encountered. But she didn't find him all that boring. When his great-granddaughter judged the old man's narrative skill, she didn't have Michaela's experience with Ned to use as a standard.

"When I was a child," old Stephan would begin, and she'd murmur at him to let him know she was listening (but that wasn't enough, she had to sit down right beside him where he could look at her without effort), "when *I* was a child, things were different. I can tell you, things were *very* different! I don't say they were better, mind—when you start saying they were you're doddering—but they were surely different."

"When I was a child, we didn't have to live the life these children live, poor little things. Up every morning before it's even light yet, out in the orchards and the vegetable gardens working like poor dirt farmers by five-thirty most of the year . . . and a choice . . . ha! some choice! . . . between running around the blasted roads and doing calisthenics for hours, or chopping wood, come the time of year there's nothing left to do in the way of agriculture. And then the poor little mites get to listen to the family *bul*letin while they eat their breakfast . . . when I was a child, we linguists lived in proper houses like anybody else, and we had our own family tables. None of these great roomfuls of people like eating in a cafeteria and everybody all jumbled in together like hogs at a trough . . .''

"The family bulletin, Mr. Verdi," Michaela prompted him. He tended to lose track.

"Oh, the *bul*letin, now that's very very important, the *bul*letin! That's a *list* the kidlings have to face every morning while they try to eat, with everything on it they have to do that day and everything they didn't do or didn't do right the day before. . . . Poor little mites," he said again.

"Hmmm," said Michaela. He would settle for "hmmmm" most of the time, since he preferred to do all the talking himself.

"Oh, yes! 'Paul Edward, you're to be at St. Louis Memorial at nine sharp, they're operating on the High Muckymuck of Patoot and he won't let them touch him unless there's an interpreter right there to pass along his complaints.' 'Maryanna Elizabeth, you're expected at the Federal Court house from nine to eleven, and then you're wanted clear across town at the Circuit Court—don't take time for lunch, you'll be late.' 'Donald Jonathan, you have three days scheduled in the Chicago Trade Complex; take your pocket computer, they'll expect you to convert currencies for the Pateets!''

"My word," Michaela said. "How do these children ever get to all those places?"

"Oh, we're very efficient. Family flyer, great big thing, revs up outside at 8:05 on the button—the five minutes to let the poor little things go to the bathroom, don't you know—and runs them into St. Louis to the State Department of Analysis & Translation, where they've got a whole army of chauffeurs and pilots and whatalls waiting, pacing up and down for fear they'll be late. They deliver everybody where they're going all day long and then bring 'em back again to SDAT at night, and we do it in reverse."

"Mmmmm."

"And then, supposing a tyke's not scheduled for the Patoots or the Pateets, well, he's got to go to *school* for two hours . . . flyer puts him down on the slidewalks in Hannibal, you see, or they run him there in the van. School . . . phooey. I say the kids that get out of it 'cause they're scheduled in solid, and then just make it up with the mass-ed computers, they're the lucky ones. Would *you* want to spend two blessed hours five days a week with a bunch of other bored-sick kids, saying the Pledge Allegiance and singing the Missouri State Song and the Hannibal Civic Anthem and listening to them read you the King James—

not that I've got anything against the King James, but the kids can read, you know, *in* a couple dozen languages! They sure don't need somebody to read to 'em. . . . And celebrating damnfool so-called holidays like Space Colony Day and Reagan's Birthday? 'Course, they do Halloween and Thanksgiving and Christmas and such, too, all that stuff . . . but would you want to do that? All that truck, I mean? Phooey . . . I can remember when we still had *classes* at school!''

"Now, Mr. Verdi," Michaela chided.

"I can. I can so."

"Tsk."

"Well . . . I can remember when my father *told* me about it."

"Mmmm."

"And when I was a tyke myself, all we had to do was the mass-ed computer lessons, at home, Now, the kids have all that to do AND the damnfool school for two hours! HOMEroom, they call it! Did you ever hear such damnfool stuff: HOMEroom!"

"Socialization, Mr. Verdi," Michaela said.

"Socialization! Damnfool!"

"Mmmmm."

"I remember what socialization did for *me*, young lady! Even when they tried to put it in the mass-ed curriculum! It made me *de*test the Pledge Allegiance and the State Song and the damnfool Civic Anthem and the whole shebang, that's what it did! Oh, I know, they say that when the kids got nothing but the mass-eds they started to act strange and their folks didn't feel like they were normal kids . . . I've heard that. I don't believe a word of it."

"Mmmmmm."

"Poor little things. You ever heard Mr. Hampton Carlyle stand up and recite *all* the verses of Hiawatha at you, little lady?"

"All the verses?"

"Well, it took him a week, you know. Including the gestures . . . You're blessed if you never had to go through that, let me tell you. And they're still doin' it to the kids, to this day! Oh, and then there's Artsandcrafts! Whoopee, let's make a little basket out of paper for the Spring Pageant and stick it full of paper flowers! And there are Special Activites. . . . Oh, I declare, Mrs. Landry, it'd gag a maggot. It's out of the Middle Ages, that's what it is."

"Mmhmmm."

"When I was a child, I had my work to do. I'd interfaced with an AIRY, and I had to know that. And I had Basque, and one of the Reformed Cherokee dialects, and I had Swedish, and I had Ameslan.''

"Ameslan?''

"American Sign Language, girl, don't they teach you anything? I had all that, and I had my mass-ed lessons to get, and I had to help out around the place. But I had time to play, and I had time to lie up in a black walnut tree and just dream once in a while, and go wading in the creek . . . these children now, Mrs. Landry, they don't have a minute to call their own. Freetime, they're supposed to get. *After* they've worked all day for the government, and *after* they've gone to Homeroom—if they can fit that in—and done the mass-ed lessons no matter what. And *after* they've put in the extra tutorials with their grammar books and dictionaries, and filled their backup requirements, and *after* they've done such stuff as run hell for leather through a shower and cut their toenails and the like, and *after* they've gone to every family briefing scheduled for them for the evening . . . if there's any time left, girl, that's theirs. That's their freetime, and precious little of it do they get. Fifteen minutes, if they're lucky.''

"Mr Verdi?''

"What? What?''

"You say they have to fill their backup requirements. What's that?''

"Shoot.''

The old man looked cross, and Michaela patted his hand and told him he didn't have to tell her if he didn't want to bother with it.

"Oh, no, I'll tell you!'' he said. "Backup . . . that's basic.''

"Mmmm.''

"You know how it works, this Interfacing?''

"No, sir. Only what I see on the news.''

"Huh. Bunch of damnfool.''

"I expect it is.''

"Well, now, the Interface is a special environment we build in the Households. There's two parts to it, each one with all the temperature and humidity regulated down to the dot, and special stuff piped in and whatnot, with the environment on one side exactly right for whichever Patoots or Pateets we've got in residence at the time, and the environment on the other side just right for humans. And between the two there's this barrier . . . you can't have cyanide gas coming on through to the kiddies just because the Patoots need it, and vice versa for oxygen and whatall, you see . . . but it's a specially made barrier that you can see through and hear through just like it wasn't hardly there at all. And we put the baby in the human side, and the AIRY's live in the other, and the AIRY's and the baby interact for a year or so and pretty soon you've got an Earth baby that's a native speaker of whatever the AIRY speaks, you see.''

"Oh," said Michaela. "My!"

"But that's for just the *first* time!" said the old man emphatically. "That's just for the very first time an Alien language is acquired as a native language by a human being. And after that, why, the human child is the native speaker and you don't have to go through all that. You just put *that* child, the one you Interfaced the first time, together in the ordinary way with another human infant, and that's backup, don't you know. The second child will acquire the Alien language from the one that was Interfaced, now there's a human native speaker available. That's necessary, let me tell you.''

"Mmmmm."

"You're not paying attention to me, are you? You *asked* me what backup was, you know, and now you're not paying attention!"

Michaela sat up very straight and insisted that indeed she was.

"You think I'm boring, do you? Everybody thinks I'm boring! Lot of damnfool phooey, if you ask me! What do *they* know?"

Michaela didn't think he was boring at all, as it happened, because the more she could learn about the habits and lifestyles of the Lingoes, the more efficiently and safely she could murder them. She considered every word that Stephan Verdi said potentially of the greatest value to her—you never knew when some scrap of information would be precisely the scrap that you most needed—and she was able to assure him with complete honesty that she was listening to every word he said and enjoying it.

"I'd know if you were lying, don't you forget," he said.

"Would you?"

"You can't lie to a linguist, young woman—don't you try it."

Michaela smiled.

"Al*read*y tried it, haven't you! I can tell by that smirk you've got on your face! Pretty doesn't cover up body-parl, girl, never has and never will!"

"Mr. Verdi . . . all that excitement's not good for you."

"Excitement? You don't excite me, you hussy, it'd take a good deal more than you to excite *me*! I've seen everything there is, in my time, and taken most of it to *bed* if I fancied it! Why, I've—"

"Mr. Verdi," Michaela broke in, "you wanted to explain to me why I can't lie to a linguist."

"I did?"

"Mmmhmm."

"Well . . . let me tell you this: if you lie to a linguist, girl, and you get away with it, if you lie to a linguist and he doesn't catch you out, it's only because he *let* you lie, for his own very good reasons. You keep that in mind."

"I will." And she would.

"Backup," she reminded him then. She'd almost lost track herself this time.

"Oh, yes. Well. You see, after Interfacing, that human child is the one and the only living human being that can speak the Alien language—and it's taken years to produce just the one. And you never know what could happen. You'd have important treaties set up, don't you know, or something else important— and the kiddy gets wiped out in a flyer accident. Struck by lightning. Whatever. You can't have that, you see. There's got to be another child coming along behind that knows the language, too, and another one behind that. Providing backup, in case anything happens. And of course grownups can't ever acquire languages like babies do, but they make a point of picking up a language as best they can every year or two, from tapes and whatall, and trying to talk to the kids that learned it Interfacing, you see. And that way, if the little one that had the AIRY's language first should go to his Maker before the backup child was old enough to work alone, well, in an emergency you could send along the grownup that had the language sort of half-assed . . . that's the only way that grownups can learn languages, most of 'em . . . and the child that was too young, and they could get by as a team after a fashion. In an emergency, don't you know! You wouldn't want that as a general thing, 'cause it doesn't work for warm spit. But in an emergency . . . well!"

"It sounds like a hard life for the children," Michaela said.

"It is. It's purely awful. Like being born in the damnfool army."

"I'm sorry," she said, and he pulled fretfully at his covers until she'd rearranged them to his satisfaction.

"It doesn't sound easy for the adults, either," she added, when she had him settled.

"Oh, phooey. They're used to it. Time they've done nothing but work all the time for twenty years, they wouldn't know what to do with themselves if they got the chance to live any other way. Phooey."

* * *

Most of the time he got a little agitated over a sentence or two in every paragraph, but he was really enjoying himself tremendously. She watched, and she'd take his pulse if he began to look flushed, while he roared at the top of his lungs about interfering damnfool women and their interfering damnfool nonsense, but she decided very quickly that Sharon Verdi was quite right. The old man's body was worn out, to such an extent that he couldn't get around anymore or do much for himself; but inside the frail assortment of muscles and bones and wrinkled flesh he was, as she'd said, fit as a racehorse. She did not need to worry about Stephan Verdi.

Only once had she seen him become so excited that she'd had to interfere and insist on a sedative. That was the day he got started talking about the Anti-Linguist Riots of 2130, with people throwing rocks at the children and setting fire to the linguists' houses . . . That was when the families had made the shift from living in individual homes like everyone else and had set up the communal Households, where there would be security in numbers. And had earth-sheltered every one of them, not only for economy's sake but also as a defense measure. So that each could be a kind of fortress on very short notice.

Talking of that, shouting that the linguists sacrificed their whole lives so the rest of the universe could live fat and lazy and at their ease, and shouting about ingratitude that would make the devil puke . . . the old man began to cry, and Michaela knew how that shamed him. A man, crying. Once Head of this Household, and crying. She'd stopped him gently, and soothed him into taking a glass of wine and a sedative, and she'd sat there beside him till he fell asleep. And since then, at the first sign that he was about to take up the subject of the riots, she headed him off expertly into a safer topic.

"You're a good child," he'd say to her from time to time.

"I'm glad you're pleased with me, sir."

"You're the best listener that I *ever* knew!"

"My husband always used to say that," she said demurely.

"Well, he was right, by damn. Does a man good to have somebody like you that can pay attention when he talks!"

"Mmhmmm."

In many ways Michaela was sorry she had to kill him. He was a nice old man. For a linguist.

Chapter Seven

Let us consider James X, a typical 14-month-old infant of the Lines. Here is his daily schedule, for your examination . . . this is an *in*fant, remember. A baby . . .

5:00 - 6:00 AM	Wakeup, followed by calisthenics or swimming, and then breakfast.
6:00 - 9:00 AM	Interface session, with one or two Aliens-in-Residence.
9:00 - 10:00 AM	Outdoor play with other children. During this play hour the adults supervising use only American Sign Language for communication.
11:30 - 12:00	Lunch.
12:00 - 2:30 PM	Nap.
2:30 - 3:00 PM	Calisthenics or swimming.
3:00 - 5:00 PM	"Play" time; spent with an older child who speaks yet another Alien language to James.
5:00 - 6:00 PM	Supper, followed by bath.
6:00 - 7:00 PM	"Family" time; spent with parents if available, or with an older relative.
7:00 PM	To sleep.

Note that this extraordinary schedule guarantees that the infant will have extensive exposure each day to two Alien languages, to the primary native language of the Household (which will be English, French or Swahili) and to sign language. But this is by no means all. Great care is taken to see that the adults directing the exercise sessions speak some different Earth language to the children—in James' particular case that morning session involves Japanese and the afternoon Hopi. That is, James X must deal with daily language input in at least six distinct languages— and the answer to your inevitable question is no . . . this does not cause James X any difficulty. Initially there may be a brief period of confusion and minimal delay in language development; however, by the age of five or six he will have native speaker fluency in all those various tongues.

Weekends will differ from the schedule above very little; there may be some sort of family outing, or a visit to a pediatrician, and on Sunday there will be an amazingly lengthy time spent in Family Chapel. These are very busy babies indeed.

(from a briefing for junior staff,
Department of Analysis & Translation)

Andrew St. Syrus had the languid good looks characteristic of his family. Skin so fair that ten minutes in the sun meant a burn, and hair the color of good English wheat. And he had a beautiful mouth. Like all the St. Syrus men, he grew a full mustache above it to serve as a counterweight of masculinity. And he had learned, painstakingly, in daily sessions supervised by other St. Syrus men, the repertoire of male body language that no St. Syrus man could afford to dispense with. Thomas Chornyak, now, if he lounged a bit in his chair you saw only a sturdy male bulk lounging in a chair; if Andrew took the same posture he appeared to be draped over the chair for the elegance of the effect, and it was fatal. Andrew sat up straight, and he kept his shoulders square, and he made damn sure every unit of his body-parl had an unambiguous message like a drone string on a dulcimer . . . I AM VERY MALE. It was a nuisance, and the Household was searching for at least two husbands from outside the Lines who could offer a substantial contribution of genes best described as hulking.

He arrived at Chornyak Household before breakfast, refused anything but a cup of strong black coffee, and went straight to Thomas' office to tell him about the kidnapping.

"My God, Andrew," Thomas said at once, both hands gripping his desk. "Jesus . . . that's awful."

"It's not pleasant."

"You're sure it's a kidnapping? Not just a mixup . . . one of those cases you read about once in a while where some woman takes home the wrong baby?"

"They'd have one extra at the hospital, if it were that."

Thomas made a face, and apologized.

"It was a stupid question," he said. "I'm shocked stupid, I'm afraid. Forgive me."

"It's understandable."

"Not really, Andrew—but go on."

"They think it must have happened sometime between midnight and the four o'clock feeding . . . that's when they noticed that the baby was gone. Somebody just waltzed up to the night nurse with a fake note saying they wanted the child for Evoked Potentials, and she handed it over like a sack of groceries."

"How could that happen? A baby is *not* a sack of groceries!"

"Well," sighed Andrew, "the nurse on duty had no reason to be suspicious. Someone's always coming after babies from the Lines for neurological testing—you know that. The man was dressed like a doctor, he acted like a doctor, the note was scrawled like a doctor's usual bad excuse for handwriting. she had no way of knowing. Hell . . . nobody argues with a doctor, Thomas—you can't blame the woman."

"She should have checked."

"Thomas. She's a nurse. A woman. What do you expect?"

"I expect competence. We expect competence in the women of the Lines, Andrew."

St. Syrus shrugged, carefully.

"Well," he said, "it's done. Never mind blaming the nurse at this point—it changes nothing. It's done."

"I'm sorry, Andrew," said Thomas.

"I know you are, and I appreciate it."

Andrew got up and walked back and forth as he talked, his hands clasped behind him. "We felt that the worst possible thing would be publicity . . . Considering the way people feel about us, they'd probably give the kidnapper board and room instead of turning him in. So we exerted a little pressure in the necessary places, and we've been promised that those media buzzards won't be allowed one word, not even an announcement."

"I see."

Andrew looked at him, narrowing his eyes, and said, "You know, Thomas, that's odd. They must be short-staffed, or confused, missing an opportunity to sic the pack on us and keep the public mind off their own shenanigans. This one is tailor-made for the bastards—I can't figure out why they're passing it up."

"Andrew, when have the actions of our illustrious government ever made sense?"

"Not lately."

"I rather expect they're concerned that people might get nervous about hospital security measures . . . copycat crimes, that sort of thing."

"I suppose. Whatever it is, thank God for it."

"Right you are, my friend. And I will tighten the screws a bit from this end, just to make sure that their motivation doesn't slip somebody's mind on its way up through the chain of command."

"I was hoping you'd offer to do that, Thomas."

"Certainly, man! Of course. You can put that out of your mind, at least. And what else can I do?"

"I don't think there *is* anything else to do."

"That's not likely. There's almost always something else to do—you just haven't had time to consider the matter. How about my pressuring the police as well as the press?"

"I think the police are doing all that can be done," said the other man, sitting down again. "They've no reason not to. It's all just a job to them, no matter whose baby is involved. And perhaps it will be all right. I mean, perhaps they'll find the scum who did this before he has a chance to harm the child."

"Not yours, is it?" asked Thomas, looking politely away from him.

"No, thank heaven, it's not. But it's my brother's, and it would have been his first child. You can imagine how he feels."

"Yes."

"As for the woman . . ." St. Syrus spread his hands wide in a gesture of complete hopelessness and stared eloquently at the ceiling.

"The mother's taken it badly, I suppose."

"Oh, my God . . . You've never perceived anything quite like it. The *lungs* on that woman! I'm surprised you can't hear her all the way here, frankly. When I left, they were sedating her so the rest of the family wouldn't have to suffer with her caterwauling. And the other women are not a whole lot better, I'm sorry to say—especially since they are all fully aware of the Lines' policy about ransoms."

"It has to be that way," said Thomas gently. "If there was the slightest chance that the linguists would pay ransoms, none of our children, or our women, would be safe. We don't have any choice.''

"I know that. The women know that. But it doesn't keep them from carrying on world without end about it.''

"In my experience, Andrew, you've got to give them something to keep them busy. Not makework, mind you, but something that will really occupy them.''

"For instance? There are nineteen adult women under my roof, and nearly that many adolescent females . . . and a miscellaneous assortment of girl children. It would take something like the excavation of a sewer system to use every spare moment of a gaggle that size.''

"What about their damnfool Encoding Project? What about their church duties? What about their ordinary obligations, for God's sakes? How can they have spare time?''

"Thomas," said Andrew wearily, "I'm ashamed to admit it, but I simply do not have the kind of control you have.''

"You haven't been Head very long . . . it will come.''

"Perhaps. But at the moment, my women claim they can't keep their mind on their hobby, and they're so angry at the Almighty that they're not speaking to Him. And so on. Drivel, endless drivel.''

"Double their schedules, Andrew. Give them some stuff to translate that there hasn't been time for. Hell, make them clean the house. Buy them fruit to make jelly out of, if your orchards and storerooms are bare. There's got to be something you can do with them, or they will literally drive you crazy. Women out of control are a curse—and if you don't put a stop to it, you'll regret it bitterly later on.''

"I regret it bitterly *now*. But this is not the moment for me to institute reforms, Thomas. Not in the middle of this mess.''

"It's a hell of a thing," said Thomas.

"Yes. And then some." Andrew sank down in the chair, caught himself and straightened up again, and lit a cigarette.

"You didn't have any warning, I don't suppose. No threats. No stuff written on your walls. Obscene letters.''

"No. Nothing like that.''

They sat silently, and Thomas concentrated on looking suitably distressed. Not that anyone in the Lines, or anywhere else, was ever going to suspect him of collusion with the government. The idea was so unthinkable that he could be certain it would go unthought. But the popular platitudes about it being impossible to lie to a linguist were based on a solid foundation. Even if you were also a linguist. He couldn't afford to be careless; St. Syrus was inexperienced, but he was capable and intelligent and nobody's fool.

"Perceive this, Andrew," he said finally. "I'm not going to just let this pass."

"Meaning what?"

"Meaning that we aren't going to sit like sticks and let it go on without taking some action of our own. I'm going to put private investigators on it, St. Syrus. Today."

"Surely that's not necessary!"

"I think it is."

"But, Thomas—"

"Andrew, this is a matter of principle. And of honor. The honor of the Lines. I want whoever is behind this to be shown, and I want the unenthusiastic law enforcement people to be shown, that we of the Lines don't take kindly to having our women and children tampered with. It's necessary to make that unambiguously clear, and without any delay that might confuse their little minds."

"It'll cost the earth, Thomas," said Andrew slowly. "Not that I mind the expense, but—"

Thomas cut him short.

"There are special funds," he said. "Special funds set aside for unusual circumstances, when cost should not have to be considered. This qualifies as one of those circumstances. Think, Andrew—damn it, man, do you want word going out on the street that anybody who fancies it can go pick off a linguist infant from a maternity ward and we'll just wring our hands and whimper in many tongues? We may be able to silence the media, but we sure as hell can't silence the criminals."

"Maybe you're right, Thomas. Hell . . . of course you're right. It's the sort of thing a criminal might do on a dare from his buddies, isn't it? Jesus."

"Andrew," said Thomas firmly, "you go home and tend to your affairs. Get all the women out on contracts if you can. Those that aren't on duty even as informal backups, find something exhausting to keep them occupied. I'll get things started here right now—first, I'll lean on the press; second, I'll hire the detectives. Leave it in my hands and go home."

Andrew St. Syrus stood up, stiffly. He was tired; he'd been up all night, and he had a full day ahead of him.

"Thomas, I'm grateful," he said. "I can't tell you how much it means to all of us, having this kind of support."

"Don't mention it, Andrew. Kidnapping is a contemptible crime. Harming babies is barbarism. I'll tolerate talk, Andrew, but I won't have the families of the Lines actually harmed. I won't stand for it. *We* won't stand for it.''

"You're absolutely right. Of course. All that chaos and hysteria I've been listening to has addled my brains.''

"Go home, Andrew. Stop thanking me, and stop agreeing with me, and go home—so that I can get this under way.''

"Of course. Of course." St. Syrus picked up his cigarettes and his flyer keys, and stood up. A back muscle he'd strained somehow jabbed at him, and he was careful not to wince. He stopped in the office door, holding it open, and drew a swift line in the air. PanSig for good-by. The necessary light touch.

"Good-bye, Andrew," said Thomas, and matched the PanSig unit politely.

Andrew was interested in PanSig; it was almost a hobby with him. He'd even managed to add three very useful units to its painfully limited lexicon, all of them producible in body, color, and odor Modes—and to get them past the PanSig Division of D.A.T. That had been a good deal harder than working out the units in the first place. He was tempted, briefly, to do the V-unit that was PanSig Body Mode for ''Thank you''; then he thought better of it, and went on into the hall, letting the door slide shut behind him. Thomas wouldn't have found it either interesting or amusing.

Chapter Eight

Gentlemen, we know the set of beliefs that you have about the linguists—every new group of D.A.T. trainees arrives here with that same set.

We will begin by telling you bluntly that most of those beliefs *are in error*. For example: there is the firm public conviction that the linguists live in luxury, surrounded by the trappings of their vast wealth. Nothing could be less accurate, men; the linguists' lifestyle has an austerity and frugality that I am absolutely certain not one of you would willingly endure. Only in the monasteries of the Roman Catholic Church could you find anything even remotely comparable as a standard of living—and if it were not for the advanced technology required by their duties as linguists, which does entail some expensive electronic equipment, a more apt comparison would be the communities of the American Amish and Mennonites. I am sure this surprises you—for excellent reasons which I am not at liberty to discuss at this time—but I give you my word it is true. And I hasten to add that the lifestyle is not imposed by any government authority.

The women of the Lines are viewed by the public as almost obscenely extravagant. Gentlemen, allow me to enlighten you on this point, with just one typical fact about these alleged extravagances. An adult woman of the Lines is allowed to own only the following garments: two plain tunics; one simple dress for official functions; one tailored garment intended for wear in church and at work in government negotiations; two pairs of coveralls; a winter cape; a rain cape; two nightgowns; two pairs of shoes—which are clingsoles; and a set of minimal underclothing. Where I have specified two of any item, this means "one for warm weather, one for cold weather." As for ornament, gentlemen—a linguist woman is allowed her wedding ring, a religious medallion or cross if she wants one, and her wrist computer. *Nothing* else is permitted, and no cosmetics of any kind.

You might think for just a moment, gentlemen, how your own wives and daughters would react to that sort of restriction. I, for one, would be afraid to go home . . .

(from a briefing for junior staff, D.A.T.)

"No," said Thomas, "I will not sympathize with you. Absolutely not."

"The compassionate linguist," said Smith. "Always eager to help."

"No," said Thomas evenly, "we have never claimed to be compassionate. There have been good reasons for that, which I do not propose to discuss with you—and if you choose to take that as meaning I won't stoop to do so, that's your privilege. My personal statement is that I don't have time to waste in that fashion, and that I resent your taking up what time I do have with this nonsense."

"We regret that you find our efforts useless, Mr. Chornyak," said the man bitterly. "We're not lofty scientists here, moving through our days in the sublime pursuit of pure knowledge—we are ordinary men, doing ordinary jobs. One of those jobs, about which *my* personal statement is that I think it is both pathetic and stupid, is to serve as liaison between you and the government in situations which both you and the government prefer not to have the public know about. And which I assume you'd be distressed to have the rest of the linguists know about. . . . But I am ordered to do this; and I do it as well as I can."

Thomas knew the taste of failure, listening to this man who was, as he said, only trying to do an impossible job because it was what he was expected to do and had agreed to do. He was sharply aware that if his own father knew what was taking place here today he would condemn Thomas in terms that would not be pleasant or give quarter. Situations like this only made the breach between public and linguist wider and more poisonous, only played into the hands of those who gained by that breach . . . and he must find time, somehow, to mend some bridges and span the gap. If only he could be six people and be in as many places at one time. If only the government would listen to the linguists' warnings that there was a limit to the number of Alien tongues it was possible for them to acquire and use on that government's behalf—which would have meant curbing the dizzying rate of expansion into space and colonization. Curbing the public greed for more room, more opportunity, more new frontiers. . . .

"Smith," he said, trying not to think about it, "I have nothing but admiration for your devotion to your duty. That is not sarcasm, that is not empty politeness, it is simply the way I feel. You don't have to explain your situation to me, I understand that it's awkward and distasteful. But I can only repeat, man, that I *told* you. Didn't I, Smith? I warned you, right here in this room, less than a month ago, and you *would not listen*. Isn't that true?"

"You warned us, yes."

"And what did I warn you *of*, Smith?"

"That if we tried to Interface that baby it would die horribly, just like all the others. You warned us, and you were right; and you are entitled to whatever warped satisfaction that gives you, Chornyak."

Thomas sat back in the chair, his lips slightly parted, holding the government man with his eyes until the red flush had spread from Smith's neck all the way to his forehead. They had not sent poor Jones into the arena this time, and it was just as well.

"All right, all right!" Smith spat at him. "That was a shitty thing to say! And I retract it. I'm sorry."

Thomas let that hang in the air. He let his face and his body and his hands do the work for him, and he said not one word. Smith didn't disappoint him.

"It's not the same thing," the man said through his teeth, his hands fiddling aimlessly with a scrap of paper on the table before him, his shoulder hunching. "It's not the same thing at all . . . it's not like somebody's kidnapped one of *our* kids and destroyed it that way. It's very, very different. You Lingoes, you don't have any feeling for your kids, you breed them like flyers come off assembly lines, they're just products to you. Shit, I've *heard* you, I don't know how many times I've heard you, talking about it . . . You don't say, 'Hey, my kid won a prize at Homeroom today, we're proud of him,' naah . . . *I've* heard you! 'That boy means two more Alien languages added to the inventories of

Household So-and-So.' 'The girl has a certain value, she in-
creases our assets by three little-known Earth languages in addition to the Alien language for which she has primary responsibility.'
JEEzus, you talk about your kids like they were stocks and
bonds, or the effing *corn* crop . . . you don't care about them! If
you cared about them, I'd feel different about this, I'd feel *sorry*
for your people, sorry about your kid, sure . . . but shit, Chornyak!
They don't mean anything to their own families—why should
they mean anything to us?''

Thomas considered it carefully, pleased to note that his earlier
consciousness of guilt had completely disappeared, and decided
that he could spare a few minutes. For the good of his battered
spirit and this dolt's soul. It had been a long day. He was, he
decided, entitled.

"Tell me, Smith," he asked, "how's your history?"

"My what?"

"How's your background in history? The usual mass-ed courses?
And surely a little something extra to prepare you for government service?"

"Yeah. So?"

"Do you remember, Smith, the sums of money poured into a
cure for the epidemic of child abuse that swept this nation
in the late 20th and early 21st centuries? Do you remember
when it was not safe to put even the most hardened and street-
wise criminal into a prison if his crime was child abuse, because
the other inmates would kill him like a mad dog, and less
gently?"

"I read about it. Everybody knows about that."

"Yes. So they do. We've stamped out child abuse, haven't
we, Smith . . . at least we've stamped out its excesses and its
obvious physical forms. We value our children now, we treasure
them, because they are the future of the human race. We no
longer leave the molding of their minds and their characters to
the random attention of ignorant pseudo-teachers in a parody of
education. We no longer leave their diets and their exercise and
their medical care to whatever chance factors happen to come
their way—our children are cared for now with the very best that
this nation can provide, for their bodies and their minds and their
spirits. And it makes no difference where they come from or
who their parents are, they are *all* cared for that way. You are
aware of all that, Smith."

"And damned proud of it. So what?"

"Well . . . Smith, do you consider yourself a man who is

fond of children? In contrast to the linguists, for example, who see their offspring only as economic resources.''

"You're damn right! They're human beings, they're not effing in*vest*ments!''

"You love children, Smith?''

"Yes, I love children! What's that got to do with anything?''

"Well, then, Smith,'' Thomas asked gently, "would you explain something to me? Would you explain to me why it is that the government has not moved to take the children of the linguists away from them? If, as you imply, we treat them coldly and callously, and exploit them—''

"You *do*, dammit! You violate the child labor laws before the poor kids are even out of the cradle!''

"Ah. . . .a forceful phrase. . . . And why is that allowed to go on, Smith? If you took your own child and put it to work in a cornfield from dawn to dark, as we linguists put our children to work in government affairs, the authorities would step in and take that child away from you for its own good, wouldn't they?''

Smith had seen what was coming, suddenly, too late, and he squirmed, and swallowed bile, and chewed on his lips.

"But nobody moves to protect our children from abuse, Smith . . . why *is* that?''

"Look—''

"And when you *did* take a child from us, Smith, one of our abused children destined for a life of unremitting toil and unrelieved grim labor, why is it that you didn't take that poor little creature for whom this government has such concern and consideration . . . and compassion, Smith, such compassion . . . and put it straight away in a good home with parents who would love it as it deserved to be loved? Would treat it as it deserved to be treated? You're a compassionate man, who *loves* children; why was that infant taken to an Interface—which is precisely and exactly what would have happened to it if you'd left it in our care, except that we would not have killed it—and put to work at three and a half weeks of age?''

"Oh, god. . . .'' The words came choked from Smith's throat, and they were forced past his lips like solid objects rather than a string of sounds.

Thomas leaned back and stared at him, all open amazement and wonder.

"Well,'' he said, "I believe you began this conversation by accusing me, and all my relatives, of a lack of compassion, Smith. As you define compassion, you and your government.

And that's very interesting. Because I have never in my entire life taken a helpless newborn child away from its mother and given it to strangers. I have never in my life taken a helpless infant and deliberately put it into an environment in which I knew it would suffer abominations and could not, could not possibly, survive. I've never done that, and no linguist has ever done that—we linguists, in our total lack of compassion and decency, Smith—we would not do that. *You* people, on the other hand, *you* people—"

He leaned across the table, and he hammered his words home with a blow of his fist for every stress.

"—you have done it *over* and *over* and *over*! And you would do it again tomorrow if you had the chance! You *dare* talk to me of compassion!"

Smith was gasping, fighting not to twist openly as he twisted inside, fighting not to writhe openly before this monster he was paid to face.

He did not want to think about it. He would not, *would not*, think about it. He had never considered that question, why it was that the U.S. government, that would have stepped in instantly if any other child, let alone whole generations of children, had been mistreated as the linguist children were said to be mistreated, not only did not interfere but paid enormous sums to cooperate in that abuse. It was not a thought that he was willing to let get the least tendril of purchase in his mind.

"Are you having a little trouble there, Smith?" Thomas asked him, smiling as a shark smiles.

"Go home, Chornyak," said Smith hoarsely. "Just go home."

"What, and leave this question just hanging there?"

"*Yeah*, leave it hanging there! I don't want to hear any more about it, Chornyak!"

"Well, I couldn't do that, Smith."

"Mr. Chornyak—"

"I have a certain responsibility here," Thomas continued. "I can't raise a major issue like this and just leave you in confusion. That's not polite. That's not decent. That's not compassionate. That's not even scientific—not when I know the answer, Smith. And I do know the answer."

"For God's sake, Chornyak. Please."

"The answer," Thomas went on inexorably, "is just as simple as it can be. If *my* children, and the children of the other Lines, did not spend their lives in endless toil, *your* children,

Smith—and all the rest of the dear little children of this United States and all its comfy colonies—could not be provided with perfect food and perfect housing and perfect education and perfect medical care and the leisure to thrive and live the good life. There would not be enough money to provide all *your* children with the good life, Smith, if ever we uncaring linguists decided that our children should know that good life, too. You *love* your children, you see, on the weary backs of ours.''

"That's not true. It's not true.''

"No? I'll listen to your explanation, then, Smith.''

"You know I can't explain anything to you, you bastard. You'd twist my words around like you've done now, you'd lay traps I can't get out of, you'd put words in my mouth—''

"And ideas in your poor little head,'' Thomas rapped out, letting all his disgust show, on all channels of communication. "If what I say is not true, Smith, teach me! Teach me the truth, and I will see that it is spread to all the other linguists. When you were a little boy, you were in the circles of children holding hands and dancing round our little ones, screaming 'Dirty stinking Lingoe, dirty stinking Lingoe!'' Weren't you, Smith? But those dirty stinking Lingoes put the food in your mouth and the soft clothing on your back and gave you the time to play and to learn and to know tender love. Would you like to come home with me, Smith, and thank them? Or you can thank me, if that's more convenient . . . I used to be one of those children in the center of the circle, I'll do as an example.''

"It's not true.''

Smith was clinging to that, because he felt dimly that it was very important that he cling to it. He did not remember why anymore. He did not remember hearing anything in the Training Lectures that had any bearing on the way he felt right now. He did not remember how he had come to be so confused or when he had begun to feel so strange and so ill, but he knew that there was a magic charm in the three words that he could use to ward off evil if he could only keep saying them and let nothing else past them.

"It's not true, it's not true, it's not true,'' he said. "It's not true.''

Thomas had no intention of telling him whether it was true or not. He had more useful things to do than continue this kindergarten exercise, and it was time he got to them.

"Smith!'' He snapped the word, cracked it like a whip, cutting through to the man's attention.

"What?"

"I want you to listen to what I'm going to say, Smith, and I want you to go back and repeat it to your bosses. Do you think you can do that, or shall I send for somebody else to do it for you?"

"I can do it." Wooden words. Wooden lips.

"This MUST NOT HAPPEN AGAIN," said Thomas, "This kidnapping trick. This government baby-killing. For the sake of many many factors you do not even dream of, I have put together a story that will keep the lid on it this time, something that we can tell the police, something that I can tell St. Syrus Household. *This* time! But I can't do it twice, Smith. I can't work miracles. I won't try—it must not be repeated, you hear me? You've had your chance, you've tried out your ignorant hypothesis about genetic differences and the imperative for putting a baby on the Lines in your cursed government Interface—and it didn't *work*, Smith! It didn't work. As I told you it would not work. And it will never work. I warn you—you tell your bosses, I warn you all—don't try it again."

He left the man nodding and mumbling in his chair; he made no effort to hide the contempt he felt for any male so easily broken, slapping down on the table the white card with the cover story Smith was to take back to whoever had the privilege of dealing with him today, and he went out the door of Room DAT40. It closed behind him with a soft sucking noise, but he was certain that Smith would be able to hear it slam in his head.

And it would of course only take Smith twenty minutes to wall off everything he'd heard Thomas say, so that it would never bother him again. Thomas knew all about that process, as did his father, and his father before him. That speech he'd made was a set piece, an extended cliché; it must come up two or three times a year. And nobody, so far as Thomas knew, had ever needed more than half an hour to put it out of their consciousness forever. They marveled sometimes, in the Lines, at the efficiency of the mental filters that kept from the masters even the realization that they were slavers . . . allowed to be slavers by the grace of the slaves, but slavers nonetheless.

It might have been possible to understand it, he thought as he headed for the roof, if it had been only their women. In the poverty of their perceptions, prevented by nature itself from ever having more than a distorted image of reality, women might very well create for themselves a picture that included nothing but the parts of reality they enjoyed looking at. That was to be expected, and however irritating it might be, it was not something that could be held against them. But it wasn't just their women who lived in fantasy, it was their men as well—and that, thought Thomas, was *not* possible to understand. You could despise them for it, or you could try to find it in yourself to forgive them for it—but there was no way to understand it. How could they manage to look straight at the truth, and, like females, not even *see* it? Or smell it. . . .God knows it stank.

Thomas found it difficult at times to stay out of the ranks of those in the Lines who settled for despising, and never mind the rest of it. That was not the way to solve the problem—it was a womanish surrender to the easy way out—but it was exceedingly tempting.

He had one more thing left to do before he could go home. He was weary, and short on patience now, but he saw no reason why Andrew St. Syrus should have to make the trip to Chornyak Household again to hear his fairy tale. What Thomas had to tell him could have been told by comset just as well as in person . . . but to do that would be to appear completely without manners or family feeling, and that wouldn't do. Resigned to the inescapable, he punched the computer keys in the flyer and gave the screen as much of his attention as he could spare from the evening traffic.

The coordinates came up, he punched them in, and the flyer turned toward the west. And when Andrew walked out onto the roof of the building where he'd been tied up in an after-dinner session of the Department of Health he found Thomas waiting for him.

"Chornyak," he said. "Something's happened."

"Yes. And it's not good, Andrew. I won't pretend it is."

"Tell me."

"There isn't any easy way to do this, Andrew. It's a matter of getting it over with, and we can do it right here as well as anywhere. Or we can go somewhere quiet and have a drink, if you like. . . ."

"No, no," said Andrew. "This will do." He leaned against the side of his flyer, near Thomas and out of the wind that was bringing in a thunderstorm. "What's happened?"

"The investigators I've hired, Andrew . . . they got to the bottom of the mess. You remember Terralone?"

"Terralone?" Andrew shook his head. "What is it? Or who is it?"

"It's a cult. A cult of lunatics, top grade. Real prize lunatics. Terraloners believe that any contact with extra-terrestrials, even if it happens to be the only hope of the human race for survival et cetera, never mind that, *any* such contact is the essence of evil."

St. Syrus took a long breath, and let it out slowly.

"Oh, yeah," he said. "Oh, yeah, I remember. Mostly, they picket."

"Picket, squawk for the threedy cameras, do the odd bit of terrorism. Badly. And have ceremonies, Andrew."

"Well?"

"Well, that's what happened to the infant, my friend. I wish it was prettier."

"You're talking rot, Thomas—there aren't any pretty ways for kidnappings to end. Let's have the rest of it."

"One of their farther-out loonies took the baby, they had a ceremony that they claim is a payment on humanity's moral debt for contaminating itself by stepping off this little rock, and the baby is dead."

"Dead how?"

"Andrew," said Thomas firmly, "you don't want to know any more than that. I'm not going to *tell* you any more than that. But the baby is dead, and there's no way to get the body back to its mother—God be praised—and it's over. They burned the body, Andrew . . . it's finished."

St. Syrus nodded, jerky and quick, and jumped at the thunderclap that rattled the flyer's shell.

"We'd better get out of this," he said, "or we'll be going home by ground transport."

Thomas put one hand on his shoulder, as gently as he could.

"They've got the son of a bitch," he said, "and he'll live the rest of his demented life in the Federal Mental Hospital in the South Bronx. He'll never set foot outside that place again—that's been seen to. And he's young, Andrew. He's looking at maybe seventy years in that place. You can tell the parents . . . he's going to pay, and pay, and pay."

"Well. It's done with."

"Yes. And there won't be any leaks to the press now either. The authorities have no more interest in a wave of copycats raiding the maternity wards than we do. The lid's on tight."

"Thank you, Thomas."

"I didn't do anything to be thanked for, friend. Bringing the child back to you safe, that would call for thanks. This?'' He shrugged. ''This isn't something you say thanks for.''

St. Syrus didn't answer, and Thomas went on.

''You can tell the parents the truth if you feel that's the appropriate way to handle it—I can't think of anything better than the truth, myself. But except for them, the story to the Lines is that the baby died in the hospital. One of those mysterious things that takes a baby out sometimes, for no reason anybody can explain. And it was cremated there at the hospital at our request to avoid the possibility of contagion.''

''Thomas, the other women in my Household aren't going to swallow that. It's been a month.''

''You tell them that it took the government this long to notify us, Andrew,'' said Thomas bitterly. ''Tell them there was a computer foulup and the baby's records got lost—tell them it took this long to straighten it out. They'll be angry enough about that to get their minds off the mourning. All right?''

''I think so. Yes . . . that should be all right. It's plausible enough.''

''If the parents want a small, very quiet, very private memorial service—and if it suits you to permit it—let them have it. No reason why not, so far as I'm concerned.''

''All right, Thomas.''

''It's all clear to you now, man?''

''The authorities get the truth—they'll know about Terralone. And the parents. Everybody else gets the killer virus story, with computer foulup for addendum. Logical, reasonable, and the end of the matter.''

''Thank god.''

''Yes. Thank god. And it won't happen again.''

''You think not?''

''Not if the government wants working linguists,'' said Thomas grimly. ''I made that very clear. You'll see security around our infants like they were solid gold, Andrew.''

''On the public wards?''

''That's their problem. If they want to move the women to the private wings at their expense, I sure as hell won't cross them; if they want to make a spectacle for the public and think up some fantasy to leak to the media, that's also up to them. But there'll be no repetition of this particular incident.''

Thomas watched St. Syrus take off, and then he headed for home, watching the streaks of lightning off to his left, anxious to get inside before the storm broke. Though Paul John would have said he well deserved the rain, and the wind, and a lightning bolt to boot. Cutting pathetic brainwashed government men to shreds and turning their heads to cottage cheese was supposed to be something a linguist resorted to only in emergencies. He'd stomped all over little Smith just because he wanted to do it, just because he was tired.

I'm getting old, Thomas thought, but I'm not getting wise. That's misrepresentation. I'm supposed to get wise. . . .

Chapter Nine

"We are men, and human words are all we have: even the Word of God is composed actually of the words of men."

(HUNTING THE DIVINE FOX,
by Robert Farrar Capon,
1974, page 8)

SPRING 2182. . . .

Thomas was home before dark, which wasn't bad considering the farcical piece of silliness he'd been involved in . . . a Special Awards Session at the Department of Analysis & Translation to honor the staff language specialists who'd just finished a new series of teaching grammars and videotapes for the eastern dialects of REM9-2-84. With the massive help of their computers, of course. And now D.A.T. would be well equipped to teach innocent government personnel a new group of outrageously distorted versions of those languages, so that they could make silly asses of themselves at embassy functions, cocktail parties at the U.N., etc. with even greater ease than they had previously been able to manage. How nice; and how nice that he'd been invited to give the Awards Speech applauding their folly. It was suitable, no doubt, and the hypocrisy of it bothered him not at all; he had waxed positively lyrical about the wondrousness of their accomplishments.

Linguists had been volunteering their services to write the teaching grammars of the Alien languages since the very first one encountered—as they had volunteered to write the teaching grammars of Earth languages down through the centuries—and the government had remained as ever staunchly convinced that its own "language specialists" knew more about grammar than linguists did. It was a kind of religious faith, damn near winsome in its naïve disregard for all observable facts. And a polite thanks-but-no-thanks . . . FATHer, we'd RATHer do it our-SELVES. Thomas chuckled, thinking that it justified any amount of hypocrisy. And he rationed these appearances carefully, accepting just that bare minimum of invitations of this sort absolutely necessary to keeping up a public image of linguist/government cooperation.

He stopped well away from the house and looked at it, slowly, scrupulously. Not because it was particularly attractive to view. Sheltered in the hillside as it was, with only the fourth floor showing above ground and the earth high over most of that, there wasn't much of it to see. But what he was looking for was some small difference, something that would catch his attention if he *paid* attention, something that deviated from the familiar. The women had a tendency to accomplish changes by altering things one infinitestimal fraction at a time, spread over months and months, so that you never saw it happening until suddenly it was just *there* . . . he well remembered a rock garden that had appeared once on the east slope of the hill, complete with three giant boulders, seemingly sprung instantaneously from the earth. And when he'd demanded to know how it got there—the wide innocent eyes, and the innocent voices.

"We had no idea you minded, Thomas!"

"Goodness, we've been working on it for six months! If you didn't want us to do it, why didn't you say something sooner?"

Sometimes you went through the fuss and expense of having their projects torn down and disposed of, as a matter of principle; sometimes you let them alone just out of exhaustion. As the years went by, you learned the value of nipping them in the bud and avoiding the entire problem. He was trying to do that now, scanning the grounds and the entrance, and the solar collectors . . . looking for detail.

The women had a sly animal cleverness that seved them well, he thought, and that only experience could teach a man to anticipate. Once, years ago, and with his father watching him in amusement, he had issued a flat order that there would be NO CHANGES not specifically initiated by males. And then when the grass stood waist high on the lawn, and the hedges looked like wild bramble thickets, he finally noticed and called the wenches in to demand an explanation.

"But Thomas, dear, you said NO CHANGES, of any kind!"

"But Thomas, we were only doing as you told us to do . . . Oh dear, it's so confusing."

His wife had looked him straight in the eye, presuming a good deal on their years together, and had asked that he please explain to them *specifically* why a change in the height of the grass or the shape of a hedge did not constitute a change. They would, Rachel had assured him blandly, do better if he would take the time to clarify that for their feeble understanding. Women! Sometimes it amused him and sometimes it infuriated him; always, it made him wonder what in the name of heaven really went on inside their heads. Better that he didn't know, probably.

Satisfied at last that nothing new was being erected on his premises one grain of sand at a time, and with the light failing rapidly, he turned his key in the antique lock that represented nothing but a concession to female sentimentality—the computer having identified him and released the barriers the moment he stepped within their range—and he went inside. Now, we would have peace. He was looking forward to the evening. He might even get some useful work done.

Except that there was no peace. Instead, there were women running up and down the stairs, there was disorder and bustle and confusion, and there was a low murmur that he recognized sadly as female nervous racket.

Thomas drew a long breath, and he stopped dead in the entrance. He did not fail to notice the row of ornamental pebbles set into the border of the threshold—that had not been there when he went off to the Awards circus, he was sure of it; he made a mental note to take it up with the ladies at the first opportunity, after he'd found out what was responsible for the disturbance he could sense all around him in place of the serenity he had been looking forward to. He let the door slide shut behind him, and coughed gently, and the racket died at once, the silence spreading from where he stood like ripples in still water; the women were passing along the word that he'd come home.

"Well," he said in the new stillness, "Good evening to you all."

"Good evening, Thomas." From all directions.

"Well?"

They said nothing, and he spoke sharply. "What the devil is going on here? I could hear the uproar all the way to the slidewalk . . . what's it all about?"

One of the older girls, one of the multitude of his nieces, came to the top of the staircase and stood looking at him.

"Well, damn it?"

"It's Nazareth, Uncle Thomas," said the girl.

"It's Nazareth? It's Nazareth *what*, child?" Knowing he'd get nowhere with her if he was cross—that would only addle her further—he hid his irritation and spoke gently.

"Nazareth . . . your daughter. She's sick."

Thomas considered that for a moment, and took off his coat to hand to the woman who had come up to stand waiting beside him. He remembered the girl now; Philippa, her name was. Superb at Laotian.

"In what way is Nazareth sick, Philippa?" he asked, heading down the stairs toward her, smiling.

"I don't know, Uncle Thomas. We've been wondering whether to call the doctor."

Thomas made a sharp noise in his throat . . . that was all he needed, one of those bloody Samurai stomping arrogantly around his house all evening . . . not that he'd stay long. Very busy men, the doctors; no time to do more than present their bill and shower their generalized contempt around in all directions. He respected the laser surgeons, who seemed to be capable craftsmen; as for the rest of them, his contempt for their ignorance was matched only by his outrage at their assumption that all humankind owed them automatic and unreasoning devotion. It was a tribute to the skill of the American Medical Association that although there had been Anti-Linguist riots again and again there had never even been an Anti-Physician rumble.

"Surely that's not necessary, child," he said. "It can't be anything serious. What's Nazareth doing, throwing up?"

His wife came then, finally, hurrying, and he turned to greet her. She hadn't time to be polite, either, of course. And she looked tired. She always looked tired, and he found it very boring.

"We've had an awful time with Nazareth," she said, without so much as a hello for preamble, "ever since dinner. She has dreadful abdominal pain, and her legs hurt her . . . her muscles keep cramping and knotting, poor thing . . . I feel so sorry for her! And she's vomited until she has nothing left in her stomach and is just retching. . . ."

"Appendix, maybe?"

"Thomas. She had that out summer before last. And an appendix doesn't cause muscle spasms in the legs."

"Her period, then? She's at the right age to start carrying on about that . . . and I've known women to claim everything short of total paralysis on that excuse, Rachel."

She just looked at him steadily, and said nothing.

"Well, then. A bit of a virus, and the drama of it all. I'm sure she enjoys all the attention."

"Whatever you say, Thomas."

There it was. That mechanical whatever-you-say that meant nothing-that-you-say. He hated it. And she was forever doing it, in spite of knowing full well that he hated it.

"You don't agree with me, Rachel," he said.

"Perhaps you might consider taking a look at her. Before you make your decision."

"Rachel, I have a lot of work to do, it's already very late, and I've lost hours in a stupid meeting as it is—not to mention this very inappropriate meeting on my staircase. Do you really feel that I need to waste yet more time fussing over Nazareth? She's healthy as a mule, always has been."

"And that is why I'm worried," Rachel said. "Because she's never sick—never. Even the appendix was only removed because she had to do that frontier colony negotiation and they didn't want to chance having her seriously ill with inadequate medical facilities at hand . . . she's always well. And no, I don't expect you to waste your time fussing over her."

"I'm glad to hear that."

"I'm sure you are."

"That will be enough, Rachel," said Thomas sternly, glad that Philippa had taken herself off when Rachel appeared and wasn't there to witness her aunt's insolence; he would have been forced to do something obvious to counteract it, if she'd been there with them.

Rachel was becoming more and more difficult as she went into middle age, and if it hadn't been for the extraordinary skill she had in the management of his personal affairs he would not have tolerated her behavior. A quick hysterectomy, and off she'd be to Barren House—it was tempting. But it wouldn't be convenient for him to have her at Barren House, and so he put up with her. He knew what she would do now . . . she'd turn on her heel and flounce off to the girldorms, her rigid back eloquently saying for her all the things she dared not say aloud.

But she surprised him. She stood her ground, and she faced him calmly, saying, "Thomas, I'm really alarmed. This isn't like Nazareth."

"I see."

"I think we should have a doctor."

"At this hour? A house call? Don't be absurd, Rachel . . . you know what that would cost. Furthermore, it's excessive and hysterical over-reaction. Is Nazareth in coma? Hemorrhaging? Is her heartbeat seriously irregular? Does she have difficulty breathing? Is there anything even remotely resembling an emergency?''

''Thomas, I told you. Severe pain—abdomen and legs. Vomiting that just goes on and on.''

''We have painkillers in the house; give her some. We have drugs to stop the vomiting, give her those. If she's no better in the morning, by all means take her to the doctor.''

Rachel drew a long breath, and clasped her hands behind her back. He knew what that meant; it meant that she had started to set her arms akimbo and her hands on her hips and then thought better of it.

''Thomas,'' she said, ''Nazareth has to be at the International Labor Office at eight o'clock tomorrow morning. She's interpreter for the new labor treaty negotiations on seldron. And that treaty's crucial . . . seldron imports are down 39 percent from last year, and there's no other source. Do you know what the situation would be in the comset industry if we lost our seldron trade contract over a labor dispute? And are you aware of the credits this Household has tied up in seldron stocks?''

''What backup has she got?'' Thomas demanded, alert now—this changed things a great deal, as Rachel knew very well. It was typical of her to take fifteen minutes getting to the point, typical and infuriating. ''Who's available?''

''There's no one to take over for her. The only other native speaker of REM34 we have is four years old—not nearly old enough. Aquina Chronyak does informal backup, but she's not fluent; she couldn't handle even trivial negotiations, and these aren't trivial. And besides that, she's booked.''

''This is a definite oversight,'' said Thomas coldly. ''We can't have this sort of thing.''

Rachel sighed. ''Thomas,'' she said, staring at his chest. ''I have told you again and again. We can only spread the language coverage just so far. Even if every one of us knew fifty languages with flawless native skill, we couldn't be in more than one place at a time. And we women cannot produce children any faster, or in any greater quantity, than we are doing already—if you have complaints, you men might turn your attention to that problem.''

Thomas was suddenly very much aware that he and Rachel had been standing there in the middle of the house wrangling for a good five minutes, and that the wrangle was on the verge of escalating into a scene. The quiet that surrounded them told him careful attention was being paid to their every word, and he cursed himself silently for not taking Rachel straight to their room the moment he saw that she was upset—heaven knew he should have sense enough by now to know that was required.

"Rachel," he said quickly, "you're very tired."

"Yes, I am. And very worried."

He took her by one elbow and began moving her firmly down the stairs toward a decent privacy, talking calmly as they went. "I don't think that either the fatigue or your worry is the result of one child who's either eaten something she shouldn't have or has some minor vi-bug bothering her. And I also do not think that it comes from your own work—as I recall, you've had only three days' interpreting in the past five. I think you've been wearing yourself out with that nonsense at Barren House."

He felt her stiffen, and he kept her moving right along.

"I mean what I say, now," he continued. "I understand that you women have a good time—" he paused to usher her through a door and close it behind them "—playing with your language. For the women at Barren House who have no family responsibilities I think it makes an excellent hobby. It's perfectly reasonable that women would want an artificial language of their own for a pastime, and I've never tried to keep you from participating. But you, Rachel, cannot really *spare* time right now for a hobby, no matter how fashionable. And I won't have you wearing yourself out at Langlish meetings and coming home so badtempered and nervous that it's impossible to get along with you. Is that clear, Rachel?"

"Yes, Thomas. It's clear." The lines bit deep in her face, and she was so taut that if he'd touched her she would have quivered like a bowstring. He ignored that, as was suitable.

"Now, I am not concerned personally about this illness of Nazareth's," he went on. "She gets excellent medical care. Whatever this is, I'm sure you've blown it up completely out of proportion. But I *am* concerned—very concerned—about the negotiations at the ILO. And I expect Nazareth to be there, and to be in a condition that allows her to carry on her duties with her usual efficiency. For that reason, Rachel, and for that reason only, I'm willing to compromise."

"In what way?"

"I'll authorize a contact with the hospital's Emergency Room computers, to be paid from Household accounts because it's a business expense—you needn't put it on the women's medical accounts. If the ER-comps think a doctor is necessary, I'll authorize that as well—but not a house call. You can take her *to* the doctors, if that actually appears to be necessary."

"Thank you, Thomas."

Rachel would have turned to leave him then, but he reached out and stopped her, feeling the jerk of her shoulder under his hand with annoyance. Too tightly strung, much too wound up . . . one more thing for him to see to if he could ever get a moment's spare time.

"Rachel," he said sternly, "I don't want any repetition of this."

"Thomas—"

"I suggest you make a few entries, Rachel. Nazareth is to go to bed one hour earlier; if that crowds her schedule, she'll just have to give up her evening freetime. I want her diet run through the computers in complete detail, and anything at all that isn't being provided in proper amounts I want straightened out. I don't want her allowed to skip any of the manual labor sessions— and I'd add swimming. See that she does twenty laps daily, unless you have permission from me for her to skip them. And don't come asking me to excuse her because she's having menstrual cramps, I won't have that sort of foolishness. Increase the vitamins she's getting, and if—as I expect—no doctor is needed tonight, you get her in for a complete checkup just as soon as she's free tomorrow."

"Before or after she swims the twenty laps, Thomas?"

If Thomas had been many husbands, he would have slapped her face, then. She knew that; and she stood before him as insolent as he'd ever seen her, holding her head tilted and ready to his hand, inviting the blow.

"Get to your daughter," he said quietly. "I am disgusted with you."

She went away without a word, leaving him with his heart pounding in his ears, taking slow deep breaths to calm himself. Thank God those last few sentences had been spoken in this room, and not as an entertainment for the Household. And he was quite preprared for the polite knock at the door that came almost immediately—that would be his brother Adam, come to presume on being only two years Thomas' junior and offer him advice.

"Yes, Adam?"

"She's a bit above herself, Tom."

"Penetrating observation on your part."

"Now, Thomas . . . sarcasm isn't going to improve the situation."

Thomas waited. You never had to wait long with Adam, who loved the sound of his own voice.

"I'm not sure I'd be either willing or able to tolerate such behavior from a woman." Adam said judiciously. "And I'm not sure it's a good idea, although your patience is admirable. You either keep a woman under tight rein, or she gets beyond you, and then it's Barren House time. Not that I mean to tell you what to do, of course, Thomas."

"My apologies for the commotion," Thomas said. "Sorry it disturbed you."

"Oh, well." Adam shrugged, being magnanimous. "You know how women are when they've got a sick kid . . . they lose what little sense they started with. Rachel's been roaring around here for the past hour as if Nazareth was on the point of death . . . she's worn herself out. I hope you've put an end to her hysterics, Thomas—that would let us all get some sleep."

Thomas nodded, keeping himself on the tight rein that Adam was recommending for the females. Ignoring the implication that because he couldn't keep his wife in order the entire Household was being disturbed and kept from its rest. As though every bedroom in this house were not completely soundproof . . . Rachel could have played a fife and drum up and down the halls, and not one soul would have had his sleep disturbed.

He knew what was behind Adam's behavior, and why Adam could never let an opportunity like this pass. It was not because he was an interfering pest, poor sod—it was because he was afflicted with a wife so vindictive and so melodramatic that no one could tolerate her company, and he had absolutely no control over her at all except the law. Which left him with an irresistible drive to control other men's women, just to prove that he did know how it was done. His control of numbers was not sufficient consolation for the way that Gillian humiliated him at every turn.

"Come take a look at something I stumbled over today, Thomas," the man was saying. "Have a glass of wine with me . . . get your mind off the fool woman."

"Thanks, Adam, I appreciate it, but I can't spare the time. I was behind before I got here, and now I'll be half the night catching up."

"You're sure? Hell . . . ten minutes, one glass of wine . . . it'd do you good, Tom."

He shook his head firmly, and Adam gave it up and wandered off to hunt somebody else who'd help him stave off the inevitable confrontation with sweet Gillian. She'd be at him for hours about the unfavorable contrast between the courtesy Thomas showed Rachel and the discourtesy Adam showed *her*, blah blah shrieking blah. Poor Adam; he was a good man, steady and reliable, but somewhere along the line he'd missed out on the essential ingredient for managing a woman: never, never for an instant, lose track of the knowledge that when you interact with a woman you interact with an organism that is essentially just a rather sophisticated child suffering from delusions of grandeur. Adam kept forgetting that, when Gillian went at him; he kept dealing with her as if she were a man, with a man's rational mind and skills. Thomas didn't think Gillian would be under the roof of his house much longer.

And then, because he at last had solitude, and silence, and peace, he put his brother's domestic difficulties out of his mind along with his own very different ones and went to his office. He sat down at the comset and waited, with his eyes closed, until the appearance of composure had been replaced by the real thing. And before he turned his attention to the stack of contracts in his computer awaiting his review, he saw to one last chore.

"I realize it's late," he told the young man with the fretful face who answered his call to the ILO section chief's residence. "And I am aware that calling your chief at home is not usual procedure." And he smiled. "Would you get him for me, please, young man?"

The screen flickered; there was a brief pause; and then the face of the ILO chief appeared, a bit fuzzier than Thomas approved of when he had to use it as a data source. Rachel must have the Emergency Room computers locked in; that always meant transmission interference.

"Donald," he said, fuzzy image or not, since it wasn't going to get any better, "sorry to bother you at home."

"Quite all right, Thomas," said the other man, his face twisted diagonally across the screen. "What's the problem?"

"You've got the delegation at eight tomorrow for those seldron labor dispute meetings, I understand, and one of my offspring's handling the interpreting."

"Fortunately," said the image. "Last time they were here we had to make do with PanSig and somebody who couldn't do much more than say howdeedo . . . some smartass from D.A.T. It wasn't very successful. It was in fact damn near a disaster. I don't want to hear, Thomas, that we're up against that again tomorrow. Those Jeelods aren't going to give us many more chances on this, they're really furious. I don't know exactly what kind of idiot misunderstanding is responsible this time, but I know we need somebody who really knows the language."

"Well," said Thomas, "we'll do the best we can, of course.

But the youngster we're sending you has come down with something suddenly—she's not at all well."

"Oh, God. That's all we need. Thomas . . ."

"Now, I didn't say she wouldn't be there," said Thomas. Remember, federal man, he was thinking, and remember good—without us you don't do anything much. "I felt you should be warned that there is that possibility, just as a matter of professional courtesy. The doctor's with her now." A minor, but useful, modification of the facts.

"The doctor?" Donald Cregg was of course aware of what a medical house call, especially at night, meant. Even through the blur and the sputter, Thomas could see the worry on his face. "It's serious, then."

"Maybe not. You know how young girls are. Every twinge, they think they're dying. It may be nothing at all. Nevertheless—just on the off-chance—I called to let you know you may be without an intrepreter tomorrow morning."

"Damn it!"

"You could call D.A.T.," Thomas needled him. "They've really been putting their backs into the federal language courses, I understand."

"Sure . . . sure, Thomas. Come on, man—who else have you got for REM34 if the kid can't make it?"

"Nobody. That's one hell of a language."

"Aren't you linguists always spouting off about no language being harder than any other language?" the image demanded.

"No human language is harder than any other human language," said Thomas. "Quite right. But Alien languages are something else again. All of them are hard, and some of them are harder than others. REM34 happens to be one of the hardest. We've got some people here good enough to translate written materials, but nobody who can interpret."

"See here, Chornyak, you've got a contract!" said the other man indignantly. "And that contract specifies that when you take on a language you put enough of your people on it to cover things like this. That's what we pay you for, for God's sake."

Thomas let a full thirty seconds go by, to give the section chief time to think over the alternatives he had to doing business with the Lines. And then he answered with politeness to spare.

"There are only just so many of us available, my friend," he said, borrowing from Rachel because it was handy, "and even if we learned fifty languages apiece we still couldn't be in more than one place at a time. We have two youngsters right now acquiring REM34 from my daughter, but neither one is exactly suited for sophisticated negotiations—one of them is four and the other is about eighteen months. In time, they'll be available, but they won't help matters tomorrow.''

"Ah, shit," said Donald Cregg. "This is damn tiresome."

"'It is. I agree with you. Maybe some of you people ought to reconsider and send some of your infants over to Interface along with ours.''

And live with dirty stinking Lingoes? And live packed into a hole in the ground like animals, with no decent privacy and no comfort and a lifestyle just above the poverty level? Thomas watched the man, not able to make out any body-parl with the comset image the only data available, but perfectly able to imagine it. Cregg would be pretending he hadn't heard that last sentence.

"Look, do what you can to get your kid there as scheduled, will you? This isn't visiting vippies here for keys to the city, Thomas, this is a matter of real urgency."

"I'll do everything possible," said Thomas.

"And thanks for the warning."

"Any time. Any time at all.''

The screen cleared, and he sat smiling at it. It was most important to keep the government conscious at all times of their dependency on the linguists. Thomas was careful not to overlook even the smallest opportunity to drive that point home and refresh the federal memory, that sieve of convenience and expediency.

He jabbed the intercom for his room, and got no answer; tried again, and heard the soft beep of the transfer mechanism before Rachel came on line from wherever she'd gotten to. The girldorms, probably.

"Well," he said abruptly, "are they sending a med-Sammy for this major crisis?"

"No, Thomas," said Rachel. "Take a half grain of codeine and a muscle relaxant and call them in the morning."

"I thought so," said Thomas with satisfaction. "You've made a great deal of fuss—and an embarrassing scene—over nothing."

"Thomas, I'm sorry you feel that way. But Natha is never sick. And she does not ever complain. You will remember . . . the time she fell picking apples and broke three ribs, we didn't hear a word from her. We wouldn't have known she was hurt if she hadn't fainted in the orchards."

"I don't remember that, Rachel, but it sounds as if she sets an example you might do well to emulate. Spunky, from the sound of it.''

"Is that all, Thomas?"

"See that she's at the ILO at five minutes till eight, Rachel—and see that she's in top form. And *that* is all."

He reached out and cut off any remarks his wife might have had in mind. Later, he'd have to try to work his way through the gruel in her head long enough to make her remember a few things about decent courtesy, and about her function as role model for younger females under his roof. It would be a nuisance, but it could be done—given sufficient patience, and sufficient skill. But not now. Right now he had contracts to see to.

At Barren House, Aquina was facing the music, and it wasn't pleasant. They had her pinned at a table in a back room, and it was Susannah and Nile and Caroline—no goodies from Belle-Anne or oil in the waters from Grace this time—who were lambasting her. And they were good at it.

"You fool, Aquina!" Susannah had said for starters. "You contemptible, wicked fool of a woman!"

"And bungling . . . don't forget bungling," Caroline added. It was Caroline who had caught her. Caroline who'd been alerted by Faye, their most medically skilled woman, that Aquina had been at the herbs in the basement cupboards. And Caroline who'd caught her coming out of the kitchens at the main house and had forced her to hand over the empty bottle in her pocket and give it to Faye for analysis. . . . not that anything sophisticated had been required. Faye knew what Aquina had taken because she knew the inventory down to the last leaf and fleck; and she'd only had to uncap the bottle and smell it to know what it had contained.

How could she have *been* so bungling? Aquina thought that was a very good question . . . except that she never, never had imagined that the other women could spy on her and follow her around. Or that Caroline could twist her arm so cruelly that she was helpless to keep her from searching her pockets . . . Who would have thought they'd be so suspicious, them with their damned ethics always on such prominent display?

"I'd do it again," she'd said, defying them. And Caroline had turned on her like a snare set free on a rabbit, and in spite of herself Aquina had gasped between her teeth, sucking air, and jerked away from the other woman. Caroline was much smaller, much thinner, much less powerful of frame than Aquina; she was also stronger than Aquina could ever hope to be, with a grip like a man's.

"You try that again, you silly bitch," Caroline hissed at her, "and so help me God I'll put you in permanent traction where you can't do anybody any more harm with your stupidity and your viciousness!"

Susannah clucked her tongue, and objected mildly. "She's not vicious, Caroline. Stupid, yes. But not vicious."

"She did her damnedest to poison a fourteen-year-old girl, and she's not vicious? What *is* that, tenderness and love?"

"Caroline . . . you know very well that Aquina had no intention of harming Nazareth Chornyak. She bellows a right good line, but she wouldn't really hurt a living creature. Come off it."

Caroline was so angry that she turned around and smacked the wall with her fist; Aquina was glad that it was the wall and not her.

"Aquina," Nile said, "whatever did you think you were doing?"

"I've told you."

"You tell us again."

She told them. The thought of having to wait forty years before Nazareth could work on the women's language at Barren House, really work on it—especially since Aquina had found her notebook, and it had turned out to be a treasure horde of Encodings, even more valuable than she had hoped—that thought had been intolerable to her. And there was only one way to shorten that forty years. . . . Nazareth had to be made barren. If Aquina could have managed that, the girl would have been kept at Chornyak Household a few more years, to finish her education and her training; but then she would have come to Barren House.

"But Aquina, you know *nothing* about medicine!"

"I can read. I know where Faye's herbals are. I'm literate."

"You could have killed her."

"No, she couldn't," chided Susannah. "Good lord. First she followed the formula with substitutions for anything that alarmed her, and then she cut its strength by half. And then she only gave Nazareth half a dose of *that*. I'm sure the child has been miserable, but she's not in any real danger, nor was she ever."

"Aquina had no way of being sure of that," Caroline insisted, and Nile nodded solemn agreement. "It's luck—just pure blind luck, *not* skill, *not* knowledge—that all she did with her nasty potion was make Nazareth sick!" And she leaned over the table and fairly hissed at Aquina. "Do you realize, you idiot, that you could have cost us not just the forty years you're whining about, but lost us Nazareth *forever*? You had *no* idea what you were doing!"

Aquina knew that they were right. She could see it now, see it clearly. She must have been half out of her mind, with frustration and with the constant worrying at the problem in her head. And she was sorry, sorry to the depths of her. But she'd be damned and fried in oil and pickled before she'd admit it.

"It was worth a try," she said defiantly. And she stared at them, breathing hard and fast and deep, until they threw up their hands and walked out on her.

Chapter Ten

They are encumbered with secret
pregnancies that never come to term.
There *are* no terms, you don't see.

They drag their swollen brains about with them everywhere;
hidden in pleats and drapes and cunning pouches;
and the unbearable
keep kicking, kicking
under the dura mater.
It is no bloody wonder they have headaches.

Hold them to your ear, lumpy as they are,
and pale;
that roar you hear is the surge of the damned unspeakable
being kept back.

Stone will not dilate
will not stretch
will not tear—
it shivers.
Cleaves.
Moves uneasily.

At its core the burgundy lava simmers,
making room.
There are volcanoes at the bottom of the sea.
Those pretty green things swaying are their false hair.

Deliver us?
Ram inward the forceps of the patriarchal paradigm
and your infernal medicine

and bring forth the ancient offspring
with their missing mouths?
I think not.

Not bloody likely.

(20th century "feminist" poem)

Thomas was nobody's fool. He listened to what the doctors
had to tell him, and he looked at the computer printouts, and he
gave it about fifteen minutes of his time. You looked at sets of
data, each one representing a possible hypothesis, until you
had only one left. The one he had was the one he would
have considered least plausible; but it was the only one the
computers had not eliminated—therefore, it must be taken
seriously. And he sent for a chief of detectives to come to his
office at Chornyak Household.

The man was called Morse, Bard Morse; he was tall and bulky
and ordinary-looking, but he proved to have a quick mind that
belied the ponderousness of his movements. He listened while
Thomas explained that someone had tried to poison a daughter of
the house, and he ran his eyes over the computer printouts
swiftly, and he came to an immediate conclusion.

"Oh, you're quite right, Chornyak," he said. "No question
about it. Did you think there was?"

"Only because it was so unlikely," said Thomas. "There's no
reason on or off this green globe for anyone to single out this one
child—she's only fourteen years old. And if the motive had only
been to score some points off the linguists, it wouldn't have been
just Nazareth who was affected by the stuff. It makes no sense to
me, frankly."

"Furthermore," mused the detective, "whoever did it isn't
worth a damn, if you know what I mean."

"I'm not sure I do."

"Well, there's various kinds of poisonings, Mr. Chornyak.
There's the kind that's meant to kill, with a great whopping fatal
dose all at one time—this sure as hell wasn't that. And then
there's the kind that's meant to kill slowly, small doses given
over a year or so, and the victim growing sicker and sicker—but
with that plan, they never would have used a dose that would
make your kid so sick so fast . . . and they would have used
something that was harder to trace and analyze. That's not it,
either."

"What else is there?"

"There's the kind where the poisoner doesn't really want to kill anybody. He does it for malice, because he enjoys seeing the victim suffer, for instance. Or he does it out of ignorance—say it was another child, that fancies himself a poisoner because he's seen it on a threedy and thinks it's exciting, but he doesn't really understand that what he's doing is dangerous."

"Well? Do you see this business as either of those?"

Morse chewed on his mustache and screwed up his forehead, and then he shook his head.

"Naw," he said. "Hell . . . it's possible it was a kid. Maybe. But how a kid would have known to put those particular herbs together, or even which ones would be poisonous, I don't see. And I don't see where a kid would have gotten them, Chornyak. Those weren't dandelion greens and daisy petals, you know, that was some pretty exotic stuff. But the malice bit . . . would that come in here? Would anybody pick out just that one child, for malice?"

"I don't know, Morse. I don't know at all."

"Is there any reason, Chornyak, why somebody would be jealous of your daughter Nazareth? Is she . . . oh, spectacularly beautiful, maybe? Spectacularly brilliant? Anything like that?"

Thomas shook his head, and laughed. "She's not unpleasant to look at, but that's as far as it goes—just a plain ordinary gawk of a girl. And as for brilliance . . . her linguistics skills tests are clear off the scales, the highest we've ever recorded in the Lines . . . but only a few of the adults know that, close family members. And none of them would be such fools as to let the information get out for general knowledge where it might cause jealousy. So far as I know, people view Nazareth as an ordinary, reasonably well-liked, very busy linguist child, with nothing to set her off. You realize that there is a sense in which *any* linguist child is unusual—but not to other linguists."

"I see," said Morse. "Well, have you got anyone on the place that's mentally just plain defective, sir? A retarded adult, for example?"

No . . . nothing like that. We never have had, to my knowledge."

"Well, you see, the malicious kind, they're always a certain kind of person. Retarded sometimes—that's why I asked—cunning, but not intelligent, you know? And whatever the situation, they love to cause a commotion. They love attention, and everything in an uproar, and the feeling of power that they're causing it all. They enjoy seeing pain, or they're indifferent to it—they're very sick people, as a rule. And always, always and without exception, they are fiendishly clever, Mr. Chornyak. They're terribly hard to catch, and they enjoy the bloody hell out of running rings around the authorities and proving how easy it is to trick everyone. This isn't *like* that, you see. This isn't like that at all. It's inefficient and disorganized and—well, it's just bumbling about, as if the poisoner was either completely confused or maybe didn't really have his heart in it. If you'll pardon a joke at a serious time, sir, if a committee was supposed to poison somebody, this is how I'd expect it to look. An amateur committee at that.''

"Ah, yes," said Thomas with satisfaction. "I see." There was nothing like getting someone to look at a problem who actually knew what he was supposed to know and could get right to the heart of it.

"It makes perfectly good sense, Chief Morse." He went on. "I understand exactly what you mean. But doesn't it leave us in a bit of a mess? That is, if this particular poisoning isn't any of the usual kinds, doesn't that mean it will be very hard to solve?"

Morse pursed his lips and rubbed at his chin with his thumb.

"I don't think it's that bad, Mr. Chornyak," he said cautiously. "We may never find out *why* this has been going on—it doesn't look as if even the poisoner knows why, you see. But it's got to be somebody that's warped more than just a little bit—someone very strange indeed. And someone who isn't clever enough to be very hard to catch. It may be tedious, and it may take a little time, but if you'll authorize the investigation we can certainly catch this person. And I might add, sir, that if you don't authorize it we will have to get on with it all the same—poisoning's not looked on with much favor by the law, you know, no matter how badly it's done. Even when the outcome of the investigation is inconvenient."

"Inconvenient? A curious word, under the circumstances."

"Well, you can see for yourself, sir—it's pretty nearly impossible that this could be anybody except a member of your family. And that always means an unpleasant time for everybody."

"Oh, I hadn't thought of that," said Thomas. "Of course. But never mind, my friend. If we've got a poisoner, let alone an incompetent poisoner, under this roof, let's get the bastard."

"I'm glad to hear you take it like that, Chornyak."

"There's some other way to take it?"

"Sometimes people are outraged at the very idea that it could be one of their own, sir. And sometimes they know who it is and they can't stand to see the person exposed—and that's perhaps the stickiest of all. You never know where you are when it's like that, because you never know who's lying to you. Or why."

"We're not one of those Gothic families with decomposing corpses in the closets, Morse," said Thomas bluntly. "There's nobody to protect here. You'll find no barriers to your investigation in this Household except those put in your way by the person responsible for the poison—naturally, you can't expect cooperation from the criminal. But as for the rest of us, the quicker you settle this the more pleased we will be."

"That's a refreshing attitude, Mr. Chornyak. I'll get on with it, then."

"Please do."

"It was explained to me by the powers-that-be about the need to keep all this very quiet, by the way. I understand . . . all those children of yours out with the public, scattered all over all the time, you're very vulnerable. You can put your mind at ease, Mr. Chornyak. I'll need a few men in here to help me, but there'll be no leaks. You have my word on that."

"Good man."

Thomas assumed the interview was over, and would have stood up to see his visitor out; but Bard Morse sat there, staring at the printout.

"Is there something else, Chief Morse?"

"Well, I was just wondering. It was one of you linguist families that had the baby kidnapped and killed by a Terralone group a while back, wasn't it?"

Feeling his ghosts coming back to haunt him, Thomas agreed that that was true. Another family, but one of the Lines.

"Well, then . . . is there anybody on your premises that strikes you as likely to have become a Terraloner on the quiet? It would be like them not to be all that bright about it. Does that give you any ideas?"

"I'd have to think about it," Thomas hedged, "but offhand I can't imagine such a thing. Our entire existence, not only now but for generations, has been interaction with extraterrestrials. I'd say we're unlikely candidates for Terralone."

"Then, is there anybody that can come and go freely in the house here, but doesn't actually live under your roof?"

"Only the women of Barren House. It's only a few blocks from here, and there's a great deal of coming and going among the females."

"I don't believe I know exactly what 'barren house' is, Mr. Chornyak. The significance of the term, I mean."

"It may seem a bit odd to you . . ."

"Try me."

"Well, of course any family is concerned with the birth of its children and their case and so on. But it's different in a linguist Household, where an infant represents such an important—in the adult sense of important—unit in the family. Much of our lives revolve around the babies, and the little ones in the various stages of language acquisition. A pregnant woman has an extraordinary importance here, as does one who has a new infant to be Interfaced. It makes it very hard on the women who can't participate in childbearing; they feel left out, and some of them become terribly depressed. They feel they have no part in it all, although that's a distorted perception, and typical female emotionalism. We tried for years to make the barren women see that they played just as important a role in the Household economy . . . and then finally, for their own good, we built them a separate residence. Nearby—because they *are* important, Morse, not only in their usual roles of interpreters and translators, but because they take so much of the care of the little girls off the shoulders of our other women. We need them, and we'd be in a bad way without them. But they are much happier with their own separate house."

He felt self-conscious, going on and on about it, but the detective kept nodding encouragement at him, and there didn't seem to be any quicker way of explaining it.

"I assure you," Thomas added, "if it was to do over again we wouldn't call the place Barren House. That seems cruel, and in the worst of taste, looking at it now. But when the place was first built, it was taken for granted that that was just a kind of working title, and that a new name would be chosen quickly—it just never happened, and I don't know why. It's a tradition now . . . and I'm certain that the women who *are* barren no longer make any connection between their condition and the name. It's just a name."

"I see," said Chief Detective Morse. "I'm sure it's very sensible if you have all the background."

"Thank you. I hope so."

"But if I may say so, sir, now that you've laid it out for me like that, it seems to me that this Barren House is the obvious place to begin looking. If you have females that are over-emotional, not quite on balance, that kind of thing, that's where they'd likely be."

Thomas thought about it. The women sitting serenely with their eternal needlework, chattering about matters that no sensible human being would waste two words on. The women going routinely to their duties with the government as they'd done all their lives, and performing all their functions as competently as any other woman. The women who were old and bedfast now, with tiny girls from the Household sitting on the edges of their beds, talking and talking, providing the absolutely indispensable practice with the languages. Good, competent, reliable women, with the usual frailties of women, and—as far as he could perceive—nothing more. But this was not his field; this was the detective's field. He had no business making prejudgments.

"You may very well be right, Morse," he said then. "I leave it in your capable hands."

"I'll have my men look around this building this afternoon, sir, just to do the obvious things. Check the kitchen for arsenic in the sugar. Check your . . . Interface, is it? . . . to be sure it's not leaking anything nasty. That kind of thing."

"I'm sure there's no problem with the Interface, Morse—if there were, it wouldn't be Nazareth who was affected."

"No, of course not, and the herbs wouldn't have anything to do with that either, sir. But it's a matter of systematic routine. We don't know what this person might try next, you see—we need to look for anything at all that's not as it ought to be. We'll just check it out, Mr. Chornyak. And once that's done, we'll go over to the Barren House place and get down to the real digging. We'll have something for you as quickly as possible, I assure you."

"Lord," said Thomas, glad to see that it was finally coming to an end, and the other man standing up. "What an absurd business!"

"Be glad it's only absurd," said Morse quietly. "It could be a lot more than that, you know. And perhaps it's a little more than absurd for the little girl that's getting the worst of it."

"She's like any other teenage girl," Thomas said absently. "She enjoys being the center of attention, and she takes advantage. I very much doubt it's half as bad as she makes it out to be."

"Just as you say, Mr. Chornyak," said the detective. "You know your own daughter, I'm sure—I don't. But let's get it set to rights, shall we? Even if she's just glorying in all the drama, that's not good for her. She'll have a serious problem with her character if that's allowed to continue."

"Absolutely right," said Thomas. "I agree."

"I'll get at it, then. And you'd help us out if you'd alert the rest of the family to expect us; that'll save us explaining the same thing over and over again. How many of you are there, by the way? In the family, I mean?"

"Oh . . .91 of us in the Household proper. Here in this building. And 42 more at Barren House."

"Good lord, there's a mob of you!" Morse exclaimed. "I'm not surprised you've got a poisoner, man—I'm surprised you don't have half a dozen! So would anybody in such a situation!"

"But we are accustomed to it," said Thomas. "We've lived this way for so many many years."

"It's astonishing! I'd have said it was impossible."

"Not to us. It's perfectly ordinary to us."

Morse whistled, still amazed, and said, "I wouldn't have thought that kind of crowding was to be found anywhere on Earth in these times, Chornyak—it takes me back, I don't mind telling you. And since that's how it is, it's a damn good thing you're here to prepare them all for the fact that there's a crew of police coming. We'd be the rest of the year just introducing ourselves and explaining our intentions, otherwise."

"We have intercom channels to every part of the buildings," Thomas told him. "I'll do an all points immediately."

"Thank you, sir. Now, if you'll excuse me. . . ."

Thomas watched him go, and then he wasted no time dawdling over the announcement. He punched the master key that brought in all the intercoms, including those at Barren House, and he told them.

"We seem to have a problem," he said. "And somebody among us has a warped idea of what constitutes decent human behavior. There will be police investigators on our premises starting this afternoon and continuing for so long as it takes to find out who is responsible for Nazareth's . . . illness. I expect every one of you to cooperate fully with these men. I expect you to see to it that they have access to whatever they need, without exception. I expect you to see to it that the children don't get in their way or make nuisances of themselves. And we intend to get to the bottom of this in short order—if you know anything, anything at all that might be helpful, you are to tell the officers at once. We don't have time for this sort of business, nor would I have thought any of us had the stomach for it. Let's get it over with. That's all."

At Barren House, the women were silent with the silence that comes of sudden shock and no warning to ease it. Aquina had gone white and shrunk against a wall as Thomas spoke, and she stood there shaking—not one of the others even looked at her.

Barren House could not, could not possibly, undergo an investigation by professional law enforcement officers. It would be quite a different matter from just having to keep their secrets from the occasional male who dropped by to settle some sort of family business or deliver a message . . . quite a different matter from distracting ordinary visitors with one of their elaborate "needlework circles" in the formal parlor. The men who would come to Chornyak Barren House now were not casual visitors, they were trained investigators, and they had every reason to believe that they were after a dangerous secret—whatever there was to find, they would find it.

And there was a tremendous lot to find, if you really knew how to search.

There were, for example, Faye's surgical instruments and medical lab, all of which would have been cause for serious suspicion even in the residence of a man, if he had no medical degree to account for them. For such things to be in the possession of women was absolutely illegal. Especially those items whose only use was for performing abortions or clearing up after them.

And there were the herb cupboards. Not just the ones that were poisonous. There was also the one that contained one of the world's most efficient contraceptives, smuggled in at terrible risk by an underground railroad of sympathetic women from all over the world.

There was the rest of the contraband. The forbidden books from the time of the Women's Liberation movement, that were permitted only to adult males. The forbidden, cherished video-tapes . . . blurred and scratchy now, but no less precious for that. All the forbidden archives of a time when women dared to speak openly of equal rights.

There were the books of blasphemy . . . that were not even known to exist. *The Theology of Lovingkindness. The Discourse of the Three Marys. The Gospel of the Magdalene*, that began: "I am the Magdalene; hear me. I speak to you from out of time. This is the Gospel of women." Those books were hidden here. Hand-lettered, and hand-bound, in covers that read *Favorite Recipes From Around the World*. They must not be found.

And there were the secret language files. They would mean nothing to the detectives, of course. But if they were carted back to the main house for the men to examine and explain, *they* would know what they were. . . .

And that was not all. That was by no means all of the secret and forbidden things that were hidden in the walls and the floors and the nooks and crannies of this place where women lived always without men.

It wasn't that the women of Chornyak Barren House were

afraid of paying the penalty for their crimes. They could face that prospect, as they had always faced it. It was the *loss*, the terrible loss . . . Every Barren House would be searched then. The boards of the floors taken up. The flowerpots dumped out. The grounds dug up. And the only source the women of the Lines had, for so many things that made the difference between a life that was unbearable and one that was only miserable would be gone. Things that women needed, things that women were forbidden to have, things that had taken scores of years and danger to accumulate—they would be gone. And the women would have to start all over again, with the men watching them to be sure they failed.

It could not be allowed to happen, and that was all there was to it; there wasn't any room for argument. The only question was: what could they do that would prevent it?

Out of the long silence, someone finally spoke, tentative, her voice thin with strain.

"Maybe we could manage," she hazarded. "Of all women on this planet we are the most skilled at communication and the most practiced at deception. Perhaps we could manage to mislead the police . . . do you think we could? They are only men, like any other men."

"Trained to search," said Grace. "Trained to ferret out secrets."

"And looking for a certain kind of person, who could get pleasure from poisoning little girls," said Faye. "A psychopath, or a sociopath . . . so far gone in her madness that she feels no need even to be careful. We all know the profile for that sort of madwoman. If we try to 'mislead' the men, in this situation, they'll learn things about us that we'd forgotten even existed to worry about. And we will destroy the Barren Houses. No, Leonora . . . we can't manage. Not possibly."

They talked it to death, ignoring Aquina still huddled by the wall but now collapsed forlornly like a bundle of rags. She had brought this on them all, and that was a burden heavy enough to collapse anyone. There was nothing that they could do for Aquina, even if they'd had time to concern themselves with her.

"We *must* come to a decision, quickly," Susannah said after a while, and the other murmured agreement. "The children tell us that the men won't get to us until tomorrow morning—but we can't count on that. It could be a ruse . . . they could knock on that door this very minute. We have to decide what we are going to do."

Like Thomas, they finally tackled it as they would have tackled a problem in linguistic analysis. They set out all the data and they formulated certain hypotheses. They proposed certain solutions, and examined each one swiftly for its merits and its flaws.

"Remember," Caroline cautioned them, "once they find out that there is even *one* secret here, that is the end—they'll worry at it until they've turned up every scrap we have to hide. And what they don't understand of the things they find, Thomas Blair Chornyak most assuredly will."

"The only real defense we've ever had," said Thyrsis, grieving, "is that no one has even taken us seriously. The men have always thought we were silly females, playing silly female games . . . they must go on thinking that."

"We can't just be unusually silly?"

"No."

They tolerated it while Aquina proposed alerting all the Barren Houses and burning them down to the ground to destroy the evidence, and let her realize for herself as she babbled that the result would be the same utter catastrophe, only done even more quickly than the men would be able to bring it about.

"You can't keep them from finding things," said Grace slowly. "That's going to happen, if they look."

"And that is the crucial point," said Caroline. "That is exactly the point. Now we have the question that matters: what would keep them from coming here at all? What would make them call it off, not *start* looking?"

When they said nothing, she sighed and went on. "Well, I can tell you. Just one thing."

"And what is that?"

"If they thought the problem was solved. If they thought no investigation was needed, you see . . . because they already had their poisoner, without need to search for her."

"Ah!" cried Faye. "Yes! That would do it! One of us has to confess, before they can start looking!"

"Convincingly," said Caroline, nodding. "Not just 'oh, I'm sorry, officer, I did it with my little potions'."

"But *who*? It won't go easy with her . . . who?"

Aquina stared at them as if they'd lost their minds and declared that that was not a question for discussion. This was her fault, she was responsible for it, and it had to be her. And they told her to just shut up.

"You'd say too much, Aquina," said Susannah, trying in spite of her deep anger at this careless foolish woman to be gentle. "You'd be sure to. You'd go all political, and you'd make a speech. And first thing you knew you'd have said one word too many . . . I'm sorry. It can't be you, Aquina.''

Then who? They were terribly afraid that they knew the answer.

It was Susannah who said what all of them knew had to be said.

"There's only one choice, really," she mourned. "Only one possible choice. Because it's not a question of choosing someone eager for self-sacrifice. It's not a question of choosing someone who is, as the men would put it, dispensable. It's a matter of choosing someone who will be believable, in view of the profile the police and the men have created for their poisoner. Dearloves, there's only one woman here who can fit those specifications . . . and they'll swallow it like a spoonful of fudge and cream. It has to be Belle-Anne."

Belle-Anne Jefferson had come to Chornyak Household a beautiful young bride. She'd been chosen for a younger son who looked like an "At Stud" ad, and there'd been high hopes. After three years of trying, when there were still no new infants to be groomed for the Interface and the doctors told Thomas Chornyak what the problem was, he refused to believe it.

"That's not possible," he'd said flatly. "I'm willing to admit a pretty broad range of possibilities in this universe, having seen many an example that's basically out of the bottom of the bottle in Terran terms—but I don't believe *this*. You look again, gentlemen, and you bring me an explanation that doesn't sound like the Uterus Fairy and The Wicked Testicle."

But they came right back with exactly the same tale. Belle-Anne Jefferson Chornyak, twenty years old and a lush ripe peach of a girl, could indeed by the force of her own will kill the lustiest little wiggler of a sperm that any man could produce.

Thomas was furious, and declared that he'd never heard of such a thing.

"It isn't common," the doctors admitted.

"Are you *sure*?"

"We're positive. You insert a sperm in that young lady, no matter how you go about it, and she just twitches her little butt and the sperm *dies*. Dead. Gone."

"Well, bypass that stage!"

"We tried that. We implanted an egg, all nicely fertilized with her husband's living sperm and healthy as you please."

"And?"

"And two days later, spontaneous abortion. I think it took her two days only because it was a new trick for her. When we tried it again on the off chance it wasn't her doing, it only took her thirty minutes from lab to basin.''

"Judas galloping priest!''

"Yes indeed. You can thank God it isn't a knack that women can master on any general scale, Chornyak, or we'd have problems . . . not that most women would have any interest in that kind of shenanigan. Most women are crazy about the drippy little creatures.''

"But Belle-Anne isn't.''

"Belle-Anne most surely isn't.''

"Have you ever seen this before?''

"No . . . there are half a dozen cases in the entire medical literature. It is truly rare. Fascinatingly rare. Oh, there are women who can work themselves up sufficiently to miscarry a fetus that wouldn't have made it anyway . . . but basically, this is a green swan.''

"And I had to get it in my house.'' Thomas swore, long and low, and the doctors grinned sympathetically.

"How does she do it? Can we bring in the therapists and convince her to cut it effing out?''

"Well . . . we don't know,'' said one of the men, and the others looked dubious. "She says she does it by prayer, as a matter of fact. You care to tackle that?''

"What? You mean the little trollop *admits* this?''

"Oh, yes.''

"Well, for . . .'' Thomas was reduced to sputtering silence, a green swan phenomenon of its own.

"It's not as if she were unaware that she's doing it, you see,'' they told him. "She's doing it on purpose. I think trying to change the young lady's head would be a waste of your time, your money, and your son's energies. She'd be very resistant— you're talking about years of therapy, at tremendous expense. Chornyak, the world is full of pretty young females . . . is it really worth the trouble?''

Which was how a pretty young woman like Belle-Anne, just turned twenty and eminently beddable, had ended up divorced and a resident at Chornyak Barren House.

The family had given Thomas a certain amount of argument about that. After all, it was a deliberate act of sabogate on the girl's part that made her unfit for motherhood; why should they have to bear the expense of her upkeep for the rest of her life?

"I say send her back to her father,'' said her ex-husband, who was understandably disgruntled, and had to face the bleak prospect of the decent waiting period as a bachelor required of him before he could take another, more accommodating, woman to wife.

"No," said Thomas flatly, and Paul John backed him all the way. "When we take anyone under this roof and accept the responsibility for their welfare, we've taken it just as it says in the wedding ceremony—for better, for worse, till death do us part. My personal preference would not be to send her back to her father, but to drop her off a tall building. But that is not the way this family does things." And that had been the end of it.

Belle-Anne would have no trouble at all convincing the policemen; she would be believed. And Thomas Blair Chornyak would not put *any*thing past Belle-Anne.

It would have to be that way, if it broke every one of their hearts.

Chapter Eleven

Religious mania can be exceedingly dangerous in the human female—especially if not caught in the early stages. The stereotype—the woman who prays publicly hour after hour, who hears voices and sees visions and is anxious to tell the world about it—that woman is easily spotted, of course. But few women fit that stereotype unless there is obvious psychosis. Instead, we see what appears to be only a charming modesty and humility of demeanor, a pleasant lack of interest in material things, an almost appealing sweetness of word and deed . . . and only when this seemingly delightful creature is far gone in theophilia do we suddenly realize what we are dealing with.

We must continue to counsel our clients to encourage their females to be religious, because religion offers one of the most reliable methods for the proper management of women ever devised; religion offers a superb cure for the woman who might otherwise tend to be rebellious and uncontrolled. However, gentlemen, however—I must caution you to insist that a man take time every few months to carry on a religious conversation with the women for whom he is responsible, however tiresome that may be. Ten minutes of carefully structured talk on the subject will almost inevitably cause the woman leaning toward religious excess to betray her disorder. It's time well spent.

(Krat Lourd, Ph.D.,
speaking on a panel
at the
Annual Meeting of the American
Association of Feminologists)

At a few minutes before eight o'clock, Belle-Anne was already sitting in the interrogation room of the precinct house, where the officers had rushed her frantically as a way of observing their promise that there'd be no publicity. Belle-Anne had not been concerned about discretion, and she was smiling at Morse as if they were both there on a holiday outing.

"Now, let me get this straight," Morse was saying. "You came in here, of your own free will, to confess to the attempted murder of Nazareth Joanna Chornyak. Because you didn't want us to mess up the house. Is that what you're saying?"

"Detective Morse," said Belle-Anne, "we work very hard to keep Barren House nice. And we get very little rest, what with the work we do as linguists, and taking care of the women who are sick, and one thing and another. We do not need a whole pack of your men tramping through the house in their boots dirtying the floors and getting finger smudges all over the walls and the furniture."

"I see."

"Furthermore, there's no reason why the other women at Barren House should have to put up with any kind of fuss at all over this—it is, after all, my idea and my idea alone. I see it as my Christian duty, to spare others the consequences of my bungling."

"Bungling."

"Yes, indeed. The good Lord told me to be careful, and I meant to be; but you see it didn't work out."

"Perhaps the good Lord made a mistake?"

"Captain!" Belle-Anne thrust her chin up and fixed him with an outraged stare. "You blaspheme!"

"I'm not a captain, ma'am, I'm a chief detective."

"Well, whatever you are, you're in danger of hellfire. I'd ask the Almighty for His forgiveness, were I you."

Bard Morse let his eyebrows rise toward his receding hairline, and turned the recorder on. This one really was a fruitcake, and he hadn't even had his breakfast yet.

"Mrs. Chornyak," he said carefully, "you do understand that if you make a confession and sign it you won't be allowed to change your mind? You can't take it back, my dear."

"I've done nothing to be ashamed of," Belle-Anne told him calmly—later he would tell Thomas that she had been "downright proud of it, if you ask me" and Thomas would agreed that he certainly could believe it—"except that I've failed in my divine mission. But the Lord knows that I did the very best I could, and

He will forgive me. Whether He'll forgive the rest of you heathens is another matter.''

"All right, ma'am, I'll try not to offend the Lord further. But I did want to be sure you understood.''

"You can be quite sure. I do.''

"All right, then . . . I've got this recorder going, Mrs. Chornyak. As you talk, the computer in the other room there will transcribe what you say, and then one of the men will bring the printout in here for you to sign, and we'll see what's to be done next. Okay, dear?''

"Yes, Captain.''

"I'm not—'' Morse began, and then he sighed and let it pass.

"Just say again what you told the man at the front desk before they brought you in here with me, Mrs. Chornyak. Just speak naturally, please, in an ordinary tone of voice. State your name, and so on, and then begin.''

Belle-Anne folded her hands on the table before her, stared him right in the eye, smiled like an angel, and recited her piece.

"My name is Belle-Anne Jefferson Chornyak,'' she said serenely. "I am a divorced wife of Chornyak Household, of this city, and I am thirty years old as of a week ago Friday. Exactly . . . well, no, I should say approximately . . . approximately a year ago, I was sitting in the garden at Chornyak Barren House, where I have lived for the past ten years. I was watching a bird on a mimosa tree, and waiting for a little girl to come from Chornyak Household to speak Hungarian with me for an hour—when suddenly, lo an angel of the Lord appeared, and he said to me 'Hark!' ''

Morse nodded at her and smiled, and made a circle with his index finger to indicate that she should continue.

"Well, as you can imagine I was very surprised. And even when I heard the Lord Himself, God the Father, speak from out of the clouds above my head, I thought perhaps I had taken a fever, don't you know? But another angel came to stand beside the first, and the Virgin Mary descended in a cloud of gold to stand between them. And she told me that it was all true. And that the Lord had given to me the task of hurrying Nazareth Joanna Chornyak home to her Heavenly Father.'' Belle-Anne stopped and gave the detective the full benefit of her brilliant gaze.

"You see, Captain,'' she went on when he said nothing, "although few people seem to realize it, there are women whose bodies are not intended for the usage of human men. I am one such woman, and Nazareth Chornyak is another. We are, Captain, the brides of Christ, and reserved to Him only, and those who abuse us will suffer unspeakable torments forever and ever. But of course if I had just gone in and told Thomas Chornyak that that was what the Lord had in mind for Nazareth he would have laughed at me."

Bard Morse could believe *that* with no difficulty, and he told her so.

"And so it was up to me, you see, although it has been a great comfort to me in my task that the angels are always at my right hand, or flying above me in their glory, singing and praising the Heavenly Father to keep up my spirits and encourage me when I falter. And since I am familiar with the use of herbs and plants, it seemed to me that it would be far better if I used such a method, a *natural* method that springs from the sweet feet of the Beloved, you see, rather than . . . oh, hitting the child over the head with a large rock, perhaps. Rocks are of course the natural creations of the Almighty, too, just as much as the plants and the grasses and the herbs that bedeck our Father's world—but I am not a violent woman. I would have tried, you know, if the Virgin had said to me, 'Take up that stone there and smite Nazareth Joanna Chornyak,' but she didn't. It was left to me to decide upon the means, and I put a little something into the child's food and drink. I'm afraid it made her awfully uncomfortable."

Morse hit the PAUSE control and stopped the tape. The woman was positively glowing.

"Would you just say a few specifics?" he asked her. "Just for our records? What substances you used, that kind of thing?"

Belle-Anne had made sure she knew all that last night, just in case the officers did show up at Barren House before morning, and what she said for the disk matched the facts the police had at their disposal. Close enough. She was sure they would not expect *her* memory to be flawless. She just had to be close, and she was.

The detective turned off the machine, and patted her hand gently, saying, "You've saved us, and your housemates, a great deal of trouble, Mrs. Chornyak. I want you to know that we appreciate it."

"Oh," warbled Belle-Anne, "I live only to serve!"

"Of course," said Morse. "Of course you do, love."

"Praise the Lord," Belle-Anne said demurely. "Praise His holy name."

"Yes indeed," Morse agreed, passing her the printout to sign while his clerk stared at the ceiling and whistled between his teeth. He would not have to tell the man to call the ambulance from the mental hospital. The clerk had been there when Belle-Anne came waltzing in, gave the man on the front desk a fervent "Hallelujah, it's another beautiful morning in our Father's world!" and followed that up with the point blank announcement that she was the Chornyak poisoner and had done it all for God and the Blessed Mother and an assortment of he-angels.

"I never counted them, you know," she'd confided to the flabbergasted desk sergeant. "It didn't seem polite . . . having to point my finger and so on."

It was this kind of thing that made Morse stay in police work. Every time he thought about retiring he'd remember something like this, and he'd realize that if he had retired he would have missed it, and he'd stay on. He wouldn't have missed this one for the world; he was only sorry he couldn't talk about it over a few drinks down at the Changing Room. It would have made one hell of a story. And it was just blind chance that there hadn't been some bored reporter there looking for an amusing drunk to take pictures of when Belle-Anne had decided to put on her extravaganza.

"Will they hang me, do you suppose, Captain Morse?" Belle-Anne asked him, her brown eyes huge in her beautiful face and fringed with lashes like chocolate velvet.

"Oh, I'm sure they won't," he soothed her, not that she seemed at all worried about it. Curious, perhaps, but not worried. "I'm sure you don't have to worry your lovely head with things like that."

No, sir. This little lady wasn't going to have to worry about anything ever again, or even think about anything. When they got through with her, there wouldn't be enough of her brain left to say the alphabet with. She had absolutely nothing to worry about.

Morse called Thomas Chornyak and told him to forget about expecting detectives prying around his place, watching Belle-Anne out of the corner of his eye as he talked to be sure she had nothing out of the ordinary in what passed for her mind. This case was all sewed up.

Thomas knew how the women loved Belle-Anne, buttburr that she was. He sent somebody firm over to Barren House to tell them. And there was the anticipated weeping and wailing and hysterics, followed by the speech Thomas had specified.

"Now, perceive this," said Adam, being avuncular as hell. "I want you all to know that we approve in principle of the wholesome interest you good ladies take in being enthusiastic Christians. I'm sure that we'll all benefit one day from your devotion. But whatever you've been up to in the way of religious fervor that caused this—excess—will have to stop. We know that Belle-Anne was never all that stable; she probably went over the edge pretty easily. And we are sure that it's all been completely innocent on your parts. But it's gone far enough. You'll go to church in the usual way, and you'll do what the Reverend tells you—and you'll let it go at that. No fancy embellishments. Is that quite clear?"

It was, they told him, still weeping and sniffling.

"And Thomas also wants you to know that while he's sure there's nobody else in this house who might feel that the Lord had picked her out personally to take care of Belle-Anne's unfulfilled divine contract, he intends to take no chances. From now on there will be guards with Nazareth when she's awake; and a comset camera will be watching her when she's asleep. Just to be absolutely sure nobody else decides she's Joan of Arc on a white unicorn sent to do holy deeds. Is *that* quite clear?"

It was, they assured him; it certainly was. All of it was entirely, perfectly, clear.

Chapter Twelve

"How do you assemble a rose window
in a universe
which has no curving surfaces?"
(Oh, poor sharp rose that is all thorns
nested within thorns—
what can you be a symbol of??)

"How do you assemble a rose window
in a universe
which has no principle of symmetry?"
(Oh, poor lopsided ugly rose that is all deficits
nested (?) within deficits—
what can you be a hunger for??)

> (from *As for the Universal Translator*,
> a 20th century poem)

FALL 2182. . . .

"This is stupid," said Beau St. Clair.

"Second that," said Lanky Pugh. "I move we cancel it."
And because he knew that Arnold Dolbe found it sickening, he
took out his pocket knife and began cleaning his fingernails, with
an air of total dedication to the task.

Dolbe tried not to moan, managed a gargled sigh, and made
useless flutters with his fingers.

"Look, men," he said. "See here. It doesn't matter if it's
stupid. Stupid's got nothing to do with it. The Pentagon says
meet on this—we meet on it. You know that as well as I do, so
get *off* me."

"Shit," said Lanky.

Showard considered the situation, and decided that Lanky Pugh offered a satisfactory model to emulate; he took out his pocket knife and began cleaning *his* fingernails, too, doing his best to make it a sort of duet for two pocket knives, matching his movements to Lanky's.

"Go on then, Dolbe," he said. *"Meet."*

"Well, I think we're up against a blank wall," said Dolbe. A muscle twitched in his right cheek, and he rubbed at it fretfully. It would get worse, he knew, and pretty soon one of his eyelids would join in the dance of twitches, and he'd be in for weeks of both, with nothing the damn med-Sammys could do for it. Dolbe felt that it was bad enough to be six feet four inches tall and weigh only one hundred fifty rattling pounds, bad enough to be bald and have a skull that was a collage of lumps and lines and irregularities, bad enough to have a face that even his mother had not been fond of—it wasn't fair that he had to be subject to nervous tics on top of that. He was miserably conscious of his burdens, of the injustice of it all, and the muscle jumped again. He laid one hand with elaborate casualness over the rebellious cheek and said, "I don't see that there's anything left for us to do. That's all."

The other men stared at him glumly, and it was written on their faces: he was not any sort of inspiration to them.

"Well, really," he said defensively, "I'm sorry I don't have the world's greatest new snazzobang plan to offer here, but I don't hear any of you doing any better."

"You're suppose to *lead*, Dolbe, remember?" Showard needled. "A major and profound principle—leaders should lead."

"Damn you, Showard," said Dolbe, looking sullen as well as twitchy. "Damn your soul."

"Thanks," said the other man, and dropped him. "That's a big help. Since you refuse to do anything but whimper, I shall just move on . . . let's run it by one more time, troops. What have we done—and what haven't we done?"

St. Clair obliged him. "We've tried computers—they don't show us useful patterns, or any other kind of patterns, in nonhumanoid Alien languages. Or so Lanky tells us, and I trust Lanky all the way when it comes to computers. Computers would help us *after* we cracked a language . . . but they're no good at the initial stage. That's one."

"Right," said Lanky Pugh. "That's one, and it's final. If computers could do it, we'd have done it."

"Human infants," St. Clair went on, "even when we follow

the linguist specs down to the last comma, don't help us . . . they can't be Interfaced with nonhumanoid Aliens. And throwing a few dozen more into the pit doesn't appeal to any of us . . . it's useless. And horrible. And stupid. That's two.''

"One, two, buckle our shoe," droned Brooks Showard.

"And then there's the linguist infant strategy—that was a bust, too. No different from any other baby . . . a complete mess. And we don't have any idea why. Which means that snatching a few more Lingoe pups and running them through the same drill would be useless, horrible, etc., see above. We've spent months analyzing it, and we've found out nothing. That's three.''

He waited for somebody to offer a comment, but nobody did.

"And that's it," he concluded. "So far as I know, that's all there is. Adults can't acquire languages . . . there aren't any other alternatives.''

"Damn it, men," said Dolbe urgently, "damn it, we've got a *mission*. The fate of this planet, and all who live on it, depends on *us*. We can't just quit . . . we have to do something.''

"I wonder," mused Lanky Pugh, thinking that if he picked his teeth with his knife Dolbe would get even more antsy, which would be just fine with him, "I wonder how that Beta-2 critter feels about our 'mission'? I mean, it's been cooped up here one hell of a long time now. . . .''

"Lanky," Dolbe pleaded, "please don't bring that up. Please. For all we know, it loves it here. We're very good to it.''

"Yeah? How do we know that?''

"Lanky—''

"Naw, I mean it. How do we know it hasn't got a wife and kids it'd like to go flicker at instead of us . . . maybe six wives and kids. Or husbands and kids. Or whatever it's got.''

"Lanky, we don't know, and we can't afford to care. Come *on*—let's stay with the subject at hand, such as it is.''

Lanky shrugged, and moved on to the tooth-picking project, noting Dolbe's shudder with satisfaction. That'd hold him.

"Brooks?" said Dolbe. "Brooks, you're our idea man. Come up with an idea.''

"You *know* what I would do," said Showard.

"Put a couple dozen linguists over a slow fire till they agreed to help us?''

"At least.''

"We can't do that.''

"Then don't bother me, Arnold!" Showard rasped. "Our problem is pretty simple here—we don't know what we're doing wrong, the only people who do know what we're doing wrong are the effing linguists, and they won't tell us! I don't see anything subtle or complex to be dealt with here . . . they have to be *forced* to help, since they won't do it of their own accord. All you nicey-nicies can sit there and blather till you decompose, but it won't change things. We're wasting our time."

"It's humiliating," said St. Clair.

"What? Failing 100 percent of the time?"

"That, sure. But what I meant was, it's humiliating that with the entire scientific resources of the civilized universe behind us we can't figure out what it is the linguists know. It's degrading."

"You're right, Beau. It is. But it's the way things are, and the way they've been ever since anybody can remember. Moping over it won't help—but forcing them to tell would. If we weren't so dainty and all abristle with scrupulosities."

"Have we got any kind of leverage at all with the linguists?"

"No. They've got all the leverage there is."

"Couldn't we go public about Honcho Chornyak playing games with us while he pretends he won't dirty his lily-whites that way?"

"Why?" Showard demanded. "What's he done, Beau? Comes to meetings when we ask him to. Never lets anything slip— follows his party line all the way, every time."

"But he wants that secret, Brooks. He does want that kept secret. We could spread it all over the newslines."

"Sure," said Dolbe. "And then he could explain to the public precisely what it is that happens to the babies they volunteer for Government Work. He'd be real good at doing that. For followup, he could tell them how we go kidnap babies out of hospitals when the parents *won't* volunteer."

"Christ . . . would he do that?"

"Ah hell, Beau! Sure he'd do it," Showard answered. "And when he got through we'd look like murderers—which we are, I might add—and he'd have it all put together somehow so there'd be no penalty for him either from the public *or* from the Lines. That's one smart man, that Thomas Blair Chornyak, and when you add in that he's a linguist you've got smart man cubed. He doesn't play littlegirl games."

"Well, like Arnold says, we've got to do *some*thing."

"Yeah. We could all go loobyloo, Beau."

"Listen," said St. Clair, "how much do we know, really, about why the babies can't hack the Interfacing? I mean, there's no question that they *can't*—I've seen that enough to believe it and plenty left over—but is there something we know about the problem that we could maybe use somehow?''

"Let's review that, men," said Dolbe expansively, *lead*ing now that somebody'd pointed the direction for him. Lead over thataway, Dolbe . . . wagons, ho, Dolbe . . . "Let's go over that one more time."

"There's nothing there," said Lanky Pugh. "I've run that all through the computer I don't know how many times—there's nothing there."

"Sometimes the human brain has an edge on the computer, begging your pardon for the blasphemy, Lanky," said Dolbe. "Let's just give it one more runby."

"All right," Showard said. "All right. First principle: there's no such thing as reality. We make it up by perceiving stimuli from the environment—external or internal—and making statements about it. Everybody perceives stuff, everybody makes up statements about it, everybody—so far as we can tell—agrees enough to get by, so that when I say 'Hand me the coffee' you know what to hand me. And that's reality. Second principle: people get used to a certain kind of reality and come to expect it, and if what they perceive doesn't fit the set of statements everybody's agreed to, either the culture has to go through a kind of fit until it adjusts . . . or they just blank it out."

"Fairies . . ." murmured Beau St. Clair. "Angels."

"Yeah. They're not in the set of reality statements for this culture, so if they're 'real' we just don't see them, don't hear them, don't smell them, don't feel them . . . don't taste them. If you can handle the idea of not-tasting an angel." He leaned back and clasped his hands behind his head, letting the pocket knife dangle. "Now, third principle: human beings are handwired to expect certain kinds of perceptions—that's where the trouble starts. The cognitive scientists tell us that whatever the hardwiring is in Terrans, it's reasonably close to whatever it is in humanoid Aliens, because the brains and sensory systems are similar enough, even if there's tentacles coming out of one humanoid's ears and not out of some other's. And the linguists tell us that because that hardwiring is close enough, you can take a brain-plus-sensory system that's not set in concrete yet—say, a baby's—and it *can* manage to make statements about what it perceives, even if it's not in the consensus set. Babies don't know what they're going to have coming at them, they have to learn. And if it isn't *too* different from what they're hardwired to notice, they can handle it. They can include it in their reality."

"So far, nothing," said Lanky. "Like I said."

"Fourth principle," Showard went on, "even a baby, even still new to perceptions like it is, can't handle it when it runs into a perception so completely different from the humanoid that it can't be processed at all, much less put into a statement."

"Babies can't make statements," said Lanky, disgustedly. "Shit. All they can do is—"

"Lanky," said Beau St. Clair, "that's all wrong. They can't attach the words you'd attach, they can't *pronounce* the statements—but they make them. Like, 'what I see there is something I have seen before, so I'll look at the other thing I *haven't* seen before.' Like 'that noise is my mother.' Stuff like that."

"Shit," said Lanky again. "Fairies and angels. Fairy shit and angel shit."

They were used to Lanky Pugh; they went ahead with it in spite of him.

"So," Showard wound it up, "that's what we know. There's something about the way the non-humanoid Aliens perceive things, something about the 'reality' they make out of stimuli, so impossible that it freaks out the babies and destroys their central nervous systems permanently."

"Like what?" Lanky demanded.

"Pugh," said Showard, "if I knew that, my central nervous system would have been destroyed permanently, and I sure as hell wouldn't be able to tell you about it."

"Aw, shit," said Lanky.

"The obvious solution," Dolbe put in, glad to have come to at least one thing he was sure he understood, "is desensitization."

"Yeah," said Brooks. "And God knows we've tried that. We've tried putting the baby in the Interface for just a fraction of a second at a time, over weeks and weeks, working up to a whole second . . . makes no damn difference. Come the time that baby somehow gets an Alien perception, it self-destructs, all the same."

"So let's think about that," Dolbe insisted. "Let's think about that seriously. The problem is desensitization. We've tried it by decreasing the exposure to the absolute minimum, and that hasn't helped. So that's out. We can't ask the baby to imagine it in advance; the baby can't understand what we're saying, and we don't know what to tell it to imagine even if it could understand. So *that's* out. What else is there, that we haven't ruled out?"

The silence went on and on, while they thought. And at last Beau cleared his throat tentatively.

"Maybe," he said. "Maybe there's something."

"Spit it out."

"Maybe it's crazy, too."

"Let's *talk* about it, man!" said Dolbe. "What is it? And you, Showard, Pugh—put those cursed knives *away*, before I go out of my mind!"

"Sure, Arnold," said Lanky solemnly, and folded the offending object ostentatiously into itself and put it in his pocket. "Now that you've asked."

"Go on, Beau," said Showard. And he put his knife away, too.

"Well," said Beau slowly, "I was just thinking. What if—just what if, now—you gave a baby, right from minute one, one of the hallucinogens? Maybe different kinds, even. What if you did that for a month or so before you ever put it in the Interface? What do you suppose you'd get that way?"

Brooks Showard stared at his colleague, as if *he'd* perceived an angel, and he came roaring up out of his apathy with a suddenness and intensity that startled even Lanky.

"By Christ, St. Clair!" he shouted. "You'd get a baby, you'd get a baby that had made itself a statement that went roughly 'Well, hell, *anything at all* might very well come along!' God *damn*, Beau, that's *it*! That is *it!!*"

Arnold Dolbe sat there, shocked stiff. He went white, and his twitches all went chronic on him at one time. "You can't administer hallucinogenic drugs to a baby!" he pronounced. "That's obscene! It's barbaric!"

The silence was vast around him, and when he finally heard it he lost all the stiffness.

"Oh, my," he said sadly. "Oh, my. I suppose, after what we've already done to babies, that was not the most intelligent remark I could have made. I forget . . . I forget, you know?"

"Brooks," said Lanky, politely looking away from Arnold Dolbe to give the man time to recover some of his composure, "you sound damn certain. Are you really sure?"

Showard made a wry face. "Of course I'm not sure. How could I be sure? But it sounds right. Even adults, if they don't overdo it for starters, can get used to having their realities altered damned drastically on LSD or synthomescaline or any of the others. A baby, with its brain still soft in the mold—in a manner of speaking—hell, it ought to get broadminded enough to be ready for anything whatsoever to come its way. No, I'm not sure, Lanky—but I'm sure enough that I want to try it. Right *now*."

"But we don't have a baby right now," Dolbe pointed out. "And unless somebody just turns up out of nowhere, like that Landry kid, we don't have any volunteer prospects right now, either. You're not suggesting that we go into the kidnapping business again, are you?"

"I'm not sure," said Brooks Showard very carefully. "I'm not sure exactly *what* I'm suggesting."

"But see here, man—"

"Naw! Shut up, Dolbe, and let me think! Will you for chrissakes let me think?"

Dolbe shut his mouth and waited, while Showard frowned and beat his fist in a slow steady drumming against the edge of the table. They all waited, and they all saw the change in Showard as he got ready to tell them exactly what he had in mind. They hadn't seen Brooks Showard with a look of optimism in so long they'd forgotten what it was like, but he looked optimistic now.

"Two things," he said at last. "I say we do two things."

"Name them," said Dolbe briskly.

"I want you, Dolbe, to go twist some arms over at NSA and have them put some real muscle into digging up dirt on the Lingoes."

"I thought you were going to talk about—"

"I'm getting to that! This is something I want out of the way first, Dolbe! There have *got* to be linguists that aren't morally the equivalent of the Virgin Mary . . . there've got to be. I want 'em. I want to know which ones are open to blackmail. I want to know what they're doing, when they're doing it, who or what they're doing it with, and how often. The works. The NSA is the right unit to do that, that's what they're for, and you, Dolbe, I want you to get them onto it. There's only thirteen of the Lines, and all of them crammed together like animals in a communal building—that ought to be the easiest surveillance assignment NSA's had in decades. Let's get that going, in case we need it later."

"Done," said Dolbe. "Consider it done."

"Okay. Now, for the business of sending the babies on the fancy trips . . . we have got babies."

"We have?"

"Yeah. We have. We've got damnall cartons and bales of babies. *Freezers*ful of babies."

"What?" And then, "Oh."

"Brooks," said Beau St. Clair, "we didn't have very good luck with those test-tube infants. Remember? They were . . .

they . . . Ah, hell, I don't know how to put it. But you remember—you were there.''

"Yes," said Showard, "I remember. And I agree with you, it wasn't the greatest. But if we've got to go monkeying around with the brains of infants, feeding them peyote with their pablum, I for one would rather start with the tubies. We've got plenty of them, there are no parents to grieve over what happens to them; it's the obvious way to go. Let's work it out on *them*. The doses. How much a baby can take without it wrecking his physical system, never mind the central nervous system. We'll start it with the test-tube babies, and we'll learn as we go along . . . And by the time somebody volunteers us another Infant Hero, gentlemen, we'll be ready. We'll know what we're doing. Don't you see? We'll bygod solve this problem!''

The whole room was crackling with the new prospect that there might, there just might, be a nugget of success somewhere in the desert of failure that had extended everywhere around them as far in space or time as any of them could remember. It was champagne time, and the bubbles already popping. Even if it meant using the tubies again.

Brooks Showard grabbed a stack of government forms lying in the middle of the table and threw them up into the air, from pure happiness, standing there and letting it rain forms on him with an expression of simple bliss.

"Hey, let's *go!*" he shouted at them. "Time's a-wasting, and all those quaint sayings from Homeroom! Let's *go!*"

Chapter Thirteen

REFORMULATION ONE, Göedel's Theorem:
For any language, there are perceptions which it cannot express because they would result in its indirect self-destruction.

REFORMULATION ONE-PRIME, Göedel's Theorem:
For any culture, there are languages which it cannot use because they would result in its indirect self-destruction.

(from an obscure pamphlet titled ''Primer in Metalinguistics,'' by an even more obscure group known as the Planet Ozark Offworld Auxiliary; they credit these statements to an inspiration from the great Doublas Hofstadter . . .)

Rachel heard the words, but it was as if they were in a language she had never studied; she could not process them. He must have seen that on her face, because he said them again, slowly and clearly. And then, when she understood, the stimulus finally overriding the shock, she curled her hands tightly into fists so that they wouldn't tremble and told herself that she must be very very careful. But it was no good, she wasn't able to be careful.

''Oh, no, Thomas!'' It was the best and the worst she could manage. ''Oh, she is too young!''

''Nonsense.''

''The child is only fourteen years old, Thomas! Oh, you can't be serious—I don't believe it.''

''I am totally serious; this isn't a joking matter. And the 'child' will be fifteen when the marriage takes place, Rachel. I've scheduled it for her fifteenth birthday.''

Rachel struck her clenched fists together and pressed them to her chest; before she could stop, she had bent forward as a woman does in the sudden pain of labor, and a low mourning croon had come from her lips. It was a sound she had not known she knew how to make; it was a sound Thomas was certain to dislike.

"My God," he said, his voice heavy with distaste. As she was aware, he despised that sort of female noise, and the obvious fact that it had been involuntary, a reflex response to pain, did not make him any less disgusted. "You sound precisely like a bawling cow, Rachel. An elderly bawling cow."

The callousness was just what Rachel needed; it pulled her back instantly from her state of emotional disarray, and when she spoke again it was calmly, and in her ordinary cool tones.

"What," she asked him, "will you men do next? First the girls married at eighteen. Then it was sixteen. Now you are prepared to see Nazareth marry at just barely fifteen . . . thirty seconds past, if I understand you correctly. Why not just move the marriage date to puberty and be done with it, Thomas?"

"It isn't necessary," he answered. "The present system, with marriage at sixteen, allows the husband to space his children three years apart and still see that the woman bears eight infants before the age of forty. Eight is quite enough, whatever the government may think about the matter, and we don't feel that a woman much past forty should go through pregnancy. There's no need for any such radical change as you are proposing."

"Thomas—"

"Furthermore, Rachel, despite your histrionics you know I have not suggested that all girls of the Lines should marry at fifteen. Only that Nazareth must do so, and only because her circumstances are exceptional."

"You would be exceptional, too, if you were under guard every moment of your life!"

"Once she's married, there'll be no need for night surveillance unless her husband is gone from home," said Thomas. "And perhaps the need for daytime guards will be less as well. In time."

"I have never understood the need for any of it," Rachel declared.

"That's very stupid of you."

"Thomas, Belle-Anne has been in the mental hospital for months, and you know what she's become. If she were released tomorrow—and that won't happen—she has no mind left at all, she's a husk! Nazareth has been in no danger since the day they took Belle-Anne away, and it is in no way stupid for me to realize that. What possible danger could there be?''

"I worry about the other females at Barren House," said Thomas. "I'm not prepared to accept unequivocally the idea that only Belle-Anne was suffering from religious mania, for one thing. And for another, my dear, there are few things easier for a copycat criminal to fake than religious mania."

"Thomas . . . it's absurd."

"Nazareth is valuable to this Household," he told her stiffly. "Far beyond the ordinary, she is valuable. Her linguistic skills would make her a prize under any circumstances, and REM34 is one of the languages most essential to the welfare of this planet—which makes her even more valuable. Finally, her genetics are superb. I expect her to provide us with infants of equal caliber. And I am not willing to take even the slightest chance that she'll be harmed, Rachel, not now, not ever. Your emotionalism is unbecoming in a woman who ought to know the value of her own child, and who claims to love her."

Rachel firmed her lips, and looked at him steadily, considering. It was just possible that he was telling her the truth, that he'd fed the data into the computers and been advised that the chance of someone following Belle-Anne's example was sufficiently great to require protection for Nazareth. It was possible. It was certainly true that Nazareth was uniquely valuable to the Line both genetically and economically. But she knew Thomas very well, and she knew that there were ordinarily many layers of motive behind the surface one that he presented with such plausibility.

For example, if he hadn't assigned those two young men to keep watch over Nazareth . . . he would have had an unsolved problem. If he were to end the surveillance he would have that problem back again. Some sort of face-saving function had been needed, because those two were so completely unpromising as linguists that they were useless for anything more than the most trivial social situations. That happened sometimes . . . a linguist would acquire the languages chosen for him like any other child, but would turn out to be utterly lacking in any ability to carry out the essential functions of interpreting and translating. It had been very convenient for Thomas to be able to give out the tale that he'd released the two cousins from their important duties as linguists to fill the equally important role of guards for Nazareth; if he released them from that, he'd have to think of something else. It would be awkward . . . there was always the danger of damage to the public's image of the linguists as infallible in all matters linguistic.

"Rachel," Thomas said, "that expression on your face is more than usually unpleasant. Please do not scowl at me in that way . . . at least wait until I've had breakfast."

"Thomas?"

"Yes, Rachel?" Oh, the overlay of weary tolerance in that voice, damn his soul!

"Thomas," she said urgently, "I can't approve of this. You managed to distract me very neatly with all the trivia about the necessity for the guards—twenty points to you, my dear. But I cannot be distracted indefinitely . . . let's return to the subject of this obscene marriage that you are suggesting."

"Rachel," said Thomas, adding practical reason to the tolerance, "it doesn't make the slightest difference whether you approve or not. It would be pleasant if you did approve, of course. I make every effort to consider your personal wishes with regard to my children whenever I can. But when you refuse to be reasonable you leave me no choice but to ignore you. And Rachel, I am not 'suggesting' this marriage—I am *ordering* it."

Rachel had been born a linguist, born a Shawnessey, and she had spent all her life surrounded by the men of the Lines. She did not misjudge Thomas. She knew him to be in many ways a good and kind and considerate man. She knew that his responsibilities were heavy, that his workload was brutal, and that at times he did things less than kindly only because he had no time to do them in any other way. As Head of the Lines, he had power; so far as she knew, he had never been tempted to abuse that power, and that was to his credit. She was willing to give him all the credit due him.

But she *resented* him; oh, how she resented him! And she resented him most at times like this one, when his total authority over her and over those she loved forced her to debase herself to him. She would choke on what she had to do now . . . but she had no other strategy available to her. She erased the anger from her face, erased the scowl to which he had objected, and let her eyes fill with the soft puzzled tearfulness that was considered appealing in women. And she sank to the floor beside Thomas' chair and leaned her head against his knee, and for the sake of her daughter, she disciplined herself to beg.

"Please, my darling," she said softly. "Please don't do this dreadful thing."

"Rachel, you are ridiculous," he said. His body was rigid under her touch, and his voice was ice.

"Thomas, how often have I asked you for anything? How often, love, have I quarreled with your decisions or questioned your good judgment? How often have I done anything but agree that you were wise in what you were about to do? Please, Thomas . . . change your mind. Just this one time. Thomas, indulge me, just this once!''

He reached down abruptly and hauled her upright in front of him like a parcel, or a child in tantrum, and he sat there laughing at her, shaking his head in mock astonishment.

"Darling . . ." Rachel said, forcing the words.

"Darling!'' He let go of one of her shoulders and he tapped her on the end of her nose with his index finger. "I am not your darling . . . or anyone's. As you know perfectly well. I am a cruel and vindictive and heartless monster who cares for nothing but his own selfish and twisted goals.''

"Thomas, I never ask you for anything!'' she pleaded.

"My sweet,'' he said, still laughing, "that is what you always say when you disagree with me. Every single time. Year after weary year. You really should talk to one of the young girls and see if they can't suggest a new routine you could use . . . you've worn that one out completely.''

Rachel's eyes stung, and she knew that tears might help her now. She'd managed to make him laugh at her, which meant that he was more relaxed, less on his guard. Tears would be the wise next move, and she owed that move to Nazareth.

She knew that. And she knew also that she couldn't do it. It was too much. Women of the Lines learned early not to give in to tears except by choice, because tears destroyed negotiations. A woman who is weeping is a woman who cannot talk, and a woman who cannot talk most surely cannot interpret. The voluntary control of tears was a skill mastered for business reasons, but it proved useful in many areas of life, and it would be useful to her now. She would *not* cry, not even for Nazareth.

She pulled away from him, stepped back and set her arms akimbo, her hands on her hips in a stance that she knew he detested, and in a voice that carried as much contempt as she could muster she said, "Chornyak—your daughter *hates* that man!''

His eyebrows rose, briefly, and he brushed at his trousers where she had leaned against them.

"So?''

"You don't feel that's relevant?''

"You know better, woman. It has no relevance at all. We linguists haven't married for any reason other than the sum of politics and genetics since . . at least since Whissler was president.

Nazareth's opinions of Aaron Adiness are of no concern whatever.''

"There is an enormous difference between marrying someone you merely feel no love for, and marrying someone you hate.''

"Rachel,'' Thomas said, sighing, "I'm trying very hard to be patient with you. But you're doing everything you can to make that impossible. I will make just one more attempt—and we will leave Nazareth's immature sentiments out of it. Aaron Adiness is superbly healthy, he comes of a Household with which we are anxious for closer ties at this time, he's talented—''

"He's nothing of the kind!''

"What?''

"Everyone knows, Thomas, that he's a mediocre linguist!''

"Oh, come now, Rachel. . . . you women may 'know' something of that kind, but it has no more foundation in fact than any of the rest of your female mythology. Aaron is a native speaker of REM30-2-699, of Swahili, of English, and of Navajo; he has a respectable fluency in eleven other Terran languages and can get by socially in four dialects of Cantonese. His Ameslan is so exceptionally fluent and graceful that he has been hired to teach it to the *deaf* at several national institutes. And I have not even mentioned the dozens of languages that he can read with ease and translate with both skill and subtlety . . . the list goes on for half a page. Not talented! Rachel, when you go out of your way to be childish you lose all claim on courtesy from me.''

Rachel was ashamed now, deeply ashamed, and she knew that she had lost. There was no hope of salvaging this. She had succeeded in turning it into a fight, and one of their better fights at that. She went on only because she no longer had anything to lose.

"It's an open secret, Thomas, that Aaron Adiness has a violent temper and an insurmountable conviction that the universe was created for his personal benefit! And that he allows both of those factors to interfere with the performance of his duties! You know it, I know it, everyone knows it . . . If he had fifty languages native and five hundred more fluent, it would *not* cancel out the fact that he cannot control his personal feelings even when he is on duty. If Nazareth hadn't been the Jeelod interpreter when the negotiations for the Sigma-9 frontier colony leases were under way, there'd *be* no colonies on Sigma-9 . . . she had to do everything but belly dance to salvage the messes Aaron made every time he fancied someone doubted his divinity. He is cruel, and stupid, and vindictive, and petty—he's worse than any woman! And if you tie Nazareth to him for life, then you are worse than *he* is!''

Thomas had gone white; for some reason, although he could easily tolerate almost any sort of confrontation with others, having Rachel forget her place in this way always enraged him so that he had to fight for control . . . and she knew it, too, damn the bitch. He regretted now having even told her of his plans for Nazareth. He should have shipped her off somewhere and had the marriage performed in her absence, as Adam had suggested; for once, he agreed with Adam that he spoiled Rachel and that it was foolish of him to do so. Certainly he got nothing from her in return for his indulgence.

"Rachel," he said, clenching his teeth to keep his voice from betraying that he was shaking with rage, "that's a common pattern when youth is combined with genius. Aaron will outgrow both his temper and his arrogance, as does any man of that sort. And Nazareth will be well advised not to remind him of her alleged rescues of his diplomatic shipwrecks—I suggest that you tell her so. Because very soon he will make her, with all her spectacular scores on the linguistics tests, look like a chimp using Ameslan. The more primitive the organism, woman, the more swiftly it matures—of *course* Nazareth was a bit further along emotionally than Aaron during the Sigma-9 contracts! The advantage is a temporary one, milady, and she'd better remember it."

"You're determined then, Thomas? You want this show horse for the Line so badly that you're willing to bind your own daughter to him for life when the very sight of him is repulsive to her? That's your idea of fair return on the value she represents to your treasuries? What's the problem, dear? Is somebody else after him?"

Thomas turned away in one swift movement, and Rachel knew she had him—he wouldn't have done that if he hadn't been afraid she'd see that in his face. But body-parl betrays, always; his abrupt move, graceless and entirely unlike him, was as revealing as any statement could have been. And it was her turn to laugh.

"Ah," she cried, "that *is* it, isn't it? You're about to lose him, a prize stallion with a spectacularly curly tail, to one of the other Lines! And that can't be allowed to happen!"

"It certainly cannot," he said, his back still turned to her.

"Well . . . if that's all it is, why not one of the other girls? You've got a houseful of brood mares, Thomas . . . why not Philippa? God knows your brother would be delighted to get rid of her, he can't stand any of his daughters, and she's a strapping seventeen. Marry *her* off to Adiness!''

''No.''

''Why not?''

''Because I wish to see what the genetic combination of Nazareth's and Aaron's abilities will produce,'' he said coldly. ''Philippa is entirely run of the mill.'' His brief moment without mastery of himself had passed, and he turned to face her easily, his voice heavy now only with the message that she turned his stomach.

''Get on with you,'' he told her roughly. ''You've wasted enough of my time. Tell Nazareth she's to be ready for the wedding on her fifteenth birthday, and let me hear no more about it. No—not one word, woman! *Get!*'' And he left their room, not waiting to see her obey.

Alone, Rachel laid her fingers loosely across her mouth, and closed her eyes, and she rocked silently. She did not cry now, either, though she could safely have done so . . . she turned *her* stomach, too. She had gone about it all wrong. She had let him catch her off guard, and she had done everything about as badly as she could have done it. She should have manipulated Thomas. Should have pretended only casual interest, even approval, when he told her his intentions. Then this evening, over a bourbon, she could have begun a discussion of the subject. She should never have challenged him directly, never opposed him openly . . . her decision to play the helpless belle had come too late, had been too rapid a transition, and had collapsed the moment he taunted her with it.

She knew she was too old and too worn with the bearing of seven children to have any erotic weapons left to use against her husband. But he was still vulnerable to other techniques, and she knew him better than anyone alive; she had only to set her self-respect aside and toady to him convincingly. She had made the sort of stupid errors a bride makes . . . a bride such as Nazareth would be, poor little girl . . . but a bride is saved from the consequences of her ignorance by the novelty of her body. Rachel no longer had that advantage. She had sacrificed her daughter to her own ego, traded her off for a few minutes of triumph over Thomas, triumph for which Nazareth would be the one who had to pay. The only shred of comfort she had was that the girl would never have to know how badly her mother had failed her, or how cheaply she had sold her out.

* * *

At Barren House the women listened to her, of course; it was courteous to do so. They made her a pot of strong tea, and they sat her down to drink it while they heard her out. But they had no sympathy to offer her.

"What did you expect?" they asked her. "You had slim chances when you started that interaction, and what little you had you threw away immediately. What did you ex*pect* the man to do when you defied him like that?"

"Oh, I know," said Rachel wearily. "I know."

"Well, then."

"Thomas is completely wrong," she said. *"Wrong."*

"He is a man. Being wrong has nothing to do with anything."

"If you behave like this often, Rachel," Caroline observed, "I'm surprised he hasn't signed the papers to put you away long before now."

"I wouldn't care if he did."

"Rachel! Think of Belle-Anne, what they've done to her, what she's become . . . you've been to see her! That's a death sentence, worse than death . . . rotting away in a state mental hospital!"

"Thomas would never put me in a state hospital," said Rachel. "The wife of the Head of all the Heads of all the Lines, in a snakepit ward? Tssk . . . that would never do. No, he'd send me to one of those places with a name like a dog kennel. Cedar Hills. Willow Lake. Maple Acres. You know the sort of place. Where I can sit all day in my rocker in a row of little old ladies in rockers, all of us doped into catatonia, waiting to be led off to bed and knocked cold for the night. Just as a change from the catatonia."

"And why hasn't he done that?"

"Because he's used to me, and he's very busy. He likes the way I keep his files in order. He counts on me to keep him from forgetting things. I make a great deal of money for the Household, and if he's right there he can be sure I don't slack off. I was a prime piece of brood stock, and he's used to thinking of me that way. He hasn't got time to break in a new woman and teach her to do all the things I do for him—it's less trouble to put up with me. After all, he doesn't have to see me for days on end. I am a convenience, with certain annoying qualities that he is able to avoid most of the time."

"A perfectly ordinary marriage," said Susannah, and the others agreed. A clever woman saw to it that as she grew older she *did* become useful in the ways Rachel had listed; it was the only security she had, and all that stood between her and the rows of little old ladies on Thorazine.

"Poor little Nazareth," breathed Rachel.

"A lot of good that does her now."

"It does her no good at all," Rachel agreed. "I say it all the same."

"Well, say it here, and then keep it to yourself," said Caroline. "The worst thing you could possibly do for her is sympathize with her. The quicker she toughens to what's ahead of her, the less power it 'will have to hurt her. Don't you dare go 'poor littling' her!"

"No. I'm not entirely a fool, though you couldn't tell it by what I've done this day. I know better than that."

"Go tell her, then, and do it properly. Before he does it."

"Duty," said Rachel. "Opportunity. Loyalty to the Lines. A woman's place. The healing power of time. Fun and games. Fables and baubles."

"Exactly. Get it over with, so that she can get used to the idea before she has to spread her legs for the Adiness stud."

Rachel shuddered, and they poured her a last cup of tea. She took a long swallow, finished it, and then stood to go face her daughter. . . . She wasn't quite sure where Nazareth was, but her wrist computer would tell her.

"Nazareth will come here afterward," she said. "You know she will."

"I hope so. Where else could she go?"

"Don't tell her I was here before her, wailing and moaning. Please."

"Of course not. She'll be far better off if she thinks this isn't bothering you at all. We know that . . .we've all had a turn in Nazareth's shoes."

Rachel stared at them.

"No, you haven't," she said bitterly. "Not one of you has had to marry a man she *hated*."

That silenced them, and they nodded. It *was* rare, because actual discord between husband and wife was not an efficient arrangement for communal living. There tended to be fewer children from such marriages, and it was hard for everyone in the Household where the couple was living. Thomas must have had genuinely compelling reasons for this match, to have gone against so much experience and tradition—or else he was counting on Nazareth's youth and innocence to be overcome by Adiness' magnificent face and body. Nazareth had not yet caught her dose of Romantic Love; he might well be counting on it overtaking her in Adiness' arms. For Nazareth's sake, they hoped that he was right and that it would take a good long time to wear off.

"We know a little something about it, then," soothed Grace. "A little something; enough to be careful, Rachel. You go ahead now, and tell her. And we'll be expecting her."

"Oh . . . Rachel?" Caroline shoved her fingers deep into her hair and looked at the other woman. "Rachel, before you go . . . have you heard the rumors about Government Work?"

"Rumors . . ."

"Rachel, do think! I realize that Nazareth is the main thing on your mind now, and rightly so, but think just for a moment. Have you heard anything about experiments with test-tube babies?"

Rachel frowned, "I don't think so," she said. "What are they saying?"

"That they're feeding the little things hallucinogens . . . and then Interfacing them with non-humanoids."

"Dear God in heaven." Even in her state of exhaustion and self-disgust, Rachel could appreciate what that meant.

"It may be only rumor," said Susannah. "It's usually rumor. It's just the kind of thing the government would love to convince the Lines they had going."

"It's . . . unspeakable. If it's true."

"Yes, it is," said Caroline. "Rachel, see if you can find out anything about it, will you? From Thomas? He may very well know."

Rachel nodded, absently, her hand on the door. She could not mourn for test-tube babies this morning. She was too entirely used up with mourning for the daughter she'd failed so shamefully.

"I'll try," she said.

"If anyone can find out, it's you," said Caroline.

"Oh, yes. I'm so skilled in my . . . marital relations."

"Rachel—just try."

"Why? What could we do?"

"It would be good," said Susannah, "to know that it was *not* true. It would be easier for us all to sleep at night, child."

When Nazareth came to them later in the day, the women were ready. In a circle of small rockers, in the common room, each with her embroidery or a quilt block or one more intricate lacy shawl to be knitted or crocheted. And their hearts resolutely hardened against the temptation to do the coddling of Nazareth that they had forbidden to her mother. Even so, the girl's despair and revulsion were hard to watch with the necessary appearance of tranquil unconcern.

She kept saying, "I can't do this."

And they kept saying, "You can, Nazareth. You will."

"I can't."

"You have no choice."

"I *do*," she said. "I do have a choice."

"What choice?"

"I will kill myself," she said. "Before I spend a lifetime with that disgusting parody of a man and his ego that is far bigger than he ever could be, I will kill myself. I *will*."

Something in her voice, some narrow edge, caught their attention. It was an easy threat, easily made, very common and frequent in young girls suddenly confronted with the unpleasant decisions of the males who controlled them. But there was a note of resolution in her words they didn't care for.

"How would you do that?" scoffed Nile, drawing up a length of emerald silk. "Perceive, Natha . . . there stand your two dear little guards, waiting for you on our doorstep. You can't even go to the toilet without those two, standing outside the door and counting off the seconds."

"They can't follow me in," said Nazareth. "They can go everywhere else, but they can't follow me in *there*. And I know ways . . . oh, I know ways that will put an end to this long before they get tired of counting seconds."

No doubt she did. Every woman did.

They looked at one another, and at the trembling girl, and the same thought was on all their faces: *we can't have this.*

"Nazareth . . . dear child . . ." Susannah spoke carefully, making certain that there was time for the others to stop her if she was misjudging the situation, "there's something you should know."

"I'm not interested in your fairy tales!"

"Not a fairy tale. A truth."

"I'm not interested—whatever it is, I do not care."

"Nazareth Chornyak," said Susannah sternly, "you hear me! Do you remember, long ago, telling Aquina about your Encodings notebook? Do you?"

Nazareth looked up at that, and her lips parted slightly; it had caught her interest after all.

"Why do you ask me that?"

"Because, child, Aquina came back and told us. And she did more than that. She found your hidingplace in the orchards, dearlove, and she's been going there every month and copying your work out for us to use."

The outrage was stamped plain and fierce on the girl's face, and they were very glad to see it there. If she could be distracted by something like this, she was still safe.

"How *dare* you!" she hissed at them. "You sneaks . . . you contemptible old *sneaks*! My notebook—my private notebook. . . ."

She was so angry she could not even go on talking, the sense of violation choking her. And they agreed with her with all due solemnity, and granted her that every single one of them would have felt just the same way. Exactly the same way.

"But what matters," Susannah went on when the storm had calmed a little, "is that among those Encodings we have found seven valid ones. *Seven*, Nazareth Joanna. And every last one of them major."

Susannah was aware of the stillness around her, the stillness of a collective breath being held. It was a terrible risk she was taking—did she have to take it twice? Had Nazareth even heard her, caught as she was in anger?

But when Nazareth finally spoke, she said none of the things they might have expected her to say. She said, "I don't want to know."

"What?"

"I do not want to know. I am not listening to you. I will not hear you. I will not be bed and brood for Aaron Adiness, who is only *filth*, do you perceive that, *filth*! I will not listen to you witches and your spells and your foolish incantations . . . I *will not* know!"

Ah. That was much better. That was ordinary young girl's panic and anger. None of that deadly dull seriousness, but ordinary frantic babble. This, they could handle, and without endangering the Encoding Project any further. But when it is necessary to be cruel, you don't drag it out; you are swift with the blow. It was over to Grace, whose laughter would hurt Nazareth far more because Grace was one of the tender ones; and Grace did not miss her cue. At the first flickers of Susannah's signing fingers, seen from the corner of her eye, Grace's clear laughter rang out and split the silence. And the others joined in.

Flinching, Nazareth cried out, "Don't *laugh* at me! How *can* you!"

"But child," said Caroline, struggling to speak over gales of mirth, "how can we not? When you're so outrageously funny?"

Nazareth was moving her head. Back and forth from side to side. Over and over and over again. Caroline had seen an animal do that once, in a zoo; it was blind, and it moved its head like that, utterly lost. And she applied the lash of pedantry along with the ridicule, cutting deep and swift.

"Nazareth, you're a linguist. One cannot *not* hear. One cannot 'refuse' to know, no matter how tempting it may be. You cannot 'refuse to know' that an angry skunk had just favored you with its perfume—and you cannot 'refuse to know' what we have just told you. You have given us seven Major Encodings; they were all valid. *You now know that.* Spare us your drivel, please."

"Oh," moaned the cornered girl, "may God curse you all. . . ."

"Dear me," said Susannah. "How you talk."

"Such manners, Missy," added Thyrsis. "Mercy."

Tears had begun to pour down Nazareth's face, and the women were delighted to see them; it was when a woman ought to weep and could not that there was cause for alarm. But they hurt for her all the same, as she tongue-lashed them.

"It wasn't enough that you lied to me," cried Nazareth, "and stole my things, and sneaked my notebook, and used my work without even asking me, and pretended all the time to be my friends! That wasn't enough, was it? No, you hadn't done enough, with just those things! That didn't satisfy you, did it? It's like the men say, you've got nothing to do, so you think up wicked plots . . . and now you are trying to blackmail me! And you laugh! You blackmail me, and you *laugh*! Oh, God curse you . . . God curse you. . . ."

That was very good, they thought. It showed that she did understand. She had a scrap of knowledge here, a scrap there . . . enough to know that Encodings were precious. The little girls heard the stories at their mother's knees, when their mothers had time to tell them, and from the women of the Barren Houses otherwise. How women, in the long ago time when women could vote and be doctors and fly spaceships—a fantasy world for those girlchildren, as fabulous and glittering as any tale of castles and dragons—how women, even then, had begun the first slow gropings toward a language of their own.

The tales were told again and again, and embroidered lovingly with detail; and prominent in their ornament were the jewels of the Encodings. *A word for a perception that had never had a word of its own before.* Major Encodings, the most precious because they were truly newborn to the universe of discourse. Minor Encodings, which always came in the wake of a Major one, because it would bring to mind related concepts that could be lexicalized on the same pattern, still valuable. "A woman who gives an Encoding to other women is a woman of valor, and all women are in her debt forevermore.''

They memorized the list, short because for so many years no one had dared to keep records written down, like the Begats of the Bible. ''And Emily Jefferson Chornyak in her lifetime gave to us three Major Encodings and two Minor; and Marian Chornyak Shawnessey, that was sister to Fiona Chornyak Shawnessey, in her lifetime gave us one Major Encoding and nine Minor; and her sister Fiona Shawnessey, in her lifetime . . .'' They learned it all, and they gave it the value women put into their voices and their eyes, and they guarded it. ''Don't tell your father, now, or any of the boys, or any of the men at all. They'll only laugh. It's a *woman's* secret.'' But of course the little girls were told that this secret was all a part of Langlish. . . .

Nazareth looked as if she would faint, and they put her head down between her knees until the color came back to her face, and then moved her to the company couch in the parlor to lie down. The couch on which no Barren House woman ever sat, because when its coverings wore out they would have to petition the men for money to have it redone. It was the emergency couch.

''Do you feel better now, Natha?''

''I hate you,'' was all she said.

Of course she did not hate them. They knew what she was thinking. If she used the motherwit of death she had learned along with the list of names, she did not destroy just her own self. Like every little girl, she had asked, ''Why can't we *talk* it, our language? In private, where the men won't hear?'' And had been told, ''Because we do not have enough Encodings yet.'' How many years would women wait for their own native tongue, just because she, Nazareth, did not have sufficient strength to cope with her life? It made no difference that she thought the tongue was Langlish, and that she did not even know that Láadan existed; the effect was the same. It was the soft net of guilt, that tightened at every move, that Nazareth hated.

She was a woman of the Lines. It might gnaw her heart hollow, but she would do her duty, because she understood— however dimly—what that duty meant. She lay there dulled, all the light in her put out by their merciless words. A prisoner hears, ''You are sentenced to life''; Nazareth felt that now, more sharply than she had ever had to feel it before. But she would learn. Every woman was a prisoner for life; it was not some burden that she bore uniquely. She would have all the company she could ever need.

*　　*　　*

Later, lying restless in her bed and listening with half an ear in case one of the invalid women might want her, Caroline wished they could have dared tell her just a little more. That they could have given her some simple gift of knowledge. Told her that there *was* a language called Láadan; that women had chosen its eighteen sounds with tender care—they hadn't wanted other women to have to struggle to pronounce it just because those whose lot it was to construct it happened to have English as their first Terran language. It would have pleased Nazareth to know that. It would have pleased her even more to know that Langlish, with its endlessly growing list of phonemes and the constant changes in its syntax, all the nonsensical phenomena, was only a charade. A decoy to keep the men from discovering the real language. It might have comforted her a little to know that the lengthy and solemn yearly meeting of the Encoding Project Central Caucus, at which all that had been done on Langlish in the preceding year was either undone or vastly complicated—by unanimous resolution—*was* the elaborate folly the men considered it to be, and just as hilarious as they considered it to be, and that it was so *deliberately*. Because the one thing the women could not risk was that some man should take the Project seriously. It would have been something to give Nazareth, to tell her any one of those things.

But they hadn't dared do it. Who could know how much resistance Nazareth, not even fifteen yet, would have under stress? All of them feared the day when some woman, driven beyond her endurance, would fling in the face of a detested man, "You think you know so much! You don't even know that the women have a *real* language of their own, one you men have never even suspected existed! You *stupid* fool, to believe that we women of the Lines would put together a deformity like Langlish and call it a language!"

Oh, yes. It would be so easy to do, and it was so tempting. Such a glory to see the man's astonished face. Not one woman in Barren House who couldn't tell a tale of the time she'd come within an inch of doing something like that. And not one who didn't bless the wisdom that had kept her from learning anything dangerous to the Native Tongue until she had reached an age, and a serenity, when words no longer leaped from her mouth in spite of her best intentions—and when she was not obliged to live all day and all night among males.

It crossed Caroline's mind, then, that they might well have to tell Nazareth some complicated lies as it was, after today. If, for example, she asked to see her Encodings in the Langlish computer programs.

Caroline's eyes opened wide in the darkness. Oh, Lord, yes! First thing tomorrow, women must be set to the task of entering Nazareth's Encodings, with the Langlish word-shapes she had given them—corrected for the current grotesque status of the language, of course, as they would certainly have done—into the computers. They had to be there for Nazareth to see, and they had to be there *fast*.

Chapter Fourteen

Oh, I never had a mommy
and I never had a dad,
but I've been the sweetest baby
that they ever could have had!
And it's not MY fault my mother
was a tube of plexiglass,
and my father was a needle
instead of a lusty ass!

I'm a tubie! (YAH!)
Little tubie! (RAY!)
I'm a tubie till I die—
do it again! (HEY, HEY!)
(popular drinking song of the 80's,
anonymous)

WINTER 2185. . . .

Arnold Dolbe felt absurd, and he looked absurd. You did not
see a government man, dressed in the obligatory antique business
suit that was the uniform of the government man, sitting in
another government man's office surrounded by eleven tiny children ranging in age from one to three years. But you did see
Dolbe, who was your paradigm government man, in just such a
situation. He was extremely uncomfortable, and the official he
had descended upon was furious . . . what would the staff *think*?
Dolbe had been told in no uncertain terms that he was to be
discreet about this; and instead he had come marching in with a
. . . a platoon . . . of flunkies, each carrying a load of brats. It
had created a sensation in the outer offices.

"Damn you, Dolbe," sputtered the official, one Taylor B. Dorcas the 3rd, "are you going out of your way to be a damn fool or does it just come naturally to you? I told you to be careful, goddam it! You call this careful?" Dorcas had gone to Homeroom with Arnold Dolbe.

He waved his arms, indicating the rows of children lined up on the chairs around his office, and demanded that Dolbe justify his disgraceful behavior. But Dolbe was accustomed to bureaucratic bellowers like this one, and they bothered him not at all; here he was on equal ground, and he knew the rules by which all the games were played. He watched the other man stolidly until he ran down, and then he spoke. With elaborate unconcern.

"There's nothing in any way immoral about appearing in public with eleven young children, Taylor," he remarked. "Spare me, please."

"I didn't say it was immoral! I said it was—making a spectacle of yourself. And of me!"

"Taylor, I'm not sure I follow you . . . but if what concerns you is the opinion of your subordinates, and their comments, you've made a grave mistake. If you've let them get out of hand to such a degree that they will even mention this meeting. Even to one another. Even over a beer. They should be blind, deaf, and numb to *all* such incidents, unless otherwise instructed by you. Tsk."

Taylor Dorcas blew air through his lips, loudly, and sat back down in total exasperation. Dolbe was right, of course; and he was a point up now because he'd been given the opportunity to deliver the little homily on management. Damn the man! Dorcas briefly considered punching his comset studs and issuing some rapid-fire orders, just to reestablish the principle that this was *his* turf and *he* was running things here . . . but Dolbe moved right in while he was still thinking it over.

"Now," he said, "these are the eleven children that we are turning over to the Department. I have their records with me on microfiche, and naturally they've been entered in your computers directly from my own office You won't need to be bothered about that."

"What, exactly—"

"Their 'birth' dates. Their various immunizations. Their medications administered, and their responses. Allergies, if any. Results of the standard battery of tests. Clothing sizes. All that sort of data."

"And their names, of course."

Dolbe's eyebrows went up precipitously.

"Their names? Their names, Taylor?"

"Well, don't they have names?"

"Why *would* they?"

"Well . . ."

"Look here, Taylor," said Dolbe, "every last one of these kids started life as the sum of an anonymous sperm and an anonymous egg. They have no parents; why would they have names?"

Taylor Dorcas snickered, and jabbed one finger at Dolbe. "You could have them all named after you, Arnold. You're as much their daddy as anybody."

Dolbe snorted, but he did not dignify his colleague's silliness with a reply.

"Well, hellfire and Congress, man, how do you keep track of them then?"

"They're numbered," said Dolbe primly. "I would have assumed that that would be obvious. Even to you."

"One through eleven?"

"No. These are not the first eleven test-tube babies we've worked with. They are eleven consecutive numbers, however. From left to right, Dorcas, please meet #20 through #30. Standard government issue infants, all in good health and now entirely yours."

"Mine?"

"Figuratively speaking, of course. I should say, to be precise, all entirely the wards of the Department of Health, Division of Children, Toddler Section, your subsection. I hope you've made the necessary arrangements."

"Yes. I have. If you'll have your . . . procession . . . take them all up to the roof, there's a large flyer waiting to deliver them to the federal orphanage. With nurses aboard to see to them during the flight, naturally. They'll be properly cared for."

"Very good," said Dolbe. "In that case, I'll get started."

"Now WAIT a minute, Dolbe!"

Dolbe had started to rise from his chair; he stopped, shrugged, and sat down again, suggesting that Taylor Dorcas try to express himself with greater clarity so that they could both get on to more pressing business.

"I need a few more details," protested Dorcas.

"All in that file, Taylor," said Dolbe, pointing to the folder he'd slapped onto the man's desk when he came into this room. It was marked TOP SECRET in letters four inches high, in three different colors and an assortment of different languages. Including PanSig symbols.

"I'll read the file," said Dorcas. "But right now I want a quick briefing from you."

"I'm under no obligation to provide you with anything of the kind."

"I'm aware of that. And you may refuse, of course. In which case, I will send for Brooks Showard and ask *him* to oblige me."

Dorcas had gained back the point and evened the score, and he smiled at Dolbe. Who smiled back. They hated each other, in an impersonal way. And Dolbe knew things. For instance, he knew that Taylor Dorcas' nickname in Homeroom had been "Dorky." But Dorcas knew some things, too. It was roughly a standoff.

"Very well. How much detail do you want?" asked Dolbe.

"As little as possible, please. I'm a very busy man."

"You have here," Dolbe said in the requisite monotone, "numbers 20 through 30 of the test-tube babies, popularly referred to as 'tubies,' temporarily in the custody of my unit. They were brought to normal term, decanted, provided standard health and social care, and are all in satisfactory physical condition. Two modifications were made in their environment, under my direction. First: from their initial day of life they were given small amounts of various hallucinogenic drugs, in gradually increasing doses. You'll find precise listings in their files. Second: at some point prior to the age of three months, each one was put into the G.W. Interface with a specimen of the Alien creature known as Beta-2, in the hope that this would lead to our cracking the language of the aforementioned Alien, which language is also known as Beta-2. The experiment was carried out eleven times, with appropriate modifications in the relevant variable— that is, in the combinations, doses, and scheduling of the hallucinogens. Results proved unsatisfactory, and the experiment has been terminated. The children are now being transferred, per regulations, to your custody, pursuant to their taking up residence at the federal orphanage in Arlington, Virginia. Any other information you may require is available in the files or on a need-to-know basis."

He did not say "END OF BRIEFING" or click his heels, but the nuance was there in the way he snapped his teeth shut at the period.

"I see," said Taylor Dorcas. "I see."

"Glad to hear it."

"You say the experiment didn't turn out to be satisfactory. I take it that means these children didn't learn any Beta-2."

"You take it correctly."

"The memorandum you sent over by pouch said something

about 'abnormal language development.' What does that mean, precisely?''

''We have no idea what it means—precisely.''

''Oh, come on, Arnold.''

''We do know what it means *im*precisely.''

''I'll settle for that.''

''*Look* at them,'' Dolbe advised. ''Do you notice anything unusual about them?''

Dorcas considered it, looking at each child in turn. They seemed quite ordinary. A bit oddly colored, perhaps, from too much sunlamp and not enough natural sunlight, but otherwise perfectly ordinary.

''They seem normal to me,'' he hazarded, ''except that they're awfully quiet. I suppose they're intimidated by all the hauling about, and the strangers.''

''No. They're always like this.''

''Always?''

''Always. They never make a sound. Not in any language.''

''But—''

''These children,'' Dolbe stated, ''have *never* made a sound since they were Interfaced. Never cried. Never babbled. You will notice that they appear to be almost expressionless, and that they change their position very little—that is, there appears to be no development of body-parl to speak of, either.''

''Good lord! What's the matter with them?''

Dolbe sighed.

''Nothing. Not so far as anyone can tell. Their vocal tracts are normal. Brain scans, in various modes, show no abnormality. Hearing is entirely normal, perhaps a bit better than normal. They should be able to talk, but they don't—and I might just add here that we have tried exposing them to native speakers of American Sign Language. No response whatsoever.''

''Jesus. How long will they be like this?''

''If I knew that, Taylor, I wouldn't be turning them over to you . . . that is, if I had any reason to believe that the condition was temporary. And you'll find specific instructions, straight from the top, to notify me if any one of them shows even the most rudimentary sign of attempting to communicate. In *any* way. It could be of the most extraordinary importance, if that happens.''

Taylor Dorcas whistled an idle tune between his teeth, and looked at the children again. They could have been dolls, he realized. And their eyes . . . he wouldn't have cared to spend much time looking into those eyes.

"They're not retarded?" he asked abruptly.

"No so far as we know. They're a little difficult to test, as you might imagine. But so far as the experts can determine, they have the ordinary intelligence of any human child. They just make no effort of any kind to communicate—or if they do, we are unable to recognize it as such."

"That's amazing."

"Isn't it."

"They're not catatonic . . ."

"Oh, no. They move about perfectly appropriately for whatever action frame they're engaged in. Feeding themselves, for instance. No, it's not catatonia, or anything like it."

"Well, haven't you got anything at all, any kind of explanation at *all*, to offer? Hell, man, the women who will care for these kids need some basis for dealing with them!"

"I'm sorry," said Dolbe. Meaning it.

"Nothing at all?"

"Nothing at all."

That wasn't strictly the truth, of course. Dolbe did have an explanation, straight from the lips of Thomas Blair Chornyak, who had graciously dropped by at Dolbe's request to see what he could contribute to the effort. According to Chornyak the problem wasn't that the tubies had no language, since only a condition like deep coma could be said to constitute true absence of language in a human being. The problem was something he called "absence of lexicalization."

"I can't be positive, of course," he'd told them, obviously fascinated, "because I don't have enough data to go on and I don't have time to gather more. But I can make a guess. And my guess is that these children have their heads full of nonverbal experiences and perceptions for which no language offers a surface shape . . . experiences for which no lexicalizations—no words, Dolbe, no signs, no body-parl units—exist. Not in the Earth languages they've been exposed to, and not in your Beta-2 language. If there is any such language."

When Lanky Pugh complained that he didn't understand, Chornyak put it into words of one syllable for them. Say a human being sees the sun come up, and wants to express that perception to another human being. The shape he gives that expression, in sound or any other mode, is a lexicalization. Human beings can presumably either find a lexicalization or coin one for any human experience, or any humanoid experience. But whatever these children were perceiving and experiencing, they either had no lexicalizations available to them for those perceptions and experiences, or they were using a mode of lexicalization that was literally impossible for human beings to recognize.

"Such as?" Dolbe had asked.

"Hell, *I* don't know. How do you expect me to give you, in words, an example of a perception for which there *are* no words? I could give you a rather strained analogy."

"Please do."

"Say they were communicating quite normally in English, but made sounds at frequencies the human ear is incapable of hearing . . . that wouldn't be precisely English, Dolbe, but let it go at that. Or say that whatever physical means they were employing to produce the words of American Sign Language were carried out at a speed so fast that the human eye was incapable of seeing it happen. That's not *it*, Dolbe—it's quite a different matter, because those would be approximately physiological problems—but perhaps it will serve as an analogy. The effects would presumably be the same."

"It's not a physiological problem, then. Or a technological one. There's not some gadget we could build?"

"I don't think so," Chornyak had said. "I'm sorry."

Dolbe had no intention of trying to explain that to Taylor Dorcas, not now, not ever. He very much doubted there was anything to it, anyway; the damned Lingoe godfather had been putting them on, he thought, or had just been carried away with the novelty of it all and spouting off the top of his head. But even if it was 100 percent correct, he intended to keep it strictly to himself and the three techs. He knew Chornyak wouldn't be talking about it.

Showard, sentimental as always, even about tubies, had asked the linguist if there was anything at all they could do to help the kids.

"I know what I would do," he'd answered. Without hesitation.

"What?"

"I'd just spread those kids around among as many native speakers of as many different Earth and Alien languages as could possibly be arranged."

"Why?"

"Because," Chornyak had said patiently, "it just might be possible that some language exists that does have lexicalizations these kids could make use of. Maybe not—but it's conceivable. It's probably the only thing there *is* to do."

And he'd had the damn gall to offer to take the whole eleven with him, back to the linguist Households, and see what he could do!

"You are aware," he'd said, "that we have the widest variety of native speakers of languages, both Terran and offworld, that exists anywhere. We're equipped to try the strategy I suggested, on the children's behalf. You're not. I suggest you let us have them."

The arrogance of the man . . . remembering, Dolbe felt his stomach churn. As if, just because business matters forced them to interact with the linguists, they would have turned innocent children over to them—even tubies! What did he think they were, anyway?

"No," he repeated, watching Dorcas, "we have nothing to suggest. Give them the same care you'd give any children. Good food. Plenty of exercise, etc. Have them watch the mass-eds. Put them in Homeroom, come the proper age. Etc., etc. And see what happens. And if anything *does* happen, notify me at once."

"All right, Dolbe, all right. If that's all you know."

"That's all I know."

"Arnold?"

"What?"

"Are the kids unhappy?"

"Do they look unhappy?"

"No . . . they don't look anything at all."

"Well, then. Why borrow trouble? May I have them taken up to the roof, now?"

"Sure. Go ahead . . . we've both got other things to do."

Dolbe called his minions to gather up the silent children and cart them back out again. As a concession to Taylor Dorcas, who'd been very civilized about it all, considering, he was careful to send the minions down back halls and direct them to isolated elevators. He could afford to be magnanimous, now. Now that he was getting the eerie little monsters off his hands at last.

Michaela Landry had shown a decent sorrow, shed a decent tear or two, when Great-grandfather Verdi went a tad prematurely to his heavenly reward. Next she had picked off an aged and decrepit uncle at Belview Household, where it had been a little more risky because there were only a few dozen people instead of the average hundred that lived in a Lingoe den. She had felt obliged after that to wait out the natural death of another old man, at Hashihawa Household, in order to avoid suspicion.

And now she was job hunting again, armed with references from three different Lines. The position they'd contacted her about, at Chornyak Household, sounded like a murderer's most beloved fantasy. Forty-three linguist women, all under one roof, and without any men to guard them! Where she could take them one at a time, with great care! Michaela felt this might be a project to fill all the rest of her years . . . after all, every one of those women was expected to die sooner or later, and in many cases sooner. She could make a leisurely life's work out of them, and perhaps grow old there herself, without ever having to search for another place.

The description given to her by the State Supervisor of Nurses had been short and to the point.

"This Barren House place has only female residents, and only twenty-three in need of nursing. None, as I understand it, requires anything elaborate. The patients are old and can't tend to themselves adequately. And they have the usual list of problems that old ladies are so fond of—arthritis, diabetes, migraines, that kind of thing. But nobody is really ill. Until now the other women in the place have apparently shared the nursing duties among them, but the employer says that there have come to be so many patients that they can't manage that way any longer. Which is not surprising, in view of the fact that all of them are Lingoes, and not proper women at all."

He had looked at her suspiciously, since she seemed to have an unusual tolerance for patients from the Lines; but she'd made him a brief speech detailing the revulsion she felt for linguists that had set his mind at rest.

"I understand your feelings, Mrs. Landry," he'd said approvingly. "I might say I share them. But why the devil do you keep taking nursing jobs with them, feeling like you do?"

"Because they pay extremely well, sir," she said. "I'm getting some of the people's money back, Supervisor."

He clucked approvingly and reached over to pat her knee, the slimy old pervert, and went on to tell her the usual details about her living quarters and her salary and her days off.

"Are you sure you're interested?" he asked, when he got to the end of his spiel. "I'm not certain this job qualifies for your campaign to get back some of the ill-gotten gains from these parasites . . . 200 credits a month plus room and board? That's not really very much, to look after 23 women . . . although there *is* the fact that none of them are very sick. How do you feel about it?"

Michaela cocked her head coyly, and let the lovely corners of her mouth curl for him. Her thick lashes came down, rose, fell again, and she looked at him from under their fringes.

"I will only be *starting* at that salary, Supervisor," she said sweetly.

He grinned at her.

"Saucy little piece, aren't you?"

"I beg your pardon?"

This time he didn't just pat her knee, his hand slid a good two inches up her thigh. Michaela managed to move away from him, but she did it in such a way that he was able to believe she had enjoyed his touch and given it up only out of modesty, and he looked absurdly pleased with himself.

"Opportunity for advancement there, eh?" he asked her, the silly grin still on his silly face. His silly flushed face.

"Oh yes, Supervisor. I'm sure there is."

"Well, I suppose you know what you're doing . . . a woman of experience like you."

"I rather expect I do, Supervisor." She looked at him sideways, and caught her breath just a little. "And *you* know a woman of experience when you see one, don't you, sir?"

"Oh, I've been around, Mrs. Landry!" he snickered. "You bet your sweet little . . . toes . . . I've been around! *Oh* yes, little Widow Landry, I certainly have!"

He hadn't been. She could tell by looking at him. If he'd taken a woman to bed more than three times in his whole life, she was a Senator. Thirty-five if he was a day, and she'd wager she knew how he spent his time. He'd have three inflatables at home, carefully rolled up in their waterproof cases: one blonde, one brunette, one redhead. And she'd bet one of them had his mother's face painted on her. Only a man of his type would even consider spending a lifetime supervising women. *Nurses.*

"Oh, and Mrs. Landry . . ."

"Sir?"

"I thought it might interest you to know that Thomas Blair Chornyak asked for you specifically. That is, the Lingoe who called on his behalf did. It seems that he recognized your name on the job-wanted notice . . . claims to have seen you once, as a matter of fact."

"Really?" Michaela was astonished. "Where could he have seen me, Supervisor?"

"I'm sure I don't know, sugar. Perhaps he was visiting one of the places where you've been working."

"Perhaps . . . but you'd think I'd remember."

She would have. The top linguist of all linguists? The most responsible of all linguists, and the pinnacle of prey for her? She would not have forgotten.

But the Supervisor didn't see it that way.

"Why on earth would you remember?" he chided her. "What conceivable reasons would your employers have had for telling you he was there? Goodness . . . let's remember our position in life, shall we? Thomas Blair Chornyak, may he rot in hell and all his relatives with him, is a *very* important man."

"Yes, Supervisor," said Michaela, blushing skillfully and allowing a small tear of dismay to appear at the corner of one eye. Which earned her a good deal more patting and exploring, in the guise of comforting the poor little thing. She hoped *he* would rot in hell, and was only sorry she wouldn't have an opportunity to help him on his way. But she kept the expression of vapid awe on her face, and used her eyelashes to good effect, until he was sufficiently agitated so that he had to let her alone or risk making some move that would be genuinely indiscreet.

Breathing hard, the supervisor moved away from her and fussed with a stack of papers on his desk, while Michaela watched him and waited. She was accustomed to wasting her time while men dawdled; her training at the Marital Academy had included the most detailed instruction in that so essential womanly skill. And finally, he told her that everything was in order and wished her good luck.

"And if you should ever need me . . ." he finished, giving her what he no doubt thought was a significant look.

That would be the day. If she ever needed him, she would kill her*self.*

"Thank you, Supervisor," said Michaela. "You've been so very kind. I'll go now, and leave you to your work."

He gave her permission to leave, and she thanked him again. And as she passed him on her way to the door, the appointment card for her interview at Chornyak Household safely in her pocket, she gave a slow and luxurious roll of her handsome hips in his direction.

With any luck at all, she'd have made him wet his pants.

Chapter Fifteen

The decision to marry a woman who has been properly trained for wifery need not be cold-bloodedly commercial. True . . . the procedure of reviewing threedy tapes of our clients, examining their genetic and personal files, interviewing those women who seem most promising, etc., is reminiscent of the personnel office rather than the romantic idyll. We agree, and we agree that the American man has no wish to proceed in that fashion. Furthermore, it is not necessary. There is no reason why a man cannot see to it that the woman he has chosen as his bride—in the *traditional* manner—is then enrolled at one of the seven fine marital academies whose graduates are accepted by this agency. In this way he can have the best of both worlds . . . the tender joy of young love, the ecstasy of finding and choosing the girl of his dreams, *and* the satisfaction of knowing that he will have a wife who is worthy of the role.

We suggest that you consider the alternative carefully, before deciding that good luck will see you through—and save you our modest fees. Do you really want to begin married life with an untrained woman whose only skill at wifery is the haphazard result of a few mass-ed courses and the confused efforts of her female relatives? Do you really want to risk your career and your home and your comfort to the fumbling trial-and-error techniques of an untutored girl? Do you truly believe that any degree of natural beauty of face and figure can compensate for a constant succession of social embarrassments and personal disappointments? (If you are a father, is that what you want for your sons?)

We think not. We think you want a wife that you can take with you anywhere without hesitation. We think you want a wife you can bring any guest home to in serene confidence. There are few more important investments a man can make in his future—don't leave *your* future to chance. We look forward to serving you.

(Brochure, from The Perfect Wife,™ Inc.)

SPRING 2187. . . . '

Nazareth waited in the government car, staring bleakly at the snarled traffic all around her; they would be late, and the others would be angry. She would have to ask the driver to go in with her and explain that the delay had not been avoidable. . . . Happy nineteenth birthday, Nazareth Joanna Chornyak Adiness.

She didn't feel nineteen. She felt old. Old and used up . . . The children of the Lines had little opportunity to *be* children, and that aged you. And having the children, first the boy born on her sixteenth birthday and then the twin girls two years later . . . that brought a certain maturity. But it wasn't either of those things that made her feel like one of those ancient wrinkled crones cackling crazy imprecations from the back of a cave. It was living as the wife of Aaron Adiness, who was twenty-five on the outside and just barely three years old on the inside, that had done it.

Aaron was handsome, and virile—exhaustingly virile—and with most people he was charming. Nazareth knew that many women envied her her husband. His astonishing facility at acquiring languages and learning them had waned as he had become older, but before that happened he had run up an impressive total. She had no idea how many languages he could read and write with ease, but certainly it ran to nearly one hundred.

It was the sort of thing the media doted on, and they never tired of filling little holes in programming with a feature about "the man who speaks one hundred languages!" Which was absurd, of course—he spoke perhaps a dozen—but the story was better when it was distorted, and it fed the unhealthy fascination the public had for anything to do with the linguist monsters. It was not all that much of an accomplishment, really, not for the human languages. For someone to be fluent in tongues from five different language families was impressive; to know one hundred just demonstrates that you have had a lot of opportunity and that you look on language learning the way others might look on surfing or chess. Human languages are so much alike that by the time you've learned a dozen well you've seen everything that human languages will ever do, and adding others is almost trivial.

But people weren't willing to believe that, and Aaron didn't mind encouraging the misunderstanding. Him and his "hundred languages". . . . Let a two-line filler come on the screen with his name in it, never mind that it said the same thing it had said dozens of times before, Aaron would be there jabbing the key to guarantee him a hard copy for his scrapbook. Which Nazareth was obliged to keep up-to-date, of course.

Living with him, subject to his whims, she felt that she walked from morning to night on eggshells. His feelings were so easily hurt that she rarely knew what had bruised them; but he would say, "You know very well what's wrong, you smug bitch!" and sulk for hours, until she had apologized not once but several times. And could be awarded his grudging forgiveness for a brief time.

If she didn't apologize, she could count on humiliation, because he would make her the butt of his wit—and it was fearsome—on every occasion offered him, the more public the better. In private, he would not speak to her at all; in public, he kept everyone weak with laughter at his jokes about her faults and her weight and her one front tooth that was crooked and any tiny miscalculation that she might have made in the course of the day . . . or the course of the night. He would set her up to fall into his traps, and sit back beaming while they roared at her misery; and he would raise one elegant eyebrow and cluck his tongue at her as you do at a pettish child and say, "Poor sweet baby, you have no sense of humor at all, do you?" It was a blessed relief to go to work and escape from him. Always.

The other women laughed at his jokes as well as the men, and Nazareth knew why. If they didn't, two things would happen to them. First, Aaron would include them in his war of ridicule. Second, their husbands would accuse them of being sullen and of being "wet blankets that spoil everybody's fun" and of being too stupid to understand even the simplest funny line. The men, most of them, thought Aaron was the most entertaining person they'd ever had the pleasure to have around.

If Nazareth was sufficiently humble, she might gain a day or two of respite, but no more. Not only did things she said hurt his feelings, and looks on her face hurt his feelings, and things she did or failed to do hurt his feelings, he could not *bear* it if she did anything well. If someone complimented her, Aaron was enraged. If she received a routine note of commendation for a job well done, he was furious. If she had a contract in hand and he had none, he was angry with a foul dark anger. She did not dare beat him at chess or cards, or win a game of tennis from him, or swim a few laps more than he could, because he couldn't handle any of those things.

And it was Nazareth who bore the brunt of it when Aaron was bested at something by another man. In public he was the good sport, there to shake the winner's hand and admire his skill; back in their bedroom he would pace endlessly around the room, raving about the bad luck and the series of mysterious accidents that had kept *him* from being the winner.

In public, his children were the apples of his eye, always tucked under Daddy's arm or bouncing on Daddy's knee. In private he detested them. They were useful only as possessions, something he could show off as he showed off his collection of swords or his cursed languages; he had no other interest in them. And he made no pretense of having any interest in Nazareth except for her sexual convenience, the money she earned for his private accounts (and how bitterly he complained about the 40 percent of her fees that went into the community accounts when he knew nobody but her could hear him!) and her value as a foil for his wit. If the day came when she could no longer be useful in any of those roles, he would have no more use for her than for a stranger . . . probably less. At least a stranger would have offered him novelty.

She might have complained, but there was no one to complain to. The men loved Aaron, since he had too much guile ever to turn his petulance on them—he had outgrown that, as Thomas had predicted that he would. And complaining to another woman would have been like shouting down a well. "If you live with a man, it's like that," they'd say, if they bothered to say anything. She believed Aaron to be far worse than most men—she knew, for example, that although her father was often angry with her mother he was always courteous to her in public, and she had seen no other man who tormented his wife as Aaron tormented her. But the women who did not have her problem had their own problems. There was no end to the inventiveness of men when their goal was to prove their mastery.

It was ironic that she had accepted this life for the sake of the Encodings, for there had not been any since the day of her wedding. It was not only that she never had an instant alone when she could have sat down and worked at them, not only the problem of a hidingplace for the work; she felt as if some sort of deadness had crept into her mind and removed forever whatever had been the source of her efforts.

I am stupid, Nazareth thought. And I am not alone in that opinion. Aaron thought her stupid, certainly; he would teach her sons to think so. And the one and only time that she had slipped and tried to tell another woman what her life was like, that woman had called her stupid.

"Good Lord, Nazareth," she had said. "You don't have to tolerate that kind of thing—you *manage* him, you little ninny. How can you be so stupid?"

Manage him. How do you manage a man? What did it *mean*, to "manage" him?

"Mrs. Chornyak, I'd better go in with you and explain."

Nazareth jumped . . . she hadn't realized that the traffic had started moving again, much less that they'd arrived.

"Thank you, Mr. Dressleigh," she murmured. "I'd be very grateful if you would do that."

"Part of my job," said the driver, carefully making the point that nothing else would have caused him to exert himself on behalf of a woman of the Lines. And then he was off, with Nazareth doing her best to keep up with him. He would explain, he would be gone, and this evening some equally reluctant hero would come to collect her. It made no difference to Nazareth; she had never had a driver who was friendly, or even very polite. Or who could be bothered to get her name right. She came from Chornyak Household, she wore a wedding ring—she would, therefore, be "Mrs. Chornyak," and never mind the details.

But when the explanations and the formalities were over, and she was finally seated in the interpreter's booth and arranging her dictionaries around her in preparation for beginning her work, she found that the universe had not forgotten her birthday after all. It had in fact prepared for her an absolutely splendid birthday gift, something she never could have conjured up for herself.

She had expected that this day would be more than usually tiresome, because the subject of the negotiation was an import tariff—never a fascinating item—and because she had no help whatsoever. Her nine-year-old backup was solidly locked into a negotiation in his own Interface language that could not be postponed; the six-year-old was down with one of the contagious childhood illnesses; and Aquina Noumarque was working in Memphis and could not come to help her either. That meant no support, either formal or informal; it was not an easy way to work.

Because her mind was taken up with the problems this would

mean for her, she didn't even realize anything was wrong until she began to hear whispers and to feel the sort of tension that is the product of body-parl shouting distress. It caught her attention at last, and she looked up from her materials to see what minor catastrophe had upset the negotiations . . . perhaps she was in luck and a government man had broken a leg? Not painfully, of course, and not seriously; she wasn't a vindictive woman.

And there sat her Jeelods in their usual coveralls, staring at heaven knows what, with an expression of grim pleasure on their square faces, and Nazareth gasped aloud.

"Dear sweet suffering saints," she said under her breath, not even stopping to be sure that the microphones hadn't yet been activated, "those are *females*!"

They certainly were. Even in the loose garments that were prescribed by their state religion, even with their hair close-cropped in a way that no Terran woman would have ever chosen, it was clear that they were females. Either they were unusual specimens, or the Jeelod woman was typically large of breast; large of breast and distinctly *pointed* of breast.

Nazareth dropped her eyes swiftly to the smooth plastic surface in front of her and fought not to let her delight show on her face. It would never do for the bitch linguist to betray her pleasure in finding herself in this situation—there would be scathing complaints to her father about the undiplomatic manner in which she had approached this diplomatic crisis.

There was a soft tap on the back of the booth, which did not surprise her—after all, they couldn't just all sit there frozen as if the sun had been brought to a standstill, someone had to do something—and she said "Yes?" without looking around, carefully bringing the expression on her face under control before she had to show it to whoever this might be.

"Mrs. Adiness . . . I hope I didn't startle you."

She turned, smiling politely, just as the man slipped into the booth and took the seat beside her. Not a government man, then . . . who was he? He was handsome, and he must have been twice her age, but he wore no uniform or insignia by which she could identify him.

"Mrs. Adiness, I'm going to speak very quickly here," he said, keeping his voice low. "I'm sorry to be so abrupt, but you will understand the necessity for bypassing the amenities. My name is Jordan Shannontry, of Shannontry Household, and I was supposed to see if I could be of service here in some peripheral fashion . . . we had word that you were completely on your own today, and REM34-5-720 has been a kind of hobby of mine.

Since I was free, and it was obvious that you would have your hands full, I came on over—but I wasn't expecting *this*.''

"Neither were the government men," said Nazareth in her most carefully noncommittal voice.

"How could they possibly not know better than this?" he asked her.

"They?"

"The Jeelods . . . surely they know the Terran culture better than this! They've been negotiating with us, trading with us, for nearly fifteen years."

"Oh, they know better," said Nazareth. "This is a deliberate tactic to stall negotiations . . . and to insult the American negotiators."

"Are you sure?"

"Quite sure, Mr. Shannontry."

"Well, damn them, then!"

"As you say, sir."

"The arrogance . . . not to mention the just plain bad manners. . . ."

"Oh, yes. The Jeelods are not noted for their exquisite manners, Mr. Shannontry. And I thank you very much for wanting to lend a hand, by the way—I didn't know there was anyone to call on."

Shannontry shrugged carelessly. "I'm not *much* to call on, my dear," he said. "I can say hello and good-bye and thank you, and very little more; and I say what little I *can* say with an accent that will have you in stitches. But I read the language easily enough, and the Department thought I could at least help with translations, look things up for you in the dictionaries, that sort of trivia."

"It was kind of you to come," said Nazareth.

"Well . . . it was my pleasure. I was looking forward to actually hearing the language in use, frankly. But I don't know what we do now, Mrs. Adiness, and it's very obvious that those men don't know either."

Nazareth permitted herself one smile, and said "Well, there is certainly nothing *I* can do, Mr. Shannontry."

"No . . . under the circumstances, there certainly isn't. Good God . . . now what?"

Nazareth looked bewildered and helpless, and waited. She was having a wonderful time. The government men could not possibly begin negotiations with female Jeelods; that was out of the question. No female, by definition, had adult legal rights, which would make any decisions vacuous in any case. Furthermore, it would set a precedent and lead to the potential for endless repetition of this tactic from other Alien peoples. There were quite a large number of extraterrestrial cultures which allowed the females of their species what appeared to be equal or roughly equal status with the males.

On the other hand, the government men had no way of knowing what precisely they *could* do, without causing an interplanetary diplomatic crisis. And the longer they just sat there, the worse it was going to get.

There went one of them now, scuttling for the door, to get some instructions from somebody higher up. Nazareth chuckled, hoping he'd run into somebody from the team that had so proudly announced a few years back that they had cracked one of the REM18 languages by use of a computer alone; it had been necessary to send a linguist to tell them, very gently, that the word they had translated as English "friend" in fact meant "one whom it is permissible to eat, provided the proper spices are used in preparation of the corpse." Nothing like a government "expert" to liven up one's already marvelous nineteenth birthday!

As the man left the room, the Jeelod negotiating team went at once into the posture of ritual absence, and Jordan Shannontry said, "Look at that, now—what does that mean?"

"They are insulted," Nazareth told him. "When they perceive an insult they will always do that. It slows things down very effectively."

"Lord help us all," sighed Shannontry. "Is there anything at all that we can do?"

"I'm afraid it isn't my place to propose a course of action," said Nazareth, quite properly. She had not trained as a wife, but she knew her role as woman linguist as well as any woman in the Lines. Her place was to interpret and to translate, to respond as best she could to direct questions posed to her regarding the language and the culture of the Aliens involved in the negotiation, and otherwise to be silent. It most emphatically was not her place to suggest strategies or diplomatic policy to anyone present.

Shannontry studied her carefully, and she flushed slightly under his steady glance, and looked away.

"This is completely unfair to you," he said emphatically. "You're far too young to be put in such a position, and I resent it deeply . . . it's unkind, and it's inexcusable."

Nazareth had no idea what to say, and she didn't dare look at him. He sounded as though he were genuinely concerned about her, but she knew better than to rely on that—any moment, he might spring the trap he was constructing with the feigned gallant words, as Aaron did, and then she would be in trouble. She kept her silence, and waited, wary as any burnt child with an unfamiliar fire to contend with.

"Mrs. Adiness," he said gently, no anger at all in his voice that she could spot, "this just won't do. My dear, if you will tell me what to say, I will go over there and *say* it. Abominably, of course—but I will say it. Just write it down for me and model it for me a time or two, and I'll take care of the matter."

"Would you do that?"

"Of course."

Nazareth was charmed. He really was going to help.

"We have plenty of time, then," she said.

"We do?"

She explained about the absence rituals lasting eighteen minutes and eleven seconds, and he made an impatient noise.

"I suppose in this case it's just as well," he muttered.

"Probably."

"Well . . . what shall I say to them?"

Nazareth thought a moment. First there would be the narrative frame that would shelter the direct sentence, and the triple particle that would disambiguate the three embeddings. Then the very simple message. . . . WE WILL BE MOST HAPPY TO WAIT UNTIL YOUR MEN ARE ABLE TO COME TO THE NEGOTIATION. The other half of the narrative frame . . . some honorifics . . .

"It will be long," she said dubiously.

"That's all right," he answered. "I'll manage. And if my barbarous accent offends their ears, it's their own damn fault. Just write it out."

She did, and she said it for him.

"Again, please."

She said it again.

"That first cluster. . . ."

She repeated it slowly, tipping her chin so that he could see clearly the position of her tongue against her teeth.

"Oh, I perceive. Like that. . . . All right, here we go. Listen to me, please—will they understand?"

Nazareth would have winced at the mangled stream of sound that represented Shannontry's oral skill at REM34, but that would have been as bad manners as those the Jeelods were exhibiting. She bit her lip, instead, and he laughed.

"That bad? Here . . . brace yourself, Mrs. Adiness, and I'll try it again."

Better. Not much, but better.

"Yes," she said. "They'll understand that, even if they don't like it very much. And it's time, I think—yes, they're turning around. Perhaps if you felt willing to go ahead before the man from the Department gets back. . . ."

"Absolutely," he said, apparently not offended by the hint of a suggestion of action. "I'll be right back."

Nazareth would never have dared leave the interpreter's booth and march right over to the Alien delegation, and she doubted that many men would have, but Jordan Shannontry seemed as comfortable as if he'd been in his own Household. She watched, as delighted as if it had been an entertainment especially for her benefit, while he faced the Jeelod women, bowed first to the left and then to the right—which showed that he had studied the culture, for all his shortcomings with the pronunciation of the language—and just said it right out. Twice. Slowly. And then again, to be absolutely certain that they had heard and understood.

The American negotiators didn't like it one little bit, and as Shannontry made his way back across the room they caught at his sleeve and made desperate "What's going on?" faces at him, but he was magnificent. He shook them off as if they were tiny children, and he did not stoop to explain one thing to them. Marvelous, thought Nazareth, marvelous! To be so certain of yourself . . . to be so controlled! To dare to behave like that . . .

He was with her in half a minute, and he touched her wrist politely, not sitting down.

"I suggest we leave at once, Mrs. Adiness," he said. "Before our federal friends can create any additional commotion. Come—I'll get you out of here, and then I will come back and explain the situation."

She was afraid to do that, but he was firm, overruling her objections and moving her briskly out of the booth and into the corridor, gathering up her work materials for her as they went so that she didn't have to bother with them. Only when they were safely outside the conference room and she was seated in the cubicle reserved for the linguists' use during breaks and delays did he say anything more.

"You're not to worry," he said. "Not at all. Whatever happens, I'll explain that you behaved precisely as you should have behaved and that there is no reason for anyone to be annoyed with you in even the slightest degree. If they want to complain, let them complain about me—you did nothing but comply with *my* instructions, and if there was an error it was *my* error. Now you just relax, dear, and wait, while I go see what can be done about all this. I assume they will send a team of men?"

"Oh, yes," she said. "Yes, of course. They are as anxious to get the tariff established—in their favor, naturally—as we are to have it firmly established in ours. This was just a—a tactic."

"Worked very well, too, didn't it?"

Nazareth ducked her head to hide her face, and agreed that it surely had.

"Well . . . we'll get it settled. And a decent Jeelod team at the table. And then, my dear, I will send someone to bring you back to the booth, and not until."

And he was gone, leaving her entirely bemused. She was not only impressed, she was astonished . . . she tried to imagine Aaron, in such a situation, and she laughed aloud. He would not have been there in the first place, not Aaron. He would work if a woman were there acting as *his* backup. He would even condescend to work on a multilingual negotiation with a woman serving as interpreter for one of the other languages. But act as backup for a woman himself? He would have gone to any lengths, made up any excuse, before he would have done such a thing.

It crossed her mind then, oddly, that it must be miserable to be Aaron Adiness and have to live in constant terror of your own ego. It had never before occurred to her.

Poor Aaron. That was a new thought. Poor Aaron.

Chapter Sixteen

Q: What do you see, Nils? Can you tell me?

A: (LAUGHTER)

Q: Try : . . it's very important. What do you see? What is it, that you're looking at?

A: It. No. Not it.

Q: Go ahead, Nils . . . call what you see 'it.' Pretend that 'it' will do. What do you see?

A: (LAUGHTER)

Q: Nils, you're not trying! You promised you would try, for the sake of science, and for my sake. Please, try, man. . . .

A: It's not a thing. It's not a not-thing. It's not an idea. It's not a non-idea. It's not a part of reality. It's not a not-part of reality. It's not a not-part of a not-part of not-reality.

Q: Nils, that's not a hell of a lot of help to us.

A: (LAUGHTER)

> (Dr. Quentun Silakady,
> interviewing an experimental subject under LSD)

Somehow Brooks Showard had taken it for granted there would be no more of the experiments that combined babies and hallucinogenic drugs. It had been hell, watching the tubies fail one after another, when they'd started with such high hopes.

And it *had* been a good idea, by God. . . . Beau St. Clair was suffering a kind of soul-destroying guilt now, that the effing med-Sammys didn't seem to be able to do much about—not and keep him conscious enough for duty, at any rate—but it had been a *fine* idea. An excellent idea, that could have been the breakthrough they'd been praying for. Except that it hadn't worked.

And considering how it turned out, considering what they had to send off to the orphanage in Arlington, Brooks took it for granted that that was the end of it. He and Beau and Lanky had agreed, too, that whatever the next move was going to be, it was up to Arnold Dolbe. Lanky'd done his share; endless variations with the computers. And Beau and Brooks had done theirs. Now it was up to Arnold.

Who surprised them. They stared at him, shocked speechless.

"Well? Why the funny looks?" Dolbe said belligerently.

When they still said nothing he turned bright red and repeated himself. "I said, *why the funny looks?*"

Showard cleared his throat and tried to speak for all of them.

"We thought . . . we thought it had been pretty conclusively demonstrated that the hallucinogen idea didn't work, Arnold. A good idea. A *damn* good idea—but it didn't work."

"I don't agree," said Dolbe.

"Hey!"

"I don't. I don't agree." Dolbe spoke doggedly, staring at them with the stubborn expression that had carried him through many a situation when he knew nothing about what he was doing. He expected it to carry him through this time, when he had at least one or two facts at his command. "I think it worked rather well."

"Dolbe, you are clean out of your pitiful mind," said Lanky Pugh. "And I believe I speak for all of us when I say that. Clear out of your pitiful mind and flying off into the never-nevers. You need total rewiring, Dolbe."

"No, I don't," Dolbe insisted. "No. *You're* wrong; I'm right."

"Well, then, kindly explain to us in what way it 'worked,' Dolbe! We didn't learn one effing thing about Beta-2. And look what happened to those tubies!"

"Precisely."

"Oh for sweet Jesus SAKES!" Showard bellowed.

"No, wait a minute," said Dolbe. "Try to control yourselves, and listen to what I have to say. It is true—we didn't make any progress with the acquisition of Beta-2. But—and this is very, very important—we did make progress with the project itself, as project. You don't seem to remember, men—but those babies did *not* die. They did *not* go mad. They did *not* suffer. Nothing happened to them.''

"Naw. Except that we destroyed their minds.''

"Oh Showard, you're worse than a woman with your damn sickening sentimentality! There is no reason whatsoever to believe that we destroyed their minds, or harmed their minds, or in any way interfered with their minds in a negative sense. None! You've seen their tests; their minds are perfectly normal.''

"Yeah? Then how come they don't communicate, Dolbe? With their perfectly normal minds.''

"We don't know that.''

"I thought the Lingoe explained it,'' said Lanky. "I didn't understand one damn thing he said, but I thought the rest of you did.''

"Never mind that,'' said Dolbe impatiently. "It doesn't matter. I don't claim that the results of the experiments were perfect— only that they did, at last, show progress. Positive advancement. For the very first time, since the beginning of this project! Now I am not for one minute willing to just let that go down the drain here, no siree. I intend to *build* upon that progress—and I must say that it astonishes me that you men are not solidly behind me.''

"Dolbe, you're such a shit,'' said Brooks.

"Thank you. I'm very fond of you, too, I'm sure.''

Beau St. Clair glared at both of them and told them to for chrissakes cut it out, they had enough trouble.

"Let me see if I understand what you're suggesting,'' he said to Dolbe. "You want us to take the new volunteer infant that came in last night, right? And start it on the drugs we wiped out the tubies with? And then you want us to Interface it, whatever it turns into. Is that right, Dolbe?''

"I wouldn't have added all the embellishments, Beau, but you have the general idea.''

"Aw, hell, Dolbe,'' Beau moaned, wholly miserable, "you know what's going to happen if we do that!''

"I don't know anything of the kind,'' Dolbe objected. "And neither do you. We have absolutely no way of knowing what will happen if that experiment is carried out with a normal human infant rather than a test-tube baby. And it was my understanding—in fact, I have referred to my notes on the meeting at which we discussed this originally, and my understanding is entirely accurate—it was my own understanding that the whole point of beginning with the tubies was so that when we once again had a volunteered womb-infant we would have had sufficient experience with the hallucinogens to be reasonably certain of what we were doing."

"He's right," said Lanky. "I hate to admit it, but he's right. That *was* the idea."

"Yeah, but that was before we saw what happened to the tubies!"

"By god, Showard, you're going to make me angry if you keep on like that!" Dolbe declared. "I tell you *nothing* happened to the tubies. You can go over to the orphanage any time and see them—they're doing just fine."

"Are they communicating?"

"They're eating. They're sleeping. They're healthy. They're up walking around, playing."

"Playing?"

"Well . . . doing things. They're not hurt."

"You're crazy."

"Be that as it may, Showard, it's time to get on with this! We've got a healthy infant, a normal ordinary born-of-woman infant, and it's only two weeks old. The mother died in a flyer accident, and the father's young; he doesn't want to be saddled with the kid and was glad to have us take it off his hands . . . he had plenty of places to put the ten thousand credits, like they always do. It's an ideal situation, *if* we move on it; there hasn't been time for the child's perceptions to even thicken up, so to speak, much less harden. And I want to get right to it."

"Great," said Beau. "Just great."

"I appreciate your enthusiasm, Beau."

Dolbe looked down at a sheet of paper in front of him, his lips moving as he read it over, and then he looked at them again.

"I've spoken to the pediatricians," he said. "We've discussed each of the previous experimental subjects. And we are agreed that the most satisfactory regime of drugs is the one used with #23—we'll follow that one with the volunteer infant."

"In what way was that the most satisfactory?" asked Beau curiously. "How the hell did they decide that? They all turned out the same way."

Dolbe refused to discuss it, saying that it was irrelevant, and Brooks Showard declared that that had to mean they'd closed their eyes and stuck a number with a pin, and Dolbe sighed deeply. Sonorously. A good and weary man, overburdened by his incompetent subordinates.

"Gentlemen," he said tightly, "whatever your personal feelings on this matter are, we have work to do. And we are keeping the government waiting. I've already notified the lab, and the drugs are on their way—we'll begin this afternoon."

"What the devil's the hurry, Dolbe?" Showard demanded. "I'd rather get drunk this afternoon, and start in the morning."

"Sorry, Showard. We don't know what the critical point is, and we aren't going to take any chances. We're very lucky to get a volunteer this young; let's not waste any time. In fact, if you hadn't been drunk last *night*, we would have started then."

"You really think this is worth a try?" asked Lanky Pugh. Lanky didn't care anything about babies or tubies either one, but he had a low tolerance for failure when he was involved in a project. Lanky was accustomed to clearing up other people's failures, not making messes of his own. He was awfully tired of this whole damned thing.

"We know," Dolbe said solemnly, clasping his hands in front of him, "that there is some crucial difference between the brain of the normal infant and the brain of the test-tube infant. It isn't possible for us to determine exactly what that difference is, in physiological or neurological or even psychological terms—but the scientists are all in agreement that there *is* a difference and they are working to identify it. There is certainly the possibility that whatever it is, it has something to do with the language acquisition mechanism in the human child. That is, it may be *precisely* the difference that we need. And we will never find out unless we try."

"Okay," said Lanky. "You're the boss."

"Thank you, Pugh," said Arnold Dolbe. "It's a pleasure to know that somebody in this room remembers that."

None of them, not in their wildest dreams, not in the depths of their most alcoholic delusions, had anticipated what did happen. They thought they had seen everything, but they were quite wrong.

. The baby tolerated the regime of hallucinogens without incident. No side effects, no allergic reactions; it seemed perfectly contented. (It *still* seemed perfectly contented, for that matter, even now.) They had put it through the regime, patiently spending the full four weeks the doctors insisted on.

And then, in suspense once again in spite of themselves, they put it carefully into the Interface with the flickering (?) thing they called Beta-2.

And the flickering thing went mad this time. At least they assumed that must have been what happened. Showers of sparks (?) flew from one end of its half of the Interface to the other. The air in the Interface took on a moiré pattern that none of them could look at. There were vibrations . . . not noises precisely but vibrations . . . thudding (?) around them. Things quivered and split off and flowed and flapped wildly. . . .

When it was over, not nearly quickly enough, the Alien was quite dead. So far as they, or the scientists, could tell. Which was just as well, since no one would have dared turn it loose and return it to where it had come from if it had survived. And there was only PanSig available for explaining to the rest of the Beta-2's, back at the old plantation or whatever they lived on, what had happened to their dearly beloved departed.

Arnold Dolbe bitterly resented the fact that Thomas Chornyak had refused to take on the job of making that explanation, or even delegating it to some other member of the Lines. It seemed to Dolbe that that was inexcusable.

"Absolutely not," the linguist had said. "You made this mess. We keep telling you, and you won't listen, and so you keep making messes. You clean it up."

"But we are not *good* at PanSig!"

"Nobody is good at PanSig," snorted Thomas. "It's not something that it's possible to be good at. It's a system of very crude and primitive signals for emergencies . . . and I suppose this is one of those. Jesus, what a mess."

At such moments Dolbe wished he had followed the Pentagon's advice and continued to let their "John Smith" types act as liaison between Government Work and Chornyak, instead of insisting that he be allowed to observe the project directly and talk with him and with the technicians without intermediary. He had hoped things would go better if they eliminated the middlemen. He had been wrong.

"Mr. Dolbe," said the linguist, "you have scores of staffers from D.A.T. who are trained in PanSig. Find somebody with guts and let him get on with this. Putting it off won't help matters . . . for all you know, that Alien was part of some kind of collective animal, or was completely telepathic. The rest of the Beta-2's may already know that it's dead."

"We know that."

"And you're scared. That's why you called me."

"We called you because you're an expert on such matters," Dolbe replied with the stiffest of upper lips. "We aren't scared."

"Then you're bigger fools than I thought," said Thomas, walking out on them. "I'd be scared shitless in your place."

Definitely, thought Dolbe, he should have let the old system stand. Then it would have been one of the John Smiths who had to be humiliated like that, and not him.

And then the linguist had stuck his head back in the door and said, "Dolbe, I'll make you the same offer I made last time. I'll take that baby off your hands."

"That won't be necessary," Dolbe whispered.

"No? Doesn't it appear to be in the same condition the other eleven children were?"

"So far as we know."

"Then let me have it—we might be able to help it."

"It will go to the orphanage, as did the others," Dolbe said, fighting to keep each word coming, something about the linguist's face making him long to crawl on the floor on his belly and beg for mercy, "and it will receive the very finest care. You may be sure of that. You can't have it."

Chornyak had given him a look that Dolbe would remember forever; but he had not said another word, and that was the last they'd seen of him.

And now Dolbe was packing. He had never expected this, never thought the day would come when he'd have to pack his things and move out of this office. His *office*. His *lab*. His *project!* It tore him apart. It twisted him, right in the guts.

The orders from the Pentagon had been very unlike the usual government messages—you could understand this set without the slightest trouble. They said: TERMINATE PROJECT. Just that. No explanation. No account of what had happened when the D.A.T. staffer told the other Beta-2's about the accident, in PanSig. No remarks of any kind. Just TERMINATE PROJECT. And their new division assignments, in a postscript.

It wasn't fair. True, everything they'd done so far had failed. But they had *learned* things! What had happened to the idea of knowledge for the sake of knowledge? Truth for the sake of truth? They'd done a damn good job, considering the magnitude of the task and what they'd had to work with.

The other men had only laughed when he told them. Laughed! And Showard, curse him, had said, "How come new assignments, Dolbe?"

"Well, of course, we'd get new assignments."

"I don't see why," Showard drawled. "Remember? It was crack Beta-2 or the world would end. Remember? The General himself told us so, him and his spaghetti and his blinding white teeth and his cute little soldier suit. If the world is about to end, I'd rather get drunk. How about you, Beau? Lanky? Wouldn't you rather get drunk?''

The only consolation in this move, thought Dolbe, who had never had even a fleeting interest in frontier colonies and wasn't looking forward to living on the one they'd picked to transfer him to, was that he'd never have to see Showard or St. Clair or Lanky Pugh again. The Pentagon had scattered the four of them as widely as they could possibly be scattered, and Dolbe found it almost unbearable that Lanky Pugh was being allowed to stay here on Earth. New Zealand might not be Washington, or Paris, but at least it was civilized. So Pugh had a certain touch with computers . . . it was still unjust.

"Never mind, Arnold," he told himself out loud. "Never mind. Just put it all behind you, and get on with what you've been ordered to do."

A team player, that's what he was. By God.

And he wasn't going to let down the side.

Chapter Seventeen

"Behavioral Notes"

ONE: That: one never has to say please.
          What does it mean? It means that please is not required because your needs are known, and without being politely asked it is still possible to refuse you.

TWO: That: one is always welcome.
          What does it mean?
          It means that there occur from time to time empty spaces which you are allowed to fill and during which your presence constitutes no real annoyance.

THREE: A shudder.
          What does it mean?
          It means that an error has been made in the translation.

(20th century "feminist" poem)

Nazareth could not have said precisely when her personal involvement with Jordan Shannontry began. She had never had a flirtation, never even a "crush," and there had been no opportunity for her to learn anything about romance from her husband. One day Jordan was simply her informal backup on duty, always courteous, always as helpful as his limited knowledge of REM34 allowed him to be. And then without any transition that she could identify he was something more, and she found herself always in a kind of breathlessness next to him. Her eyes went more and more to his strong hands as they turned the pages of his books and worked deftly with the microfiches; she knew those hands so intimately that she could see them with her eyes tightly closed . . . the texture of the skin and its color, the elegance of the joints, the haze of dark soft hair, the bend of the wrists. All of it seemed to her to have an endless fascination so that she could never tire of exploring it again; and when his hands touched her, accidentally or in the course of their joint duties, she went absolutely still, as a rabbit freezes when the owl swoops down upon it. Presumably, this was the "love" about which she had heard so much . . . she had no real way of knowing. And the negotiations dragged on and on.

Jordan was kind, and that was probably her downfall. She wasn't accustomed to kindness from men, and had rarely encountered it. The men of her Household, in the brief bits of time they had with her, were simply correct; and she had never had any contact with other men except as an interpreter. The interpreter was paid no more attention than a business machine, especially if she was a woman; after all, as Thomas said so frequently, a circuit will carry any message you want to send over it, but you do not assume from that fact that it understands what you have said. It was his standard response to accusations that the linguists allowed their women to take part in affairs properly reserved for men.

As for small girls interpreting, or women past thirty. . . . they were invisible. Nazareth much doubted that the men they worked with even knew they existed for more than a few seconds at the beginning and end of each negotiation. They disappeared from the male consciousness in just the same way that the miniature earphones—so annoying to the wearer for an instant or two after they were inserted—faded out of awareness.

Jordan Shannontry not only treated her kindly, he paid her compliments. He had remarked once on the tasteful arrangement of her hair. He had mentioned that she had a lovely throat. A lovely throat! On a very bad day, when nothing at all went right and every one of the men at the table was cross and on a nervous hair trigger, Jordan had brought in a yellow rose and laid it across her dictionary. No one had ever given Nazareth a rose before, not even on her wedding day. When she looked at him now, she could scarcely breathe for the thudding of her heart, and since that could well have interfered with her effectiveness as interpreter she was careful *not* to look at him. Only at his hands; she allowed herself that. She had thrown the yellow rose away, rather than chance its being found no matter how carefully she tried to hide it; there was no way that she could have explained how she had come to have it in her possession.

The day came, as it inevitably had to come, when there was only one more session of negotiations left, one more day when they would sit side by side in the interpreter's booth. She knew she wouldn't see him again afterward unless she made some sort of effort herself. What sort, she had no idea . . . she had heard of "affairs" but was completely ignorant of how they were initiated. One thing she was dead certain of—whatever was done would be done by the man in the situation, not the woman. But surely she had to let him know that she was willing?

She did not let the word "adultery" come into her mind, adultery being an offense second only to murder . . . she had a feeling that within the Lines it might well be considered *more* serious than murder. She had gone no further in her imagination than lying in Jordan's arms, both of them fully and decorously clothed, and perhaps talking together . . . perhaps his lips might touch her hair. So far, and no further.

All that last day she thought, whenever she was not actually interpreting; but no graceful stratagem came to her, and as the hours passed and she knew that if she didn't act she would never have another opportunity her anxiety became panic. And that was how it happened that she found herself, walking down the corridor behind her escort to the government car with Jordan beside her, turning suddenly to him and reaching up to whisper into his ear "I love you, Jordan, I love you so very very much!" And then running. Running full tilt past the flabbergasted government aide, and almost leaping into the car. Slamming the door behind her, praying that the driver would hurry.

"Something wrong, Mrs. Chornyak?" the man said when he reached the car. "Never saw a lady linguist take off like that before, I must say. You all right?"

"A little sick at my stomach," she managed. "I'm sorry."

"No problem," he said. "We'll get you home, then."

She waited through that afternoon, having no idea what might happen next, alternately wishing she had done nothing at all and wishing she had done far more, wishing there were someone she could talk to and knowing there was nobody she trusted that much. And it would not be fair, even if she had had someone; whoever it was, by her telling she would have implicated them in what she was about to do. She would not do that.

Every soft signal from the comset made her jump, but none of the calls was for her. And then, a few, minutes after eight o'clock, Rachel found her out in the gardens and told her that Thomas wanted to see her in his office.

"Oh, damn," said Nazareth, "I'm in no mood to hear about the next contract, or whatever complaints there are on this one, or whatever else Father has to talk about!"

"Really."

"Well, I'm not. I'm worn out."

"Nazareth, your father didn't ask me to come find out if you were willing to go to the office. You know that. He sent me to tell you he was waiting for you there. Please don't trouble me with your nonsense."

"I'm sorry, Mother. It was rude of me. . . . I guess I really am tired."

"No doubt you are," said Rachel calmly, and went on about her business, saying only, "Don't keep Thomas waiting now, dear; he doesn't like that."

No, he didn't; that was true. Whatever he wanted, the longer she put off hearing about it the more unpleasant it would be, and so she hurried.

When she opened the door of the room set aside for the Head of the Household, her father was at his desk, as she had anticipated. But she had not been expecting to see Aaron there with him, sitting in the armchair, nor was she expecting the bottle of wine open and already half-empty on the desk. She stopped in the doorway, surprised, and Thomas motioned to her to let the door close and join them.

"Sit down, my dear," he said. "Make yourself comfortable."

Nazareth was wary instantly; they both had that satisfied expression that went with some new and delightful project that would mean endless annoyance for her but carried some advantage for them. What had they scheduled her for now? Aaron wore an expression that could only be described as a smirk; it had to be something he was really confident she would detest.

"Nice to see you, Natha," he said, all cordiality and cooing welcome. "You do look lovely."

There was a time when Nazareth would have explained to him that the reason she was so grubby was because she'd been out working in the gardens when Rachel came to get her, but she no longer bothered. She kept still, and waited to see what they had for her. Work on a frontier colony, maybe? Someplace that would involve a dozen frantic transfers from one means of transport to another? She detested travel, and they both knew that.

She expected something dreadful, but she did not expect what it turned out to be.

"Nazareth," her father said, "we had a visitor this afternoon."

"Nice man," Aaron put in.

"Indeed he is," said Thomas. "And a gentleman."

"Well?" asked Nazareth. "Does it concern me, this gentleman? Or is this just a game and I don't know the opening move?"

"Nazareth, it was Jordan Shannontry."

Nazareth went very still. What was this?

"Nazareth? Did you hear what I said?"

"I heard you, Father."

"Have you anything to say?"

"As you said," she began, cautiously, so cautiously, "he is a nice man. He's been very helpful. Not like having a real backup, of course, but still it gives me a break now and then. A hard worker."

"He had a rather disturbing story to tell me, Nazareth," Thomas said.

"Oh? He did? Did something go wrong? Nobody spoke to me about it, Father—I didn't know."

"It had nothing to do with your professional functions."

"Oh?"

"Nothing at all." Thomas poured himself some wine and looked at her over the top of the glass, handing the bottle on to Aaron. "According to Shannontry, you ended your working day today by accosting him in the hall—in public!—and blurting into his ear that you 'loved him very very much'. And then bolting like a badly trained horse."

"Oh," she said again. "Oh."

" 'Oh?' Is that all you have to say? I assume Shannontry would not make up such a wild hairy tale—but you *are* my daughter. I'll listen to you if you care to deny it."

He watched her, and when she said nothing, stunned into total silence and as unable to move as if she'd been fast-frozen, he went on.

"I thought as much. He was completely at a loss, inasmuch as he is a respectable married man with numerous children, and you are alleged to be a respectable married woman, etc. And inasmuch as he cannot conceive of what made you take such a bizarre notion."

Finally Nazareth could speak, although the hoarse words were not in a voice she recognized as hers.

"He told you. . . . He actually came here, to this house, and he *told* you!"

Thomas raised his eyebrows, and Aaron looked even more delighted.

"Certainly," said Thomas. "What would you have expected the poor man to do?"

"I believe, Thomas," her husband suggested, "that she thought he'd come climbing up a ladder to her window—figuratively speaking, of course, since what he'd have to do is come down through a tunnel—perhaps with a band of strolling musicians warbling lovesongs. Or send a messenger with a note begging her to flee with him to . . . oh, to Massachusetts at least."

"Is that what you expected, Nazareth?" asked Thomas gravely. "Are you that much of a fool?"

She bit her lip and hoped she would die, and he kept on.

"*Certainly* he came here and told me, and I would have been most surprised if he hadn't! He is well aware of his obligations as a gentleman—and when something as idiotic as this happens, it is a gentleman's duty to go tell the female's father of her ridiculous behavior. In his place, any man of breeding would have done precisely what he did. Did you think he would just ignore it, you utter ninny?"

"I didn't think he would . . . tattle!"

Thomas sighed, and exchanged a long look with his son-in-law.

"My dear child," he said, "that is not a very well-chosen word."

"It seems to me to be exactly the right word."

"Well, that's not bright of you. When a young woman misbehaves in the manner that you took it upon yourself to misbehave this afternoon—and I must tell you, Nazareth that I was *very* surprised—some responsible person witnessing the incident has to inform the family, so that they can decide what to do about the situation. Since Shannontry was, thank God, the only person who knew precisely what you had done, he had no choice but to tell us himself. And I'm certain it wasn't pleasant for him."

"He came here," Nazareth repeated dully, through the fog of his words, "and he told you, and he told Aaron—"

"Of course not! God, girl, you leap from one stupidity to another like a goat! He came here and he told *me*, because I am your father, and the Head of this Household. He did not tell your husband; as is quite proper, he left that unpleasant duty to me."

Thomas had told Aaron! Her own father! The room wavered and twitched before her eyes like a comset screen with interference; things took on the look of flat cardboard cutouts; she stared fixedly at a point behind Thomas' head. In her ears a single high tone keened unbearably on and on . . . This world, she thought.

This world. Only a male god could have created this repulsive, abominable world.

"Nazareth!"

She didn't answer, but the vicious slap of the word caught her attention sufficiently that she raised her head a little and looked at her father; it seemed to her that Aaron's grin had spread all around her like spilled syrup on a steep floor. It came at her from everywhere.

"Nazareth, Jordan gave me his word, as a gentleman and as a man of the Lines, that he had never given you *any* reason to assume that he was interested in you other than to the extremely limited extent necessary to allow you to function together in the course of your professional duties. He was shocked, and very saddened to find that a woman of your heritage and alleged good breeding would read improper advances into simple courtesy."

He gave me a rose, Nazareth thought. He said that my throat was lovely . . . and he gave me a rose. But she did not tell them that. Perhaps he had not told them that.

"I am equally shocked, Nazareth, and equally saddened. I value the reputation and the honor of this house highly, and it is not pleasant to know that you have no concern for either. To have a Chornyak daughter thrust herself upon a man like a common whore. . . . Nazareth, it leaves me speechless."

AND WHY DO YOU GO ON TALKING, THEN? It was a scream, but it was silent.

"You must realize that you put a fine man—a fine Christian man—in a most awkward position. You repaid his courtesy to you and to this Household with insult, and you shamed us all. And you laid upon Jordan Shannontry a distasteful obligation—which, to his credit, he carried out at once. If I were cruel enough to tell your mother how you have betrayed your upbringing, it would break her heart—she is a decent God-fearing woman, Nazareth Chornyak Adiness! As we are decent God-fearing people one and all beneath this roof! What, in the name of all that's holy, could you have been thinking of?"

"I don't know."

"You don't know?"

Aaron spoke then, still grinning, hugely pleased. "She's telling the truth, Thomas," he said. "She really doesn't know. You have my word for that, and I am in a position to guarantee its accuracy. Her ignorance is impenetrable, in every sense of the word."

WHAT ARE YOU GOING TO DO TO ME?

It was all she could think of. What would they do to her? Take her away from her children? Make up some story? Put her in an institution as they had poor Belle-Anne, and only last month Adam's troublesome Gillian? She was too old to whip, and she had no money or privilege to be taken away—what would they do? What *could* they do? And Aaron . . . he was the injured husband here, when was *he* going to begin telling her what filth she was?

Thomas must have been thinking the same thing; he said, "Aaron, do you have anything to say to this fool I seem to have married you to?"

Aaron chuckled, and had some more wine. The bottle was empty.

"Your husband is taking this with remarkable calm, I should mention," Thomas told her. "I know very few men who would have seen it as he does. And I want him to know that I am impressed by his good sense."

"Well . . ." Aaron made a deprecating gesture. "Thomas, you'll have to admit, it's really funny."

FUNNY?

"I'm not sure I see that, son."

"Well, look at her!" Aaron laughed, waving the hand that wasn't holding the wineglass. "Can you imagine a man like Jordan Shannontry having any interest in a woman like Nazareth? Come on, Thomas—it's disgusting, sure, but it's funny. My *daughters* would have had better sense, infants that they are, but not Nazareth! No sophistication, her hair any old way, God only knows what she was wearing . . . no grace, no elegance, no conversation, and as much erotic appeal as your average rice pudding. . . ." He was laughing openly now, the hearty laughter of the grownup who watched the tiny baby do one of those "cute" things suitable only for tiny babies.

"I have a feeling I wouldn't have been able to muster up your sense of objectivity, Aaron," Thomas said. "If it had been Rachel, for instance. Not that Rachel would have done anything so ludicrous. Rachel has a sharp tongue, but she is not a fool. And she has managed to read one or two books that weren't grammars in her lifetime."

Aaron just shook his head, and wiped the tears from his eyes.

"I can just see it," he said weakly, and did his version of the blushing maiden on tiptoe whispering tender confidence into the bashful lover's ear. "Oh JORdan," he bleated in falsetto, "I LUUUV you. . . . very. . . . very . . . much . . ." He wiped his eyes again. "Oh my God in heaven, Thomas, it's funny. It's so damn funny."

The corners of Thomas' mouth moved a little, as if something were tugging at them; and he admitted that in fact it did have its comic aspects.

She sat in her chair, numb, carved of wood. She could not feel anything except the laboring of her heart, and she had no desire to. She sat, as her father first chuckled, and then laughed, and finally as the two men leaned back in their chairs and roared at the magnificent hilarity of it all.

"Nazareth . . . thinking that Shannontry would. . . ."

"That idiot child . . . thinking . . . *say*ing. . . ."

She saw no reason to bear any more of it, but she couldn't move. Her legs wouldn't obey her. She sat there while they gasped and laughed and presented one another with ever more elaborate descriptions of what it must have been like when she "accosted" Jordan, what the government men must have thought, how she must have looked as she scuttled for cover, and she was nothing but a bruise twisted round a core of shame; but she couldn't move.

They did at last stop laughing, after she had decided they never would. Thomas made a quick motion of his fingers, and Aaron nodded, set down his wineglass, and left the room, walking past her without so much as a glance.

"Well, Nazareth," her father said. "That husband of yours is a remarkable man, I must say."

He settled himself, and straightened in his chair, and looked at her for just a moment with the smile still on his lips. But when he spoke to her again his voice was cold and hard and there was not even the memory of laughter in it.

"Know this, Nazareth Joanna Chornyak Adiness, daughter of my Household," he said, as if it were an oath. "Know this. Your husband is a man of enormous tolerance, and enormous good sense, to be able to see the very real humor in this. Jordan Shannontry is a man of honor, and he will put it out of his mind—he has handled it exactly as it should have been handled. I have no intention of making anything more of it, either . . . because it is nothing at all. But . . . Nazareth, are you listening to me?"

"Yes."

"Nobody is angry with you. This isn't worth our anger. It's just nonsense, foolish stupid nonsense, and evidence of how extraordinarily stupid you can be. But do not *ever* let it happen again! Hear me, Nazareth—not ever. You will be sharing a room with your cousin Belle-Anne before you can turn around, if ever I hear even a hint of such a thing again."

"Yes."

"All it takes to put you where Belle-Anne is is the signature of two adult males of your Household. Don't you forget that, girl. You can count on me for one of them—and I believe I can count on Aaron for the other."

"Yes."

"Don't misunderstand me, now! I do not mean that if a man comes to me to report that you've raped him in the halls of Congress we'll take action against you! I mean that if I ever hear so much as a *hint*, so much as a rumor at third hand, so much as a whisper, that you've in any least way compromised the honor of this Household and the name of Chornyak . . . do you understand me?"

"Yes."

"I wonder. You appear to understand very little. Ignorant female, how dare you behave like a common street trollop!"

"I don't know."

"You don't know . . . one can only wonder what you *do* know! Now get out of here, and go see if you can think of some way to apologize on your knees to your husband, and a way to demonstrate to him your appreciation for his kindness, which you *do not* deserve."

"Yes."

Somehow, she got out of the room and out of the house and fled into the orchards. Safe in the darkness, she put her arms around an apple tree, clinging to it with all her strength as the world swung and dipped around her. After a little while, she realized that she was saying the litany of the Encodings aloud. Over and over again, like a charm against evil. She had bruised her mouth against the tree's rough bark.

If they had been angry, if they had punished her, she thought she could have borne it. But they weren't angry. For all Thomas' fierce exit speech, words he no doubt felt bound "as a gentleman and a linguist" to flay her with, they hadn't even been cross. She was like a little child, a very little child, that had soiled itself and admired its handiwork. It was a matter for laughter, not discipline, except that you must fix it firmly in the child's mind that nice people didn't do such things. For its own good.

It was nothing at all. If she had had the skill and the leisure to write it all down, and to somehow bring it to pass that men would read it, it would only bore them. What a fuss a woman makes over nothing at all; that is what they would say, and they would forget it at once. And there were no words, not in any language, that she could use to *explain* to them what it was that had been done to her, that would make them stop and say that it was an awful thing that had been done to her.

Nazareth ran her hands over the tree a last time, and stood up to ready herself to go into the house and face Aaron. Carefully, she brushed every trace of the earth and of the apple tree from her skin and from her clothing. She tidied her hair, and disciplined her face to a mask of false calm. She had no reason to give Aaron Adiness any additional scrap to humiliate her with, and she did not intend to.

Nazareth was never again to feel even the smallest stirring of affection, or even of liking, for any male past toddling age. Not even for her own sons.

Chapter Eighteen

There are times when I cannot help feeling a certain uneasiness—almost guilt—about the education of the little girls in our Households, and of the older girls as well. It's true that they have the mass-ed computer lessons, and the socialization of Homeroom, and the endless training in languages. But they get nothing more. We are so careful about our male children; we hire them every kind of special tutor, we provide them with every sort of special instruction; we do everything that *could* be done to ensure that they will learn how to be men in the finest sense of that word. We take that as a sacred responsibility.

But we do almost nothing to help our little girls grow to be womanly women. We don't even send them to the Marital Academies, because we can't do without their services for that long. We leave them, instead, to the erratic attentions of the women of our Barren Houses. . . . It isn't right, and I am aware that it isn't right. And one of these days I fully intend to do something about it. Something carefully planned, not something haphazard. At the very first opportunity, once the pressure from our business dealings begins to be a little less the dominant force in our lives. I feel that we owe our women that much, and I am not too proud to admit it.

> (Thomas Blair Chornyak,
> during an interview with
> Elderwild Barnes of *Spacetime*,
> in a special issue on education in the United States)

FALL 2188. . . .

Michaela Landry's first reaction to the living arrangements provided for the feeble and ill women of Chornyak Barren House was that it showed the men of that Household to be even more callous than other men, which was saying a good deal. She had looked at the situation, twenty-three women in twenty-three narrow beds, all in one big room with twelve beds down each side in rows that faced each other; and she had felt shock, and distaste, at how *cheap* the Chornyak men would have to be to treat these women so. Surely they could have managed at least the partitions used in the children's dormitories at the main house, to give their women a semblance of privacy and a place of their own! But no, they were all dumped here like charity patients on a public ward in the oldest hospitals . . . and even there, Michaela thought, there were curtains to be drawn for those women who did not choose to be on public display. Not here. Here, if one woman must undergo some intimate procedure, or was ill in a way that would distress others to watch, someone would bring panelled screens—a practical use for their everlasting needlework—and set them up around the bed. And the moment the situation was back to normal, the screens would be taken away and the woman left in the midst of a crowd again.

But gradually she came to understand that it wasn't precisely as it seemed to her. The room had high windows along both sides, so that there was always a soft flood of light, and it had ordinary big windows at either end that gave every woman a view of the Virginia woodlands outside. In the spring it was flowering trees and carpets of wildflowers; in the autumn it was a spectacle of scarlet and gold and yellow. For most of the women, who could rarely leave their beds, it meant nothing that the patches of woodland were really only skillful plantings of wild things in an ample yard, and that just past the edge of the glory of dogwood or scarlet maple there was a slidewalk and a public street; from where they lay it looked like the inner heart of a woodland.

If the room had been cut up into cubicles, only a few of them could have watched the procession of the trees through the cycle of the year, and the others would have only had glimpses when someone had time to wheel them down to the windows. And the sunlight would not have been there to cheer them except for that segment of the day when the sun was at their particular small stretch of the clerestory windows. They would not have looked up and seen open air and two panoramas of the glory of the outdoors, and the faces of the other women who had been their relatives in law if not by blood for most of their lives. They would have looked up to see a flat barren wall, and to wait and hope that someone would come along and look in and perhaps stay for a few moments.

"It was our own choice," one of the oldest had told her when she felt settled in enough to mention it. "The men, now, they had every intention of putting 'private rooms' on this floor. A decent privacy, they called it. We wanted none of that." And she had laughed softly. "Once they realized they didn't have to spend any money, they were delighted to let us have our way; in fact, they felt positively magnanimous about indulging us in our exotic fancies."

"But don't you tire of always being together?" Michaela asked. "I understand that it's far more beautiful this way . . . this openness of light and air, and the views at the end of the room . . . but don't you *mind*, always being in a crowd like this?"

The old lady patted Michaela's hand reassuringly.

"Sometimes," she said. "Sometimes we think 'if I have to look at those stupid faces on those stupid women for one more minute I will go completely out of my mind!' Of course; each of us does. And that is why there are four bedrooms downstairs, my dear. Separate, proper bedrooms. When one of us truly can't bear living in this room any longer, we take a week's rest—or longer, if we like—in a proper bedroom downstairs. And when you go down there you always think you'll want to stay at least a month—but in three days you're hankering to come back up here."

"That's very hard to believe," Michaela said.

"Well, my dear, you must realize that all of us, or almost all of us, grew up in linguist Households, scores of us under a common roof. We've spent our childhoods in dormitories, we've always eaten in communal dining rooms and shared communal bathrooms. We're much more used to being together all the time than your average person is today."

"It's so strange," Michaela said. "At first, it must have been so hard."

"No," said the old lady briskly, "I don't believe it was especially hard. We went into the communal dwellings after the Anti-Linguist Riots, for security . . . there was safety in numbers. And to have the Interfaces right there, you see. They cost an enormous sum, and there couldn't have been an Interface in a small private home. And it was for security, as well as for economy, that we earth-sheltered all the Households instead of . . . oh, buying up old hotels, or something of that kind. But the main thing that you must understand, and that you don't understand because you are too young, my dear, is that in the days when the Households were built almost *all* people in this country lived very crowded lives. Almost all people everywhere did! Only the very wealthy could afford private homes, then, you see; and most people were jammed into apartments and condominiums . . . the crowding was just terrible. In that situation, the linguists were probably not much more crowded than the average person, and I daresay they were quite a lot more comfortable. Because the Households were carefully planned, you see."

Michaela shook her head, embarrassed. "It's hard," she said. "Hard to imagine. Things have changed so quickly."

"Mmmm, I suppose so, child. But the situation that *you* are familiar with, where anyone with a few thousand credits who feels a little crowded can just move out to a frontier planet or asteroid and have all the room he wants . . . that's very *new*. Why, I can remember when there was only *one* settlement in space, my dear! And to be able to go out to that one, miserable bare hardscrabble that it was, Mrs. Landry, you had to have an enormous fortune at your disposal. Long before frontier colonies became routine, child, we were all jammed in together on this planet Earth in a way that people today would literally find intolerable. And think what I would miss, if I were given a room of my own!"

She waved her hand for Michaela to look around the room, and the other woman had to smile. On almost every bed, sitting most carefully on the edge so that they would not joggle bodies already stiff and aching, were the little girls from Chornyak Household. They came running all day long, in flocks, back and forth between the two buildings. And every patient, unless she was so ill that she could not participate, had two or three little girls of various ages perched on her bed, holding her hand, and talking. Talking, talking, by the hour. If one left, another would come at once to take her place.

Old Julia Dorothy, whose voice was so weak that she could no longer carry on any vocal conversation, was as much the center of the hum of girlchildren as anyone else; while they went to the others to keep up their skills in oral languages, both Terran and Alien, they went to Julia Dorothy to hone their skill with Ameslan and sat on her bed with their fingers flashing and their faces moving constantly in the mobile commentary that went with the signs. Julia Dorothy couldn't speak aloud, but her fingers were as nimble as spiders, and her old face with its wrinkles and seams was so articulate that at times Michaela—with not even the fingerspelling alphabet at her command—felt that she could grasp something of what Julia was signing.

These women, she had to accept it, were content. Ill, perhaps: feeble, certainly; old, beyond question. But content. They knew they filled a valuable role, that they were a resource without which the community of linguists could not have functioned. The little girls had acquired languages, and they had to *use* them, or they would fade and be lost. Their mothers and fathers and uncles and aunts had no time to talk with them in their multitude of foreign tongues; if they weren't on duty on government contracts, they were on duty in the running of the Households. The children could not usefully practice with one another, because except for the English and Ameslan that they all knew, the rest of the languages were parcelled out among them two or three to a customer, and those two or three completely different. A child might have one other younger child who shared her Alien language, preparing to be backup, but the chances were rare that the two of them would be free at the same time except during the hours spent in Homeroom or before the mass-ed computers.

Only Michaela's patients, who could no longer go out to work with the contracts or fill other useful roles in the economy of the Households, could do what these women did. They were a priceless resource, and they knew their value. When a four-year-old girl was the only person other than her eighteen-month-old backup who could speak some one Alien language on this entire planet, she could run over to Barren House in search of a willing partner in conversation. If no one there had even scraps of the language, the child—with a skill that astonished Michaela—would simply set about *teaching* it to whichever of the old ladies had caught her fancy and had free time.

Michaela listened because she was charmed, though she understood almost nothing of what she heard.

"You see, Aunt Jennifer, it's almost like an Athabaskan Earth language! It has postpositions, and it's ess-oh-vee. . . ."

"Aunt Nathalie, you'll like this one! It has sixty-three separate classifiers, and every last one of them gets declined at both *ends,* can you believe that?"

"Aunt Berry, wait until you hear! Aunt Berry, watch my tongue! Do you see? It's a whole set of fricative liquids, Aunt Berry, *six* of them in complementary distribution! Did you see that one?"

They might as well have been discussing the latest overturn in physics for all that it meant to Michaela. But she loved to watch. The eager faces of the children, and the way they labored to make themselves so clear and to go slowly—because, they told Michaela, it is so *very* hard for someone like Aunt Jennifer to learn a new language, you know. And the unbelievable patience of the old women, nodding solemnly and asking the child to repeat it again . . . they would spend twenty minutes with the aunt trying a sound, and the child shaking her head and modeling it, and the aunt trying it again, over and over, until at last the little one would say "That's not it, but it's *almost!*" and clap her hands. But she would not joggle the bed. . . .

"Don't you get tired?" Michaela asked once when the last of the children had finally gone home to dinner one very long day.

"Tired of the children?"

"No . . . not that, exactly. Coming and going like they do, I suppose you don't have any one of them long enough that it's all that tiresome. Not if you really like little girls, and you seem to."

"Well . . . in the particular, Mrs. Landry, some of them can be maddening. They are normal little girls. But in the general, of course we like little girls."

"But see here, don't you get tired of always talking about languages like you do? I would go mad, I'm sure I would."

"Oh, there's nothing more interesting than a new language, my dear."

"Really?"

"Really."

"Ugh," said Michaela. "I don't think I can believe that."

"Besides," put in Vera from the next bed, "when we are actually conversing in the languages—not trying to learn one, or learn about one—we talk about everything in the world and in the worlds beyond."

"It's not just lessons all the time, then? So long as you're talking Jovian, for example, you could be talking about dinner or the threedies or anything else at all?"

"That's quite right, Mrs. Landry," said Jennifer. "There is of course no such language as Jovian—but you have the rest of it right."

"No Jovian?"

"Well, child . . . is there any such language as Terran? Or Earthish?"

"I suppose not. No, of course there isn't."

"Well, if our globe requires five thousand languages or more, why should Jupiter have only one?"

Michaela sighed. "I had never thought about it," she confessed. "It just never. . . . never came *up* before."

And then they explained to her that the humanoid languages weren't given Earth names like "Jovian" anyway. At the very beginning it had been tried, but it had been a waste of time; people couldn't even pronounce them, much less remember them.

"So they're numbered, you see. Like this one . . . do you perceive, my dear? REM41-3-786." Pronounced "remfortyone; three;seven-eighty-six."

"What does it mean? Or does it mean anything?"

"REM . . . that's a historical remnant. Long ago there was a computer language called BASIC, that had a word REM for "Remark," that was used a lot. When they first began putting Alien languages into computers, they were still using REM, and it's hung on. So they all have REM first now, and it doesn't 'mean' anything except perhaps 'here comes the number of an Alien humanoid language.' "

"And then?"

"Then comes the number that tells us which humanoid species is referred to. On Earth, there's only the one . . . some planets have several. The '41' in this number says that the language is one of those spoken by the 41st species with which we've Interfaced. The number '1' won't ever turn up, because it *does* mean Terran, in a way."

"Now you've lost me."

"Well. The digits from 1-1000, with Terran—serving as a sort of cover number for *all* Terran languages, don't you see—being #1, those are reserved for the humanoid species. One thousand may not be nearly enough, of course, but we haven't reached that total yet."

"I see . . . I think. And who has #2?"

"Nobody at all," answered Jennifer. "That number is set aside in case it happens that the cetaceans of this planet turn out to have languages of their own as we primates do. If we ever could get to the bottom of that, those languages would be summarized by the numeral 2."

"My goodness."

"Yes. So that's that much, REM41. And then comes a number from 1 to 6, that classifies the language for one of the possible orderings of verb and subject and object. This one is a 3—that means its order is verb followed by subject followed by object. Very roughly speaking, of course."

"We wouldn't need that one, for all we know," said Anna, "if we ever acquired a non-humanoid language."

"Why? Would they all have the same order?"

"No, dear. There's no particular reason to expect that nonhumanoid languages would *have* verbs, subjects, or objects, you see."

"But then how could it *be* a language?"

"That," they told her, "is precisely the point."

"And then," Anna finished, "there's the final number. 786 in this one. That just refers to the numerical order the languages are acquired in. So, we have it all. REM41-3-786 . . . it means this is an Alien humanoid language spoken by the 41st encountered humanoid species—which may speak many many other languages besides this one, of course—and it has VSO order and is the 786th language we've acquired. That works out better than referring to it as . . ." Anna paused and looked around. "Anybody know the native name for REM41-3-786?"

Somebody did; it sounded to Michaela like "rxtpt" if it sounded like anything at all, and there was quite a bit more of it.

"It *is* interesting," she said slowly. "This kind of thing . . . I wouldn't have thought that it could be, but it is."

And they all smiled at her together as if she'd done something especially praiseworthy.

She was having a very hard time; she slept badly, and woke from nightmares drenched with sweat. She was losing weight, and the women fussed at her to let the other residents of Barren House take over at least a portion of her duties.

"It's my job," said Michaela firmly, "and I will do it."

"But you are up half a dozen times, every night! Someone else could do part of that . . . or take one night in three . . ."

"No," said Michaela. "No. I will do it."

It wasn't the disturbed sleep that was making her thin and anxious, and certainly it wasn't the work itself. She had almost nothing to do in the way of actual nursing. Medications now and then, a few baths to give, and injection, diet lists to make up; really almost nothing. She didn't even have to see to making up the beds or caring for linen, because Thomas Chornyak had hired someone from outside to take care of such things. As for sleep, she had not had an uninterrupted night within the span of her memory. Women had always had to be up and down all night long; if there weren't sick children, there were sick animals, or sick people of advanced age. If there were none of those, there would be a child with a bad dream, or a storm that meant someone had to get up and close windows—there was always something. A nurse only extended her ordinary female life when she learned to be instantly awake at a call, on her feet and functioning for as long as she was needed, and instantly asleep as soon as she could lie down again. It had never kept nurses, or women of any kind, from listening respectfully as the physicians whined about the way their vast incomes were justified by the fact that they were awakened during the night to see to patients. They would have said, "It's not the same thing at all!" As of course it was not. Women had to get up much oftener, stay up longer, and were neither paid nor admired for doing it. Certainly it wasn't the same thing.

The cause of Michaela's condition was something unique to Michaela, not one of these universals of womankind. When she had taken this post, she had intended to put an end to the women of Chornyak Barren House one by one, as plausibly and randomly as she could manage . . . adding forty or more notches to her bow. She had even considered killing all of them at once as a political statement; of course she would have been caught and punished, but it would have been a way of letting the linguists *know* they weren't getting off scot free with their murders of innocent babies! She would have been a heroine to the public, who felt as she did about the matter; she had thought it might very well be worth it.

And she had gone so far as to select Deborah as her first victim. Deborah was ninety-seven years old; she had to be fed an enriched gruel and pureed fruit and vegetables with a soft tube. And no little girl went to talk to Deborah, although to Michaela's consternation almost every little girl went to sit on the old lady's bed to stroke her forehead and pat her hands for a few minutes during the day.

"She doesn't know you're there, sweetheart," Michaela had told the child the first time she saw that happen. "It's very kind of you, but it's useless—Deborah hasn't been aware of anything for a very long time."

The child had turned clear eyes up to her, disturbingly adult eyes: she could not have been more than six years old. And she had said: "How do we know that, Mrs. Landry?"

Michaela had admitted that she could not be absolutely *sure*, of course—but there was no reason to believe anything else, and the doctors would tell her exactly the same thing.

"And that means," said the little girl reprovingly, "that while we do not know for *sure*, Aunt Deborah might very well lie there every day unable to speak or move, and wish and wish and wish that someone would come sit with her and pet her a little. Isn't that so?"

"Child, it's so un*like*ly!"

"Mrs. Landry," and it was a rebuke, no question about it, "*we* are not willing to take that chance."

Michaela had not interfered again. But it had seemed to her in some way a little unwholesome that the children should be thinking about what Deborah might or might not be feeling, and it reinforced her opinion that she was the logical first victim. She had anticipated that she would take care of that rather promptly.

And now she'd been here half a year almost, and Deborah still lay there silent and unmoving under the hands of the little girls and the other women of the house. Michaela could not bring herself to do the act. Worse, with every passing day she felt herself less and less willing to kill *any* of them. They were not what she had expected. They were not what she had always been told they were. They did not fit the profile of the "bitch linguist" that everyone she had known believed in, that was the staple character in obscene jokes and foolish stories that children used to frighten one another. "Hey, you think the Lingoe males are shits," people would say. "They're angels of charity and goodness compared to the Lingoe *bitches!*" She had expected it to be easier than the other times—but it hadn't turned out that way.

Here were women who had spent their lifetimes in unremitting work. The twenty-three who were her patients were not victims of illnesses, for the most part; they were simply exhausted. Like very old domestic animals who had been worked until one day they lay down and just could not get up again; that's what they were like. They were *not* indifferent to the problems of the public . . . they were concerned about the affairs of the Chornyaks, certainly, but so was anyone concerned about their own families. But they cared just as much for the problems of the public at large as did any other citizens. They were just as interested in the latest events in the colonies, just as excited about the newest discoveries in the sciences, just as eager to hear of events in the world and beyond. The aristocratic disdain, the contempt for the "masses," all that list of repulsive characteristics she'd been brought up believing marked the woman linguist—none of it was to be found in them. Not in the women she tended. And not in the other twenty who were not her patients.

They were not perfect, were not saints—if they had been, it would have been easier, because they would have been so *other*. Some of them were petty and silly. Some did everything to excess—for example, there were the absurdities of Aquina Chornyak, which seemed endless. But it was just the sort of distribution of imperfections that you would expect to find in any group of women of such a size. No more, and no less. And their devotion to one another, not just to the invalids who might have called to any woman's compassion but devotion even to the most irritating among them, touched Michaela's heart.

She had not seen anything like this outside the Lines. But then outside the Lines women never were together in this way. Every woman was alone in her own house, tending to the needs of her own husband and her own children, until she was of an age when she was sent to a hospital to die—all alone in a private room. Women, asked to consider living as did these linguist women, would have said that the prospect was horrible and declared that nothing could make them choose such a life; Michaela was sure of it. But perhaps they would have been to one another as the linguist women were, if they'd had the opportunity; how could anyone know? It didn't matter, because other women were never going to have what these women had, they were always going to be shut up, one or two to a house, never going out except as the displayed possession of some man.

These women, living as they did, were wonderful to watch. She envied them what they had, but she could not hate them for it—she had seen in her first post, at Verdi Household, that the women of the Lines were as totally subjugated to the men as any women anywhere. They went out into the world to work, but they had no privileges. The situation was in no way their fault.

How was she to kill them?

But if she did not kill them . . . then the awful thought could not be kept out of her mind: perhaps she was wrong to have killed the others. Not Ned; she would never believe she had been wrong to kill Ned. But the other linguists? They had been male linguists, but still . . . it was a seed she could not allow to grow and yet it grew when she was sleeping. What if the male linguists were as innocent of the things she had been taught all her life long to blame them for as the women were? What if she had killed not to do her part in freeing her nation of a pestilence but out of a naïve belief in a stereotype that had no basis in reality? So many things that "everybody knew" had turned out, under her own eyes, to be lies. What if all the rest of the beliefs about linguists were lies, too? And when she remembered that the only evidence she had had for the conviction that linguists were to blame for the baby-slaughter at Government Work was the word of Ned Landry, her stomach twisted viciously. When had Ned Landry ever known *any*thing, about anything? What if he had been entirely wrong?.

Michaela lost more weight, and slept even less, and the women made her herb teas and fussed over her and threatened to call Thomas and tell him his nurse was sicker than her patients.

"You would not really do that," she said.

"No. We would not really do that. But we would insist that *you* do it—and we will, if you don't begin to improve.

She was still fretful, still not at ease in herself, as the time for the Christmas holidays drew near. And then one morning something happened that settled at least one part of the issue for her.

It was a morning when she was doing something that required her nursing skills instead of just her woman-wit. Sophie Ann Lopez, born a Chornyak but married into the Lopez family of the Lines, and then come home to Chornyak Barren House when she was left a widow at eighty, was not one of the bedfast ones. She was ninety-four, and she did not get things done speedily, but she got them done. She was up each morning with the birds, and the absolute limit of her concession to her advancing years was the cane she used for going up and down stairs. The moment she reached the level she was headed for she'd put the cane somewhere, and then in an hour or two everyone would be calling, "Has anybody seen Sophie Ann's cane?" She hated the cane, and nothing but the almost inevitable prospect of months in bed with a broken hip from tumbling down stairs made her give in and accept even that minimal aid.

But in the cold of mid-December Sophie had caught some sort of infection; it had spread to her kidneys, and finally it had been necessary for a surgeon to come with his lasers and do a bit of minor surgery. It had gone uneventfully, behind the panelled screens with their riot of wild roses and blackberry vines in brilliant wools against a background of deep blue, and the surgeon was off to some other task, leaving Michaela to watch over Sophie Ann as she gradually awoke from the anesthetic.

For a while Michaela had thought her patient was only mumbling noises. And then, struggling through the sedative layers, had come recognizable words.

"It won't be long now," Sophie kept saying. "Not long now, I tell you!"

She kept it up until Michaela was first amused and then curious.

"What won't be long now, dear?" she asked, finally.

"Why, Láadan! What a silly question!"

"What *is* it, Sophie? Is it a celebration?"

Michaela leaned over and stroked the thin white hair gently away from the damp forehead where it clung in limp strands.

"They'll see, then," babbled the old woman. "They'll see! When the time comes, when we old aunts can begin to talk Láadan to the babies, it won't be long! And then they'll be talking pidgin Láadan, but when they speak it to *their* babies . . . then! Then! Oh, what a wonderful day!"

It was a language?

"Why, Sophie Ann? Why will it be wonderful?"

"Oh, my, it won't be long now!"

It had come a scrap at a time until Michaela thought she had at least the rough outlines. These women, and the women of linguistics for generations back, had taken on the task of constructing a language that would be just for women. A language to say the things that women wanted to say, and about which men always said "Why would anybody want to talk about *that?*" The name of this language sounded as if Sophie were trying to sing it. And the men didn't know.

Michaela stood thinking, tending Sophie Ann, and wondering if this was only the anesthetic talking; the old woman seemed very sure, but Michaela had known surgical patients to be very sure of dragons and giant peacocks in the operating room and similar outrageous delusions. If it was true, how could it have happened? How could they have kept it a secret, how could they work on it and not have the men know, supervised as they were? And how could anyone invent a language? Michaela was quite sure that nobody knew just how the first human language had come to be; she was equally sure that God was supposed to have played a prominent part in the becoming . . . she remembered that much from Homeroom. Hadn't there been something called a Tower of Babble? Babbling? Something like that?

It was inevitable that Sophie Ann's racket, and Michaela's questions, would draw the attention of the other women; they came pretty quickly. Caroline came, wrapped in her outdoor cape, just back from an assignment, and cocked her head sharply to listen.

"Oh, goodness," she said at once, "what nonsense she's talking!"

"Is it?"

"It certainly sounds like it. What's she been saying, Mrs. Landry?"

"Something about a secret language for women," Michaela told her. "She calls it Ladin . . . lahadin . . . Latin? Almost like Latin, but with a lilt to it. And she keeps saying that it won't be long now, whatever that might mean."

"Oh," Caroline laughed, "it's just the anesthetic!"

"Are you certain of that?"

"Mrs. Landry, Sophie is almost one hundred years old!"

"So? Her mind is as clear as your own."

"Yes, but she is talking about something from long long ago . . . you know how very old people are! They cannot remember what they did five minutes ago—her cane, for example, which she never knows the location of—but things that happened half a century ago are as fresh in their mind as their own names. That's all this is."

"Please explain, Mrs. Chornyak," said Michaela firmly. "I'm afraid it's a complete muddle to me."

Caroline held the screen with one hand and unwound her cape with the other, talking easily. "Mrs. Landry, when Sophie was a little girl the women's language *was* a secret, I expect. Women were much more frightened then, you know; at least the women of the Lines were. They were afraid that if the men found out about the women's language they'd make them stop working on it, and so they tried to keep it a secret. But that's all been over for many many years."

"There is a woman's language, then?"

"Certainly," said Caroline cheerfully. "Why not? It's called Langlish, Mrs. Landry, not whatever Sophie was mumbling about Latin. And it's not a secret at all. The men think it's a silly waste of time, but then they think that everything we do except interpreting and translating and bearing children is a silly waste of time. You can almost always find somebody working on Langlish in the computer room, my dear . . . you're perfectly free to go watch if you like."

"But it's for linguist women," said Michaela.

"Did Sophie say *that?*"

"No . . . but I assumed it would be."

"That would be a warped sort of activity," Caroline observed. "And a *real* waste of time . . . no, it's not reserved for linguist women. We are constructing it, because we have the training. But when it's finished, when it's ready for us to begin teaching it, then we will offer it to all women—and if they want it, it will be *for* all women."

"Sophie Ann called it a pigeon. A pigeon?"

Caroline frowned, and then she saw what the trouble was. "Not the sort of pigeon you're thinking of, Mrs. Landry," she said. "Not the bird. It's pidgin . . . p-i-d-g-i-n."

"What does that mean?"

"Is Sophie Ann all right, Mrs. Landry?"

"Absolutely. I wouldn't be chatting with you if she weren't."

"I'm sorry; I ought to have known that. A pidgin, then. . . . when a language in use has no *native* speakers, it is called a pidgin."

"I don't understand."

"Say that a conquering nation spoke Hungarian. And they conquered a people who spoke only English. They would have no language in common, you see. But they would need to communicate for trade, for administration, that sort of thing. In such a situation they would work up between them a language that wasn't quite Hungarian and wasn't quite English, for use only when the two peoples *had* to communicate. And a language like that, the native language of *no*body, you perceive, is called a pidgin."

"Is that a good thing? For women to learn one of these pidgins?"

"No . . . it isn't. But say that the conquered speakers of English for some reason became isolated from the rest of the world. Say they had children who were born hearing the pidgin and grew up using it and perhaps began to prefer it to English. And by the time *they* had children, it was the only language the children heard, and it became a native tongue for *them*, for the children. Then it would be what is called a *creole*, Mrs. Landry. And it would be a new real language. It would develop then like any other language, change like any other language, behave like any other language."

"So . . . women here who know this Langlish only from a book or a computer, they speak it to children. And the children would speak it, but it's not a real language. But if they speak it to their own children. . . ."

"The situation is very different from the classic one," said Caroline. "We women are not precisely a conquered people with an existing language . . . but the analogy is close enough. Basically, yes; it would then become a native language. Remembering, of course, that all children of the Lines are multilingual and have a *number* of native languages. It would become one of their native languages."

"For all women to learn, if they chose to."

"Of course."

"*Would* they choose to, do you think?"

Sophie Ann was wide awake now, looking at them with an anxious expression that caught Michaela's attention at once; she turned to her patient and touched her soothingly, stroking her arm.

"It's all right, Sophie Ann," she said. "It's all over."

"I've just been explaining to Mrs. Landry about Langlish," Caroline told Sophie Ann. "You were talking about it before you woke up, dearlove—a lot of nonsense, I'm afraid. About long ago, when it was kept secret."

Michaela saw the look of consternation on Sophie Ann's face, and spoke quickly to reassure her. "It's all right, dear," she said, knowing that the old woman must be embarrassed at her confusion. "Really! Caroline has explained it all to me. It's all right."

"Well," said Sophie Ann weakly. "Well. I'm sure . . . I'm sure everyone talks a lot of drivel under an anesthetic."

"Oh, they certainly do," Michaela reassured her. "Doctors and nurses don't pay any attention—it's never anything but nonsense—it was just that in your case it was such *interesting* nonsense."

Caroline kissed Sophie's forehead and went away, and Michaela settled to her care, saying no more. But she knew, nevertheless, that this was the very last straw. She could not harm these women.

She stood calmly before Thomas' desk and listened to his courteous objections, but she was absolutely firm. He could of course force her to go through the formal procedure of contacting her brother-in-law and having him petition for her release, if he chose to do so. She knew no reason why he should, because he would have no trouble finding a replacement for her; but whatever he did, she was not going to change her mind.

She did not tell him her problem was that her life's mission was to murder linguists and that she found herself in the uncomfortable dilemma of having for patients only linguists she could not bring herself to kill. She provided him with logical reasons, instead.

"My patients are endangered by this situation," she told him when he asked for reasons. "There's no way that I, a single nurse, can provide so many sick women with adequate care. And while I am not in the least afraid of hard work, Mr. Chornyak, I *do* have standards. When the work reaches a point where it's literally impossible for me to do, my patients' welfare must become my primary concern. I can't any longer pretend that I can fill this post, sir."

"But surely they haven't suddenly become so much sicker than they were?" Thomas asked.

"Oh, no . . . not at all. They are in fact remarkably healthy, all things considered. But they are also remarkably long-lived, these women of your Household. And as more and more of them become extremely aged, sir, they require constant attention to their personal needs. Almost every one of them, Mr. Chornyak, must now be helped even for such simple matters as bathing and eating.''

> And I always have a dozen or more willing pairs of hands ready to help me with those tasks. Even the four-year-olds are contented to sit with a bowl of rice and spoon it one tiny morsel at a time into the mouth of a beloved aunt. And I have seen two seven-year-old girls bathe a frail lady of ninety as competently and gently as any adult woman could have done, chattering the whole time about their verbs and their nouns. . . .

She thought of all this, waiting, but she said none of it. She had learned enough to know that if Chornyak for one moment suspected that the women of Barren House had any leisure to spend tending others he would find a means for them to put it to gainful work instead; even for the four-year-olds, he would have had strong opinions about the ''waste'' of their time.

''Well, Mrs. Landry,'' said Thomas slowly, ''I do see your point. I'm afraid we've been rather inconsiderate, as a matter of fact. When I hired you, I thought there was very little for you to do—but I haven't paid any attention to the facts of the matter, and I should have realized that the situation was a progressive one. I apologize, of course, but you should have spoken to me sooner—it appears that our old ladies are determined to live forever, doesn't it?''

Michaela had been braced for strong protests, intricate arguments, and a great deal of linguistic manipulation along the lines of doing one's duty and keeping one's word. But Thomas didn't behave as she had anticipated.

''Fine,'' he said, nodding agreement and making a quick entry to his wrist computer. ''Fine. You may consider yourself released from your contract as of the end of this month, my dear.''

Taken aback, but grateful that it had been so simple, Michaela thanked him.

''Not at all,'' Thomas said. ''I regret that you were obliged to ask, and I apologize on behalf of the younger women at Barren House, who most assuredly should have spoken to me about this long ago and spared you the task. And now that that's settled, may I offer you a different post, Mrs. Landry?''

"A different post?"

"Yes, my dear. If you would be so kind as to give me your attention for just a moment."

"Of course, sir."

"If I understand you correctly, what's needed at Barren House is primarily strong backs, not nursing skills. Isn't that right?"

"For the most part, yes."

"How many nurses do you think should be available, for all this bathing and feeding and so on?"

"Two at least, perhaps three."

"Very well. We'll begin with two, and add another if it becomes clear that it's necessary. If you agree, what I'll do is find two strong and willing women looking for work as—what do they call them? practical nurses?—all right, I'll hire two of those. One in the daytime and one at night?"

"No, sir, I'm sorry; you need two in the day, and then one on duty during the night in case she's called. They could manage nicely if both were there all day and they alternated spending the night on call, first one and then the other."

"Well, let's give that a try. And then I'd want you to stay on for two purposes, Mrs. Landry. Neither would be very burdensome, as I perceive it, but you must feel free to tell me if I am mistaken."

"Yes, sir. Thank you."

"My father is vigorous and alert. But he has spells of severe vertigo that trouble him frequently, he has what I understand are mild infections of the urinary tract, he needs someone to keep track of his diet because he has a tendency to gout—as well as a tendency to gluttony, unfortunately. He's acquired a disgraceful sweet tooth."

"He needs a nanny with a nursing license, in other words."

"Exactly. He's not bedfast except when he's suffering from one of his illnesses, off and on, but we need someone at hand for those times. We also need someone who will notice that he *should* be in bed, because we often don't see it soon enough. I'd like you to move here to the main house to look after Father, as described, but also check in once a day at Barren House to see that everything's being done properly there. And to do anything that actually requires a trained nurse. And of course if someone there became seriously ill, you could stay at Barren House until the crisis was past and we would manage without you here temporarily. Could I persuade you to do that, my dear? It would be a tremendous help to us all."

Michaela was delighted. This would let her carry on her vocation of death without having to exercise it on the women; it would let her maintain her relationship with the women of Barren House—which, to her complete astonishment, had come to be something that she treasured—and it would save her the nuisance of hunting for a new post, learning the ways of a new family and patient, all those tiresome things. It was a pleasant surprise, something she had not expected at all and found very welcome.

And perhaps she would be able, once in a while, to see something of the progress of the woman's language. She had no skills that would let her be part of the work, and she had better sense than to get in the way by trying to help with things she understood not at all. But if she stayed on, and if she observed carefully and discreetly, perhaps she could stay in touch with the project. Now that the women of Barren House knew that she was aware of Langlish, they might talk to her about it sometimes, even teach her a few words—it was at least possible.

"Do you need time to think it over, Mrs. Landry?" Thomas asked her.

"No," Michaela answered. "I'd be delighted to accept. It wasn't that I wanted to leave, sir—it's very beautiful here, and I'm happy with the post. It's just that the situation as it is currently set up had become impossible. What you propose should solve it, and I'd like to stay."

"Wel'll have to put you in a guest room, I'm afraid—and there are no elevators. And no private bath."

"I don't mind that, sir. Really."

"It's settled, then?"

"If you're satisfied with the arrangement, Mr. Chornyak."

"Then I'll proceed at once to find the two practical nurses . . . you don't mind staying on at Barren House until they're hired and then getting them settled in their duties, I assume."

"Not at all. I'd be pleased to do it. And if I can do anything else to help in this transition period, Mr. Chornyak, please let me know. For example, sir . . . I know the Nursing Supervisor well. If you would call him to authorize it, I could probably find competent women quickly and make the necessary arrangements. There's no reason why you should have to trouble yourself about that."

"Would you do that?"

"Of course."

"Excellent, Mrs. Landry. I'll call the man, and we'll get all this out of the way. Now, if you'll excuse me, I have a great deal of work to tackle."

Michaela allowed her lashes to fall, modestly presenting him a gesture that would imply the ancient courtesy without demanding it of her, and then looked at him carefully. Yes; he liked that.

Thomas found himself much taken with Michaela Landry. There was something about her, some quality he could neither define nor describe, that made him feel somehow . . . oh, *taller*, when she was near him. Taller and stronger and wiser, and in every way a better man. He had no idea what it was she did, and hadn't time to observe her to find out, but he knew that he enjoyed it. When she was in the room, he found that he tended to move to be closer to her, if he could do it without seeming obvious. And he fell quickly into the habit of calling her to his office each day to discuss various minor matters having to do with the health of Paul John or the Barren House patients.

While she was with him, once the actual purpose of the discussion was accomplished, he noticed that without any awareness of having changed the subject he would suddenly be in the midst of some other discussion entirely. His own projects, his plans, his problems . . . not indiscreetly, of course. He never let slip anything that it was improper for her to know, or for any nonlinguist to know. But their talk went far beyond the remotest outer fringes of what could be called *nursing*. And she didn't seem to mind at all. She was the most remarkable listener Thomas had ever encountered. Never bored, never uneasy and anxious to leave him and get on with something else, never wanting to put her own two cents in. She made him feel that every word he said was a pleasure to her ears . . . which could not be true, of course, but was a delightful illusion and a credit to her womanhood. If only Rachel could have been like that!

When he found himself sharing her bed, scarcely three months after the move to the Chornyak Household had been accomplished, he was a little disappointed. Not in her performance; she was as skilled in his arms as she was at everything else she did, and he would have been very surprised if that had not been the case. But he had somehow thought of her as a woman of exceptional virtue, still entirely faithful to the memory of her dead husband—a respectable widow of sterling character and decorous charm. He could not help being disappointed that she wasn't as he had imagined her to be.

On the other hand, there were advantages to the arrangement. It reinforced his conviction that no matter how admirable a woman might seem, no matter how superior to the usual run of her sex she might appear to be, might in *fact* be, nevertheless all women are truly weak and without genuine strength of character. It was instructive, and it taught him the necessity for keeping an eye on the other women of his Household, an eye that went beyond surface judgments; he had been lax about that, he thought, without realizing it.

They were frail reeds, women, especially in the hands of an experienced man like himself, and a man who was—as he was—a master of the erotic arts. If he'd had any doubts about that mastery, due to his advancing years and Rachel's dutiful lukewarm attentions, Michaela's rapt ecstasy at even his most casual efforts would have swiftly dispelled them. She was never in any way indelicate, never demanding, never lustful—lustfulness was abhorrent in a woman, and had she shown any sign of it he would have instantly dispensed with her. But despite her modesty he could always perceive that his touch carried her to the heights, and he realized that her husband had no doubt been one of those bumbling incompetents in the bedroom.

It pleased Thomas to be able to show Michaela how a real man made love to a woman, and he found her reciprocal pleasure precisely what he would have asked for. He had never disappointed her, when her body was what he preferred: and if he wanted to talk rather than make love she was as contented with his words as with his caresses. If he fell asleep, he could be certain that when he woke she would be gone, the bed fresh, the room made neat, and no rumpled and frowsty female presence to interfere with his comfort. Unless he had specifically asked that she stay, in which case she would have somehow managed to arrange her hair and tidy herself without disturbing him, and would be fragrant and ladylike beside him, waiting on his pleasure. An entirely satisfactory woman, this Michaela Landry. As nearly a flawless woman as he had ever encountered. Under the circumstances, he was willing to forgive her her inability to resist his advances and live up to his earlier expectations.

It is unjust, he reminded himself, to expect of a female more than her own natural characteristics allow her to accomplish.

Unjust, and always a source of discord. He could not imagine Michaela ever being a source of discord, but he took very seriously his responsibility not to destroy that quality in her by spoiling her or allowing her to take liberties. She was perfect, just as she was; he wanted no changes.

Chapter Nineteen

Gentlemen, I'd like to get one crucial point settled before we do anything else here today. I want to begin by *properly* defining the medical specialty known as gynecology; I want that straightened out and out of the way so that we may move on to other matters. If you'll bear with me . . .

For those of you considering gynecology out of a sense of compassion and selflessness, the definition will not matter. For those considering gynecology for the sake of pure research, for the opportunity it provides to add to the sum of scientific knowledge, the definition will be irrelevant. But for the rest of you, who may be wondering if you have made a serious error—I strongly urge that you listen very carefully to what I am about to say. It is of the utmost importance that you do so.

Gentlemen, gynecology is not just "health care for the female human being past puberty." That definition, seen far too often in the popular press, is a distortion that can be a genuine threat to your self-respect—if you accept it. You must *not* accept it; it is an error, understandable in the layman perhaps, but not in the professional man of medicine.

Let me tell you what gynecology is. What it really is. Gentlemen, it is health care for your fellow *man*—whose women you are maintaining in that state of wellness that allows the men to pursue their lives as they were intended to pursue them. As this country desperately needs them to pursue them. There are few more distasteful burdens, few more severe impediments, a man can find himself saddled with than a sick wife, an ailing mother, a disabled

225

daughter—*any* female in poor health. It is the gynecologist who sees to it that a man does not have to bear that burden or struggle against that impediment.

Gentlemen . . . I know that you have all heard jokes about the gynecologist "serving" women. They are ignorant jokes. By keeping women healthy, the gynecologist serves *man;* few duties are more truly essential to the welfare of this nation and its people. Never forget that, gentlemen, for it is the truth as God is my witness. . . .

> (from a welcoming address,
> Northwestern Medical University,
> Division of Gynecology, Obstetrics, and Feminology)

SUMMER 2205. . . .

Nazareth lay in the narrow hospital bed and waited for the doctors to appear. She was indifferent to the peeling paint on the walls, to the ancient metal beds, to the rows of strangers who shared this decaying ward with her; she was not used to either luxurious surroundings or to privacy. But she was not indifferent to the manner in which she was treated, the hostility that was the primary message whenever anyone spoke to her, no matter what the actual words used. It was cruel of the nurses to have spread the news to all the other patients that she was a linguist and subject her to that hostility—but they inevitably did it. How else were people to know? It was not as if her skin had been pale green, or as if linguists had horns to identify them to the unsuspecting public. . . .

Once, years ago, she had been in the hospital to have her appendix removed. And because she was only a child, and still very naïve, she had asked the nurses specifically *not* to tell anyone she was a child of the Lines.

"Why not, Miss Chornyak? Are you ashamed of it?"

She had wanted to ask, "Aren't you ashamed of your hard hearts?" But she had kept still, warned by the swift sting of their response. And of course the nurses had told the others not only that she was a linguist, but that she had asked them not to tell. Of course.

She understood all of this much better now. Doctors despised the nurses, but that was not the problem—doctors despised *everyone* except other doctors, and were trained to do so. But the public despised the nurses, too, and that *was* the problem. Nursing, Nazareth understood from the histories, had once been an admired calling; there were worlds on which it still was. Nurses had once been called "angels of mercy". . . . there had even been male nurses. But that was before so many of the nursing functions had been turned over to computers. Once the bedside computers, the healthies, had taken over all the record-keeping, all the decision-making not done by doctors, had begun dispensing all medications and injections automatically, the role of the nurse had gone rapidly downhill. And when the healthies were programmed to interact with the patients and provide even the *words* of comfort—words that the nurses unfortunately had thought they did not have time to provide—that was the end of the road of prestige.

Now nurses bathed patients, changed beds, fed the helpless, tended sores and wounds, disposed of wastes and other foul bodily excretions, saw to the cleansing of the dead . . . all the distasteful and unattractive things that are natural to sickness. It was a rare woman now who went into nursing for any reason other than that she needed the money badly, or that some male who had power over her felt that *he* needed the money. Thus the nurses despised *themselves;* it was no surprise to Nazareth that they took out on the patients the frustration that was their daily and nightly portion.

Nevertheless, it hurt her that they must add to their usual unpleasant behavior still one more dose of viciousness, just because she was a linguist. It hurt her not just physically—although that did hurt, because they were needlessly rough as they tended her—it hurt her simply because they were women. Women hurting other women . . . that was ugly. And it hurt her because they were deformed of spirit through no fault of their own and there was nothing whatsoever that she could do to help them.

The doctors would come when it pleased them, of course. They would stay for so long as it pleased them to stay, and leave when it pleased them to leave. She wanted badly to get up and walk in the hall, to distract her mind from the pain of her body, but she didn't dare. Like washing windows to make it rain, if she left this bed for five minutes she could be certain that the doctors would make their rounds while she was away from the room; she stayed where she was, therefore, and went on waiting.

When they did come at last they were not in a good mood. She had no idea what had caused them to be so cross. Perhaps the stock market had "plunged" . . . it was forever "plunging." Or perhaps a patient had dared to question something they chose to say or do. Or perhaps they had wanted pink eggs and hummingbird's tentacles for breakfast. A doctor needed no *reason* for his irritation—irritation was his birthright, along with the title now reserved to him alone. No longer were there "doctors" of anthropology and physics and literature to offend the *real* doctors and confuse the public; they had put a stop to that, as they had put a stop to so many things that were unseemly and inappropriate.

"Mrs. Chornyak."

"Adiness, doctors," she corrected them. The smile that went with the words was not for them, but amusement at her own perversity . . . as if she took pride in bearing Aaron's name! She had never once corrected any of the government staffers whose principles for system of address consisted entirely of the rule "a linguist is a linguist is a linguist" and called everyone of the lines by whatever name-of-a-linguist happened to be most familiar to them.

"Mrs. Adiness, then. Sorry."

"Quite all right, doctors."

"Any problems?"

"No," she said. "But I have a question."

They looked at one another, body-parling. WHY THE HELL DO WE HAVE TO PUT UP WITH THIS INSUFFERABLE BITCH? And one of them said, "Well? What is it?"

"Could I be discharged?" she asked.

"Your surgery was when?"

"Day before yesterday."

"Pretty short time, isn't it?"

"Laser surgery heals quickly."

Body-parl again, MEDICAL OPINIONS, YET, FROM THIS USED-UP OLD PIECE . . . HELL OF A NERVE SHE'S GOT. Nazareth ignored it.

"You think you're well enough to leave? Then by all means, leave." The senior man in the pack leaned across her, jolting the bed; she would have gasped with pain except that she would have endured *any* pain rather than show weakness in front of these elegant specimens. He punched the DISCHARGE stud in the bedside computer, and when the questionmark came up he punched in ANY TIME TODAY.

"There you are," he said, and off they went, telling her over their collective shoulders that if she had any other questions she could ask the nurses. And Nazareth knew that to be true. She could certainly ask the nurses questions. They wouldn't answer them if it could possibly be avoided, but she was free to ask. It made no difference to her anyway, now that she had permission to leave.

* * *

The message went through to Clara's wrist computer, and Clara went straight to Nazareth's husband. It was luck that Aaron was still in the house; she caught him just leaving, and impatient to be on his way.

"She wants what?" he asked her crossly. "Do speak up, Clara."

"She's being discharged today, Aaron," said Clara. "And she doesn't want to come back here. Now that she is most assuredly and officially barren . . . she wants to go straight to Barren House from the hospital. For good."

Aaron stopped then, his attention captured at last. "Isn't that a little unusual?" he asked. "Irregular?"

"If you say so, Aaron."

"You know very well what I mean," Aaron snapped. "Wouldn't the usual thing be for her to come back here and spend a few weeks lounging about indulging herself and *then* move over to Barren House?"

Clara could have told him of many women who had come back from illness or surgery and taken up their lives beside their husbands just as before, and who had remained honored in the Household until they were widowed because their husbands wanted them to remain. But she didn't bother. Aaron was not capable of feeling as much affection for any human being as he felt for one of the dogs; and he was not capable of feeling *any* affection for a woman. Had he thought of his mother as anything more than part of the furniture? she wondered. Probably not. There were men like him everywhere, men who felt toward women the kind of ugly prejudice that had once been attached to racial differences . . . but Aaron was unquestionably the worst example she had ever known. It would be a waste of time to try to break through what Aaron felt toward the females of his species, and she had no time to waste.

"It's up to you," she told him. "And to Thomas, of course."

"Hunnnh." He stood there, scowling at her as if she had brought great trouble and worry upon him through sheer incompetence.

"What's the procedure?" he demanded, finally. "Do I have to put it to Thomas formally, or what?"

"I'd recommend that, Aaron," said Clara, carefully looking at the floor. Or what!

"Is he here?"

"He's still in his office, I believe."

"*Damn*, what a nuisance!"

"You can deal with it whenever it's convenient for you," said Clara coldly. "I'll notify Nazareth to wait until you have time to attend to the matter."

"Never mind," he said. "I might as well get it settled, and then I'll give you a message for Nazareth on my way out. Keep yourself within reach, would you?"

"Certainly."

"I'll get back to you, then."

He turned and took the stairs down to the lower floors two at a time, while Clara watched him with the perfect hatred of long practice.

"So she's to be discharged today?"

"So Clara tells me."

"Isn't that awfully quick?"

Aaron shrugged and smiled. "You know how she is. If she sets her mind to something, that's the end of it."

"Very like her mother."

"No doubt."

"And she wants to go straight to Barren House from the hospital rather than coming home?"

"Yes . . . wants the women to send her things on ahead. I suppose she'll want her books sent, but I won't permit that. She doesn't need them with her, and I'm used to having them here."

"Of course," agreed Thomas. "Well . . . what do you want to do about this?"

"I say we should let her have her way," said Aaron carelessly. "Why force her to come here if she'd rather not? She's been through quite an ordeal . . . first the illness, then all that lasering and mauling about . . . if it would make her happy to go on to Barren House, why not let her?"

"You don't mind, Aaron? Are you sure?"

The two men looked at each other, and knew they were thinking the same thing. IF SHE COMES BACK HERE, EVEN IF SHE SAYS NOTHING AT ALL ABOUT IT, SHE'LL BE A CONSTANT REPROACH. THE WOMEN WILL LOOK AT HER, AND THEY'LL LOOK AT US AND THEIR EYES WILL SAY "YOU STINGY CHEAP BASTARDS" EVEN IF THEY KEEP THEIR MOUTHS SHUT. THE WOMEN THINK WE SHOULD HAVE AUTHORIZED THE BREAST REGEN-ERATIONS FOR HER . . . THEY WILL FIND A WAY TO CONSTANTLY REMIND US THAT THAT IS HOW THEY FEEL.

"I wouldn't want to stand in her way at a time like this," said

Aaron solemnly. "It would be unkind, and unreasonable. I think—unless you have strong objections—that she should be humored in this. After all, she can still come here to see the children as often as she wishes . . . and her services continue to be available to the Household as always. Why cause her unnecessary distress?"

"You're very logical about it," Thomas observed. "I'm glad to see that."

The room was quiet, both of them thinking, and then Aaron decided that there would be no better time than this moment, while Thomas was apparently pleased with him.

"Thomas," he said, "Nazareth and I haven't been very . . . happy . . . together."

"Well . . . she was always odd. It's not difficult to understand."

"Do you suppose under the circumstances that—" Aaron stopped, judiciously, as if the words were difficult for him to use.

"Well? That what?"

"How would you perceive the prospect of a divorce for us, Thomas? For Nazareth and me?"

The older man frowned, and his body went rigid; he made Aaron wait. And then he said, "We don't approve of divorce, Adiness."

"I'm aware of that, sir. I don't approve of it myself, nor does my family."

"It was all that divorcing and musical beds that damn near wrecked this country in the twentieth century," Thomas stated with considerable fervor. "We've been a long time coming out of that, a long time returning life to its right and natural form. . . . I'm not sure I care to contribute to holding back the progress of that change."

Aaron spoke cautiously; it wouldn't do to give Thomas the idea that he wasn't for the American Way and the Sanctity of the Home and all the rest of it. Hell, he'd been to Homeroom, just like everybody else: he knew the drill.

"There is no *law* against divorce," he pointed out.

"No. But it is mightily disapproved of. Ordinarily the public disapproves of it *very* strongly unless the woman in question has been institutionalized for life, or is a flagrant adultress . . . lord knows the closest poor Nazareth ever came to adultery was that idiot caper whispering into Jordan Shannontry's ear. I'm afraid that's not flagrant enough. I don't think a divorce could be managed without a lot of public outcry . . . especially not in the present circumstances."

"Sir, is this a matter of your own personal convictions, or is it a question to be settled on the basis of public reaction?"

"I do *not* approve of divorce!" Thomas snapped. "Where my personal opinions are concerned, a contract is a contract—and the marriage contract is as valid and binding as any other. Divorce, except in the most extreme cases, is nothing more than self-indulgence. This nation is under severe enough strain from the shocks of contact with the Alien civilizations, and the drive to settle the space colonies and bring them up to a decent living standard . . . it is *crucially* important that we preserve our cultural fabric and set it well above our personal convenience."

Thomas was going to turn him down, Aaron thought. For the sake of the effing public and its little pointy heads. And the fact that Aaron would be condemned to spend the rest of his life with a woman so mutilated that no decent man could look at her without revulsion was not going to sway him. It was bitter, and he was not ready to accept it. Not quite yet.

"Well, sir," he said, "I will of course abide by your decision. But I think you should know that I don't think I could force myself to share your daughter's bed now . . . not as she is now. And a man needs sexual release if he is to be useful to his Household . . . I'm certain that you know that as well as I do, Thomas."

Ah. Thomas felt that, and he narrowed his eyes to consider its implications. This was a new factor in the equation. He was quite certain that no one in the Household, not even Rachel, suspected his relationship with Michaela Landry. He had been discreet to such a degree that he had almost suspected himself of a mild paranoia on the subject, and he knew there was no question about being able to trust Michaela. But Aaron had always been crafty, sly, given to meddling when he thought there was advantage for him . . . If he *did* suspect, and saw himself denied "sexual release" while Thomas dallied outside Rachel's bed, he could make a lot of trouble and make it safely. However stodgy the American public of 2205 might be about divorce, it wasn't a patch on their feelings about adultery. It was done, of course. In moderation, and with taste. But to be caught at it was unforgivable. How much did Adiness know?

The dark handsome eyes looked back at him, guileless and open—much too guileless and open for his tastes—and Thomas knew he could not be sure. What had he said? That he was certain Thomas knew of a man's needs for sexual release as well as he did? No, he could not be sure.

The decision made, Thomas didn't dawdle.

"Do you think," he asked, "that you could do this with *extreme* delicacy?"

"Of course, Thomas."

"And with the utmost degree of courtesy?"

"What do you mean, sir?"

"I mean that, *for a change*, you would treat Nazareth as if you valued her. I mean that you would speak to her courteously in public, that you would no longer make her the source of your reputation for clever conversation and delightful jokes—oh, I'm not a total fool, Adiness, however much I may refrain from meddling in the marital arrangements of others! And I mean that when you encountered Nazareth by chance before others you would defer to her as to a lady for whom you felt respect. I will not have it said that we first allowed her to be mutilated to such an extent that she was no longer acceptable to you, and then kicked her out of the Household brutally as a divorced woman, with no excuse but our economies! Surely you are capable of understanding that."

"Indeed, sir—I understand precisely what you mean. And you can count on me."

"I have your word as a gentleman?"

"Absolutely."

Thomas steepled his fingers then, and peered at Aaron over the top of them."

"In that case," he said, "perhaps it would not be an entirely unacceptable idea. There's a young girl in our dorms . . . her name is Perpetua. Have you noticed her, Aaron?"

He had. She was lovely. Thick brown hair, huge brown eyes, a body lush and promising, and a gentle manner that roused him every time she moved or spoke. Aaron had indeed noticed Perpetua, as had every other man in the Household.

"I may have," he said.

"In about a year, Perpetua will be sixteen. And needing a husband. I'd like to keep her here, Aaron."

"I see."

"You would have been divorced a respectable length of time by her sixteenth birthday, or very soon thereafter . . . and Perpetua would make you a good wife. It would be a suitable alliance, in every sense of the word."

The old fox, Aaron thought. He was going to make a trade of it. Aaron Adiness, at stud again for Chornyak Household—or no divorce. But he thought he could find considerable consolation in being sentenced to serve as stud for Perpetua. It would be the intervening year that would be difficult.

Thomas knew that, too.

"You would have to be *quaintly* beyond reproach during your year as a bachelor," he said, measuring the words out. "Move into the bachelor rooms, be there in your bachelor bed every night without exception . . . I will not have it said that you divorced Nazareth simply to marry Perpetua."

"It will be said no matter what I do, sir."

"It's one thing to have it said because people have small twisted minds; it's quite another to have it said because you provide an excuse to say it."

"You want my word again."

"Indeed I do."

A year of total celibacy . . . the prospect dismayed Aaron more than he had thought it would. But life with Nazareth meant permanent celibacy broken only by the occasional quick flutter on the sly. . . . They would watch his every move, if he remained married to Nazareth; he'd be fortunate if he could find himself some draggled trollop once a year. Aaron shuddered; there were worse things than a year of monkhood.

"I swear it, Thomas," he said swiftly. "I understand the conditions, and I'll abide by them. To the letter."

"Huhnh." The sound was not pleasant, nor was the expression on his father-in-law's face.

"I'll know if you don't," said Thomas grimly. "And I'll break you. If you deviate by so much as a wink, young man. The reputation of this Household, the reputation of the Lines, means infinitely more to me than any single member. The public already has reason enough to criticize about the manner in which we 'send our females out to do men's work,' without adding scandal."

Aaron put on the haughtiest expression he had in his repertoire.

"You have my word," he repeated. "It should be sufficient."

"I wonder."

Aaron flushed, but he said nothing. There was nothing to say. Either the fellow would trust him or he wouldn't, and there was nothing Aaron could do to influence him except sit there and allow himself to be as transparent as possible. He had nothing to hide, for once—he would abide by the conditions and consider that a reasonable price for freedom from Nazareth.

"All right, then," said Thomas suddenly. "All right. I am not ordinarily disposed to see any excuse for divorce . . . but this is an unusual situation. And there's *some* precedent—there was Belle-Anne. All right, Aaron; under these circumstances, and with your promise, I won't oppose you."

Aaron let out his breath, not realizing until he did so that he'd been holding it. It was a great relief. Too bad he couldn't have had one more night in Nazareth's bed before she'd gone off for the surgery, but it hadn't occurred to him. As it hadn't occurred to him that she wouldn't insist on coming back here and making his life a hell just for the satisfaction of doing so—in her place, he certainly would have gloried in the chance for revenge. It was typically female that she was either too stupid or too cowardly to seize that chance. He found himself almost grateful to her; he was not a brilliant man, but he was not so foolish that he didn't know how large an account of bitterness he'd run up with her in the years of their marriage. He'd had a lot of fun doing it, but he knew it hadn't ever been any fun for Nazareth; like all women, she had no sense of humor whatsoever. Like being colorblind, or tonedeaf. A curious deformity.

And now he and Thomas had managed to bring off a very efficient little bit of action here. All in one swoop, they'd gotten rid of Nazareth and the annoying reminder she would have represented, they'd arranged to keep Aaron in the house *and* fathering more infants—something that would have been impossible otherwise—and they'd settled the matter of a suitable husband for the luscious Perpetua. Aaron knew that in spite of Thomas' facade of objections he must be pleased; this was the sort of thing the man considered an efficient example of household management. He had been damn near smiling when he told Aaron to go ahead and notify the Chornyak attorneys. Aaron felt that they were damn clever, he and Thomas . . . he was only sorry that there was no way he could brag about this little coup.

Clara saw him come up the stairs from his meeting with her brother, and read the smug satisfaction on his face correctly, but she wasn't quick enough with her "Aaron!" to stop him as he went rushing out the door. It was clear to her that the two men had been willing to let Nazareth do what she wanted: it was also clear that Aaron had forgotten all about the fact that his wife was waiting for the decision. Unless perhaps he, or Thomas, had sent her a message directly?

Thinking hard, she didn't hear Michaela until her name had been spoken twice, and even then she jumped.

"You're too tired, Clara," Michaela observed. "You're asleep on your feet."

"No . . . I was just thinking. And worrying."

"Can I help?"

Clara explained, and Michaela touched her hand lightly.

"I'm on my way to Mr. Chornyak's office right now," she said, "to ask him about a new medication for your father. If you want to come along with me, we could bother him together . . . safety in numbers and all that."

"I'm not afraid to speak to him alone, my dear," Clara said. "That's not it. I'm just trying to get my bad temper under control before I do it. I'll wait until you're through."

"Well, I *am* afraid to go alone," Michaela declared, "because the medicine I want costs almost three times as much as what your father's been taking; so please come with me out of Christian charity, Clara. He won't carry on so if he has to split the thunder and lightning between us."

Clara looked at her, and Michaela could see by the glint in her eyes that she wasn't fooled by the easy chatter, but she said only, "All right, Michaela," and went with her without further comment.

And of course, as Clara had suspected, neither of the men had thought to send Nazareth a simple yes or no. Much less the news that she was about to be divorced.

"Thomas!" Clara had been shocked. "Dear heaven, Thomas . . ."

"What, Clara?"

"I mean that. . . . It's just. . . ."

"Clara, will you please quit stammering and sputtering and speak your piece? Nazareth doesn't care a thing for Aaron, never has, and you know it as well as I do. What's the problem?"

Clara was helpless, and felt both helpless and absurd. There wasn't any way to explain it to him. It had nothing to do with whether Nazareth cared about Aaron Adiness. It had to do with first undergoing that explicit demonstration of how little she was worth to the men, when they refused the money for the breast regeneration; and it had to do with then undergoing the mutilating surgery itself; and it had to do with the way a woman was treated in the public wards, especially a linguist woman; and it had to do with the pain and the grief that Nazareth would be feeling right now; and it had to do with what it would be like for her, on top of all the rest, to be told causally, by wrist computer, "Oh by the way, Aaron's divorcing you—thought you'd want to know."

She could have made him understand, of course, if she'd had hours to spend explaining it to him. Thomas was a shrewd judge of the effects of language upon others, and he was—despite the silly exchange between herself and Michaela—never an unreasonable man. But there was no way to make him see it quickly and efficiently, and Thomas had no patience with long rambling speeches about subjects he had had no interest in in the first place. He was staring at her, and Clara knew that he was annoyed, and she felt as if she were going to strangle. I'm getting old, she thought, and I must be losing my wits along with my other youthful charms.

"Clara," said Thomas, "I know you're fond of Nazareth. But it was Nazareth who *asked* to go directly to Barren House, you know—it's not as if Aaron had tried to *send* her there. I assure you, I would not have allowed him to do that, Clara. We are only doing what Nazareth, herself, asked for."

"I know that, Thomas."

"Then I truly do not understand why you are so upset."

Michaela stepped smoothly into the widening breach, certain that Clara would welcome the help.

"Mr. Chornyak," she said, all deference and propriety, "I think what's worrying Clara is that Nazareth must just hear this news by wrist computer, without even a human face attached. Just that little tinny noise, saying that she's being divorced and good riddance to her, if you see what I mean."

"I don't see what you mean," Thomas answered. "She detests her husband, she doesn't want to come home, and she's being told that she doesn't have to put up with either husband or Household for even one more day. It seems to me that she should be dancing in the halls. But as long as the two of *you* understand what you mean, it really doesn't matter whether I do or not. I have never pretended to be an expert on the emotional notions of women."

"Yes, sir," Michaela said.

"Well? Have you and Clara got a solution to this dreadful difficulty that I'm too thick-headed even to perceive?"

"Mr. Chornyak, I need to see the hospital anyway—I should have gone over there long ago. I might need to send one of my patients there sometime, and I should at least be familiar with the place. Unless you have some objection, sir, I could take the message to Nazareth and have a look around the facilities at the same time."

"I have no objection at all, Mrs. Landry," said Thomas. "If you have the free time, and you feel it's advisable, by all means go ahead."

"Thank you, sir," Michaela said. "And I have just one other item to talk to you about before I go, please."

While Michaela was quickly outlining to Thomas the advantages of the new medication that justified the expense of its purchase,

238 / Suzette Haden Elgin

Clara slipped away without saying anything more, her gratitude written plainly in the set of her head and shoulders and the shaping of her hands.

The hospital was ugly, but then hospitals always were. Michaela had never worked in a luxury ward among the wealthy, but always in places like this. She paid very little attention to its looks, concerned only to make sure that it was clean—and it was. And she was equally unimpressed by the sass from the nurses.

"Either tell me at once, without any further nonsense, where Mrs. Adiness is, or I'll call Thomas Blair Chornyak and tell him that you've misplaced her," she told them. "Perhaps with his personal assistance we'd be able to locate her."

"Well, there's no need to be unpleasant!"

"You're wasting my time, nurse, and your behavior is beneath contempt. You are here to *serve*, not to obstruct healing, and whether you happen to fancy a particular patient or not should not be your concern. Now take me to Mrs. Adiness."

She was as skilled at genteel tongue-lashing laced with aristocratic venom as she was at listening to boring stories; it was one of the skills that the marital academies assumed a woman might need if she married into a wealthy family where human beings were still employed as domestic servants. The nurse recognized the tone without difficulty, and had had no training in defense against it . . . she came bustling out from behind her narrow counter, flushed and pouting, and took Michaela to Nazareth's bed without asking any questions about the possible source of the authority in that voice.

"There," she announced, pointing. "There she is. Somebody to see you, Mrs. Adiness."

Michaela stared at her fixedly until she turned and flounced off, muttering about ingratitude and who did people think they were anyway; and then she turned to look at Nazareth.

"Mrs. Adiness," she said courteously, "I'm Michaela Landry, the nurse that your father employs for Barren House. I'm ashamed to use the word 'nurse' after that specimen, but I promise you I'm not here to demonstrate the depths to which my profession sometimes manages to fall. I don't think we've met except in passing. . . . How do you do, Mrs. Adiness."

She extended her hand, and Nazareth took it briefly, saying, "Yes, of course, Mrs. Landry, I remember you. It's very kind of you to come by."

She looked bruised, Michaela thought. If it were possible for someone to carry bruises of spirit and mind as well as body, she would be carrying them. Thin, *ugly* thin . . . a bad color, the characteristic unhealthy look of the cancer patient . . . and that skewered knot of hair. Even here. Poor thing.

"Mrs. Adiness," she said, "it's all right for you to go on to Barren House from here; they sent me to tell you. And your father asked me to come and help you. . . . He didn't want you to have to make the trip by yourself." It was an easy lie, and it cost her nothing; she made a mental note to tell Thomas that she'd said it. And it ought to have been true, because this woman most certainly was not well enough to have left the hospital by herself and made her way to Barren House all alone. From the taut look of her she would have done it, and without a word of complaint, but she had no business making an effort of that kind. Or any other effort. Michaela wanted her tucked into a comfortable bed and under *her* care, and she wanted it fast. And as for the news about the divorce, she would pass that on after she had this woman comfortable, and sheltered, and away from prying eyes. Not one minute before.

"Mrs. Adiness. . . ."

"Please, Mrs. Landry . . . call me Nazareth. I would prefer it."

"As you like, ma'am, and you might consider calling me Michaela if that's not awkward for you. Now, can you dress and get your things together while I arrange for a cab?"

"A cab?" Nazareth was astonished. "The robobus goes right by here."

"Is that how you got here?"

"Of course," Nazareth answered, and added, "And I don't have any money."

"Well, I do."

"Money of your own?"

Michaela smiled. "It's one of the few benefits of being both widowed and a nurse, Nazareth. My brother-in-law is my legal guardian, but he is required to leave me part of my salary since I don't live in his home. I don't have very *much* money, but I can manage the price of one short cab trip."

"I can't let you spend your money on me," Nazareth objected immediately, and Michaela laughed at her.

"All right," she said. "You are the lady of the house, and I am the employee, and I'm not about to cross you. I'll get the cab for myself and let you take the bus, and I'll be at Barren House before you. It will be so much nicer that way, not having to be crowded in the cab."

She was utterly surprised when Nazareth only nodded, as if that made perfectly good sense, and she sat down at once on the edge of the other woman's bed, careful not to jolt her as she did so.

"Oh, my dear," she said, not caring if she seemed disrespectful, because this was mute pain that she faced and tending pain was a function that she was not able to set aside for the sake of good manners, "I didn't mean that! Of course not! And I will not let you go to Barren House in any other way than under my care, and in decent comfort. Please understand that, and forgive me my jokes . . . I only meant to make you smile, Nazareth."

Nazareth only looked at her and said nothing at all, and something in Michaela gave way, some knot she had not realized was even tied inside her. "You're very tired, Nazareth," she went on, "and you need care, not clever conversation. I'll get the nurse to help you dress."

"Please, no!"

Michaela was firm, and there was steel in her voice. "I promise you, my dear, that nurse will be as gentle and as tender with you as if you were her newborn and beloved child. You have my word on it."

"You don't know . . . . ."

"Oh, but I *do* know! I most assuredly do know. And I promise you. She will come, and she will be respectful, and she will be kind, and she will treat you with flawless attention. She will not dare do anything else—as for what she may be thinking, that is *her* narrow little twisted mind, and you are to ignore that as you would ignore any other deformity. For politeness' sake. And I will get the cab and take you home."

"I'm not a child, Michaela . . . you don't have to. . . . "

"Don't talk! Hush. If you were a child this would be much simpler, because I could just pick you up and carry you, whether you kicked and screamed or not. But you're taller than I am, unfortunately, and I'm going to have to have some help—must you make it even more difficult for me than it is?"

She hated saying that, because all her impulses were to treat this hurt one tenderly, but it was exactly the right thing to say. The idea that she was causing trouble for the nurse sent to fetch her stopped Nazareth's objections immediately.

"I'm very sorry, Mrs. Landry," said Nazareth. "Please proceed."

Please proceed! Such a funny, awkward woman, and what a

very hard time she must have had with her whole personality akimbo like that . . . and that swift, ever so correct "Mrs. Landry!" Putting her in her place. Her dignity would see her back to Barren House, Michaela thought, and that was far more important than anything else right now.

Chapter Twenty

Then consider this, please: to make something "appear" is called *magic*, is it not? Well. . . . when you look at another person, what do you see? Two arms, two legs, a face, an assortment of *parts*. Am I right? Now, there is a continuous surface of the body, a space that begins with the inside flesh of the fingers and continues over the palm of the hand and up the inner side of the arm to the bend of the elbow. Everyone has that surface; in fact, everyone has *two* of them.

I will name that the "athad" of the person. Imagine the athad, please. See it clearly in your mind—perceive, here are my own two athads, the left one and the right one. And there are both of *your* athads, very nice ones.

Where there was no athad before, there will always be one now, because you will perceive the athad of every person you look at, as you perceive their nose and their hair. From now on. And I have made the athad appear . . . now it *exists*.

Magic, you perceive, is not something mysterious, not something for witches and sorcerers . . . magic is quite ordinary and simple. It is simply language.

And I look at you now, and I can say, as I could not say three minutes ago—"What lovely *athads* you have, grandmother!"

(from "The Discourse of the Three Marys," author unknown)

242

Nazareth went to Barren House bruised, as Michaela had seen that she was, and numb. The news that she was being divorced hardly penetrated that numbness, so that by the time she became aware of it any chance that it might cause her discomfort was long past. But after a while, under the competent hands of the women, she began to let that numbness go, and she realized that she was like someone who goes home at last after a lifetime of exile.

No more Aaron; he avoided her, and when he could not avoid her he was overpoweringly polite. No more being alone with him, where he did not feel obliged to be polite. Her children only a few steps away, and the little girls routinely here at Barren House in any case. And a kind of freedom. She would never have to bear a man's eyes upon her scarred body. She would heal, and she would add to her usual clothing the garment with the false and foolish breasts, and she would go out to work as she always had; and no man would ever see her naked, or touch her body, again. Not even, so long as she was conscious, a doctor. Not ever.

She wandered about Barren House at first, absorbing it as if she had never been there before, luxuriating in the voices of the women, glorying in the bed that she could have all to herself without the snoring bulk of a man always waking her, always crowding her against the wall. It was luxury; she had not anticipated that it would be, because she hadn't known what it was that she lacked.

Finally, when Michaela agreed that it was time, the women told her about the woman-language called Láadan, and explained the nonsense called Langlish. Nazareth sat and listened to them in amazement, saying not one word until they were finished, and then she said, "You women. You women and your fairy tales!"

"It's true!" they protested. "Really, Nazareth . . . it's true."

"All my life you've told me that the tale of *Lang*lish was true."

"That was necessary," Aquina retorted. "We are a better judge of what's required than you are."

"And now, after a lifetime of lying, you expect me to believe that you are suddenly telling the truth?" Nazareth shook her head. "Go away with your bedtime stories," she jeered, "tell them to the little girls. Along with the unicorn and the bandersnatch and the Helga Dik! Leave me in peace."

"Nazareth," Susannah chided. "You should be ashamed of yourself."

"Should I?"

"You know you should. We've been waiting for so many years to show you this—I've grown to be an ancient crone able only to cackle and hiss while I waited. And now you won't *let* us show you."

"Show me, then," said Nazareth, who loved Susannah dearly. But she could not resist teasing Aquina. "Aquina," she asked, "does it have one hundred separate vowels, this Láadan?"

"Oh, you're impossible!"

Nazareth chuckled at Aquina's disappearing back, and Susannah told her again that she should be ashamed of herself.

"I am," Nazareth said, with great satisfaction. "I'm so very ashamed I can hardly hold my head up. Now show me."

"It's down in the basement," they warned.

"Of course. With the tub of green bubbling slime that you sacrifice a virgin to every Monday morning. Where else would it be? I can walk to the basement, I'm not crippled—lead on, please."

She followed them, laughing again as they pulled the scraps of paper from the backs of drawers and the middles of recipes files and other assorted nooks and crannies. But she sat down and looked at the assembled materials when they handed them to her, and she stopped laughing as she read. Once she said, "It would be so easy for all this to be lost! And so awful."

"No," said Faye. "It would be a nuisance, but not a tragedy. It's all in our memories. Every last scrap and dot of it."

Nazareth said nothing else at all. She had begun, laughing and dubious, but enjoying herself; now, as she examined the materials, she grew more and more tense, and they wondered if they had bothered her with this too soon. She was still far from well.

"Nazareth," asked Susannah cautiously, "are you all right, child? And are you pleased?"

"Pleased!" Nazareth handed the little stack of papers to them as if it were a spoiled fish. "I'm disgusted!"

The silence spread, and they looked at each other, bewildered. Disgusted? They knew about Nazareth; there was no other woman in the Lines as good at languages as she was. But were they really so far from what was needful in a language that Láadan disgusted her?

Nazareth stood up, swaying a bit, but she pushed them away when they would have helped her and went back up the stairs ahead of them. "There's no excuse for this,'" she announced with her back to them. "No excuse!"

"But it's a good language," Aquina cried, saying what the others hesitated to say. "You have no right to judge it like that, on ten minutes' casual examination! I don't care *what* your damn test scores are, or how distinguished your damn Alien language is, you have no right!''

"Aquina," Grace said disapprovingly. "Please."

"It's not that," Nazareth said, tight-lipped. "It's not that there's anything wrong with the language.''

"Then what *is* it, for the love of heaven?" Aquina demanded.

Nazareth turned on them, where they stood uneasily in the kitchen keeping an eye out for a stray child who might hear something she should not hear, and said, "What is inexcusable is that the language isn't already being used."

"But it can't be used until it's finished!"

"What nonsense! No living language is ever 'finished'!"

"Nazareth, you know what we mean."

"No. I *don't* know what you mean."

Caroline came running then, exclaiming over the racket they were making and the stupidity of keeping Nazareth standing like that, and herded them all into one of the private bedrooms like disorderly poultry, which was precisely what she compared them to. When she had the door closed and her back against it, she said fiercely, "Now! What *is* all this?"

They told her, and she relaxed against the door and let her hands fall to her sides. "Good heavens! I thought it was an earthquake at the very least . . . all this fuss because Láadan doesn't suit little Nazareth? Mercy!"

"But it does suit me, Caroline," Nazareth insisted. "Not that it would matter if it didn't—but it does."

"It isn't finished, you know. They're right."

"They're wrong."

"Oh come on, Natha!"

"I assure you, this language that they have just shown me is sufficiently 'finished' to be *used*. It obviously has been for years, while you played with it and fiddled about with it . . . when I think, that there are little girls of the Lines six or seven years old that could already have been speaking it fluently and who know not one word! I could kill you all, I swear I could."

"Nonsense."

"You know what you're like?" Nazareth demanded. "You're like those idiot artists who never will let their paintings be put on the wall because they always have to add just one more stroke! Like those novelists never willing to let their books go, who die unpublished, because there's always just one more line they want to put in. You silly creatures . . . the men are right, you're a pack of silly ignorant *fools* over here! And at all the Barren

246 / Suzette Haden Elgin

Houses, obviously, since you're all muddled equally. Dear heaven, it makes me almost willing to go back to Chornyak Household, not to have to look at you!''

''Nazareth—''

''Be still!'' she commanded them, not caring at all how arrogant or unpleasant she might be. ''Please, go away and let me have a little while to think about this! I'm too upset now even to talk to you . . . go *away!*''

She was trembling, and if she hadn't been who she was they knew she would have been crying, and it bothered them to leave her like that. On the other hand, it was clear that their presence was not any comfort to her, and so they did as she asked.

''We'll wait for you in the parlor,'' Susannah said quietly as she went out the door. ''That's the safest place to talk about this—when you are willing to talk, child.''

She wasn't long, and when she joined them she was calm again. They handed her a stole to work because it required no attention whatsoever and would leave her free to talk and to listen. And they sent someone to watch the door and divert any little girls that came along to the basement to ''help with the inventory,'' if they didn't seem willing to simply go back to Chornyak Household because everyone was too busy to keep them company.

''Now then,'' Caroline began, stabbing at the sampler that said ''There is no such thing as a primitive language,'' in elaborate cross stitch, ''if what you say is true this is the most important day of my life, of many of our lives. But it seems very unlikely to all of us, Nazareth—think, you've been here only a few weeks, and you haven't been yourself until just the past day or two. We have been here, some of us, for more than twenty years. And we have been working at the language all that time, in every spare moment we could steal. Don't you think that if the time had come to bring the Encoding Project to a close and start teaching the language we would have noticed it? Without you to tell us?''

''No,'' declared Nazareth. ''I *would* have thought so, if anybody had described this absurd situation to me. But I would have been wrong. It must be that you are so close to the matter that you can't see it—it takes someone with fresh perceptions to peer past the claptrap.''

''And so the good Lord has blessed us with you, Nazareth Joanna Chornyak Adiness . . . how lucky for us to have the benefit of your 'fresh perceptions.' ''

"Caroline," Nazareth persisted, "I have never been able to get along with anybody. I know that. I don't know what's wrong with me, but I do know that I'm scarcely able to get through a paragraph without offending two people and hurting three others. And I am sorry . . . I have always been sorry. I have always wished someone would tell me how to be better. But however awful it sounds to you, put in the only way I know how to put it, that language is *ready*—'finished,' if you prefer—and for it not to be in use is a shame and a scandal."

"Nazareth!" Caroline was annoyed now, and annoyed that she was annoyed. "You're very good, of course—but we are not so bad as all that! We do not need you, to instruct *us* in linguistics."

"But you do." Nazareth was as determined as stone.

"You presume," said Grace stiffly. "We have all been trying to make allowances, but you go too far."

"All right," said Nazareth, "I presume. But tell me what it is that the language lacks, and I will listen with an open mind. What doesn't it have? What do you think it needs before you will call it finished?"

Well . . . they mentioned a bit here and a piece there, and Nazareth scoffed. Not one thing that they mentioned, she told them, that couldn't be supplied from the existing mechanisms of the language. Or by adding a bound morpheme—an ending, a little extra piece somewhere in the word. They made their objections until they ran out of objections and she countered every last one of them.

Finally, Caroline said, "Nazareth . . . the vocabulary is so limited."

"Is that it?" Nazareth stared around her. "Is it the size of the vocabulary that's bothering all of you?"

"Well," Caroline told her, "we know what a language has to have. We did all those things long ago, and you are right about the ones we've been discussing. But we can't begin speaking Láadan to the babies until there is a vocabulary sufficiently large, sufficiently flexible—"

"To what?"

"What?"

"Sufficiently large enough and flexible enough to *what*, Caroline? Write the *Encyclopedia Galactica*? What are you waiting for? The specialized lexicons of the sciences? The complete lexicon of wine-tasting? *What*, precisely?"

Now they were genuinely cross, and their needles flew.

"Certainly not! We simply want it to be possible to speak it with grace and ease in the affairs of ordinary life!"

"Well," Nazareth pronounced, "it is ready for that."

"It isn't!"

"How many words do you have? How many freestanding whole words, even without all those that would come from adding the affixes?"

"About three thousand," said Susannah. "Only that."

"Well, for the love of Mary!" Nazareth cried, and they all shushed her together.

"I'm sorry," she apologized, "but really! Three thousand! The way you were carrying on . . . I thought perhaps you had only a few hundred lexical items."

"Nazareth," said Susannah, "English has hundreds of thousands of words. Do think—and don't shout, *please*."

"And Basic English, in which the entire New Testament has been most adequately written, has fewer than *one* thousand. As all of you know quite well."

"But we cannot have the language begin in a state that requires constant paraphrase," Caroline objected. "Bad enough that it must begin as a variant of a pidgin—at least let it have an adequate vocabulary!"

Nazareth took a long slow breath and laid the length of wool in her lap.

"My dears," she said, as seriously and as patiently as she could, her voice steady and her eyes holding theirs, "I tell you that language is ready. Ready to use. And what is more, you know it. All of you, every last one, you know languages with no more lexical items than this Láadan of yours has. You are telling *yourselves* fairy tales, and I don't understand why. If we begin today, if those of you tending infants for the main house begin this very day murmuring to those babies in Láadan instead of English, it will not be until they are adult women and are doing the same for the *next* generation—or maybe the generation after that, because no language has ever, as far as anyone knows, been started in this way—it will be at the very least the generation after those infants before Láadan is a creole. And still another before it can be called a living language with the status of other living languages."

They showed her defiant faces, and she could hear their minds ticking, spinning the excuses; she stopped them before they could work their way into another tangle.

"Now, wait!" she said. "I know as well as you that in the days when every educated person learned Latin as a second language for the carrying on of scholarly and legal discourse, people managed. It must have been a barbarous sort of Latin, but they *managed*. Do not go jumping from what I've said to still more reasons for delay! If it takes five generations, or ten, before Láadan goes beyond being a barbarous auxiliary language and becomes our native tongue, that is all the more compelling reason to begin at once! Of course it will be dreadful at first, there's no way it could be anything else . . . but my dear loves, we are talking of at least one hundred years to get past that, if we begin this very day! And you sit there, and you tell me that we must wait until we have . . . what? Five thousand words? Ten thousand words? Ten thousand words and ten thousand Encodings? What arbitrary number have you set as your goal?"

"We don't know. Not exactly. Only that what we have isn't enough."

Nazareth frowned, and bit her lip, and Susannah reached over to put the neglected stole back in her hands.

"Crochet, Natha," she directed. "That is what we women do . . . ask the men and they will tell you. Any time they come here, they find us chatting and needling away. Frittering our time. Use your hook, please, child, and don't look so *intense*. It makes wrinkles."

Nazareth obeyed, absentmindedly putting the small hook through its paces, but she did not change her expression.

"There is something more," she stated flatly. "Something that you're hiding. This 'limited vocabulary' excuse is just as phony as the 'not enough Encodings' you gave me when I was a little girl. You use it to soothe the children, and I'm not a child—it won't placate me. I want to know the truth. No more lies, now."

"Nonsense!"

"You are forever saying that!" protested Nazareth. "You could save yourselves a lot of trouble by getting a parrot to say 'nonsense' for you all the day long. And it won't wash . . . there's something else. Something I'm too stupid to see. Something that isn't just a question of whether the language is 'finished' or not. And I know exactly who to ask, too! Aquina Chornyak— what is the *real* problem here, hiding behind a silly wordcount?"

When Aquina didn't answer, Nazareth reached over and pulled her hair. "Aquina! You tell me! What sort of radical are you, anyway?"

"All right," said Aquina. "I'll tell you—but they won't be pleased."

"Never mind that."

"The real problem is because decisions have to be made, and these . . . persons . . . won't make them."

"What decisions are these?"

"You feel that Láadan is finished, right?"

"In the sense that any language is finished. Its vocabulary will grow, as the vocabulary of any language grows."

"All right, then. Suppose we begin to use it, as you say we should do. And then, as more and more little girls acquire Láadan and begin to speak a language that expresses the perceptions of women rather than those of men, reality will begin to change. Isn't that true?"

"As true as water," Nazareth said. "As true as light."

"Well, then, milady—we must be ready when that shift in reality begins. Ready to *act*, in response to the change! Once that begins we will not be able to go on sitting here in the parlor tatting and twiddling and playing at revolutionary ideas. We will not be able to spend our days like placid cattle, thinking of the time, centuries away, when someone will have to *do* something! And that is where the sticking point is, Nazareth—there's not a woman in this house, or in any of the other Barren Houses, with guts enough to come to a decision about what we are to do *then*. That's what keeps us, as you put it, adding one more brush stroke and one more line and going 'oh no not yet!' and 'nonsense!' and 'pray spare us!'"

"Oh," breathed Nazareth. "I understand. Yes."

"Do you understand, Nazareth? Do you really?" Caroline's voice was bitter and angry. "Consider, for example, what Aquina would have us do! We would start stockpiling emergency rations and supplies, if she had her way, and bundling them into packs that we could carry on our backs as we fled into the wilderness, each of us with one kidnapped girlchild on our hips, fleeing just one step ahead of the hordes of men determined to slaughter us all!"

"Caroline, you exaggerate," Aquina scoffed.

"Not much. I've heard you often enough."

"They wouldn't dare kill us. They'd incarcerate every last one of us that *knew* Láadan; and they'd dope us silly till we forgot every word. They'd destroy our records, they'd punish any child who used a single syllable, and they'd stamp it out forever—but they wouldn't kill us. I never said they'd kill *us*, Caroline; it's Láadan they would kill. And we'd have to get away before they could invent some new and horrendous 'epidemic incurable schizophrenia' allegedly brought back from a frontier planet in a bag of grain . . . but they wouldn't kill us."

"You hear her?" Caroline challenged Nazareth. "That is what we listen to, endlessly."

"I hear her," Nazareth said. "I see your point, Caroline. And I also see Aquina's. And there are many many other possibilities."

"Certainly there are," Caroline agreed. "It's as absurd to think the men could get away with shutting us all away in instituions as it is to think they could kill us. And if Aquina didn't so love wallowing in extremes she'd know. that. They would have to move against us a few at a time, even if they invent half a dozen epidemics from outer space that are conveniently contagious only for females. But the men know the power of a new language just as well as we do—and they *would* stop it, Nazareth. The day we begin to use Láadan, the day we let it out of the basement, that day we put its very existence at risk. You were right about the tub of green stuff bubbling away down there, Nazareth—but we don't have any virgins to sacrifice."

"You are afraid."

"Of course we are afraid!"

"What I think they will do," said Faye, "the only thing they can possibly do, is break up the Barren Houses. Isolate us from one another. Keep us away from the rest of the women, certainly nver let us near the infant children. It won't be hard for them to teach the babies that elderly women and barren women are witches, horrid old repositories of wickedness to be feared and avoided—that's been done before, and it's always been a smashing success! Some of us they'll shut away . . . some of us they'll isolate in the Households. Can't you imagine the publicity campaign as they 'decide' that they were in error all these years putting us in separate buildings and 'welcome us back to the bosoms of our families'? The public will love it. . . . and they'll stamp out every vestige of Láadan. And every vestige of Langlish, while they're at it, just in case it might give someone ideas again someday. And Láadan will die, as every language of women must have died, since the beginning of time."

"Unless we get away before they realize that it's happening," hissed Aquina. "That's the only chance we have."

Nazareth got up and went to the window, staring out across the open green through the trees, silent and troubled.

"Nazareth," pleaded Grace behind her, "if Aquina is right—allowances made for her embellishments, of course—do you perceive now what it means?"

"Yes."

"And they can't muster up the courage," said Aquina with contempt, "to decide what must be done and *do* it."

"Because we don't *know* what we must do," said the others. "We have talked and talked and talked about it . . . we don't know."

"We must choose one Barren House," said Aquina steadily, "the most isolated and the most easily defended, and we must be ready to go there with as many girlchildren as we can take with us, at the first hint that the men know what's happening. It isn't a difficult decision. And we must be ready to move on from there, if we have to."

"It would mean leaving our children!"

"And never seeing our families again."

"And publicity—think of the lies the men will give to the media!"

"All the old ones, upstairs . . . we'd have to abandon them!"

"No wonder you've been stalling," said Nazareth, turning around again. "Marking time. No wonder."

"Oh, not you, too!" moaned Aquina. "I can't stand it."

Nazareth came back and sat down, and took up the foolish stole again. "Perceive this," she said with absolute certainty in her voice, "no matter what it means—either we do not really believe in the Encoding Project, in which case the men are right and we are just silly women playing silly games to pass the time—or we must begin."

"Damn right!" said Aquina.

"You must remember," said Nazareth, glaring at Aquina, "that it will be many years before the men notice. They're used to hearing the little girls practicing Alien languages they've never heard before and may well never hear again, not to mention any number of Terran languages completely unfamiliar to them. So long as we convince the children that it's a secret to be kept from the men—like so many other secrets we've taught them to keep, loves—ten years will go by, perhaps more, before the men suddenly realize that too many little girls are making the *same* unfamiliar sounds. Dear heaven, they're so entirely convinced that the Project is only Langlish, and so entirely convinced that we can barely find our way to the bathroom without a map! It may be decades before anything actually needs to be done, in the way that Aquina means. Please do realize that."

"But—"

Nazareth cut Aquina off, raising her hand in the ancient gesture of teachers. "But I agree with Aquina that the decisions have to be made, and made right now, in case they are someday needed. She's absolutely right. If we did need to make some sort of move, there'd be no time then to decide what it should be, and anything we did in panic would be certain to be the wrong thing. We must make the plans, however unlikely it is that we'll ever have to use them, and put that behind us.''

"Thank heaven for someone with sense!''

"Thank *you,* Aquina,'' said Nazareth. "Now, you others, can we proceed with this?''

Proceed. From an endless Project, going on generation after generation, to "can we proceed?'' It was too much, and they were stunned by the prospect.

"It's not complicated,'' Nazareth assured them. "Word should go out to all the Barren Houses as quickly as can be managed, using the recipe-codes. In each Barren House those women who are best at speaking Láadan are to begin practicing it with one another, never mind how badly they do, until they are at ease enough to serve as roughly adequate models. And then, they are to begin using Láadan and only Láadan with the female infants of the Lines whenever there are no men about.''

"Or women still living in the Households.''

"Or women still living among men, yes,'' Nazareth agreed. "Whenever it is as safe as it ever will be safe. Meanwhile, those who know almost nothing about it will turn to and *learn.* Without drawing the attention of men, and without slacking on our other duties.''

"And the planning?'' That was Aquina.

"And the planning must begin,'' said Nazareth. "In every Barren House, there must be meetings to discuss alternatives. For every choice of action that you feel the men might take when they learn that they've been duped, there needs to be a corresponding action that all the women are agreed upon and are prepared to move on at a moment's notice. The results should be exchanged among the Barren Houses until there is a consensus— until we all understand just what we would be expected to do in each possible hypothetical crisis. And we will do whatever we *must* do to prepare.''

"Just like that, Nazareth?''

"Just like that. You've put it off far too long already.''

"Well,'' said Susannah. "Well! Someone must go upstairs and tell the others. They have a right to know.''

"And someone,'' Caroline pointed out, "must set the tables for dinner and call in the sentries before they decide we've all died in here.''

They folded up their work and put it away in the deep needle-work bags with the jumble of yarns and laces and scraps hiding the useful false bottoms. And tried to decide whether to rejoice or to weep.

"Is it a time for celebration, do you think?" hazarded Grace.

"Who could know? It's a time for terror. That much is certain."

"It's stepping out into the void," said Susannah solemnly.

"And it's all Nazareth's fault," said Nazareth.

In the abashed silence, she added, "Any beginning is also an ending, you know. You can't have just the one."

Chapter Twenty-one

You go from us
into a new becoming;
we rejoice for you and wish you an easy journey out
into the Light.

The winds will speak to us of you,
the waters will mention your name;
snow and rain and fog, first light and last light,
all will remind us that you had
a certain way of Being
that was dear to us.

You go back to the land you came from
and on beyond.
We will watch for you,
from Time to Time. Amen.

(funeral service for The Lovingkindness Church)

Michaela woke before dawn, with a pounding headache, drenched in an icy sweat. Before the soft tone of the Household alarm that roused everyone—unless sick or given some special dispensation—at five o'clock in the morning. Here in the depths of the hill that sheltered Chornyak Household there was nothing else to wake you . . . no light filtered in here below the earth, except in the long halls that ran down either side of the building, where there was some illumination from the ground floor sky-lights extending the full length of both halls. And there was no sound . . . no birdsong, no thunder, no traffic from the streets or skies, nothing. It was absolutely still, and absolutely dark. And except in the dormitories the linguists had constructed the sleepingrooms to offer the maximum possible amount of soundproofing; it was, after all, the only privacy there was within the houses of the Lines.

If the couple who had the room next to yours chose to while away the night in erotic pleasures or forbidden rituals—something Michaela could not imagine in the linguists, who seemed to her almost excruciatingly proper, almost puritanical, but then you never knew—you would never know about it. You would never hear a moan, a gasp of pleasure, an obscene incantation, even a scream of ecstasy at orgasm. The builders of these houses had insisted on that, and it had been very wise of them.

But with the dreams that had been tormenting her nights lately, Michaela needed nothing to wake her, not even the alarm. The dreams were more than sufficient. Dreams in which each of the men she had killed lined up before her and held out imploring arms, begging for their lives back, whimpering pitifully like babies trapped in cellars or small animals caught in fences. . . . She shuddered, and threw back her damp sheets, loathing the feel of them against her skin.

It was so ridiculous, damn it! Except for Ned Landry—and by God, she would kill *him* again in an instant, if she were given the chance—every one of those men had gone peacefully and probably gratefully to his grave. Every last one had been at the end of a long and fruitful life of hard work; every one had reached that stage of life where none of the physiological systems could really be counted on any longer, and the body began to betray the embarrassed spirit; every one of them had been more than ready for some rest. Rest she had given them. Painlessly. Sweet rest.

Grandfather Verdi, for instance. It was absurd that she should dream of him begging for his life back! He had been so anxious, in a completely healthy way, to be rid of it.

"Like a baby, that's what," he would grumble. "Like a baby! Diaper me and bathe me and oil me and powder me, powder me and diaper me like a baby! And feed me baby *food*, too, filthy stuff! No way for a man to go on, Mrs. Landry, no proper way at all! Bunch of flaming damnfool, that's what it is!" And he would tug furiously at the diapers that shamed him so, and toss on his pillows, and curse the magnificent genetic heritage that tied him to a world he was good and sick of. . . . he would not have been asking for that life back. He would have been thanking her for the blessing of release. And it was the same with the others.

Except for Ned. And as for Ned . . . if she had dreamed only of him, groveling and begging and pleading for mercy, she would have positively enjoyed it. She hoped he was burning in hell. Slowly. With some devil always keeping him *waiting*. She did not regret having killed Ned Landry, any more than she regretted it when she destroyed a polio virus with a vaccine for the children. Same sort of filth, same sort of pestilence, same sort of service to humanity, getting rid of Ned Landry. She was staunchly glad she'd done that.

But the others? It was absurd, and she knew it was absurd, and still they haunted her nights. Even though they were all men. Even though they were all Lingoes. Even though, by rights, they deserved killing.

Pain lanced through her head with the thought, and she smiled grimly into it . . . *you* deserved *that*, Michaela! Because you are a liar. You are a liar, all the way from your head to your toes. THEY DESERVED KILLING. . . . You know better now. And that was the problem. She thought she had escaped from the problem when she left Barren House and redefined her targeted victims so that they would always be only male linguists, but she had been wrong.

Paul John Chornyak, for example. Ninety-five years old. At an age where death would be no more surprising than the sun coming up in the mornings. A bit of a nuisance to Thomas and the other senior men, because he'd once been Head and couldn't forget it, insisting on attending meetings and being part of the business decisions of the Line. Not that his mind wasn't still sharp, it was; but his memory wasn't what it had been, and his patience was a toddler's patience. She served his meals away from the communal diningroom now, except for Sunday dinner and holiday meals and the odd occasion when he just suddenly decided that he by damn did not *wish* to eat alone in his room. And even that happened only in the evenings, when he was like most very old people and knew he faced a nearly sleepless night . . . he hadn't really needed any sleep to speak of for years, and he got bored waiting for morning. It made him petulant, and he would sometimes insist on going to the diningroom for his evening meal just to cut into the span of the endless evenings and nights. Breakfast, though, and lunch—those Michaela served him in his room, staying with him if he wanted her, listening to him talk. Which meant that any day, any day at all, she could ease him on his way as she had eased the others on, ridding the burdened world of one more linguist.

But she loved the old man.

That brought her *wide* awake; and she lay there staring at the ceiling, shocked at her own thoughts. It was true. She loved him. She had loved Grandfather Verdi, too; she knew that now. She loved the old women at Barren House. She loved Nazareth Chornyak, whose face she'd begun to seek out first whenever she went into a room where linguists were; she knew she made excuses to touch Nazareth as she passed her, to brush an imaginary thread from her tunic or straighten an imaginary wrinkle . . . to rub aching muscles after a day of difficult work . . . yes, she loved Nazareth as well. It seemed to Michaela suddenly that she was running over, brimful and running over, with love. For Lingoes! For filthy, effing Lingoes, unspeakable Lingoes, that she'd hated all her life as did any decent citizen, that had taken her baby and killed it and given her a hunk of metal in exchange . . . Where had all that love come from? She had not known she had it in her, that ability to love.

Thomas, now, she felt no love for, any more than she'd felt love for Ned. She had turned her attention to convincing him that he had seduced her, because she knew his power and respected it and she knew no other way to make use of it. But she felt no love for the man. Loving someone who considered you only one small notch above a cleverly trained domestic animal, and made no secret of it—that is, loving any adult male—was not possible for her. It would be a perversion, loving your masters while their boots were on your neck, and she was a woman healthy of mind. Like most women she had suffered one violent case of the Romantic Love that everyone learned about in Homeroom and had spoonfed to them (with a giant spoon) by the media. When she was very young. And like most women, that one case had cured her for life.

It had been her good fortune that it had happened to her *before* she met the man she was to marry, sparing her the soul-destroying experience of ''falling in love''—and then out of love again—with her own husband. She *serviced* Thomas, as she had serviced Ned, and she had no reason to believe she'd lost her touch. Thomas would never be like Ned, never a fool, never swift-melting putty in a woman's hands, no. But she worked at it very hard, and she was extremely careful; she knew that she was as nearly indispensable to Thomas now as it was possible for any woman to be, with such a man. As indispensable as poor Rachel, at least; probably more so. And he would be wondering where she was—it was past time for her to be seen up and about her duties.

''I'm tired,'' she said aloud. ''I'm absolutely worn out. I

cannot get out of this bed and go upstairs and be a nice lady.''
After which, of course, she stood up, stripped the bed of its
sheets for the laundryroom, pulled on a robe for her definitely
necessary trip to the nearest shower room, and headed out into
the corridor to begin her day. At least in the daytime she was too
busy to be haunted by her row of little old ghosts, with Ned as
their token youngster. She shut the nonsensical plaints of her
victims up in her room along with her bone-weariness, and went
gracefully about her business.

She was very late; when she reached the diningroom it was
nearly empty. All the children had gone long since, and even the
section where the adults ate was thinly populated. Mostly by the
very senior men, who no longer went out on negotiations, and
who reminded her unpleasantly of what she'd only just put out of
her mind. She stood in the doorway trying to decide where she
should sit and seriously considering skipping breakfast altogether.
She could go straight on to Barren House, where they'd give her
a cup of good tea and some fresh-baked bread, and where she
could count on good company and good conversation. Versus
sitting with one of these men and being told what the world was
coming to and how it was all the fault of either the President or
the women, depending on which had most recently irritated the
old gentleman in question.

There was a touch on her arm, and she jumped; she hadn't
heard whoever it was coming up behind her. Clingsoles were
wonderful for a house with scores of busy people coming and
going; they kept down the racket. But they gave you no warning
that someone was near you, which could be inconvenient at
times.

It was Nazareth who had touched her, though, and that was
a note of hope at last in this otherwise miserable morning.

"Natha," she said. "You're late."

"So are you. Disgustingly late. Come have breakfast with me,
and we can be disgustingly late together."

"Here?"

"Of course not here. Come on, I happen to know that there's
a health crisis at Barren House that demands our immediate
attention, Nurse Landry. I'll vouch for it if necessary. You don't
want to eat with those old creakers, do you?"

"Not particularly," Michaela admitted. "But I expect I ought
to do it anyway. Sort of a public health service."

"No, you come along with me, I need you worse than they
do; I feel this terrible pain coming on," said Nazareth. And

before anything more could be said she had moved Michaela out the door, across the atrium—where the latest A.I.R.'s had not yet come out of their privacy area, which meant nothing at all to be seen there—and through the service rooms onto the street. Nazareth wasted no time in anything she did, and years of experience with her brood of nine had given her a firm way of bustling another person along that was impressive even to a professional nurse who did professional person-bustling. At the slidewalk, Michaela applied the brakes, both to catch her breath and for the principle of the thing.

"Hey!" she protested, laughing. "It's too early for running! I wasn't brought up jogging and hoeing before daybreak like you mad linguists—could we walk now? Please?"

"We could. But I had to get outside before someone saw me and invented an emergency for *me*."

"They do that, do they? I suppose that's why I see you here at the big house so rarely."

"Absolutely right," said Nazareth. "My father devoutly believes that a linguist not in use is a linguist being wasted, and he allows *no* linguist to be wasted. I stop by very early to see whichever of my kidlings happens to be around, and then I hightail it back home."

Home. That would be Barren House.

"You could get caught, going by the diningroom," Michaela noted.

"Yes . . . but how else was I to get your attention? I assure you that if I stood in the atrium and shouted at you I would *definitely* get caught. It was safer to slip in and grab you, you perceive."

The walk had started to turn into a jog again, and Michaela knew Nazareth couldn't help it; hurrying was as natural to her as eating and drinking. But she stopped, and reached out to turn the other woman round to face her.

"Let me take a look at you," she said, holding Nazareth firmly with a hand on each shoulder. "No, Nazareth, don't go tugging away from me! I'm not at all sure you're well . . . perhaps I should suggest to your father that you spend another few days at the hospital, since it's so pleasant there? Hold still, woman, so that I can *see* you! They'll still feed us, if we don't get to Barren House till noon—hold *still*."

Nazareth smiled at her, declaring that she gave up, and Michaela looked her over thoroughly in the morning light; it was more reliable than indoor light. Still much too thin, she thought. *Much* too thin. Tall as she was, a good four inches taller than Michaela, the gauntness was still obvious. Especially in the plain tunics she wore. Her hipbones stuck out, still.

"I won't eat more," announced Nazareth with determination, reading her mind. "Don't bother instructing me, Nurse. I eat enough already. I have always been a gawk—just ask my erstwhile husband—and I am not going to change to one of those motherly types at my advanced age."

"Hush," said Michaela, and laid a gentle finger to Nazareth's lips, getting a kiss for her trouble; she moved her hands to trace the stark cheekbones, and narrowed her eyes to study the face of this self-proclaimed gawk. Yes, she was too thin; but the look of intolerable strain was gone. There was a touch of color in her cheeks, her eyes glowed with the beginnings of health, and she had let her hair down from that vicious knot she'd always worn it in and put it in a single braid down her back.

"Really, Nazareth," Thomas had commented the first time he'd seen the change of hairstyle. "At your age." Michaela was delighted that Nazareth had ignored him.

"You look better, Nazareth," she said, finally satisfied. "So much better."

"I *am* better, that's why. Nothing like chopping away all the dead wood and decay at one whack to improve the basic structure."

"When I remember how you looked in the hospital that day. . . ."

"Don't remember," advised Nazareth sensibly. "Don't think of it. You think of the past too much . . . it's not good for you."

And how did she know that? Michaela stared at her, thinking how dear she was, and Nazareth clucked her tongue at her.

"Could we go on now, do you suppose?" she demanded, pretending to be cross. "If you're through with inspection? I'm willing to eat, if you'd give me half a chance. And I happen to know that Susannah made spice bread this morning, Michaela."

"It'll all be gone."

"If you keep us standing here like this, it certainly will."

Michaela took her hand, and they hurried, cutting across the greenspace and leaving disapproving glances behind them from the pedestrians standing sedately on the slidewalks. They would think she was a Lingoe, too—it crossed Michaela's mind as she stretched her legs to keep up with Nazareth's brisk stride, and she marveled that it did not bother her. What bothered her was the prospect of missing out on Susannah's pulitzer among spice cakes.

*　　*　　*

She had a long and busy day, and she gave no more mental space to her dreams; she was occupied with the living. And when she got back to Chornyak Household in midafternoon, ready to make her daily report to Thomas—a farce, but their most discreet opportunity to make arrangements for the nights, and therefore observed punctiliously—she found the house hushed and a message from Thomas that she should not go to his office that day.

"Is something wrong, Clara?" she asked, surprised; Thomas *never* omitted her "report" if he was in the house, because he was determined that it should be looked upon as an unchangeable item in his daily schedule. "It's awfully quiet. . . . has something happened?"

"It's Father, child," Clara said.

Paul John? Michaela would have run, then, answering the call like an old fire horse answering an alarm, but Clara caught her wrist and held her fast.

"It's no use, child, and there's no need for you to go," said the other woman. "He's gone—and everything's been seen to."

"But why wasn't I *called?* He's my patient! Why didn't someone send for me, Clara? I was only at Barren House!"

"Michaela, dear child, my father had come down to make a pest of himself in the computer room—" Clara began.

"Oh heaven, your *father* . . . and I am standing here complaining at you! Oh, Clara. . . ."

Clara patted her hand and went right on. "He'd taken it into his head that there was something he wanted changed in one of the tax programs, and he was standing there talking, telling them how they were doing it all wrong and he wouldn't tolerate it—and he just *went,* child. In the middle of a phrase. It couldn't have been easier."

"But—"

"And," Clara continued, "we women were seeing to our dead many and many a long year before ever we had a nurse in this house. There was no need to disturb you."

"I'm sorry, Clara," Michaela said softly. "Of course there wasn't. When did this happen?"

"Oh, perhaps an hour ago, dear. I'm sure someone's gone over to Barren House with the news by this time . . . it's not the sort of thing we announce on the intercoms . . . but you must have just missed them."

Michaela drew a long breath, and realized that she was shivering. She was ashamed of herself.

"Clara, I'm so sorry," she said again.

"Don't be, my dear; Father was ninety-five, you know. It was to be expected, and I'm not grieving. If he'd been sick, now; if he'd suffered—that would have been another thing entirely. But this was just as he would have wanted it. He died right in the middle of telling someone what to do. It's all right. Really."

Michaela tried to smile, and then Clara was gone, saying something about arrangements to be made, and she could, blessedly, sit down at last. She was as weak as if she'd been tapped like a tree, and all her blood drained away. And she knew why. It wasn't grief, though Paul John had mattered greatly to her; Clara was right that he had died as he would have preferred to die. It was because of what she had thought the instant Clara told her, what had come into her mind the instant she heard the news.

OH THANK GOD, NOW I WILL NOT HAVE TO KILL HIM.

That is what she had thought. She was sick with relief, and sick *at* her relief. She stayed there a long time, in the unusual stillness of the house, wondering what sort of wickedness wound on itself she nurtured.

After a while a message came through on her wrist computer, from Thomas. Unfortunate incident, but not unexpected, etc. Michaela's services would, however, still be needed, etc. She was expected to continue in her position . . . he would meet with her the following day to discuss the necessary changes in her duties, etc.

Michaela acknowledged the message. And then, when she was sure she could walk without trembling, she went to her room.

Chapter Twenty-two

Now, the only song a woman knows is the song she learns at
birth,
a sorrowin' song, with the words all wrong, in the many tongues
of Earth.
The things a woman wants to say, the tales she longs to
tell . . .
they take all day in the tongues of Earth, and half of the night
as well.
So nobody listens to what a woman says, except the men of
power
who sit and listen right willingly, at a hundred dollars an
hour . . .
sayin' "Who on Earth would want to talk about such foolish
things?"
Oh, the tongues of Earth don't lend themselves to the songs a
woman sings!
There's a whole lot more to a womansong, a whole lot more to
learn;
but the words aren't there in the tongues of Earth, and there's
noplace else to turn. . . .
So the woman they talk, and the men they laugh, and there's
little a woman can say,
but a sorrowin' song with the words all wrong, and a hurt that
won't go away.
The women go workin' the manly tongues, in the craft of makin'
do,
but the women that stammer, they're everywhere, and the
wellspoken ones are few. . . .

'Cause the only song a woman knows is the song she learns at
birth;
a sorrowin' song with the words all wrong, in the manly tongues
of Earth.

(a 20th century ballad,
set to an even older tune called "House of the Rising Sun";
this later form was known simply as
"Sorrowin' Song, With the Words All Wrong")

SUMMER 2212 . . .

Time passed, in the ordinary way of time passing, in the cycle
of the seasons and the less predictable but equally endless cycle
of the government negotiations for conquest and expansion of
territory. Languages were acquired, and infants born and Interfaced,
and yet more languages acquired. Sophie Ann died, peacefully,
in her sleep; and Deborah was gone now, too, with the little girls
tending her to the last. Susannah's arthritis kept her in a wheel-
chair now, but did not keep her from baking her spice bread.
Nazareth remained thin, Caroline abrupt, Aquina excessive. They
tried not to think of what Belle-Anne had become, because there
was nothing they could do about that; and when Aquina could
not keep from thinking about it they soothed her through the
horrors and kept careful watch on the herb cupboards until the
spasm of memory had eased. Time went by, no different from
any other time.

And Nazareth had been right. Every tiny girl in Chornyak
Household knew Láadan now, and used it easily. It wasn't going
as rapidly at the other Barren Houses, but the reports coming in
from them were not displeasing. A few of the older girlchildren,
already out of infancy when the teaching of Láadan began but
still too young to be much involved in government contracts, had
begun to pick up the language on their own . . . haltingly, of
course. But then, the women were even more halting, and they
managed. "Latining by," they called it, remembering Nazareth's
comment about what the "international" Latin must have been
like. They managed. And the men had noticed nothing.

One of the first things that Nazareth had done as the Project
was put into effect was to prepare a manual alphabet for Láadan.
Like the fingerspelling alphabet of Ameslan in concept, but very
different in form, because it had to be something that only the
trained and seeking eye could see. The tiniest movements, and
made by fingers lying still and unseen in laps—that was all it

could be. It was splendid training for the little ones, and for all of them; if you could learn to follow those miniature motions and understand them, all the while behaving as if you weren't doing so, following ordinary body-parl was absurdly simple by comparison.

The children loved it . . . there's never been a child who didn't love a "secret language" and this one was wondrously secret. It let them sit in Homeroom, for example, demure and seemingly attentive while the teachers droned away in their twentieth century rituals; the eyes of the little girls gave away nothing, but their fingers were busy. "STUPID poem! Will he never stop? How long is it till the bell? He's an old fool!" And much worse, of course. It was exciting, it was just dangerous enough, and it was theirs alone. There was no need to worry about them forgetting that they must keep it a secret. You couldn't have gotten them to betray Láadan short of using thumb-screws and the rack, because it was theirs, and it was theirs together—nothing else met that description.

It was happening just as Nazareth had told them it would happen, and they willingly granted her that. But there were some things that were surprising, nevertheless. For instance, there was the speed of it.

"It's happening so fast!" Thyrsis said, and yelped; she had stabbed her finger with her embroidery needle. She put the finger to her mouth, to catch the drop of blood before it spotted her work, and said, "How can it be so fast?"

"Nazareth, you said it would take a long time," agreed one of the others. "Generations, you said. . . . I remember very well."

"And it will be generations," Nazareth said, "before it is anything more than an auxiliary language. That's unavoidable. I don't see any change in that constraint."

"But they use it constantly, and they love it so. And they do strange things."

"For example?"

Susannah chuckled. "For example . . . when I thought I'd introduce a new word yesterday, for that new way of dancing that we saw on the threedies. You remember, Grace? The one that looks as if the youngsters are all trying to dislocate their shoulders?"

"I remember," Grace said. "I would swear it had to be painful."

"Well! I thought I had a decent proposal for a word, and I suggested it. And one of the littlebits *corrected* me, I'll have you know!"

"Corrected you? How could that be—did you make an error in the morphology? At your age?"

"Of course not, it was a perfectly good Láadan word, formed in accordance with every rule. But she did. She said, 'Aunt Susannah, it could not be that way. I'm very sorry, but it would have to be *this* way.' "

"And she was right?"

"Goodness, how would I know that? I don't have native intuitions about Láadan, you know!"

"Nor do the children."

"Ah, but they seem to think they do. Already."

"It's not possible."

"No . . . but she said 'This way, my mouth knows that it's right.' "

They all shook their heads, admitting bewilderment. And Nazareth said, "I admit it's happening far more quickly than linguistic theory would allow. But I think I know why, really. I think we just hadn't realized how much *fun* it would be for the children. They have so little fun, we ought to have realized . . . but I never thought of it."

"Do you notice," Caroline asked, "do you notice how close they are, to one another?"

"The little girls?"

"Of course, the little girls! Even the older ones, who are just able to use Láadan enough to make the tiny ones laugh at them . . . they are . . ."

She stopped, because there was no word for it in any language she knew, and she wanted to use the *right* word.

"Oh," she said. "I know . . . They are *héenahal*." And she sighed. "Such a relief, to have a language with the right words in it!"

"Well, no wonder they are so knit together, then," Nazareth observed. "Remember that some of them have had that blissful resource from the day they were born."

"I cannot imagine it," Grace said emphatically. "I try, but I can't. What that must be like. Not to be always groping, because there aren't any words—while the person you want so desperately to talk to gets tired of waiting and begins talking of something else. To have a language that works, that says what you want to say easily and efficiently, and to have *always* had that? No, loves, I cannot imagine it. I am too old."

"It's working, then," Thyrsis said. "We can truly say that it's working."

"Oh my, yes," Nazareth answered. "You surely could not,

for even one instant, believe that *this* reality is the one that you and I were born to deal with? Yes, it is working, and very very quickly.''

"And," Aquina pointed out, "we are no more ready to deal with the new one than we were the day Nazareth told us to get off our butts!''

"Aquina, don't start!''

"Well, we aren't.''

"There's no hurry, Aquina.''

"No hurry? God almighty, the men are slow, but they are not deaf and blind! How long do you think this can go on, before they notice?''

"A very long time," Caroline said confidently. "They think we are all fools. They believe that our entire attention is devoted to setting up descriptive matrices for the eighty-four separate phonemes of Langlish at the moment, for instance.''

"Eighty-five.''

"Eighty-five now? Dear heaven . . . you perceive? Nothing is so outrageous that it doesn't just reinforce them in their conviction that we have vanilla pudding for brains. And when they are that secure in their perceptions, we are quite safe.''

"Still," Aquina fretted, "still! They aren't ordinary men, they are linguists. Trained to observe. They're sure to notice, and we aren't ready.''

"Aquina," Thyrsis protested, "must you? When we are so happy?''

"Yes. I must. Somebody has to.''

Nobody answered her, and their fingers flew at their work in a determined WE-ARE-IGNORING-YOU unanimity, but that didn't stop her.

"What we really need," she said solemnly, "what would really solve the problem once and for all, is a colony of our own. A colony just for women. Somewhere so far away, and so lacking in anything worth money, that men would never be interested in taking it away from us.''

Nazareth threw up her hands, embroidery and all.

"Aquina," she cried, "you are outrageous! A colony! We cannot even buy a piece of fruit without a man's written permission, and you want us to buy tickets on the spaceliners . . . We can't travel beyond the city limits without a male escort *and* a man's written permission, but you want us to take off for the stars and set up a colony. . . .'' She broke down, helpless with laughter, but managed to use both hands to smooth Aquina's white hair, to show there was no malice in the laughter.

"Oh, I know," grumbled Aquina, "I know. But it would be so wonderful."

"We'd take vacuum bottles of frozen sperm along," chuckled one of the others. "For the little girls we'd be kidnapping. Wouldn't we, Aquina? And we'd sneak them through customs as . . . what . . . shampoo?"

"I know," said Aquina again, "I'm an old fool."

"Well then. . . don't be a tiresome old fool, Aquina."

"But the men *will* notice," she insisted. "Never mind my fantasies, you know they will notice. And we aren't certain what to do."

"My dear," chided Nazareth, "that's not so. You have a list. Eleven possible male reactions. Eleven logical moves in response, one for each hypothesis. We did that five years ago."

"Oh, we made *lists*! But we haven't done anything to get ready to carry them out! We have other lists for that! The pre-lists, to get started preparing for the *real* lists. . . . It's stupid. It's bizarre. It's inexcusable! We should already have begun, long ago."

"Oh, dear. . . ."

It was an argument that went round and round like a canon, and it would go on as long as there was privacy and leisure enough to sustain it, because it had no answer. If Aquina was right, then they were indeed seriously behind. But they were so busy! The only ones who had the free hours that might have gone into actually setting one of the plans in motion were those too ill or too old or otherwise unable to do any of the tasks involved. And there was no way out.

The governments of Earth had no limit in their greed; every new Alien people contacted meant new Alien treasures to be sought after, and a new market for the products of Earth, and that meant a new Alien language to be acquired. There were never enough infants, never enough Interfaces . . . again this year a resolution had come up in the United Nations, proposing that the linguists should be compelled by law to establish one of the Households in the Central American Federation, one in Australia, one somewhere else—it was not *fair*, the delegates thundered, that all the Households should be located in the United States and in United Europe and in Africa, when everyone needed them equally! And then of course the delegations from the African confederations and from United Europe had leaped up to protest that they could hardly be included in the accusations of linguistic imperialism, since it was the United States that hoarded *ten* of the thirteen Lines.

It kept happening. As though they were a public utility, or a military unit, and not private citizens and human beings at all. It made no difference, because there was no way that the Lines could be compelled to spread themselves "equitably" around the world at the pleasure of its populations. But the constant pressure to do more, to be more, never let up. Why, the governments wanted to know, couldn't each linguist child be required to master at minimum two Alien languages instead of one, thus doubling their usefulness? Why couldn't the women of the Lines be required to use the fertility drugs that would guarantee multiple births? Why couldn't the time each infant spent Interfacing be increased to six hours a day instead of three? Why . . . there was no end to their whys, and nothing but the stern grip of the Judaeo-Christian paradigm kept them from adding a question about why the men of the Lines couldn't take a dozen wives apiece rather than one.

As there was no end to their demands, there was no end to their prying. The linguists had spotted the men from the various intelligence services within days of their being planted in the Households, and had been much amused. They might have been fine secret agents, but they were rotten plumbers and carpenters and gardeners. And the ones assigned to so enflame the passions of the women that they would manage to marry *into* the Lines had been hilariously obvious.

The women of the Barren Houses had no time, in such an atmosphere, to set contingency plans in operation. Every day there was less time. Even these brief gatherings in the parlor, armed with the needlework for excuse, just to discuss what there was not time to do and to fret about it, were becoming more and more rare. And more brief, with everyone but the very oldest obliged to meet multiple deadlines.

As they were obliged now, all of them leaving in a rush except Susannah, who no longer went out to work on negotiations, though she still put in long hours as a translator and at the computers storing data. Aquina had to leave, for all her determination to *do* something; and Susannah was left alone with Nazareth and the usual flurry of everything being up in the air.

"I can't believe it," she said. "Surely you aren't on holiday, Natha? Aren't there at least six places you're supposed to be, at the same time, fifteen minutes ago?"

"Yes," laughed Nazareth. "And I'm late for all of them."

"And still sitting here?"

"I'm trying to make up my mind which of the six to be late to first, dear Susannah."

"Mmmm. . . I perceive. And I perceive something else, Nazareth Joanna Chornyak Adiness."

"What else do you perceive, with those wise old eyes?"

"That *you* are not worried," Susannah pronounced.

"Ah! What very sharp eyes you have, grandmother!"

"But you aren't. *Are* you?"

"No. I'm not worried."

"Everyone else is, my dear. Not just Aquina. If it were only Aquina it wouldn't matter. But *everyone* else."

"I know."

"They try to keep from thinking about it, but they are upset."

"Yes."

"Well, then—why are *you* so serene. Nazareth? What aren't you saying? Why are you unconcerned?"

"I don't know."

"Truly?"

"Truly."

"Nazareth?"

"Yes, Susannah?"

"Do you know something we don't know? Again? As you knew that it was time to begin teaching Láadan, and we didn't know? As you knew that it would work, that teaching, and we didn't know?"

Nazareth gave the question serious consideration, while Susannah sat looking at her steadily.

Finally, she answered, "Susannah," she said slowly, "I am so sorry. But there's no way to explain. I'm not *able* to explain."

"Perhaps you ought to try, nevertheless."

"If I could, Susannah, I would. And when I can, I will."

"And how long will that be? Before you feel that you might be able to begin to attempt to try?"

"Nazareth began folding her work away, smiling.

"My crystal ball is broken. Susannahlove," she teased. "And I must go, or it won't be just six places I need to be at once, it will be a dozen. I have to clear some of them away."

Chapter Twenty-three

On this view, sentences are held together by a kind of "nuclear glue" consisting of mesons, alpha-particles, and meaning postulates, all swirling in more-or-less quantitized orbits around an undifferentiated plasma of feature bundles. Thus, the earlier notion of a grammar as an abstract yet concretely manifested generative-recognition algorithm is abandoned, and is replaced by a device (to return to a more traditional sense of that word) in which features specify and are specified by other features in various combinations, subject, of course, to obvious constraints which need not concern us here. Whatever else may be said in favor of this position, it is at least unassailable, and this in itself represents a significant advance in the Theory of Universal Grammar as this field had traditionally been conceived. Opposed to this at the present time stands only the Theory of Universal Derivational Constraints, which, although it is likewise unassailable, suffers from a lack of plausibility. . . .

Coughlake makes what is perhaps the best possible argument in favor of the Unsupportable Position when he says that derivational constraints should be left unrestrained, since, he argues, they have been exploited for too long already by non-derivational chauvinists attempting to exert a kind of interpretivist imperialism, a *pax lexicalis*, as it were, over the realm of syntax.

INSTRUCTIONS: You have thirty minutes. Identify the distinguished linguist who is quoted above, and specify the theoretical model with which he is to be associated. Then explain, clearly and concisely, the meaning of the quotation. DO NOT TURN THE PAGE UNTIL YOU ARE TOLD TO DO SO. BEGIN.

> (question taken from the final examination
> administered by
> the Division of Linguistics,
> U.S. Department of Analysis & Translation)

This was a splendid, and a rare, occasion. Looking down the tables spread with the heavy white linen (real linen, taken from chests in the storage rooms where is had been folded away along with other Household valuables rarely used), looking at the gleaming silver and crystal, Thomas wondered just when they had last done this. It had to have been years ago, unless you counted the Christmas dinners . . . and even for those, they didn't bring the linens from the chests, or invite guests from the other Households. This opulent display was in honor of his seventieth birthday . . . and the last one, come to think of it, could only have been for some other Head-of-Household's seventieth birthday. Long ago, in this house, it would have been the celebration for Paul John. As if the number seventy had some significance.

But it was of course only an excuse. To stop the round of work and study and breeding and training and recording. To spend time in eating and drinking and good fellowship. To spend time renewing acquaintances, seeing old friends you might not have seen except in passing for years and years. Such excuses were few and far between, with only thirteen Heads of Lines to turn seventy.

They'd been enjoying themselves, no question about it. First there had been the magnificent food, such food as the public was led to believe the linguists gobbled *every* night, and the fine champagne, and the exotic wines from the colonies. All of that with the women still at the tables, and the conversation restrained by their presence to politics and shop talk . . . but delightful nevertheless.

And now the women had gone off to whatever it is that women do when they are alone together—gossip, Thomas thought, always gossip—and the time for real conversation had come. The solid useful talk of men, who know and enjoy one another and can speak freely together. Not gossip, certainly. The bourbon had come out, and the best tobaccos; the room had a warmth that it never had at Christmas. Thomas smiled, realizing that he was genuinely contented, for that moment at least. So contented that even the thought of the latest D.A.T. catastrophe could not distract him. Not tonight.

"You look smug, Thomas," his brother Adam observed, pouring him some more bourbon. "Downright smug."

"I feel smug."

"Just because you survived to seventy?" Adam needled him. "That's not so remarkable. Two more years, and I'll have done the same."

Thomas just grinned at him and raised his glass to touch the other man's in a satisfactory clink of mutual congratulation. Let Adam pester; nothing was going to spoil his mood tonight.

He pointed down the table with his cigarette, at the huddle of men in splendid formal wear complete with neckties. "What are they talking about down there, Adam? If it's as good as it looks, I may move down where I can get in on it. Which is it, sex or the stock market?"

"Neither one. Surprise."

"Oh? Not women, not money?"

"Oh, it's women, Thomas. But not their arms and their bosoms and their bottoms, my dear brother. Nothing erotic."

"Good lord. What else is there to talk about, when one talks of women?"

He paid attention then, trying to hear, and scraps of it floated up to him over the general hum.

"—damned angel, all the time. Can't believe—"

"—one single ache or pain, can you believe it? It's unheard of, but God what a relief! I was—"

"—how it used to be, whine and nag and whine and nag from morning till night—"

"—how to account for it, but—"

"—damn, but it's *good*, you know, having—"

Thomas shook his head; he couldn't hear enough. Just a word here and a phrase there, drowned in satisfied discourse.

"All right, Adam," he said, "I give up. What are they talking about?"

"Well . . . I don't know anything about it myself, living as I do in single blessedness. But if they are to be believed, something has come over all the women."

"Come over them? They all looked just as usual to me—what do you mean, come over them?"

"According to them—" Adam made a large gesture, to include all the men at the tables "—the socialization process has finally begun to take hold, and the women are recovering at last from the effects of the effing feminist corruption. High time, wouldn't you say?"

"That's what they're saying?"

"That's it. Women, they tell me, do not nag any more. Do not whine. Do not complain. Do not demand things. Do not make idiot objections to everything a man proposes. Do not argue. Do not get sick—can you believe that, Thomas? No more headaches, no more monthlies, no more hysterics . . . or if there still are such things, at least they are never mentioned. So they say."

Thomas frowned, and he thought about it. Was it true? When had he last had to put up with insolence from Rachel? To his astonishment, he found that he could not remember.

He raised his glass high and shouted down the table, to get their attention; and because it was, after all, his celebration they turned courteously to see what he wanted of them.

"Adam here tells me all our women have gone to open sainthood," he said, smiling, "and I'm ashamed to say that I not only haven't noticed, I don't find it easy to believe—it's a good deal more likely that Adam's confused. But if he's not, it sounds like a damn drastic change . . . is it all of them? Or just a few?"

They answered without any hesitation. It was all of the women in the Households. Oh, perhaps the very oldest were still a bit cross now and then, but that was age—even old men could be annoying. Except for that, it was all of them, all of the time. As Adam had said, the distortions of the twentieth century had apparently finally been laid to rest, and the new Eden was come on Earth.

"Well, I'll be damned," Thomas declared.

"No doubt, brother, no doubt," Adam said, with a foolish smirk on his face. Adam had had too much bourbon.

At the next table Andrew St. Syrus raised a hand and said, "Let me just take a poll, Thomas . . . all right? Tell me, all of you—how long has it been since you sat and listened to a woman nag? Or watched one sit and blather endlessly about something that no one in his right mind could possible have any interest in? Or blubber for hours over nothing at all? How long?"

There was a murmur, and some consultation, and then they agreed. It had to be at least six months. Perhaps longer. They had only begun to notice it recently, but it must have been going on quite a long time.

"But that's amazing!" said Thomas.

"Isn't it? And wonderful. And all in time for your seventieth!"
And up came the bourbon glasses in a toast.

"Oh, and those tiny ones," said someone across the room.
"Oh, to be fifty years younger!"

A roar of laughter went around the room, with the usual jeers
about dirty old men, but there was support from the other tables.

"They are so incredibly *sweet*, those tiny tiny girls," mused
the fellow who'd brought it up. A Hashihawa, he was; Thomas
could not remember his first name. "And they have the most
charming concepts. Chornyak, perceive this, would you? I have
a granddaughter—hell, I have two or three dozen granddaughters—
but this one in particular, she's an adorable little thing, name of
Shawna, I think. At any rate, I heard her just the other day,
talking to one of the other little girls, and she was explaining so
gravely how it was, that what she felt for her little brother was
not 'love' qua 'love', you know, it was. . . . I don't remember
the word exactly, but it meant 'love for the sibling of one's body
but not of one's heart.' Charming! Just the kind of silly distinction a female *would* make, of course, but charming. Ah, it'll
be a lucky man of a lucky Line that beds my little Shawna,
Thomas!"

"What language was she speaking?"

The man shrugged. "I don't know . . . who can keep track?
Whatever she Interfaced for, I suppose."

And then the examples began coming from others. The charming examples. The so endearing examples. Just to add to the
conversation and explain to Thomas, who clearly had not noticed
what was going on around him lately. Not a lot of examples,
because the subject went rather quickly to the more interesting
question of the next Republican candidate for president of the
United States. But at least a dozen.

Thomas sat there, forgetting his bourbon, something tugging
at him. Adam was staring blearily at him, accusing him of
thinking of business instead of celebrating like he was supposed
to do. But he wasn't thinking of business. Not at all. He was
thinking about a dozen examples, a dozen "charming" and
"endearing" concepts, from nearly as many different Households.
That should have meant roughly a dozen different Alien languages for the examples to have come from. But it didn't sound
that way. Few of the men had remembered the actual surface
shapes of the words, but Thomas had been a linguist all his life;
he didn't need all the words to be able to perceive the patterns.

They were all, every one of them, from the *same* language. He would have staked his life on it.

And that could mean only one thing.

"Sweet jesus christ on a donkey in the shade of a lilac tree," said Thomas out loud, stunned.

"Drink up," Adam directed. "Do you good. You're not half drunk enough."

He was not drunk at all, he was stone cold sober. And a whole bottle of bourbon would not have made him drunk at that moment.

It could only mean one thing.

Because there was no way that the little girls of all those different Households could all be acquiring a single Alien language, all at the same time. *No way.*

And it began to fall together for him. Things he had half noticed, without being aware that he noticed them. Things he had seen from the corner of his eye, heard from the corner of his ear—things he had sensed.

He looked at the men of his blood, the men of the Lines, laughing and hearty and slightly tipsy and contented, surfeited with the rare pleasure of the evening and one another's good company. And all he could think was: FOOLS. ALL OF YOU, FOOLS. AND I AM THE BIGGEST FOOL AMONG YOU. Because he was Head not of just Chornyak Household, but of all the Households, and that was supposed to mean something. That was supposed to mean that he always knew what was going on in the Lines, before it could go farther than it ought to go.

How could it have happened? Where could his mind have been?

He said nothing to the others, because of course he could be wrong. There could be some other explanation. There could be some cluster of related Alien languages spread out among the Lines by coincidence, something of that sort. Or he could be imagining the patterns, distracted by the liquor he so rarely drank. He put it aside and concentrated on fulfilling his role as host for the rest of the evening, because it was his duty to do so and because he would not spoil this for everyone else when he might be mistaken.

It dragged on, interminably, all the pleasure gone from it for him. Adam passed out and had to be carried to a cubbyhole in the dorms reserved for just such undignified accidents. Adam could not control his women, and he could not handle his liquor, and no doubt it was unpleasant for him to have to always compare himself with Thomas, and so he drank until he could compare no longer. It seemed to Thomas that this celebration, that had become a mockery, would never end.

When at last it was over, as had to happen despite his distorted time perceptions, Thomas was weak with a mixture of relief and dread. And glad that he could get away now to his office, where no one would dare go at night without his express invitation, and where Michaela Landry would be waiting for him as he had instructed her to be. He had expected to be in an unusually good mood at the end of this evening, and he had wanted her to be there, to talk to.

He still wanted her to be there, frantic as he felt. Not for her body—he had no interest in her body tonight. But for her blessed skill at listening with her whole heart and her whole mind. And for the fact that he could trust her absolutely.

He felt that if he could not have talked to someone about this he would have gone mad. He *could* talk to Michaela, bless her.

"Michaela, do you understand what I'm telling you? Do you follow what I'm saying?"

"I'm not sure," she said carefully. "I'm not a linguist, my darling . . . I know nothing about these things. Perhaps if you would not mind explaining it to me again, I might understand."

He badly needed to say it all again, that was clear to her. And for once she badly needed to *hear* it again. To be sure that he was saying what she thought he was saying, and to learn what he had learned. Because the women had not told her, of course, any more than they would have told any other woman who had to live among the men. Not even Nazareth. And Michaela had not guessed.

"Michaela," said Thomas sternly, "if you would pay attention, you wouldn't have any problem—it's not beyond you to understand this."

"Of course, Thomas. Forgive me—I will listen very very carefully this time."

"Now you know about the Encoding Project, Michaela; you're in and out of Barren House constantly, you couldn't possibly not know. For generations our women have been playing at that game . . . constructing a 'woman's language' called Langlish. You must have at least heard them speak of it."

"I think I do remember something about it, Thomas."

"Well, it's nonsense, and it's always been nonsense. In the first place, it is impossible to 'construct' a human language. We don't know how any human language began, but we damn well know that it wasn't because somebody sat down and created one from scratch.''

"Yes, my dear.''

"And in the second place, if it were possible to do such a thing, it certainly could not be done by women . . . as is made painfully clear by the travesty they've produced. Eighty-plus phonemes. Switching the obligatory word order—by committee, mind you—every two or three years. Sets of *hundreds* of particles. Five different orthographies, for different situations. Eleven different separate rules for the formation of simple yes/no questions. Thirteen—'' He caught himself then, remembering, and apologized. "None of that means anything at all to you, Michaela. I'm sorry.''

"It's very interesting, Thomas,'' she said. "And I'm sure it must be important, when a person understands it.''

"It *is* important. It bears out everything that I've said about the folly of both the Project itself and the women involved in it. It is exactly what you would expect to see happen when a group of women took on an entirely absurd task and worried at it in their spare time for interminable years. With committees and caucuses thrown in. It is what I would have predicted, and I do understand the result—and that is the problem.''

"I'm so sorry, my dear; now I really don't follow you.''

"Michaela, I've made a point of checking up on the progress—or regress—of Langlish every six months or so. It's puerile, mechanical, a kind of overelaborated Interlingua beside which Interlingua looks as authentic as Classical Greek. It has always been like that. It has been a source of amazement to the men of the Lines that our women could produce such a monstrosity . . . and has been proof enough, if we had needed further proof, that language acquisition skills are not directly correlated with intelligence. But—and this is the point—out of that travesty, that 'Langlish,' there could not possibly have developed any coherent system that could be learned and spoken by little girls throughout the linguist Households. It is impossible that that could have happened.''

Michaela noted the signs of strain in the muscles of his neck and shoulders, and moved to a different position where the turn of his head to look at her would ease them.

"But you seem to think that it has happened,'' she said. "Or do I still misunderstand?''

"No. . . . I think it has happened. I don't understand it, it makes not the remotest sense, but I think that it has happened. And I will not have it, Michaela!''

"Certainly not," she said promptly. "Of course you won't."

"I won't have it," he continued, as if she'd said nothing. "I have never believed in being overly strict with our women, but this I will not permit. Whatever it is, unless I have somehow got it entirely wrong, it's dangerous—it has to be stopped, and stopped *now*, while it involves only a handful of little girls and a gaggle of foolish old women. Damn their conniving souls!"

"Will they tell you the truth about it, Thomas, do you think? If they're frightened, I mean. I suppose this Langlish must mean a good deal to them."

"I don't expect to have to have them *tell* me," he said, his face grim and his eyes blazing in a way she'd never seen him look before. "I will put everything else on my schedule for tomorrow aside. I will go to Barren House immediately after breakfast—I may damn well go *before* breakfast. And I will stay in that warren of iniquity until I get to the bottom of this if it takes me a week. I'll turn out every cupboard in the place, I'll look at every program in the computer . . . and while I'm there, to demonstrate to them that I am not quite as stupid as they may have thought, I will search every container and contraption they allegedly use for 'needlework,' with shears in hand if that's what it takes. I'll get to the bottom of it, Michaela. Whether they are 'fond' of it or not. Whether they dare try to lie to me or not."

"I see, Thomas. My, what a lot of trouble for you."

"And if it is what I think it is. . . ."

"Yes, my dear? Then what?"

"Then," and he struck his desk with his fist so hard that she nearly jumped—not quite, but nearly—"then I will stamp it *out*. Every last vestige of it. I will destroy it as I'd destroy vermin, and I'll see to it that it's done in every one of the Households. And there will be no more Encoding Project, Michaela, I give you my word on that. Not ever. Not *ever* again."

Thinking that she must be more careful than she had ever been before, Michaela told him how wonderful it was that he could do all that, and so swiftly and surely. And then she asked him, "But my dear, I don't think I see *why* you must trouble yourself in that way. It's only a language, and they know so many languages already! Is it because they've done this without your permission . . . taught it to the children without asking you first?"

He stared at her fiercely, as if he would bite her, and she sat absolutely still and deliberately tranquil under his gaze until he was satisfied with glaring and clenching his teeth and knotting his brows.

"This Langlish, if they've actually pulled it together sufficiently for children to use it, would be as dangerous as any plague," he told her flatly. "Never mind why, Michaela. It's complicated. It's way beyond you, and I'm glad it is. But it represents danger, and it represents corruption—and it shall not happen."

"Oh, my dear," Michaela breathed, "if it is so very dreadful as all that . . . perhaps you should not wait until tomorrow. Perhaps you should go tonight—yes, I am *certain* that you should go tonight!"

She knew no surer way to keep him from going straight to Barren House than to offer it as her emphatic suggestion, and he responded as she had anticipated.

"If I could be sure that I am right, I would go at once," he said. "But I'm not quite that sure. There's no need for hysteria."

She shivered carefully, and made her eyes wide to tell him that she was frightened, and he laughed.

"Michaela, for heaven's sake. Nothing could possibly happen before morning, even if I am right—and I'd look like a madman charging over there in the middle of the night if I've made an error. Don't be absurd."

He went on about it for quite a while; for him, he did a considerable amount of repeating himself. It was the whiskey, she supposed, or the shock of having to entertain the suspicion that the women had put something over on him. Or both.

She let him talk, feeling as if she were not really there in the cramped room but looking at it and at him through a tiny hole in a distant fabric, far from here, high in space and time. Whatever his problems might have been, they were about to be solved; as for her, she had no problems now because he had solved them. For good and for all. Peace filled her like dark slow water . . . the light in the room was gold melting and flowing.

Here was a murder that she could carry out as she had Ned's, in good conscience. Here was a service that she could do, for the women of the Lines. She was no linguist and never could be, she couldn't help them with their language and would only be a burden to them if she tried—but she was as skilled at killing as they were at their conjugations and declensions. She, Michaela Landry, could do something that not one of them, not even silly Aquina with her notions of militancy, could have done. She could save the woman's language, at least for a time—perhaps long enough, certainly for a good while—and she could pay in some measure for her sins. If there had been deaths before at her hand that were not justified, if she had done harm, this would be a kind of recompense.

And no need to wait for opportunity, no need to be clever, because she had no intention of trying to escape. Not this time. She was tired, so tired, of playing the role of Ministering Angel while something in her writhed over questions she couldn't answer, and the men she'd killed tormented her nights with their pleading. Now there would be an end to that, and the Almighty had mercifully granted her the privilege of a *worthy* end!

When he had fallen asleep, worn out with drink and with talk, she took a syringe from the nurse's case that she kept always with her at night in case of an emergency, and she gave Thomas a single dose of a drug that was swift and sure. He made no sound, and he did not wake; in ten minutes he was quite dead, and past all hope of heroic measures. She moved him to the floor, long enough to close the couch that served them for a bed, and then she bent and maneuvered him onto it again—she had not spent all these years lifting and turning patients for nothing. She was strong enough, even for a man of his bulk, gone limp in death. She dressed him as he'd been dressed for the banquet, loosening the necktie, making it look as if he'd just stretched out there to take a nap. He often slept in his office, and no one would be surprised that he'd done so after the celebration.

And then! Ah, the wicked nurse, her sexual advances spurned by the upright moral Head of Household even in his slightly tipsy state, fell upon him and repaid his years of kindness with murder most foul! Out of nothing more than her wounded pride. . . . She could easily imagine the newslines and the threedy features. . . . CRIME OF PASSION! VINDICTIVE NURSE CRAZED WITH LUST AND MADDENED BY REJECTION, SLAYS TOP DOG LINGOE! It would be a seven days wonder. Maybe eight days. Maybe, since it was Thomas Blair Chornyak, much longer. It should buy the women many months, even if some other of the men had begun to notice what was happening, because the transfer of power for such an empire as the Lines constituted could not be a simple matter.

She had never been so calm, or so content. She was sorry that she would have to leave Nazareth Chornyak . . . dear Nazareth. But if Nazareth had known of this, she would have been grateful to have Michaela do for her what she could not do herself. It was a fitting gift to leave for her.

Michaela took her nurse's case and went to her own room and her own bed; she fell asleep at once and slept without a single dream to disturb her rest. And she didn't bother to undress. When they came for her in the morning, as they would the moment they saw the empty syringe beside the corpse, she would already be dressed to welcome them.

Chapter Twenty-four

It was a time when there was no splendor . . . do you understand? It was a time when the seamless fabric of reality had been subjected to an artificial process: dividing it up into dull little parts, each one drearier than the one before. And *uniformly* dreary, getting drearier and drearier by a man-made *rule*. As if you drew lines in the air, you perceive, and then devoted your life to behaving as if those air-territories bounded by your lines were real. It was a reality from which all joy, all glory, all radiance, had been systematically excluded. And it was from *that* reality, from that linguistic construct, that the women of Chornyak Barren House were attempting to extrapolate. It couldn't be done, of course. You cannot weave truth on a loom of lies.

Aquina kept saying that we had to decide what to DO . . . well, imagine a person standing on a block of ice, planning and planning and planning. Planning ways to get about on the ice, ways to decorate it, ways to divide it up, ways to cope with all the possible knowns and givens of a block of ice. That would be a busy person, provident and industrious and independent and admirable, isn't that so? Except that when the ice melts, none of that is any use at all.

We women had set a flame upon the ice, and it was inevitable that the ice would melt. In such a time, having never known anything but life upon the ice, you cannot *do;* in such a time, you can only *be*.

I would have explained, if I had known how; it wasn't that I was trying to keep anything secret. It hurt me that I didn't know how to explain. I would wake up in the morning and think, perhaps *this* will be the day when the words that would explain are given to me; but it never happened. I grew to be very very old, and it never did happen.

> (a fragment from what is alleged
> to be a diary of Nazareth Chornyak Adiness;
> it bears no date)

The meeting was an unusual one, in every way. Every place at the table was filled, and it had been necessary to bring in extra chairs to seat the overflow that couldn't be fit at the table proper. Not only were the full complement of men from Chornyak Household there, but a delegation of three senior men and two junior from each of the other twelve Lines, attending in person. Ordinarily this outside representation would have been handled by computer conference to avoid the inconvenience and over-crowding . . . And looking at it now, seeing everyone jammed in elbow to elbow at the table, those in the chairs lining the walls already uncomfortable before the meeting even began, James Nathan wondered if he had made a mistake when he chose this alternative.

At *his* elbow, David Chornyak was wondering the same thing, and he and James Nathan stared at each other in quick consternation, and then looked quickly away. It was too late now, whether it had been an error or not; they were all here, and the best thing to do was get on with the business of the day as swiftly as possible.

"Go on, Jim," said David under his breath. "Let's get this over with."

James Nathan nodded, and pressed the small stud beneath the table. He disliked the sound of the thing . . . his grandfather Paul John's choice of a falling minor third would not have been his choice. But the tones did stop the muttering and get everyone turned to face him, which was their function.

"Good morning, gentlemen," James Nathan began, "and my thanks to all of you for coming here in person. I know you're not particularly comfortable, and I regret that. I'm afraid we've never had any need for conference facilities here at Chornyak Household."

Nigel Shawnessey, whose Household in Switzerland *did* have conference facilities, cleared his throat elaborately and gave the ceiling a significant glance. He considered this a ridiculous imposition, carried out only as a vehicle for a display of dominance. And wholly unnecessary. Nobody had ever challenged Chornyak House for the position of Head of the Lines, and so long as the Chornyaks continued to produce men of the traditional caliber nobody ever would.

James Nathan had not missed the bit of body-parl, and he knew what it meant, but he didn't agree. Filling the shoes of Thomas Blair Chornyak had not been easy; stepping into them at forty-six had come perilously close to being beyond his abilities. Nobody had ever anticipated such a thing, with his father in robust health and only just turned seventy . . . the Chornyak men filled their posts well into their eighties ordinarily, and sometimes longer than that.

There had been nothing ordinary about having a Head murdered by a madwoman. And the effort of assuming Thomas Blair's role, so suddenly and without any of the usual mechanisms of transition, had brought painfully home to James Nathan the need to keep a tight rein on the Lines. Which was, even as he thought it, so awkward and unfelicitous a phrase that it made him smile. A tight rein on the Lines, indeed . . . thank God he hadn't said that aloud! And he had been adamant about this meeting—under no circumstances would he have called it at Shawnessey Household, and found himself obliged to run the meeting while Nigel Shawnessey played host, with all the intricate burdens that would have laid upon the Chornyak men as guests. Thomas would have done it that way, and never given it a thought, but he was not Thomas, and he knew it. Oh no . . . he might be young, and he might have tumbled into the Headship a bit abruptly, but he was not stupid.

"Our agenda today," he said smoothly, "is a single topic, and a most unusual one. The last meeting of this particular kind was held in 2088, when the decision was made to build Chornyak Barren House, and we were fewer in number in those days. I've called the meeting only because the time I was having to spend listening to complaints from all of you about this matter had begun to take up an absurd proportion of my days—and my nights. And I insisted on having all of you here in person because leaks to the media would have been more than usually unacceptable in this case. Security on the comset network isn't adequate, as all of you know to your sorrow—and it would be very distasteful to have this affair become a topic for the popnews commentators."

"Damn right," said half a dozen men heartily, and the rest made noises of agreement.

"Very well, then," said James Nathan. "Since we understand one another, we will move at once to discussion. Our subject today, gentlemen, is . . . the women."

"Where are they, by the way?"

"I beg your pardon?"

"Well," said the man from Verdi Household, "talking of leaks and distasteful indiscretions and so on . . . where are the Chornyak women while this meeting is going on?"

James Nathan answered in a tone that made his resentment of the question clear. "Arrangements have been made," he said stiffly. "You needn't concern yourself."

"Arrangements? What sort of arrangements?"

Verdi was damned rude, and he'd have to be set right at the first opportunity. But not now, thought James Nathan, not now; this was not the place for personal discussions.

"Most of the women are at negotiations," he said. "Those who were free have been given a variety of assignments off the grounds. There are no females at Chornyak Household today except those under two years of age—I assume my colleague will trust us to prevent any serious indiscretions in those infants."

Point scored; Luke Verdi flushed slightly, and said no more.

"Now," James Nathan went on, "I've heard essentially the same story, and the same complaints, from every one of you. I am personally aware of the situation as well; this Household is not immune. But we need a summary from someone, to make sure that we are in fact dealing with a *general* problem; this is far too grave a matter to be settled hastily. I need not remind you that we must anticipate a strong reaction from the public, no matter what we decide to do."

"The hell with the public," said a junior man from Jefferson Household.

"We're in no position to take that stance," James Nathan told him, "even if it were consistent with the policies of the Lines—which it is not."

"It's none of the public's damn business, if you ask me."

"I didn't ask you, and I won't. But I *am* going to ask for that summary, and I know precisely whom to ask. Dano, would you do the honors?"

Dano Mbal, of Mbal Household, was an imposing man and one accustomed to narration. He was very good at it. Narration, oration, declamation—all male linguists were trained for those, as they were trained in phonetics or political strategy; all three were essential skills in the use of the voice as a mechanism of power. But Dano had gifts that went beyond the training. He

288 / Suzette Haden Elgin

could read you a list of agricultural chemicals and keep you on the edge of the chair. And he inclined his head slightly now, to indicate that he was willing to be spokesman.

"The problem," he said, "is not difficult to summarize. It can in fact be done in three words, thus: WOMEN ARE EXTINCT."

He waited a moment, to let that sink in and to let the laughter subside around the room. And then he went on.

"*Real* women, that is. We have living females of the species homo sapiens moving about our Households, but that is all that can be said for them. They are homo sapiens, they are female, and they are alive. Nothing more, gentlemen, nothing more."

One of the younger men opened his mouth to ask a question, but James Nathan was alert for interruptions, and he silenced him before he could make a sound, raising one hand.

"Please go on, Dano," he said, underlining the message that the man was not to be interrupted.

"I believe," said Mbal, nodding at James Nathan, "that we all first began to realize that something odd was happening with the women on the night that Thomas Blair Chornyak was so brutally murdered . . . I remember well that it was a subject of discussion that night. Except that we all thought, then, that it signalled some sort of change for the *better*! Gentlemen, we were quite wrong."

He paused just long enough to fill a pipe with the aromatic tobacco he was addicted to, and to light it, and then he said, "Gentlemen, our women have become intolerable. And what is most astonishing about this is that we find ourselves curiously. . . . helpless? Yes, I think helpless is the word . . . helpless to bring any accusation against them."

This brought a murmur of protest too widely scattered to be silenced by a gesture. The idea of men helpless against women was absurd, and the men were quick to say so. Dano listened to them courteously, and then he raised his broad shoulders and spread his open hands in a *gesture* of helplessness.

"Well, gentlemen!" he said. "I will stop, then, and hear the accusations. As you would phrase them."

He waited while they shuffled and muttered, and then he grinned at them.

"Ah, yes," he said. "Just as I thought! You are eager enough to have them accused—but you are no more able to give those accusations surface shape than I am. Can a man 'accuse' a woman of being unfailingly and exquisitely courteous? Can a man 'accuse' a woman of being a flawless mother or grand-

NATIVE TONGUE / 289

mother or daughter? Can a man, gentlemen, 'accuse' a woman
of being an ever willing and skillful sexual partner? Tell me . . .
can a man point a finger at a woman and say to her, 'I *accuse*
you of never frowning, or never complaining, of never weeping,
of never nagging, of never so much as pouting?' Can a man
demand of a woman that she nag? Can he demand that she sulk
and bitch and argue—in short, that she behave as women used to
behave? In the name of sweet reason, gentlemen, I ask you—can
one accuse a woman, name her guilty, for ceasing to do every
last thing he has demanded that she *not* do, all his life long?''

The silence was thick, heavy in the air; they were all thinking,
and they had forgotten that they were cramped and crowded into
this room. Each of them had his own women in mind, and each
of them had an image of those women listening to him as he
made some sort of speech about how they were so goddam
COURTEOUS and COOPERATIVE and REASONABLE and
PLEASANT. . . . Oh, no. It was true. There was no way to
accuse them of those things. A man would look and sound like
an idiot. A kind of sigh, a sigh of being burdened and oppressed,
went round the room.

"I take it it *is* a general problem, then?" asked James Nathan.
"None of you disagrees with Dano Mbal's description?"

The contributions came thick and fast, from every corner and
from every Line.

"It's as if they weren't really even *there* at all!"

"They look right at you, and they don't interrupt or fidget—
they fold their hands in their laps and give you what is supposed
to be their full attention, right? More attention, God knows, than
they ever *used* to give. But somehow you know, you *know*, that
their minds are a thousand miles away. They're not really looking at you—and not really listening!"

"They might as well be androids, for all the good they are;
androids would at least be uniformly attractive."

"They are so goddam cursed *boring*!"

It went on for some time, and James Nathan let it go. He
nodded now and then, encouraging them, wanting them to get it
all out in the open, wanting the consensus of sullen anger that he
could feel building. None of it was new; he'd been listening to it
for what seemed to be years and years—though as Dano had
said, it couldn't really be that long. Whatever it was, it was true
that at the beginning it had seemed to be something desirable.
What man would not be pleased to have his women always
serene, always compliant, always courteous, always respectful?

Dano Mbal spoke again.

"It used to be," he said, "that when a man had done something in which he could take legitimate pride, he could go home and talk to his wife and his daughters about it, and that pride would *grow*—it would be a reason to do even more, and to do it even better. We all remember that . . . it was important to us. But now, now, it would be just as satisfying to go outside and talk about our plans and our accomplishments to a tree. As so many of you have said—it's not that they interrupt, it's not that they won't give a man all the time he wants—it's that they are simply not really there at all. There's no feedback from them that couldn't be obtained from a decently programmed computer. It is as frustrating to address your remarks to our women as to address them to your elbow."

That was true. They all agreed. No question about it, it was the same for all. And there was the other side of the coin, which each secretly suspected mattered only to him, and which would not be mentioned aloud.

It used to be that a man could do something he was *ashamed* of, too, and then go home and talk to his women about it and be able to count on them to nag him and harangue him and carry on hysterically at him until he felt he'd paid in full for what he'd done. And then a man could count on the women to go right on past that point with their nonsense until he actually felt that he'd been justified in what he'd done. *That* had been important, too—and it never happened anymore. Never. No matter what you did, it would be met in just the same way. With respectful courtesy. With a total absence of complaint.

And it used to be that three or four women would go off in a corner and talk to each other and make a man feel left out somehow . . . but that was normal. You could raise hell about it and make them leave off their woman-gibberish. It was annoying, but you could do something about it, and you knew where you were. They never did that anymore, either. They were *always* at your disposal . . . it was as if they had no need to talk to one another any longer. But you couldn't complain about that. You couldn't raise hell about it. You couldn't order them to stop it. You knew what they would do if you were fool enough to try it. Those pleasant, serene, obscenely courteous faces . . . they would look at you, with nobody home back of their eyes, and they would say "Stop *what*, my dear?" And there'd be no answer. Stop giving me your full attention when I ask for it? Stop doing without the gossip and gabble I always ridiculed you for? It was out of the question.

"Gentlemen," said James Nathan, "am I correct that it's

unanimous? Our women are a constant irritation? A total royal pain in the butt? Impossible to live with? Useful only for the occasional bed session, and even then it's like fucking a well-bred rubber doll? Do I have it right, gentlemen? Am I leaving anything out? Overstating the case? Is there *anyone* here who feels that his women are an exception, or that the rest of us have gone over the edge?''

"No," they said. No, he had it exactly right. And by *God* they would not stand for it.

"All right, we're agreed. We can't live with the bitches, and we can't find any way to cure them of whatever it is they've come down with."

"It's unbearable, Chornyak," blurted young Luke. "It's unbearable!"

James Nathan nodded slowly, pleased. This wasn't going to take as long as he'd expected. He'd thought there would be a lot of hedging and waffling, a lot of "perhaps I am exaggerating the situation" and "it may well be that I have only imagined this" and similar offputting. There'd been none of that.

"The question, then, is what we are going to do about it," he stated flatly.

"Damn right."

"Except," Emmanuel Belview pointed out, "that there isn't anything we *can* do about it. That's precisely the problem. They're fucking *saints*—how are we going to punish them for *that*?"

"I don't think we should punish them."

"What?"

"What? What do you mean, not punish them?"

He held up both hands against the clamor, and hushed them.

"If we can't live with them," said James Nathan, enjoying himself very much, "let's live without them."

"What?"

The immediate racket was so completely disorganized that he could only laugh, and wait; and he was sorry he wouldn't have anyone to listen to him talk about the disorderly way they'd behaved, after this was over. It would have been a relief to talk about it—to talk to a real woman about it.

"Gentlemen? Could I have a little quiet, please?" he tried.

"I said," he repeated when he finally had them reasonably attentive again, "let's live without them, since we can't live with them. We need them for many things, I know that. Not only for breeding. We need them, and need them badly, to do their share in the interpreting and translating booths. We're spread so thin already that we couldn't begin to keep up with the work without them—we can't afford to dispense with them. But, gentlemen, we do *not* have to live with them!''

''But—''

''They are total wet blankets,'' he continued. ''They take every smallest fraction of pleasure out of life. Being with them is like being sentenced to life imprisonment with some terribly charming elderly maiden aunt that you hardly know and don't care to know better. And I repeat, we do not have to *do* it!''

He leaned forward to make his point.

''Gentlemen,'' he said, ''the solution is right under our noses. I opened this meeting by telling that there hasn't been one like it since the day our forefathers met to work out the establishment of the first Barren House. Right here. In this room, at this table. And for almost the same reason, different only in scope— because the barren women were an intolerable pain in the ass and they had to be gotten out of the men's hair. Without—and this is crucial!—without sacrificing any of the essential services they provided. We have only to follow the excellent example they set us!''

''By God,'' said one of the Shawnesseys. ''He means build them houses. By God!''

''Exactly!'' James Nathan struck the table with his fist, and beside him David was laughing openly, delighted. ''The precedent already has been set. The barren women have had separate houses, have lived apart from the men, all these years. It's been no problem. It hasn't interfered in any way with their performance of their duties. It has worked superbly, agreed? Well! We need only extend that privilege to *all* our women. Not move them to the Barren House, those buildings aren't large enough or suitably equipped. But build them houses of their own, gentlemen. Women's Houses! Every one of the Households has land enough to build a separate women's residence, put it close by as we've done with the Barren Houses . . . where it will be convenient when we need to see a woman for some reason, sexual or otherwise, but where the women will be *out of our way.*''

''It could be done,'' said a senior man cautiously.

''Of course it could.''

James Nathan could see the relief spreading over them, the loosening of the tension that had held them when they first came into this room. They were thinking what it would be like . . . to have the women out of their lives and yet close enough for those times when only a woman would do.

The objection that he was waiting for, the one about the cost, came almost immediately.

"I was waiting for that," he said.

"Chornyak, it would cost millions. Thirteen separate residences? There are a hell of a lot of women in the Lines, man. You're talking about an immense sum of money."

"I don't give one scrawny damn," he told them.

"But, Chornyak—"

"I don't care what it costs," he went on grimly. "We have the money. God knows, we've never spent any. We have money to build ten Women's Houses for each of the Lines and not even dent our accounts. You know it, and I know it—that's one of the very rare benefits of a hundred years of avoiding all conspicuous consumption. The money is there. We have always lived in ostentatious austerity to keep the public happy. . . . we've done enough, and we're entitled. Let's spend that money, before we all go raving mad."

"It's the public that will go raving mad," said one of the men, "They'll never stand for it. There'll be *riots* again, Chornyak! Remember the 25th Amendment to the Constitution? No mistreatment of women allowed. We'll never get away with it!"

"Perceive this," James Nathan insisted. "There won't be any real problem. Not if we do this properly. We point to the precedent, to the Barren Houses . . . we go on and on about how happy our women are to go to them, which is true. And we take pains, gentlemen, we take exquisite pains, to make these Women's Houses superb places to be. We will not leave ourselves open to even the hint of a charge that we are abusing or neglecting our women! We spend whatever it costs to build them fine houses, beautiful houses, houses furnished and equipped with all the crap women always want, everything they could possibly need within the limits of reason. Our comsets are falling apart, for example, we've let that go on as an ecomony measure—we'll put brand new systems in for the women. We'll give them gardens—they're all crazy for gardens. Fountains. Whatever. We'll build them residences that the public can go through, if they insist, and satisfy themselves that we are providing the women with every comfort, every convenience, every facility. Let them send teams of inspectors out if they like . . . they'll find nothing to criticize. And gentlemen, the public will *envy* us."

They thought about that, and he saw a few grins as they began to understand.

"The men will envy us," he said simply, "because we get to

live every man's dream. No women in our houses to foul up our lives and interfere with us—but women in abundance just a few steps away, when we choose to enjoy their company.''

"The *men* will envy us,'' said Dano Mbal. "The *men*.''

"Isn't that what matters?''

"It brings the obvious to mind, Chornyak.''

"Explain it to me . . . it may not be as obvious to me as it is to you.''

"Mention the men,'' said Dano, "one thinks of the women. Their women will not envy ours, shut off in separate buildings in that fashion. They will pity our poor women—you know they will. And that is a good thing in its way, since the smaller the population that envies us the less trouble there will be. But what about *our* women, James Nathan? They're not going to just smile and curtsey and move next door into an upgraded harem, man! This is going to put a considerable dent in their saintly demeanor, because they are going to fight like tigresses.''

"Let them fight, then,'' said James Nathan. "What can they do? They have no legal rights in this matter, so long as they cannot claim that they're being deprived of anything— and I have explained to you that we would make absolutely certain they couldn't make that claim. Nothing but the best for our women, I promise you! So they fight it, so they have hysterics, so what, Dano? Men have been able to control women without difficulty since the beginning of time—surely we are not such poor examples of the *male* homo sapiens that we cannot continue in the ancient tradition? Are you suggesting, Dano Mbal, that we men of the Lines are not *capable* of controlling our women?''

"Of course not, Chornyak. You know I am suggesting no such thing.''

"Very well, then. The women have only themselves to blame for this, my friends. *They* have decided, in some incomprehensible female way, to turn themselves into multilingual robots—it was not we men who set them on that course. They've made their beds, as the saying goes; let them lie in them. They have no money, they are legally not even of age . . . what can they do to stop us?''

"They can bitch. They can raise hell.''

"Then the more quickly we get this done, the more quickly we'll be rid of their bitching and their hell-raising. I move we vote. At once. Time's a-wasting, gentlemen.''

*   *   *

There was a certain amount of discussion, a few objections, some grudging compromises had to be made . . . that was to be anticipated. It was how the game was played. But in the end they agreed unanimously, as James Nathan had known from the start they would. And when that point was reached, and the vote properly recorded, he punched the keys that would display the holos he'd had prepared especially for this meeting. He intended to spend plenty of credits; they had the money, they could afford to spend it, and he'd been serious about that. But there was no reason to *waste* money, and he'd spent many careful hours with David, the two of them working out every detail of the basic plan. There was no reason at all why the residences couldn't be sufficiently uniform to allow for purchasing all the materials in huge quantities, at correspondingly huge savings.

In the Barren Houses, when the announcement was made, the women first sat shocked into total silence, staring at one another. And then their eyes began dancing, and they smiled, and then they laughed until they had no strength left to laugh any more.

"We were going to flee into the woods. . . ."

"With babies on our backs . . ."

"Dig ourselves forts in the desert . . ."

"Oh, dear heaven. . . ."

"We were going to be shut up in the attics . . . oh, lord. . . ."

Even Aquina had to admit that it was funny, although she felt obligated to warn them that this was probably all just a trick to lull them into a sense of false security. Before the men began the *real* action against them.

First they said, "Oh, Aquina, don't start!"

And then they all thought of it together, and they backed Nazareth to the wall.

"Nazareth, you *knew*."

"I didn't."

"You *did*. That's why you always stalled . . . always said that it would be all right, always did your best not to be here when we had planning sessions. You *knew*. Nazareth Joanna, *how* did you know?"

Nazareth stared at the floor, and at the ceiling, and everywhere except at them, and begged them to let it pass.

"Can't you just be satisfied?" she asked them. "We don't have to flee anywhere, we don't have to erect battlements and woman ramparts and move into caves with lasers at the ready . . . we just have to go on about our business, with a great deal

less inconvenience than we've ever had to put up with in all our
lives.''

"Nazareth," said Caroline, "if we have to tie you to a tree,
you are going to explain."

"I was never *able* to explain anything," Nazareth wailed.

"Try. At least try."

"Well."

"Try!"

"Perceive this . . . there was only one reason for the Encoding Project, really, other than just the joy of it. The hypothesis
was that if we put the project into effect it would *change
reality*."

"Go on."

"Well . . . you weren't taking that hypothesis seriously. I
was."

"We were."

"No. No, you weren't. Because all your plans were based on
the *old* reality. The one *before* the change."

"But Nazareth, how can you plan for a new reality when you
don't have the remotest idea what it would be like?" Aquina
demanded indignantly. "That's not possible!"

"Precisely," said Nazareth. "We have no science for that.
We have pseudo-sciences, in which we extrapolate for a reality
that would be nothing more than a minor variation on the one we
have . . . . but the science of actual reality change has not yet
been even proposed, much less formalized."

She didn't like the way they were looking at her, or the way
they were moving back. She hadn't liked it before, when they
were crowding her, but this was worse. And inevitable; she had
known it couldn't be avoided.

"What did *you* do, then, Nazareth," Grace asked her in a
strange voice, "while we made fools of ourselves?"

Nazareth leaned against the wall, and looked at them bleakly.
It was hopeless. Probably the little girls who spoke Láadan well
could have said what she needed to say, but she couldn't even
begin. *I had faith?* Could she say that?

Faith. That dreadful word, with its centuries of contamination
hiding all the light of it.

"Please," Nazareth said, giving up. "Please. I love you. And
everything is going to be all right. Let that be enough."

It was Aquina that saved her, however.

"Good lord," Aquina cried, struck with still another call to
arms. "We don't have time for this! We have to decide how we
go about offering Láadan to women outside the Lines. . . ."

Dear Aquina.

"Now that," said Nazareth solemnly, "is something that I do believe I *can* be helpful with. If you'll let me make a pot of tea and if we could all sit down and talk about it. . . ."

Chapter Twenty-five

```
1Ø REM HERE WE GO AGAIN
2Ø GOTO 10
```

It was Lanky Pugh's personal opinion that this latest hooha from Government Work should have been located offplanet. *Way* offplanet. Preferably somewhere out behind the Extreme Moons.

But the Pentagon didn't feel that way about it. In the first place, they assured him it was perfectly safe for G.W. to be right where it was. El Centro, California, wasn't just a ghost town—it was a ghost *location*. Nobody, but nobody was ever going to drop by the godforsaken broiling spit in the middle of a giant rockpile that had once been a town called El Centro . . . in a time when you couldn't be too particular about what square foot or two of this earth you stood on. That time was long gone, now.

The real reason, however, was that the scientists who were required for this project couldn't be allowed to go offplanet. Some of them might have been willing to do without their labs and their creature comforts, but the government wanted them right there at hand. Right on tap, where you could pick up your comunit and give a call and say, "My God, Professor Blah, will you come take a look at *this*?" And Professor Blah could be right there, in about half an hour maximum. The Pentagon was almost violently against the idea of having any of their Professor Blahs more than a half hour out of range.

And so they were set up in an underground installation, all nicely cooled and decorated so you could hardly tell you weren't at a motel, in the middle of effing nowhere. Lanky Pugh, and a whole platoon of servomechanisms, and the Professors. And what they had going this time surprised even Lanky, who had really believed—when they closed down Arnold Dolbe's unit—that the U.S. Government had come to the end of its string regarding the Interfacing of human babies and nonhumanoid Aliens. The shutdown had been very convincing, and Lanky had approved of it with all his heart. He'd been glad the baby project was over, glad to see the discreet removal of the media notices calling for volunteer infants, and damn surprised when he found out that it was just one more song-and-dance to a federal tune.

Here they are, opened up with a brand new project, this one going on just below the surface of the ground for all the world to see, if the world cared to trek out to El Centro, California. This project's Interface had cost the taxpayers a cool billion if it had cost them a nickel—you didn't provide a shared environment for humans and whales in the middle of an effing desert for any kind of discount rate.

There was a turnstile, and a chipper little servomechanism sitting beside it to chirp at people. "Hello, folks! Welcome to the Cetacean Intersection! Please insert your credit card in the slot that you see outlined in red on the top of the turnstile, and step right through! Please follow the yellow line that you see straight ahead of you on the floor of the building! It will take you right to the Interface! Thank you, folks, and please come back and see us again."

Nobody, to Lanky's knowledge, had ever bothered to go through the turnstile and follow the yellow stripe and watch the solemn pair of small whales swimming in their half of a regulation Interface . . . a little oversized, but otherwise regulation . . . with an equally solemn tubie watching them through the barrier. There was nothing to see, nothing to hear, and nothing at all to experience that was worth the 135° hell of rocks and cracked earth and Nothing that stretched as far as you could see in every direction above the ground.

It was fancy, all right, and if anyone ever did come look at it it would probably impress the hell out of them. Lanky had to give the government credit; they'd spared no expense. There was even a very small automated souvenir shop, where you could buy a toy Interface to take home to the kids.

The real project, though, was two levels lower, encased in the same earthquake-proof concrete shell, but sunk deep into the bowels of the blasted earth. And what went on down there, far underneath the whales swimming round and round and round and the tubie watching, was something else altogether.

"Let's just assume," the Pentagon briefer had said, "that

what the linguists tell us is true. Just for the sake of getting on with this. Let's assume that the problem is simply that the human brain cannot tolerate sharing perceptions with a non-humanoid brain. We've had plenty of evidence that that's true.''

"Yeah, we sure have," Lanky had agreed. "Damn sure we have."

"And then let's just set aside the other matter. Let's just ignore, for now, the fact that the linguists know a solution to the problem that they're unwilling to let us in on. The hell with them, gentlemen! The government of the United States has for chrissakes got savvy enough, and technology enough, and everything else enough, to either figure out what it is that the linguists know or to find some other way around the problem.''

"Damn right," said Lanky. "Way to tell 'em.''

"Now what it boils down to is this . . . what we need, men, is a brain that's just a little bit less humanoid and just a little bit more Alien. A kind of bridge between the two, don't you see?''

Lanky didn't know whether he saw or not, but the professors had all seemed to follow what was going on without any difficulty. They trusted him with the computers; he trusted them with *their* tools. And it sounded just about as crazy, no more and no less so, than any of the rest of the G.W. projects.

The idea was to use genetic engineering, and the government's overflowing tanks full of tubies, and gradually, one step at a time, alter the brains and the perception systems of the tubies to make them alien. Or Alien, as the case might be.

The Pentagon man had felt obliged to caution them.

"We can't move fast," he'd said. "We don't dare move fast, because we don't know exactly what it is that we're after. But we have thousands of tubies for you gentlemen to work with, to modify in whatever way you care to—and if you run out, well, there's plenty more where those came from. You just let us know what you need.''

The professors sat with microscopes and nearly invisible messes on slides and in Petri dishes, and they made their slow changes. Lanky didn't know how they did that. Whether they poked the little embryos with the scientific equivalent of pins, or blasted them with lasers, or ran currents through them, or what. He most emphatically did not want to know. He knew enough about G.W. projects to last him all the rest of his life. He stayed carefully away from the profs, he ran the data they gave him without allowing any of it to register in his memory—that's what you have computers for, so you don't have to put stuff in your own memory—and that was all he did. Just doing his job, thank you very much.

He had asked one question. He had asked, "What are you going to call it?"

"Call what?"

"Well . . . you're down here to fool around with the embryos till you get something we can Interface. Something that's not quite human and not quite humanoid and not quite Alien either. I believe you'll get it . . . don't see why not. But what are you going to call it?"

"Mr. Pugh," the eggdome had said, looking at him just exactly the way he looked at the stuff under his microscope, "please go away and let me work."

All right. Lanky had gone away as requested. It didn't hurt his feelings, being talked to like that. After what Lanky Pugh had been through, he didn't have any feelings left to hurt. He gave the professor one wave to acknowledge the message and went on up to watch the whales swim around.

One of the things he planned to do, before he left this fancy hell, was figure out how to get into the Interface and go for a swim with those whales in that beautirul blue water. Round and round and round, in a lovely endless loop.

Appendix
From: *A First Dictionary and Grammar of Láadan*

As is true in the translation from any language into another, many words of Láadan cannot be translated into English except by lengthy definitions. A miscellaneous sampling is given here to illustrate the situation; it consists mainly of samples from the "ra-" prefixing forms of the language.

doóledosh: pain or loss which comes as a relief by virtue of ending the anticipation of its coming

doroledim: This word has no English equivalent whatsoever. Say you have an average woman. She has no control over her life. She has little or nothing in the way of a resource for being good to herself, even when it is necessary. She has family and animals and friends and associates that depend on her for sustenance of all kinds. She rarely has adequate sleep or rest; she has no time for herself, no space of her own, little or no money to buy things for herself, no opportunity to consider her own emotional needs. She is at the beck and call of others, because she has these responsibilities and obligations and does not choose to (or cannot) abandon them. For such a woman, the one and only thing she is likely to have a little control over for indulging her own self is FOOD. When such a woman overeats, the verb for that is "doroledim". (And then she feels guilty, because there are women whose children are starving and who do not have even THAT option for self-indulgence . . .)

lowitheláad: to feel, as if directly, another's pain/grief/surprise/joy/anger

núháam: to feel oneself cherished, cared for, nurtured by someone; to feel loving-kindness

óothanúthul: spiritual orphanhood; being utterly without a spiritual community or family

ráahedethi: to be unable to feel lowitheláad, above; to be empathically impaired

ráahedethilh: 1) to be unwilling to feel lowitheláad, above; to be empathically impaired 2) to be musically or euphonically deprived

radama: to non-touch, to actively refrain from touching

radamalh: to non-touch with evil intent

radéela: non-garden, a place that has much flash and glitter and ornament, but no beauty

radíidin: non-holiday, a time allegedly a holiday but actually so much a burden because of work and preparations that it is a dreaded occasion; especially when there are too many guests and none of them help

radodelh: non-interface, a situation which has not one single point in common on which to base interaction, often used of personal relationships

raduth: to non-use, to deliberately deprive someone of any useful function in the world, as in enforced retirement or when a human being is kept as a plaything or pet

rahéena: non-heart-sibling, one so entirely incompatible with another that there is no hope of ever achieving any kind of understanding or anything more than a truce, and no hope of ever making such a one understand why . . . does not mean "enemy"

rahobeth: non-neighbor, one who lives nearby but does not fulfill a neighbor's role; not necessarily pejorative

rahom: to non-teach, to deliberately fill students' minds with empty data or false information; can be used only of persons in a teacher/student relationship

ralaheb: something utterly spiceless, "like warm spit," repulsively bland and blah

ralée-: non-meta (a prefix), something absurdly or dangerously narrow in scope or range

ralith: to deliberately refrain from thinking about something, to wall it off in one's mind by deliberate act

ralorolo: non-thunder, much talk and commotion from one (or more) with no real knowledge of what they're talking about or trying to do, something like "hot air" but more so

ramime: to refrain from asking, out of courtesy or kindness

ramimelh: to refrain from asking, with evil intent; especially when it is clear that someone badly wants the other to ask

ranem: non-pearl, an ugly thing one builds layer by layer as an oyster does a pearl, such as a festering hatred to which one pays attention

rani: non-cup, a hollow accomplishment, something one acquires or receives or accomplishes but empty of all satisfaction

rarilh: to deliberately refrain from recording; for example, the failure throughout history to record the accomplishments of women.

rarulh: non-synergy, that which when combined only makes things worse, less efficient, etc.

rashida: non-game, a cruel "playing" that is a game only for the dominant "players" with the power to force others to participate

rathom: non-pillow, one who lures another to trust and rely on them but has no intention of following through, a "lean on me so I can step aside and let you fall" person

rathóo: non-guest, someone who comes to visit knowing perfectly well that they are intruding and causing difficulty

raweshalh: non-gestalt, a collection of parts with no relationship other than coincidence, a perverse choice of items to call a set; especially when used as "evidence"

sháadehul: growth through transcendence, either of a person, a non-human, or thing (for example, an organization, or a city, or a sect)

wohosheni: a word meaning the opposite of alienation; to feel joined to, part of someone or something without reservations or barriers

wonewith: to be socially dyslexic; uncomprehending of the social signals of others

zhaláad: the act of relinquishing a cherished/comforting/ familiar illusion or frame of perception

A First Dictionary and Grammar of Láadan is published by the Society for the Furtherance and Study of Fantasy and Science Fiction, Inc. For further information send SASE to Láadan, P.O. Box 1137, Huntsville, AR 72740-1137.

Afterword
Encoding a Woman's Language

Native Tongue (1984) inaugurates Suzette Haden Elgin's powerful trilogy about the invention of a female language. As the first volume of this trilogy, *Native Tongue* introduces us to the patriarchal culture of a future Earth, where a small number of linguistically skilled women are banding together to fight their second-class status by secretly creating a women's language. The sequel, *The Judas Rose* (1987), follows the story of that language, Láadan, as it evolves from the private creation of a very few women to a shared language that subversively links women worldwide, and then as it is discovered by the patriarchal church and state it was created to oppose. The concluding book in the trilogy, *Earthsong* (1994), turns from the question of a gender-based language to the broader question of alternate and gender-linked forms of nourishment, as women try to spread the news of another way of feeding the world, aurally rather than orally.

Central to this trilogy, as to most of the science fiction of Suzette Haden Elgin, are two interrelated convictions: "The first hypothesis is that language is our best and most powerful resource for bringing about social change; the second is that science fiction is our best and most powerful resource for trying out social changes before we make them, to find out what their consequences might be" (Elgin, "Linguistics"). Elgin's definition of feminism can be gleaned from the type of social change she is most interested in making: the eradication of patriarchy and its replacement with "a society and culture that can be sustained without violence" (Elgin, "Feminist" 46). The belief that "patriarchy requires violence in the same way that human beings require oxygen" links the Native Tongue trilogy to Elgin's bestselling non fiction book, *The Gentle Art of Verbal Self-Defense*: both are concerned with feminist linguistic interventions, the production and/or teaching of "gentle" linguistic strategies to counter, and thus change, verbal violence (Elgin, "Feminist" 46).

Fifteen years after it was first published, and despite a number of years out of print, *Native Tongue* retains a cult following and remains an important contribution to the canon of feminist science fiction as well as to feminist debates about the significance of language. Its importance is far more than academic, although it also serves as a historical document highlighting the particular concerns of feminism in the early 1980s. With all of the changes feminism has wrought in American society, *Native Tongue* and its sequels remain exciting for the sense of expanded social possibilities they embody.

The themes of the Native Tongue books have been woven throughout Suzette Haden Elgin's life and work. She received her Ph.D. in linguistics, with a focus on the Navajo language, from the University of California at San Diego in 1973, at the age of thirty-seven. Earlier degrees were in French, English, and music, all of which came into play in her later teaching. Elgin taught at San Diego State University until she retired in 1980, at which time she began the Ozark Center for Language Studies near Huntsville, Arkansas. She is the founder and president of LOVINGKINDNESS, a nonprofit organization that investigates religious language and its effect on individuals, as well as the editor and publisher of *Linguistics and Science Fiction,* a bimonthly newsletter interested in language issues in genre fiction. She writes prolifically in a variety of forms, including fiction, poetry, and essays, and she now draws prolifically as well. Her best-known work, however, is the popular series of books that begins with *The Gentle Art of Verbal Self- Defense*, which teaches readers how to identify and defuse verbally violent or combative situations.[1]

Elgin's most basic tenet is that language is power: "If speaking a language were like brain surgery, learned only after many long years of difficult study and practiced only by a handful of remarkable individuals at great expense, we would view it with similar respect and awe. But because almost every human being knows and uses one or more languages, we have let that miracle be trivialized into 'only talk'" (Elgin, *Language Imperative* 239). Overlooked because it is so inherent, language may in fact be "our only real high technology" (Elgin, "Washing Utopian" 45). It is certainly our most prominent social technology, the primary way human beings manipulate the material world (De Lauretis 3). Yet our very familiarity with language leads to its undervaluation. How can something as everyday as talk shape reality?

Elgin subscribes to a widely discussed but highly controversial theory that in linguistics is called the Sapir-Whorf hypothesis.[2] This hypothesis claims that languages "structure and constrain human perceptions of reality in significant and interesting ways" (Elgin, *Language Imperative* xvi). Based on a study of American Indian languages, this hypothesis proposed that languages vary dramatically and in ways not easily anticipated, and that such variations encode dramatically different understandings of reality, so that people speaking different languages actually see the world in widely divergent ways (Bothamley 473). How we perceive the world depends upon our linguistic structures in both the words we choose and the larger metaphors they encode. These structures, for example, powerfully affect our understandings of gender. Assumptions about gender roles are everywhere encoded in our language, particularly in our habit of binary thinking, through which the paired terms *male/female* become associated with other pairs: *active/passive, strong/weak, right/left,* and so on. The work of feminist anthropologist Emily Martin provides an excellent example of this idea. In "The Egg and the Sperm," Martin examines the metaphors used by gynecology and obstetrics textbooks to describe female reproductive processes. Dominant social assumptions about gender roles, she discovers, color the books' scientific descriptions of conception: the egg is represented as waiting passively for the sperm to compete for the privilege of entering it. Linguistic structures for representing gender lead researchers to focus on characteristics that accord with their conceptual presuppositions. Thus, a passive egg/active sperm model prevails over another model, which might involve a "sticky" egg capturing sperm (1–18).

According to the Sapir-Whorf line of thinking, language structures our perceptions not only through word choice, but through metaphors and metaphor systems, with benefits, limitations, and concrete consequences. For example, as Elgin points out in *The Language Imperative,* the language we use to talk about menopause influences how we experience it. The description of menopause as "a natural event" will produce one set of effects; with this model, a woman going through menopause is likely to interpret any negative experiences as annoyances (minor or major) rather than medicalizing them. However, if menopause is described as "a medical condition characterized by a lack of estrogen," the menopausal woman is more likely to interpret her experiences in terms of pathology, leading to medical intervention as well as increased concern on the part of the woman, her family, and her friends. This *linguistic* shift has an effect on the woman's material reality (75–80). It is important to point out that there is no way out of this dilemma produced by the linguistic construction of reality. Because the language we use has developed alongside human history, we are inevitably embroiled in these issues. While no form of speech is inherently better than another, the effects of different speech acts are often very different, and Elgin encourages us to judge speech on that basis. Summarized briefly, Elgin's linguistic position has powerful feminist implications: The language we use to describe and operate in the world affects the way we understand the world, our place in it, and our interactions with one another. Changing our language changes our world.

This idea is not unique to Elgin, nor to linguistics. Other feminist thinkers have also addressed the ways that language shapes our perceptions. French feminist philosophers Hélène Cixous and Luce Irigaray have both considered how language reinforces existing gender relations. Cixous argues that the subordinate position of women has its foundation in the Western habit of thinking in dual, hierarchized oppositions. Holding that the logical and linear structures of modern Western languages reproduce the values and prejudices of patriarchy, Luce Irigaray further claims that women need our own language if we are to free ourselves from domination. This idea that language matters in the day-to-day existence of humans thus brings together a variety of different disciplines and links different feminist projects. This idea is also not unique to feminist theory; it has been addressed by such philosophers as Ferdinand Saussure, Jacques Derrida and Michel Foucault.

It also has far-reaching social and political implications. Elgin wrote what she has called the "thought experiment" of the Native Tongue books in order to test four hypotheses:

> 1) that the weak form of the linguistic relativity hypothesis is true [that human languages structure human perceptions in significant ways]; 2) that Gödel's Theorem applies to language, so that there are changes you could not introduce into a language without destroying it and languages you could not introduce into a culture without destroying it;[3] 3) that change in language brings about social change, rather than the contrary; and 4) that if women were offered a women's language one of two things would happen—they would welcome and nurture it, or it would at minimum motivate them to replace it with a better women's language of their own construction. ("Láadan")

Elgin admits that the experiment did not produce the desired outcome: the fourth hypothesis was proven false when her constructed women's language, Láadan, failed to be taken up in any meaningful way. But the broader questions she raises, concerning gender, language, and power, continue to resonate.

•

Should we be surprised to find these urgent feminist concerns addressed in a work of science fiction? That has been the initial response of some feminists. For example, when Carolyn Heilbrun reviewed *Native Tongue* in 1987 for the *Women's Review of Books,* she described herself as "a non-reader of science fiction" (17). Despite her self-confessed "resistance to SF (not that I dislike it, but that I can never figure out what's going on)," Heilbrun gave *Native Tongue* a glowing review: "There isn't a phony or romantic moment here," she observed, "and the story is absolutely compelling" (17). It is worth asking why science fiction has been anathema to many feminists, and worth offering a quick list of the reasons science fiction *deserves* a feminist audience. Feminist distaste for science fiction must be more than simply a response to its relatively low status as "genre fiction," since other forms of genre fiction, from the detective novel to the romance, have their staunch feminist adherents. Responding to the historic linkages between science and its traditional values—especially masculinist objective rationality—feminist readers and critics have challenged science as a method of inquiry about the world. They have tended to avoid scientific issues, themes, plots, and images, focusing instead on the crucial projects of reclaiming forgotten women writers, questioning the gendered nature of the literary canon, and imagining alternative forms for literary expression (Squier 132–158).

"Toys for boys": all too often, this phrase has seemed to accurately sum up the science fiction genre. But precisely because science and science fiction have seemed the rightful terrain of men at their most macho, feminists should give the genre their renewed attention, revitalizing its form and its content. The issue is, as Elgin has taught us, linguistic at its core. Until we abolish the culturally enforced hierarchical relations between science and the humanities that maintain literature as an insignificant, invisible, and feminized part of our culture in relation to significant, visible, masculinized science, we haven't made the large-scale linguistic transformation that Elgin herself calls for. We are still representing the world by gendered binary pairs (male/female; science/literature), and ceding to males the science half of the two-culture divide. *Science,* in short, is as open to feminist redefinition as any of the other words in our lexicon. Rather than abandoning it, we simply need to encode it anew and reclaim it as one of our native tongues.

The scientific study of alien species, a classic science fiction focus on the future, and a feminist preoccupation with the science of linguistics connect science fiction and feminism in the three

interrelated narratives that compose *Native Tongue*. The primary story
follows the development of the woman-language Láadan by the women
of the Linguist Lines, especially the protagonist, Nazareth Chornyak
Adiness. A parallel story line traces the U.S. government's secret
attempts to break the linguistic monopoly of the Lines by successfully learning, or "Interfacing" with, a non-humanoid alien
language. A third narrative strand follows Michaela, a nonlinguist, as she attempts to avenge her infant, who was killed in a
state experiment to break the language monopoly; instead she finds
surprising commonality with the linguist women. While these three
narratives do not always connect smoothly, taken together they
explore the constructive power of language, the origin of gendered
oppression, and the material and social commonalities between
women.

Elgin explores the nature, power, and significance of language
through the distinction between humanoid and non-humanoid languages, and the different worldview each constructs. Any language
is a limited set of perceptions and expressions; the rough similar-
ity of humanoid languages, and thus the rough correspondence of
their worldviews, is what allows them to be Interfaced. Dramatically
different worldviews separate humanoid and non-humanoid languages, and thus the realities they construct, which explains the dan-
gers of Interfacing humanoid and non-humanoid languages. The
government technicians, in an effort to work through the problem
of non-humanoid languages, articulate the relationship of language
to reality:

> "First principle: there's no such thing as reality. We make it
> up by perceiving stimuli from the environment—external or
> internal—and making statements about it. Everybody per-
> ceives stuff, everybody makes up statements about it, every-
> body—so far as we can tell—agrees enough to get by, so that
> when I say 'Hand me the coffee' you know what to hand me.
> And that's reality. Second principle: people get used to a cer-
> tain kind of reality and come to expect it, and if what they
> perceive doesn't fit the set of statements everybody's agreed
> to, either the culture has to go through a kind of fit until it
> adjusts . . . or they just blank it out." (140)

Elgin puts it this way in the epigraph to chapter 13: "'For any language, there are perceptions which it cannot express because they
would result in its indirect self-destruction'" (145). Thomas
Chornyak describes the failure to Interface with non-humanoids as
an intrinsic limitation: "It was distressing, but it was not ridiculous.

No human being could hold his breath for thirty minutes; that was a natural barrier, and one learned not to fling oneself at it. No human being, so far as he knew, could share the worldview of a non-humanoid. It was not ridiculous" (66). The Government Work technicians articulate the intrinsic limitations more specifically as "'human beings are hardwired to expect certain kinds of perceptions'" (140). Language, then, is both biological, in that our biological brains can form certain kinds of perceptions, and cultural, in that every language and culture uses a smaller set of perceptions and expressions from the larger set of hardwired possibilities.

This imbrication of the physical and the social is demonstrated most forcefully when the technicians pursue the experimental Interfacing between human infants and non-humanoid aliens despite warnings of disaster from the linguists. The leader of the group, Showard, finally concludes, "'There's something about the way the non-humanoid aliens perceive things, something about the "reality" they make out of stimuli, so impossible that it freaks out the babies and destroys their central nervous systems permanently'" (141). One infant, in an attempt to Interface with Beta-2, the resident non-humanoid alien, had convulsed so violently that it "literally turned itself inside out" (48). That the problem is not simply one of human linguistic and cognitive limitations is demonstrated by the subsequent experiment, in which the technicians try to alter consciousness and thus worldview by feeding the infants hallucinogens (186). This time, when they get the dosage "right" and Interface the infant, it is the alien being, Beta-2, that goes mad and dies, showering sparks throughout the Interface (188). The infants who survive the experiment cannot, so far as other people can tell, communicate in any way comprehensible to humans, although they appear normal and healthy.

The constitution of reality through language is more than simply a psychological effect in *Native Tongue*. As the Interfacing experiments reveal, language has the power to fundamentally reorder the material world, producing vibrant life or violent death. Moreover, language is constitutive in a number of other ways. A large part of the popular prejudice against linguists stems from their ability to manipulate verbal and non-verbal language. John Smith, a government liaison to the linguists, "knew that there was absolutely nothing an ordinary citizen could do if a linguist decided to structure an encounter in such a way that that citizen would look like a perfect ass" (63). And he knows this is also true of the linguist women: "Oh, they observed all the forms, those women; they said all the right words. But they had a way of somehow leading the conversation around so that words came out of your mouth that you'd never heard yourself say before and would have taken an oath you couldn't be made to say" (63). Examples of this linguistic power dynamic abound, both between linguists and citizens ("Thomas tilted his head a fraction, and Jones felt deeply inferior for no reason that he could understand" [63]) and between male and female linguists. For example, Rachel is unable to countermand her training as a linguist and resort to tears ("Women of the Lines learned early not to give in to tears . . . because tears destroyed negotiations" [149]) and she thus fails in her attempt to dissuade Thomas from marrying Nazareth to a powerful linguist she hates. In fact, a frequent refrain in the book is "you can't lie to a linguist."

The prodigious control the linguists maintain over the deployment and interpretation of language extends to the power male linguists wield over the female linguists. When Nazareth's love for Jordan Shannontry is exposed, leading to her familial humiliation, the worst pain comes from her inability to express the experience: "And there were no words, not in any language, that she could use to *explain* to them what it was that had been done to her, that would make them stop and say that it was an awful thing that had been done to her" (201–02). Elgin contrasts this despair with the relief felt by the women of Barren House when they can finally use the "right words" of Láadan (267). Along with its constitutive and manipulative powers, language also has the power to produce emotional comfort through consensual validation. Thus English expresses the experiences of the men and especially the linguist men relatively well and completely, creating in them a sense of justification and self-righteousness. For the linguist women, on the other hand, the available language fails to match their set of experiences, and they feel a host of negative emotions.

Despite their appreciation for the power of language and their grip on well-known linguistic principles, linguist men are unable to evade the constitutive power of gender relations. Thus the linguist men fail to apply this information to their own families. The constitutive link between language, gender relations, and reality is expressed in the women's search for a believable suspect for the attempted poisoning of Nazareth. Precisely because religious and reproductive rebel Belle-Anne is already assumed to be insane, she can act as decoy and confess to Nazareth's attempted murder, thus distracting the men of the Lines from the subversive activities taking place in the Barren House. Belle-Anne's tale of heavenly mandate and the hordes of he-angels does not fit the reality set of her immediate acquaintances and it is dismissed as the ravings of a madwoman; ironically it is precisely because she has already been *disbelieved* that she is now believed.

The linguist men are aware that the women are constructing a women's language. Their assumption that women have inferior linguistic skills blinds them to the women's true strategy: the women's decoy work on the false project of Langlish, an elaborate and unworkable female tongue, screens their *real* work on Láadan. Viewing the Langlish Encoding Project as harmless and time-consuming, the linguist men are trapped by their assumption of female inferiority, encapsulated in their convenient repetition of the fact that language skills are not correlated with intelligence (15–16). Only after Láadan is spoken and taught to the little girls does anyone recognize the power of the project. Even then, despite all of the evidence presented at the family celebration to all the men of the Lines, only Thomas recognizes the "'danger'" and "'corruption'" present (281) in what appears to the others as "charming" and "endearing" (276).

In certain ways, Láadan is deceptively simple. Encodings are "'the making of a name for a chunk of the world that so far as we know has never been chosen for naming before in any human language, and that has not just suddenly been made or found or dumped upon your culture. We mean naming a chunk that has been around a long time but has never before impressed anyone as sufficiently important to *deserve* its own name'" (22). When the women create Láadan, then, they are not simply creating new words. They are, in fact, reordering what is significant and not significant, perceived and not perceived.

Láadan, the true women's language, is both the culmination of and the evidence for the idea that language can change reality. While Láadan is still a secret, the men describe the women as constantly frowning, complaining, weeping, nagging, pouting, sulking, bitching, and arguing (289). Further, they frequently accuse women of talking endlessly about things no one would find important, and even then of never getting to the point (264). Verbal exchanges between male and female linguists are contentious and combative. Once Láadan is in place, however, women are happy, effective, self-sufficient. This reordering has profound effects on the world of the linguist men as well as the women. After Láadan has been in general circulation for about seven years, the men notice a change in the behavior of the women. Adam reports to Thomas, "'Women, they tell me, do not nag anymore. Do not whine. Do not complain. Do not demand things. Do not make idiot objections to everything a man proposes. Do not argue. Do not get sick—can you believe that, Thomas? No more headaches, no more monthlies, no more hysterics . . . or if there still are such things, at least they are never mentioned'" (275). But what appears to be a good change, a benign change, from the initial point of view of the men, is revealed as something both larger and more disturbing.

When the men of all of the Lines get together to discuss the "problem" of cooperative, cheerful women, the stakes of their behavior become clear: "'It used to be,' [Dano Mbal] said, 'that when a man had done something in which he could take legitimate pride, he could go home and talk to his wife and his daughters about it, and that pride would *grow*—it would be a reason to do even more, and do it even better'" (290). In his mind, Adam continues the corollary:

> It used to be that a man could do something he was *ashamed* of, too, and then go home and talk to his women about it and be able to count on them to nag him and harangue him and carry on hysterically at him until he felt he'd paid in full for what he'd done. And then a man could count on the women to go right on past that point with their nonsense until he actually felt that he'd been justified in what he'd done. *That* had been important, too—and it never happened anymore. Never. No matter what you did, it would be met in just the same way. With respectful courtesy. With a total absence of complaint. (290)

The new language, with its new set of values and perspectives on reality, thus changes the way the men and women of the Lines relate to one another. In effect, the women are no longer playing the linguistic games that support a binarized and hierarchized version of gender. The male response to the new world created by Láadan is, ironically, to do just what the women have desired: to move all of the women into their own residence. A shift in language has thus produced, albeit slowly, a real, measurable, and enjoyable change in their daily lives.

Of course, language is not entirely all-encompassing; knowledge can exist outside of language, which is precisely the urgency to produce new Encodings. We can see this in the book through Nazareth's unexplainable sense that the women's elaborate contingency plans are missing the point (271), the idea that even babies make (unpronounceable) statements about experience (141), and the experience of the LSD tubies, who are silent because for them, perception of reality is not linguistic (167). But the success of Láadan in emancipating women from oppression materializes the ways in which language can, quite literally, alter reality.

Elgin's second main concern in this novel is gender relations, and more specifically, the balance of power between the sexes. The world of *Native Tongue* takes place in a period of dramatic feminist setback. March 11, 1991, sees the landmark passage of the Twenty-fourth Amendment (repealing the Nineteenth Amendment that granted universal female suffrage) and the Twenty-fifth Amendment (affirming women's universal secondary and protected status) (7–8). Women's subordinate status is so ingrained and unquestioned that Aaron Adiness, as a young boy, believed his grandfather was a liar because he said women were once "allowed" to vote, be members of Congress, and sit on the Supreme Court (17). While the injustices of a male-ruled world are made clear, Elgin also demonstrates the complexity of effort and institution required to maintain such an unequal and dehumanizing system. The male assumption of female inferiority rests on three main tenets: that women are biologically inferior, that there is a natural hierarchy of the sexes, and that a woman's value derives from her basic reproductive usefulness. Women are variously described as more primitive than men (151) and as "rather sophisticated child[ren] suffering from delusions of grandeur" (110). Both statements presume not only that women and men have different biological complexities, but that a more complex organism is more intelligent and more worthy of rights; such claims were frequently used in nineteenth century science to justify racism, and have been widely criticized since. Evidence to the contrary in the novel, such as Nazareth's incredible linguistic ability, is explained away with the oft-repeated fact that "language acquisition skills are not directly correlated with intelligence" (279).

The idea of biological hierarchy grounds the society's gender relations, which mandate female subservience and male protection rather than equality. When Rachel and Thomas fight about Nazareth's prospective marriage to Aaron Adiness, Thomas is driven to rage by what he sees as Rachel "forget[ting] her place" (151). More than twenty years later, as the men discuss Nazareth's cancer and the appropriate medical response to it, Thomas remarks, "'We do feel —and, I might add, we are obligated to feel—more than just a ceremonial regard for the women in question'" (10). Even something as presumably female-oriented as gynecology is reinterpreted to focus on men: "'Let me tell you what gynecology is. What it really is. Gentlemen, it is health care for your fellow *man*—whose women you are maintaining in that state of wellness that allows the men to pursue their lives as they were intended to pursue them. As this country desperately needs them to pursue them'" (225).

Women are valued to the degree that they serve the needs of men. Thus, Thomas values his daughter Nazareth for her linguistic skills and her genetic heritage, since both bring great benefit to the men of the Lines (147). When she is poisoned, he is persuaded to seek medical care not because she is in pain, but because she has a crucial role to play in the following day's important labor treaty negotiations. As he puts it, "'I am not concerned personally about this illness of Nazareth's. . . . She gets excellent medical care. Whatever this is, I'm sure you've blown it up completely out of proportion. But I *am* concerned—very concerned—about the negotiations at the ILO'" (107). Nazareth is not a special case. The women are valuable for their languages, which bring money and prestige to the household, as well as for their reproductive abilities, which bring more money and prestige to the Lines through the production of linguistically skilled children. When a woman can no longer breed, she is removed to Barren House, the cruelly named woman-only space apart from the main house. Although once in the Barren House women are free (by definition) from the burden of reproduction, women there are still expected to translate. When they are too old or sick or frail to serve as official translators, they act as informal partners for the little girls to practice their many languages (206–07). Those activities seen as useless from the male perspective, such as tending to others (219) or working on Langlish (216), must be done in spare moments that don't interfere with the primary tasks of teaching languages and running the household. Women's subordination means that men rule the household unquestioningly. They take credit for the creation of children (11), they choose the spacing of their children (146), and they have free license to abuse their wives verbally, if not physically (175). Men outside the Lines can even choose their wives from and send their daughters to an array of sophisticated wife-training schools. As Nazareth muses bitterly upon accepting her marriage to Aaron, "Every woman was a prisoner for life; it was not some burden that she bore uniquely" (159).

Though subordinate to men, women can reframe even their most subservient behaviors to resistant ends. Thus Michaela, the ideal deferential listener, plays the role of executioner to the men whose trust she wins by flattery and manipulation. Although most of the women in the novel do not go as far as Michaela does, they are hardly resourceless victims. While they cannot fully escape their subordinated status, they do find ways to challenge their subordination. Aaron remarks, "This business of letting them have pocket money, and making exceptions for flowers and candy and romance media and bits of frippery was forever leading to unforeseen complications . . . astonishing how clever women were at distorting the letter of the law!" (16–17). Women thus use an exception meant to keep them contented in ways never anticipated: to exert small bits of female control and thus sabotage, without directly challenging, male rule. The practice of incremental change is another popular tactic of resistance. Making small changes over long periods of time, changes that are so small that they escape male notice, women frustrate the men while exerting their own control. Even if all they do is annoy the men, they are also putting them on notice that their control must be *maintained*.

The women adopt the stereotypes men hold as covers for their own subversive activities. Needlework, that quintessential female activity, is used to disguise the women's serious strategy sessions: "'Crochet, Natha,' [Susannah] directed. 'That is what we women do . . . ask the men and they will tell you. Any time they come here, they find us chatting and needling away. Frittering our time'" (249). Because sewing is assumed to be useless and a waste of time, everything associated with it, including conversation, is assumed to be harmless. The women of Chornyak House frequently remark that the image of frivolity and stupidity provides the best defense against the men of the household. Under these assumptions the men neither look for or see the evidence of conspiracy, of the teaching of forbidden women's history, of the women's medicine, contraception, and abortifacients. Some women even use the most stereotypical of male/female relations—romantic love—to manipulate, and thus resist, men. Michaela ruminates:

> Thomas, now, she felt no love for, any more than she'd felt love for Ned. She had turned her attention to convincing him that he had seduced her, because she knew his power and respected it and she knew no other way to make use of it. But she felt no love for the man. Loving someone who considered you only one small notch above a cleverly trained domestic animal, and made no secret of it—that is, loving any adult male—was not possible for her. It would be a perversion, loving your masters while their boots were on your neck, and she was a woman healthy of mind. (258)

Although women are quickly disabused of their belief in romantic love, they continue to rely on it as a source of resistance, a way to remain useful and convenient to men.

Perhaps the most extreme version of female rebellion in the novel is found in Belle-Anne, who functions as an effective foil to Michaela. Belle-Anne's specific rebellion is to refuse pregnancy at all costs, but in such a way that force won't change anything. As the doctors observe, "'You insert a sperm in that young lady, no matter how you go about it, and she just twitches her little butt and the sperm *dies*. Dead. Gone'" (127). Her ability to sabotage her own reproductivity enables her to escape both marriage and living among men. Unfortunately, it also makes her appropriate as a sacrificial lamb when Aquina botches her attempt to make Nazareth barren and thus accelerate her entrance to Barren House. Belle-Anne confesses to poisoning Nazareth in order to forestall the search that would inevitably expose all the women's secret sources of resistance—linguistic, social, and medicinal.

Since resistance can be produced from within patriarchy, patriarchy must be continually reproduced. The eternal small battles between the men and women demonstrate that gender hierarchy and sexual enslavement must be continually maintained through a variety of tactics. The most common tactic used at Chornyak House is the simple and expedient one of keeping the women busy. Thomas advises the head of another Line, "'Double their schedules, Andrew. Give them some stuff to translate that there hasn't been time for. Hell, make them clean the house. Buy them fruit to make jelly out of, if your orchards and storerooms are bare. There's got to be something you can do with them, or they will literally drive you crazy. Women out of control are a curse'" (86). This rationale also allows the women their Encoding Project (16). By assigning them amounts of work unheard of outside the Lines, the men assume the women won't have either the time or the energy to scheme. The women, of course, counter this with traditional women's activities that double as subversive covers, such as needlework and the ingenious recipe-code.

Another primary tactic for controlling women is the manipulation of information. The men manipulate history in order to eradicate a precedent of female autonomy by reinterpreting through the contemporary trope of male indulgence: "'Men are by nature kind and considerate, and a charming woman's eagerness to play at being a physician or a Congressman or a scientist can be both amusing and endearing; we can understand, looking back upon the period, how it must have seemed to 20th century men that there could be no harm in humoring the ladies'" (72). This form of manipulation seeks to control aspirations. Another kind of linguistic manipulation seeks to grant women the illusion of control and input while strictly circumscribing the options they can exercise. During one argument, Thomas says "'Rachel, . . . it doesn't make the slightest difference whether you approve or not. It would be pleasant if you did approve, of course. I make every effort to consider your personal wishes with regard to my children whenever I can. But when you refuse to be reasonable you leave me no choice but to ignore you'" (148). Women's supposed autonomy is thus predicated on their fundamental agreement with men.

Other types of manipulation are even more insidious. Nazareth discovers how kindness can function like manipulation when Jordan Shannontry begins to act as her backup in negotiations with the Jeelods. He pays her attention and compliments that culminate in presenting her with a yellow rose. When she tells him she loves him, however, he tells her father, and she becomes a victim of abuse and ridicule from both her father and her husband (193–97). The manipulation of religious feeling, as well as emotional feeling, is touted as another way to control women (130). As Nazareth remarks, "There was no end to the inventiveness of men when their goal was to prove their mastery" (176). The tactics used are multiple, and they are interesting not only for their variety, but for their very existence. By demonstrating the need to constantly reinforce mastery, Elgin demonstrates the instability of the dynamic, and it is this inherent instability that creates the possibility of change and thus of successful rebellion.

Indeed, *Native Tongue* begins with a preface that sounds a note of hope. Written in an even more distant future by a woman who holds the title of executive editor, the (fictional) preface explains that the novel is being published by a coalition of institutions, including the Historical Society of Earth, WOMANTALK, and the Láadan Group (6). This strategy of retrospective annotation implies that the experiment that was Láadan really did change the world, demonstrating the contingency of any system of oppression.

Elgin's novel explores other familiar feminist issues, such as the inability of resources to keep up with modern global—and in this case, intergalactic—capitalism, the gendered structure of government, the malleable nature of power, the gendered relationality of labor, and the distinction between the artificial and the natural. But it is the book's two main themes of constitutive language and linguistically enforced gender relations that reflect Suzette Haden Elgin's primary contribution to feminist thought.

Native Tongue was originally published in 1984 by DAW Books, a respected science fiction imprint. Contemporary reviews were positive to mixed. While conservative journals faulted the book for what was seen as lack of characterization or social logic (*Publishers Weekly*) and boring didacticism used to rationalize her language experiment (*Booklist*), more progressive and feminist outlets praised the book for its significant themes. *Fantasy Review* noted that "Elgin is on strongest ground when she writes of male/female relations, the work of the linguists, and the feminists' struggle to hide the development of their own language from the men. Though structurally flawed, her novel is well-written, its people are strong characters, and its themes are well worth considering" (Taormina). Carolyn Heilbrun, writing in the *Women's Review of Books,* praised as "exciting" Elgin's understanding "that until women find the words and syntax for what they need to say, they will never say it, nor will the world hear it." The *Voice Literary Supplement* praised her for "hav[ing] insight into cultural survival, colonialism, pidginization as well as into anger other than her own" (Cohen). These reviews all appear to agree with Elgin that oppression and language can be linked, and that language can also be a tool of revolution.

Native Tongue is frequently compared to Margaret Atwood's *The Handmaid's Tale,* another feminist, dystopian science fiction novel. The novels have similar settings: near-future versions of the United States where women have been stripped of their rights and are under the legal and often physical control of men. But where *The Handmaid's Tale* was praised for the spooky possibility of its imagined future, the scenario in *Native Tongue* has, according to Elgin herself, been dismissed as "improbable" and something that "could never happen in the United States" ("Women's Language" 176). *The Handmaid's Tale* was a bestseller and has been considered a classic since its 1986 publication, while *Native Tongue* went out of print in 1996 and maintained only a small, though enthusiastic, following among readers and scholars.

The context of the early 1980s, when Elgin was writing *Native Tongue,* is important in understanding both the social concerns that motivate the text and its intellectual position. Feminism in the late 1970s and early 1980s, especially academic feminism, was concerned with several sets of questions. Central among these was the question of whether gender is essential or constructed. If gender is essential, biological, and material, then the differences between men and women are set in nature. If gender is constructed, then it has nothing (or little) to do with our bodies and everything to do with social expectations and socialization. This debate had practical consequences, because an answer, even a contingent, personal answer, helped to point one towards an appropriate strategy of revolution. If gender is essential, then feminists should work for equal valuation of the inherent qualities of both men and women. If gender is constructed through socialization, then we should emphasize different relations and social practices that would challenge gender roles. This larger question carries other issues along with it. If gender *isn't* essential, as most feminists seemed to conclude, then on what can we base collective action? Is separation an effective political strategy? How would—or should—sexuality change along with gender roles?

A second major concern of 1970s and 1980s feminism, as previously noted, lay with the power of language to structure and express, and thus make possible, different perceptions. Julia Kristeva, Hélène Cixous, and Luce Irigaray all advocated variations on the idea that language as we know it encodes masculinist perceptions and values, in effect rendering women silent. They advocated the adoption of a women's language that is non-linear, sensual, and true to women's experience in patriarchal culture. As noted, Elgin's novel endorses the view of language as constructivist. In its very structure, *Native Tongue* highlights the power of language to construct reality. In its juxtaposition of various points of view, and its alternation between narrative and historical documents concerning the oppression of women in its various forms, the novel necessarily "engage[s] active reader involvement in the de/construction of textual meaning" (Rosinsky 107). By choosing such a structure, Elgin not only avoids burdening her narrative with history, but also enacts the very constitutive power of language she demonstrates.

Native Tongue must be viewed within the history not only of feminist thought but also of the science fiction genre. Science fiction is often traced back to Mary Shelley's 1818 *Frankenstein, Or, a Modern Prometheus.* Read variously as a political tract, a philosophical critique of Romantic individualism, and a birth myth, this brilliant novel presents a solitary scientist who constructs a human being in his laboratory out of a mixture of human and animal parts. The experiment goes awry, and the monster—alien and unnamed—escapes only to wreak havoc on its human creator, other human beings, and itself. Shelley's interrogation of the limits of humanity and the role of technology in human life forms the basis of much of science fiction today. Even our fascination with outer space and aliens reflects the genre's special concern with questions of identity and technology. Despite its origins in the mind of a young woman, science fiction as it developed—from H.G. Wells, Jules Verne, and C.S. Lewis in Europe to Isaac Asimov, Philip K. Dick, and more recently William Gibson in the United States—has been a genre dominated by white men as authors and readers. As science fiction gained popularity in the United States during the early part of the century through pulp novels and pulp magazines, the stories of exploration and high technology resonated with American expansionist ideals and the concomitant stress on technological innovation. Yet as far back as the teens in the United States, Charlotte Perkins Gilman articulated a strong feminist critique of such expansionist ideologies in *Herland,* while in Great Britain in the 1920s Charlotte Haldane grappled with the implications of eugenics and compulsory motherhood in her dystopian *Man's World.* It was not until the 1970s and 1980s that women made the strongest impact on science fiction, using it as an important medium to think through some of the claims and conflicts of feminism. Naomi Mitchison, Marge Piercy, Ursula LeGuin, and Joanna Russ all used the generic conventions of science fiction, often with modification, to examine and interrogate the actual, and possible, gender relations of modern life. And it was only when men and women of color, like Samuel Delaney and Octavia Butler, began to play an increasingly important role in forging a resistant science fiction that the genre gave a far-reaching and serious critique to the racializing agenda of science.

In its exploration of the constitutive properties of language, Elgin's novel harks back to Mary Shelley's emphasis (in chapter 12 of *Frankenstein*) on the role of language in forming the creature's sense of self and world. Like the women in *Native Tongue,* the monster must learn an alien language; like them, the ability to name opens up a whole world:

> I found that these people possessed a method of communicating their experiences and feelings to one another by articulate sounds. . . . This was indeed a godlike science, and I ardently desired to become acquainted with it. But I was baffled in every attempt I made for this purpose. Their pronunciation was quick, and the words they uttered, not having any apparent connection with visible objects, I was unable to discover any clue by which I could unravel the mystery of their reference. By great application, however . . . I discovered the names that were given to some of the most familiar objects of discourse. . . . I cannot describe the delight I felt when I learned the ideas appropriated to each of these sounds and was able to pronounce them. (Shelley 107)

If Elgin's novel continues the tradition of Mary Shelley's feminist analysis of the constructive aspects of language, it also evokes other recent works of science fiction: Neal Stephenson's examination of the way language functions as a virus in his widely read and critically acclaimed *Snowcrash,* and Greg Bear's exploration of DNA as a language technology for species adaptation to global change in *Darwin's Radio.*

Thus this reprinting of Elgin's novel marks a significant new moment in science fiction, for it signals a convergence of the genre's three major strands: the original (though frequently unacknowledged) strand of feminist cultural critique running from *Frankenstein* through to *Herland*; the tradition of technoscientific experimentation of science fiction's male-dominated high modernist period (from Wells through Clarke and Asimov); and the postmodern strand of science fiction linking an examination of social technologies (language, race, gender) with a new focus on biotechnological interventions. Finally, in her attention to aging and to interspecies communication, her invention of the Barren House and the Interface,

Elgin draws attention to two contemporary issues which are increasingly the focus not only of science fiction but of fiction of all genres: the receding limits of human life and the vanishing boundaries between species. As contemporary biomedicine's assault on the limits of the probable encodes as mundane what only months ago was coded as revolutionary, these issues increasingly function to break down the distinction between science and other forms of culture, between science fiction and other sorts of fiction.

Read as a work in this new, hybrid genre for which we do not yet have a name—this genre that does not differentiate science from other kinds of culture, but instead performs a detailed analysis of the networks between them—*Native Tongue* seems both powerfully prescient *and* strikingly dated (or, to put it more positively, of historical interest). The novel is prescient in its attention to the experiences of aging and menopausal women, who were given short shrift in feminist theory until the late 1990s. In its invention of Barren House, *Native Tongue* provides wonderful meditations on the different consciousness of aging, the pains and pleasures of growing—and being—old.[4] Looking to the present and future, the novel also nudges us to realize that we are living and working through precisely the kind of linguistic shift, or re-encoding, that Suzette Haden Elgin explored in *Native Tongue*. The increased emphasis on nonsexist language and the integration of feminist challenges to simple or deterministic ideas of gender or biology have changed the workplace environment, helped to make space for nontraditional families, and catalyzed a civil rights movements for lesbians and gay men and for disabled persons. As the biomedical revolution reshapes the entire human lifespan, with interventions ranging from assisted reproduction to hormone replacement therapy, our language is also registering the cultural shift in our definitions of the human. Thus our lexicon now includes the terms *biological mother, surrogate mother, genetic mother,* and *postmenopausal mother,* in addition to the older terms *adoptive mother, unwed mother,* and *natural mother.* Along with assisted reproduction, fetal surgery, cloning, and interspecies organ transplantation are changing the human narrative so dramatically that what seemed like science fiction in 1984 now seems to us in the new millennium as increasingly unremarkable fact. Test tube fertilization and cloning, which Elgin depicts in the novel, seem now not wildly futuristic but, in other contexts, realities, as well as moral dilemmas. In addition, the novel's portrait of intergalactic capitalism anticipates the actual trend in the 1990s —with the decline of Communism and the rise of multinational corporations and the Internet—toward global capitalism.

At the same time, the novel serves us well as historical record of the dystopian visions central to a particular stage of feminism, for the life of linguist women mirrors in its stringencies the harshest social critiques of second stage feminism: patriarchal domination, sex as an instrument of control, women subject to the whims of their male masters and categorized solely by their sexual and reproductive capacities. Yet *Native Tongue* reflects the partial vision of its era, too, particularly in its insistence on seeing men and women as unified groups necessarily opposed to one another in thought, action, and desire. Contemporary readers may well wish for another project that would encode a newer language, one that complicates the idea of a "native tongue" by challenging its basis in a fixed and gendered identity.

While Elgin's novelistic vision of the future was dystopic, the strategies of language she and her characters employed provide new avenues of critique and change. Just as the novel both reveals language to be based on gendered assumptions and provides new ways to think about both language and reality, we can explore the ways language helps encode other power hierarchies, including those of race, class, sexual orientation, and even the human over other species. In doing so, we can employ new linguistic strategies to challenge these power structures and encode a reality more equitable for all.

Susan Squier
Julie Vedder
Pennsylvania State University
June 2000

NOTES

1. Elgin's nonfictions series has grown quite extensive. In addition to the original *Gentle Art of Verbal Self-Defense,* it includes *The Last Word on the Gentle Art of Verbal Self-Defense* (1987), *The Gentle Art of Written Self-Defense: Letters in Response to Triple-F Situations* (1993), *Genderspeak: Men, Women, and the Gentle Art of Verbal Self-Defense* (1993), and *The Gentle Art of Communicating With Kids* (1996), among others.

2. While linguists have, for the most part, discarded this theory in favor of the school of thought pioneered by Noam Chomsky— which contends that the capacity for language is wired into our brains by evolution, rather than developed as a result of our environment—the idea survives in many other disciplines. All the same, there is some confusion about the actual meaning of the Sapir-Whorf hypothesis. The "strong" version, which Elgin claims no one has ever advocated, says that our language determines our perception of reality (*Language Imperative* 52). It is this version that is often discredited. The "weak" version, to which Elgin subscribes, also known as the linguistic relativity hypothesis, says only that our language structures and constrains our perception of reality. For a discussion of all these competing theories, see Steven Pinker, *The Language Instinct,* especially pages 55–82.

3. Gödel's theorem argues that within any fixed system, there are truths that exist, but are not provable within the system (Hofstadter 101). In other words, no system is complete, and in any attempt to include new things, the system necessarily changes. In the case of *Native Tongue,* the fixed system is a masculine, violent, hierarchical culture and language. Elgin's experiment was to see what would happen if she tried to "prove" the truth of a women's language. For a detailed discussion of Gödel's theorem, see Douglas Hofstadter, *Gödel, Escher, Bach.*

4. This theme appears in *Earthsong: Native Tongue III,* which has as its central character a linguist woman who communicates with the spirit of one of the oldest old who has just died—a linguist woman who helped to create Láadan.

WORKS CITED

Bothamley, Jennifer. *Dictionary of Theories.* London, Detroit: Gale Research International, 1993.

Cohen, Debra Rae. Rev. of *Native Tongue. Voice Literary Supplement* October 1984: 18.

De Lauretis, Teresa. *Technologies of Gender: Essays on Theory, Film and Fiction.* Bloomington: Indiana University Press, 1987.

Elgin, Suzette Haden. "A Feminist Is a What?" *Women and Language* 18.2 (1995): 46.

———. *The Gentle Art of Verbal Self Defense.* 1980. New York: Barnes and Noble, 1985.

———. "Laadan, the Constructed Language in *Native Tongue." Suzette Haden Elgin's Website* (www.sfwa.org/members/elgin/Laadan.html) Online. March 2000.

———. *The Language Imperative.* Cambridge, MA: Perseus Books, 2000.

———. "Linguistics and Science Fiction." *Suzette Haden Elgin's Website* (www.sfwa.org/members/elgin/SHE_info.html) Online. March 2000.

———. "Washing Utopian Dishes; Scrubbing Utopian Floors." *Women and Language* 17.1 (1994): 43–47.

———. "Women's Language and Near Future Science Fiction: A Reply." *Women's Studies* 14 (1987): 175–181.

Heilbrun, Carolyn. Rev. of *Native Tongue* and *Native Tongue II: The Judas Rose. Women's Review of Books* July–August 1987: 17.

Hofstadter, Douglas R. *Goedel, Escher, Bach: An Eternal Golden Braid.* New York: Vintage Books, 1979.

Irigaray, Luce. *This Sex Which Is Not One.* Trans. Catherine Porter. Ithaca, New York: Cornell University Press, 1985.

Martin, Emily. "The Egg and the Sperm: How Science Has Constructed a Romance Based on Stereotypical Male-Female Roles." *Signs: Journal of Women in Culture and Society* 16.3 (1991): 1–18.

Rev. of *Native Tongue. Booklist* November 1984: 342.

Rev. of *Native Tongue. Publishers Weekly* 225 (1984): 98.

Pinker, Steven. *The Language Instinct*. New York: HarperCollins, 1994.

Rosinsky, Natalie. *Feminist Futures: Contemporary Women's Speculative Fiction*. Ann Arbor: UMI Reseach Press, 1984.

Sellers, Susan, ed. *The Hélèn Cixous Reader.* New York: Routledge, 1994.

Shelley, Mary. *Frankenstein, Or, A Modern Prometheus*. 1831. New York: Signet Classics, 1965.

Squier, Susan. "From Omega to Mr. Adam: The Importance of Literature for Feminist Science Studies." *Science, Technology, & Human Values* 24.1 (1999): 132–158.

Taormina, Agatha. "Womanspeak." *Fantasy Review* November 1984: 31.

CONTEMPORARY WOMEN'S FICTION FROM AROUND THE WORLD
from The Feminist Press at The City University of New York

A Matter of Time a novel by Shashi Deshpande. $21.95 jacketed hardcover.

Allegra Maud Goldman a novel by Edith Konecky. $9.95 paper.

Almost Touching the Skies: Women's Coming of Age Stories. $35.00 cloth. $15.95 paper.

And They Didn't Die a novel by Lauretta Ngcobo. $42.00 cloth. $13.95 paper.

An Estate of Memory a novel by Ilona Karmel. $11.95 paper.

Apples from the Desert: Selected Stories by Savyon Liebrecht. $19.95 jacketed hardcover.

Bamboo Shoots After the Rain: Contemporary Stories by Women Writers of Taiwan. $35.00 cloth. $14.95 paper.

Bearing Life: Women's Writings on Childlessness. $23.95 jacketed hardcover.

Changes: A Love Story a novel by Ama Ata Aidoo. $12.95 paper.

The Chinese Garden a novel by Rosemary Manning. $29.00 cloth. $12.95 paper.

Coming to Birth a novel by Marjorie Oludhe Macgoye. $30.00 cloth. $11.95 paper.

Confessions of Madame Psyche a novel by Dorothy Bryant. $18.95 paper.

David's Story a novel by Zoë Wicomb. $19.95 cloth.

The House of Memory: Stories by Jewish Women Writers of Latin America. $37.00 cloth. $15.95 paper.

Mulberry and Peach: Two Women of China a novel by Hualing Nieh. $12.95 paper.

Paper Fish a novel by Tina De Rosa. $20.00 cloth. $9.95 paper.

The Present Moment a novel by Marjorie Oludhe Macgoye. $30.00 cloth. $11.95 paper.

Reena and Other Stories by Paule Marshall. $11.95 paper.

The Silent Duchess a novel by Dacia Maraini. $19.95 jacketed hardcover. $14.95 paper.

Songs My Mother Taught Me: Stories, Plays, and Memoir by Wakako Yamauchi. $35.00 cloth. $14.95 paper.

Sultana's Dream: A Feminist Utopia by Rokeya Sakhawat Hossain. $19.95 cloth. $9.95 paper.

The Tree and the Vine a novel by Dola de Jong. $27.95 cloth. $9.95 paper.

Truth Tales: Contemporary Stories by Women Writers of India. $35.00 cloth. $12.95 paper.

Two Dreams: New and Selected Stories by Shirley Geok-lin Lim. $10.95 paper.

What Did Miss Darrington See? An Anthology of Feminist Supernatural Fiction. $14.95 paper.

With Wings: An Anthology of Literature by and About Women with Disabilities. $14.95 paper.

Women Working: An Anthology of Stories and Poems. $13.95 paper.

Women Writing in India: 600 B.C. to the Present. Volume I: 600 B.C. to the Early Twentieth Century. $29.95 paper. Volume II: The Twentieth Century. $32.00 paper.

You Can't Get Lost in Cape Town a novel by Zoë Wicomb. $13.95 paper.

To receive a free catalog of the Feminist Press's 180 titles, contact: The Feminist Press at The City University of New York, 365 Fifth Avenue, New York, N. Y., 10016; phone: (212) 817-7920; fax: (212) 987-4008; www.feministpress.org. Feminist Press books are available at bookstores, or can be ordered directly. Send check or money order (in U.S. dollars drawn on a U.S. bank) payable to The Feminist Press. Please add $4.00 shipping and handling for the first book and $1.00 for each additional book. VISA, Mastercard, and American Express are accepted for telephone orders. Prices subject to change.